*Books by Roberta Gellis
from Jove*

A TAPESTRY OF DREAMS
THE ROPE DANCER
FIRES OF WINTER
MASQUES OF GOLD
A SILVER MIRROR

FIRES OF WINTER

ROBERTA GELLIS

JOVE BOOKS, NEW YORK

This Jove book contains the complete
text of the original trade paperback edition.
It has been completely reset in a typeface
designed for easy reading, and was printed
from new film.

FIRES OF WINTER

A Jove Book / published by arrangement with
the author

PRINTING HISTORY
Jove trade paperback edition / September 1987
Jove edition / June 1990

ISBN: 0-515-10030-7

Jove Books are published by The Berkley Publishing Group,
200 Madison Avenue, New York, New York 10016.
The name "JOVE" and the "J" logo
are trademarks belonging to Jove Publications, Inc.

PRINTED IN THE UNITED STATES OF AMERICA

10 9 8 7 6 5 4 3 2 1

CHAPTER 1

Bruno

MY MOTHER WAS a castle whore. My father, Sir William Fermain, holder of Jernaeve keep, took the whore Berta to his bed in spite of his wife. That poor lady had borne my father a third daughter who survived only a few hours, like the other babes before her. Once her lord had taken her, my mother touched no other man, and in the third month of her master's keeping she conceived me. Moreover, even after the lord called her to him no more, she remained chaste, and for the whole time she suckled me also.

My mother, like most of the people of Jernaeve and the lands beholden to it, was fair of hair and light of eye, but I am dark—like my father. Yet, because my mother was what she was, he would not acknowledge me even as a bastard of his get.

I only learned these things later. When I was very young, three or four years old, I only knew that the dark man in fine clothing hated me, and that if I ran or hid or wept, I would be beaten, but if I defied him or fought him, he would only cuff me once or twice and then let me be. I am accounted a brave man. I learned that from my father's handling—but there are better ways to learn.

In those early years, before I understood what rank

1

meant, I often begged my mother to leave the keep, or if she would not, to give me to one of the serf families in the outer bailey. I would not have grieved much about being parted from my mother. By the time I could conceive that there were other places to live, most of her hopes had soured. She was plying her trade again, and I was a nuisance. She kept me clean and fed but preferred my absence to my presence. In any case, although I did not know it then, she had not the power to be rid of me. My father would not acknowledge me—but he would not let me go either. The lady of the keep had lost two more babes over those three or four years, and little as Sir William Fermain liked a whore's child, I was a living son.

Moreover, as the years passed, I came to look more and more like a Fermain. I could not have displayed the aquiline nose or the square, stubborn chin of the Fermains in those early years, but my skin was already darker than that of the local people, my hair so dark a brown as to be safely called black, and my eyes the same. I had grown happier also because my father had ceased to torment me—not that I ever grew to feel anything for him other than fear and angry resentment. The reason I became less a target for his cruelty was that from the first time an old man-at-arms put a blunt wooden sword into my hand, I knew, as if by instinct, how to handle it. It was the same with horses. I was running among their feet out of love for them as soon as I was steady on my own, and riding was my greatest pleasure from the moment I was set astride.

Had my father ignored me completely, I would have been perfectly happy, but as my skills in horsemanship and swordsmanship increased, he watched me often with an expression that made me uneasy, and he brought others to look at me. One man I recall in particular, then only because he looked so much like my father that I was doubly afraid, but since then for many reasons.

I was six years old at that time. I remember clearly because one day my mother gave me a small round metal helmet and a leather jerkin sewn all over with metal scales. She told me my age then and that the helm and hauberk were gifts from my father. She smiled at me and kissed me too—a thing I could not remember her ever doing—and said I would make her a great lady yet. She was then suckling another boy child, one whose father she could not name, but she let him scream on the heap of straw where he lay while she dressed me in my father's gift.

Many years later I realized that the gift and the new attention he was paying me made my mother think he intended to recognize me soon. The lady of the keep was great with child again, and my mother believed that when that babe died, my father would give up hope and make me his heir. Poor woman, her hopes were never to be realized because my father's wife at last bore a babe—a daughter—who clung to life. I saw Audris, who had been baptized in haste, since she was not expected to live, only a few hours after she was born. She was a tiny, scrawny creature, but strangely beautiful, brought to my mother to nurse because my father's lady wife was dying. The memory of how she looked—of all the sights and sounds of that night—are very vivid because I was so frightened at first.

It was late at night and I was wakened by the men with torches who accompanied the woman carrying the whimpering babe. Being wakened would not have impressed me; it was no unusual thing because of my mother's trade, but the crowd of finely dressed people and their loud, excited voices as they discussed the lady's coming death branded each detail on my mind. Young as I was, it was all too clear that they were glad of the poor lady's perilous condition. I had never even seen her close, yet that grieved me. Now I know that it was no dislike of the lady herself that bred such callousness. What they desired was that my father be free to wed a different woman, one who could breed him a strong heir.

I saw, too, the indifference with which the babe, Audris— they told my mother her name; I do not know why—was thrust at my mother. The child was still wet with the water of baptism and carelessly wrapped in an old shawl though it was autumn and the night was chill. My mother listened to all they said, for they spoke before us as if we were beasts with no understanding—or, perhaps, they thought their language would be strange to us. But a whore must learn the tongue in which the men who use her speak, and my father had seen to it that I was tutored in proper French and used it.

Initially my mother had taken Audris with an indifference equal to that with which the babe was handed over, and I could feel tears sting my eyes. Here was another such as I, of no account to anyone, unwanted, unloved. But as my mother listened to the talk of those who had invaded our hut near the stable wall, a strange expression crossed her face. I was the only one who saw, for she had lowered her head in seeming submission to the high-born ones. In Berta's eyes there was a malicious gleam and an immovable stubbornness in the set of her mouth. As soon as those who had come were gone, she put Audris to her breast—and the babe sucked. Then my mother laughed softly and bade me bring my good clean shirt to her. With that, she patted Audris dry and wrapped her more carefully in a clean shift of her own, holding her close to warm her.

When Audris had taken her fill—and it was a good meal she made for a creature so tiny—my mother patted her until she brought up wind, then made me rise from my pallet, which was warm from my body, and laid Audris therein, covering her with my blanket. She threw her own blanket over me to keep me from growing chilled and bade me watch by the babe, with stern words about what I should do if she cried or began to spit up what she had eaten. Then she made up the fire so that it blazed in the hearth like a fire of winter. I saw Audris better in that light, and she looked so strange in the sudden flare and sudden dark that I had to see her better. Finally, my mother snatched up my half brother and went out with him.

I knew I would never see him again, but that did not trouble me. My mother had so taken the other two babes born to her down to the serfs in the lower bailey. When she took the first child, I had never been there, but my mother told me, when I cried for the babe she had carried away, that there was always a woman who had lost a babe among them or among the people of the village beyond the wall or on the outlying farms. It was the first I had heard of any place other than the keep and the inner bailey, and the tale had distracted me from the loss of my toy—for it had been an amusement to watch the comic expressions on the face of the little one and see the wavering of his arms and legs and the attempts to move himself. I was so lonely in those days, forbidden to play with the other children and constantly in fear of my father. By the time Audris was brought to us, I was accustomed to losing my siblings and I had enough, in my practice of arms and riding, to fill my days.

Before she left, my mother had lit the lamp with a long sliver of wood first thrust into the blaze of fire in the pit in the earthen floor. When I was younger and the little leaping flame from the twist of linen set into the soft fat in the pottery bowl had fascinated me, I had been forbidden to touch the lamp. I gave that only a glancing thought now. My mother would not be back for some time, I knew, and I had to see Audris more clearly. A stool lifted me high enough to reach the low shelf on which the lamp was set, and I brought it nigh and examined my half sister in the flickering light.

I could see at once that she *was* different from the babes my mother had borne. Unlike them, she was not red, nor was her head bald and strangely pointed. Her cheeks were very pale, almost as if no blood coursed under her skin, and she had hair, silvery white. And as I gazed at her, she opened her eyes, which were not a cloudy blue but clear and very, very light, almost silver like her hair. I had never seen so lovely a babe; my mother's were all ugly when they were newborn, though each had a certain charm even then, and they grew handsome after a week or two. Audris, though, was like a faery thing; I shuddered looking at her, wondering if she were perchance a changeling. It could have happened, I knew, because no one cared about her and likely no one had been watching.

So fearful was that thought that the flame shook in my hand and I lifted the lamp away; Audris cried out then, not a raucous howl like my mother's other babes, but a soft mewling. I made haste to climb the stool again and set the lamp back on its shelf so I could pat the child silent as my mother had bidden me. In stroking her, I must have pushed aside the fold of cloth that held one arm, and she worked it free and found one of my fingers around which her little hand closed softly. I had had that experience before, but this was different somehow, partly because Audris's grip was so much gentler than that of the other babes but also, I think, because I knew my mother could not give away this child, and I hoped I would have someone with whom to play. It did not occur to me then that, being the lord's daughter, Audris might merit a finer wet nurse than my mother or might be kept from such as I. I had seen how little she was regarded and did not then understand the difference between a whore's bastard and the legitimate daughter of the lord of the keep.

Nonetheless, we were not separated. Partly that was owing to how sure my father was that this child too would die, and partly it was owing to the fact that he was busy seeking another wife, out of whom he expected strong sons, who would make a daughter near worthless. He was much away, and I remember my joy in those months and remember also feeling that it was Audris who had somehow brought all my happiness with her. Nor was that all childish foolishness. The nurse of a nobleman's child has many privileges and an easy life; thus, my mother did not wish to have Audris taken from her, and she closed her door to the men who were used to finding it open. That pleased me, for they often disturbed my sleep with their grunting and groaning and thrashing about, and Audris herself, as she grew stronger, amused me more and more.

Audris talked and walked early. It was a strange thing to see and hear, for she was very tiny, no larger than other babes months younger. She was my pass also to lovely places like the keep garden, where my mother would often set me to watching her while she washed clothes or did other tasks. And with Audris, I was free to play by the hearth in the great hall, for we had all moved from our hut to the third floor of the south tower in the keep a few weeks after Audris came to us. My father had come to my mother's hut through the first snow of winter, choking in the smoky interior while he stared at Audris, who was squalling lustily at that moment—her voice having grown stronger—and beckoned my mother out. When she returned, she was laughing softly but triumphantly.

"I have won what I played for. Today we move into the

keep.'' She spoke in her native tongue—mine was French, for though I understood English, I was rarely allowed to speak it.

And then, during the dog days of August, my father died. Perhaps he brought home the sickness from some keep or town that he had visited. I knew nothing of it at the time he died; I have often wondered since I have been a man whether I would have been glad or whether his loss would have shaken me. I never loved him, yet he had been a central core in my life, and I might have felt strange to know he was gone forever. But by the time I heard he was dead, I was too terrified to care.

My father's sickness had spread throughout the keep and all had fallen into chaos. I knew something was wrong because my mother began to cook our meals on the small hearth in our chamber, and she kept us close within our tower. She told me angrily, when I begged to go out to my lessons, that the man who had taught me was dead and that so many were sick there were not folk enough to tend them.

I later learned that when my father's strong hand was gone and there were none to bid them nay, most of those who still had their health had fled. They carried the seeds of the plague with them, so that the village and outlying farms were also reaped by Death's scythe, the sickness lingering some weeks. That was why Audris's uncle, Sir Oliver Fermain, delayed so long in coming to Jernaeve. I believe that if he had known Audris was alive, he would have come at once. But hearing of the deadliness of the disease, he must have thought so small and seemingly weak a child had died; thus, there was no sense in exposing his family and himself.

At the time, however, all I knew was that I was alone with no one to help me or tell me what to do. Those I had depended on were gone, for my mother had disappeared and the man-at-arms who taught me had died, and those I approached later drove me away. My mother was also dead then, but I did not know that either because she had left the tower—for what reason, I will never know—telling me only to stay within and to keep Audris with me. She had gone down to the village, where she had been slain, I suppose by someone who thought she carried sickness.

I obeyed my mother's order all the first day she was gone, for there was some food left from the breaking of our fast and I shared that with Audris for our dinner. By evening we were very hungry and Audris was crying, so I dared creep down the stairs. The hall was empty, the fire dead—a thing I had never seen before because Jernaeve was stone built, and even in the hottest days of summer the hall was cold. I do not think I have ever known such fear, not even when my father beat me for no reason. To be alone, all alone! It was unthinkable. In those few moments I looked death in the face, believing the whole keep was empty save for Audris and me.

I have never forgotten that I looked back toward the doorway to the tower stair, tempted to run back to be with Audris, but my stomach ground within me and I had only soothed away her tears by promising to bring her something to eat. I would have gone hungry longer to save myself the eerie trip across the silent hall and out and down into what I feared would be an equally silent bailey, but I never could bear to see Audris cry. So I ran quickly across to the door and down the wooden stair of the forebuilding, beginning to weep with relief when I heard sounds coming from the bailey.

My tears of relief were shed too soon. What I had heard were the beasts—the dogs in their kennel, the horses in a small paddock and stable, and the few cows kept in the upper bailey pens for their milk. Usually there was a hog or two and a sheep being fattened for slaughtering. The last two were gone, already butchered and eaten, I suppose, and no more brought up because my father and his steward were both dead and there was no one to give the order. I did not think of that then, of course; I was simply overjoyed to see the animals alive, for I knew by instinct that someone must have been feeding and watering them. Most of my fear dropped away, and I thought of one of the grooms who lived with his wife and children in a hut near ours against the stable wall. He knew me and had always liked me, allowing me to "help" with his duties—which was more hindrance, I am sure—around the horses, and I believed he would help me now. Perhaps his wife would give me food.

I received my first shock on the way to his hut. A man came out of the chapel, and I ran toward him in joy at seeing another person—but he screamed at me to stay away, and when I stood for a moment, too shocked to move, he cast a stone at me. I suppose he was sick and his cruelty was for my own sake, but at the time it was a terrible blow. I was to receive another, even worse. When I came to the groom's house, his wife was sitting in the doorway.

Before I could even speak, she spat at me, screaming, "Whore's bastard, how dare you live while better than you died!" Then she began to struggle to her feet, gesturing menacingly, and added, "The lord is dead. He can protect you no longer."

That was how I learned my father was dead, and partly why I gave little thought to it. I was too shocked and frightened to do more than flee before the groom's wife could reach me, terror lending speed to my feet. But I saw before I was halfway across the bailey that she could not follow, and then rage steadied me. I was sure my father had never protected me—at that time I had no idea of the effect of simply being the lord's son—and I believed I had won the little favor I had received by my own natural skills. That was in a sense true, for if I had not shown a natural aptitude for riding and handling a sword, my father would have turned his back on me totally. But my rage was mingled with a new fear. I remembered the man who had thrown a stone at me and the physical threat implied by the gestures of the groom's wife. Did those who survived blame my father for the loss of their families? Did they intend to revenge themselves on me—and on Audris, who was even more the lord's child?

I have long since learned that the woman was almost mad with grief and have forgiven her, especially since the notion she set into my mind, to avoid everyone in the keep, may have preserved my life and Audris's by keeping us free of the sickness. The anger she woke in me, by reminding me of the praise of my tutor and the approving looks of so harsh a critic as my father, was also useful to me. It gave me the feeling that I was able—urged on by the pangs of hunger—to provide for myself and Audris.

By then, I was near the kitchen sheds built against the wall of the keep. With the stealth natural to a small boy, whose curiosity often drove him to invade places, like the smithy, where he would not be welcome, I crept into the kitchen yard, keeping well inside the lengthening shadows. Seeing no one, I sidled into a storage shed, where I found a knife stuck into a round of cheese, as if someone had been about to cut a portion and been called away and forgotten. I finished the work, though it was not easy, the knife having rusted and stuck to the cheese. Still, I managed, and then having the knife in my belt and knowing—as I thought, being very ignorant—how to use it, I felt much bolder and went from shed to shed, gathering what I could carry.

For many days—recently, thinking back, I decided it must have been nearly a month—I kept Audris and myself hidden. I stole wood for our fire and food for our bellies and emptied the vessels of soil, mostly going out in the late evening, just before dark when the shadows were deepest and most plentiful. Near the end of the time, I went out in the early morning also, into the garden where the fruits were ripened. For drink, I stole milk, if any remained in the shed by evening, and I fetched water from a small spring in the garden in one of my mother's pots because I could not lift the pail that went down into the well in the lowest floor of the keep. I was afraid to go down into the dark too, but I did not admit that. By then, I was very bold and proud. I think I must have believed, for a time anyway, that we would always live that way.

I was well content that it should be so, for Audris was very good and minded me. I kept her as clean as I could and took her with me for an airing when I went to the garden, teaching her to hide and be still on those few occasions when someone came in. I wonder now whether it was those lessons, for I was frightened and she may have felt my fear, that made her so shy of strangers all the rest of her life. But at that time she was happy, playing only with me. I was happy too, but as the weeks passed, I began to miss my pony and the practice with my sword.

Soon I was trying to devise a way to steal a ride and at the same time keep Audris safe. Usually I left her sleeping, tied by a cord to the leg of the bed so that if she woke she could not burn herself in the fire or fall down the stairs, but I knew that a ride would take longer than my short forays for food and that it would be dangerous to leave her tied too long.

Still, thinking about the pony made me wonder if he would remember me, and I could not resist a short visit to the stable. I had been there once, perhaps two weeks earlier to take some straw to add to the rushes on the floor; these were becoming thin and matted, and it was growing cooler as the summer waned. Then, although feed had been thrown into the troughs, the stable was filthy. This time it was different. Plainly, someone had been at work. I remember how my heart sank at the sight—I suppose I knew then that life would revert to its normal pattern and I would sink into nothing again instead of being provider and protector, a person of the first importance. I could not even stay to see the pony but turned and ran, and because I was already running, escaped the outstretched hand of a groom. I heard him calling after me, but I had become most adept at concealment and escaped him easily.

That did not lift my spirits, though, and it was a long time before I fell asleep that night. Nor was I wrong in my feeling that my life was about to change again. On the very next day, not long after Audris had wakened me and I had given her some fruit and cheese and sour milk with which to break her fast, a tumult of sound rose from the hall below us. That place, dead and silent for so long, was suddenly full of people, all talking, shouting orders, wielding rakes and brooms to rid the place of the rotten old rushes, starting a roaring fire to burn cleansing herbs, and such-like. The noise startled Audris, used as she was for so long to no noise except that which we made ourselves, and she began to weep. I hushed her fiercely, thrusting her into the corner of the room farthest from the door, and ran back, struggling to close it. This I could not do, for the locking bar was down and it was above my head and too heavy for me to lift, so it caught against the seat into which it normally dropped.

Had the door closed, Audris and I could have spent the
day much as usual, since, young as I was, I knew no
sound could pass the thick stone walls or the thick wooden
floor and door. As it was, I was frightened to death that
the smallest noise we made would betray us, and I held
Audris in my arms to keep her still and silent. I could feel
her little body shaking with fear—poor child, it was my
fault, for she would not have been afraid, I think, if I had
not myself been terrified. I tried to calm her by telling her
over and over that as long as she was with me, I would let
no harm come to her. It was a stupid promise and I knew
it, but I could think of nothing else to say to comfort her.

Of course, our silence could not keep our presence
secret long. I should have known that the cleaning would
not stop with the hall. By early afternoon, our door was
flung open suddenly, and a tall woman with thick bronze-
colored braids entered. I shrank back, but there was no
shadow in the south tower where windows facing southwest and southeast allowed sunlight to pour into the room.
For one moment the woman stood frozen, staring at us,
then she cried out and ran forward.

Perhaps I cried out too. Audris's thin little arms were
clasped tightly around my neck. I remember how she
screamed when the woman pulled her away from me and
lifted her, holding her firmly with one arm. With the
other, she urged me to my feet and hurried me down the
stair to confront a man, who looked so much like my
father that I thought for a moment the groom's wife had
lied when she told me the lord was dead.

In the next moment I realized he could not be my father
because he asked, "Who are you?"

I had learned early that to display fear brought a harsher
punishment than defiance, so I answered boldly, "I am
Bruno, Berta's son." And then I recognized him as the
dark man my father had brought to watch me at my
training, and I knew he, too, was a lord and would protect
a lord's child against the common folk, so I added, "The
child is Audris, Lord William's daughter."

The woman was rocking Audris in her arms, trying to
quiet her, and Audris was struggling to be free, shrieking,

"Boono, Boono," which was the closest she could come then to my name.

"Set her down, Eadyth," the dark man said, and Lady Eadyth obeyed.

Audris ran to me at once, and I whispered, "Hush, you are safe now." She quieted, slipping her hand into mine and trying to hide herself behind me.

"I am Sir Oliver Fermain," the dark man said, "Sir William's brother, and I have come . . ." He hesitated, staring at Audris, who was half hidden behind me. Then his mouth set hard, and he went on, "I have come to hold Jernaeve for Demoiselle Audris."

There was a moment of heavy silence in which grief and fear gripped my throat and closed it. I was very innocent and was afraid of the wrong things. It never occurred to me that Sir Oliver need only slay both Audris and myself, and Jernaeve keep with all its rich lands would be his own and his children's after him. It would have been so easy. Who was to say that we had not died of the disease as so many others had done? Certainly not his wife whose children would profit. Nor did I fear that I would be thrust out of the keep altogether and left to make my own way, which would have been within Sir Oliver's right. A whore's child has no proper place. The horror in my mind was that Audris would be taken from me.

During that silent moment, Sir Oliver had been looking at what he could see of Audris. Suddenly, he frowned and turned his head to his wife. "Take the child away and clean her and dress her properly."

"She *is* clean," I cried, heedless of angering him in the agony of losing the one creature who had ever valued me above others. "I could not wash her linen. I—"

"You are nowise to blame," Sir Oliver said sharply, raising his voice above Audris's renewed shrieks, but these grew fainter as Lady Eadyth carried her away.

My eyes followed her, until the dimness of the hall and the mist of tears that rose obscured Lady Eadyth. Then I fought back the tears, knowing they would only gain me a beating. I suppose I knew, too, that it was right for Audris to be cared for by a woman, and the fact that Sir Oliver was praising me, saying it was a miracle that I had kept

the child alive, also eased my bitterness. I had had few
words of praise in my life, only now and again, grudgingly
uttered, by the man-at-arms who trained me. Thus, despite
my grief, I was able to answer Sir Oliver's questions so
that in the end he knew everything. And it was he who
told me, as kindly as one is able to give such news, that
my mother was dead.

I felt no grief over my mother—all my grief and loss
was confined to Audris—but knowing my mother was
gone for good gave me a sense of being adrift with nothing
to cling to. I do not remember that I made any response to
Sir Oliver; perhaps my expression was enough, for he put
his hand on my shoulder and himself led me down to the
kitchen, where he bade one of the cooks feed me. I must
have told him that Audris and I had had no dinner; there
was food in the tower, but we had been too frightened to
eat. And as the cook hurried to find cold meat and some
pasty for me, Sir Oliver told me that when I was full I
might amuse myself as I pleased until bedtime and that I
should sleep in the tower that night, until he could make
new arrangements for my care.

Looking back, I wonder what he planned. Not, I suspect, what actually happened. It was Audris, I believe,
who forced Sir Oliver to take me into his own household.
He was a good man, honest and honorable, but I do not
think he intended to raise a whore's son with his own
children. Perhaps I am wrong. He knew, although he
never said it and I had not claimed it—my mother had
made clear to me that it was forbidden—that Sir William
was my father. In any case, it is foolish to speculate on
what can never be proven. What happened, happened, and
my life has been shaped by that, not by what might have
been.

Audris could not be quieted. She screamed until Sir
Oliver bade his wife bring her back to me, and even when
she became more accustomed to her aunt and the new
servants, she would not be parted from me for long. Lady
Eadyth tried a few times more over the following days to
separate us, but Audris began to scream the moment I was
out of her sight. So instead of being cast out completely or

raised among the servants, Sir Oliver took me into his family.

His sons tried to overawe me at first and called me "whore's son," but I stared them down with such pride that even Alain, who was older than I by more than a year, did not dare raise a hand to strike me. And when I was matched with him in swordplay, I beat him so quickly and so soundly that he came to be in awe of me. I think when they saw my skill in riding and fighting, Alain and young Oliver wished to be my friends, and we were easy enough together doing those things that boys do, but I could never take them into my heart. I could not forget that they *had* called me "whore's son" at first, and they tormented Audris when they could.

I think Sir Oliver noticed their hatred of Audris, for he sent them early to be fostered. After Alain was sent away, I expected to go too, but Sir Oliver kept me in Jernaeve. He never gave a reason. Well, he was not a man for talk. At first I thought it was for Audris's sake. Later, I realized it was because he did not wish to foist me on a noble family as if I were gently born. Poor man, now I know I was a burden on his loyal heart. He knew me for his brother's get, yet my father had never recognized me. But he took over my training himself, teaching me the skills of a knight rather than those of a man-at-arms, and I learned that he paid for my armor—true mail, not the boiled leather of a common soldier—out of his own purse.

By the time I was fifteen, I was growing restless and a little bored in Jernaeve. Like any youth, I thought that I knew all there was to know and was impatient with lessons. And my case was worse than many others because Sir Oliver did not allow me to put into practice what I had learned by going in his stead to oversee the outlying manors or to collect the dues from the small keeps beholden to Jernaeve. So when he loosed my tether and sent me with a troop from Jernaeve to answer a summons from the king to fight in France, I was wild with joy. I went as squire to Sir Oliver's substitute, a man called Sir Bernard, and I learned two salutary lessons.

The first was about women. When we came to London, I was burning with desire for a woman. Not that I was a

virgin. Knowing too much of the uses of women from my
youth, I had sought out one of the castle whores—in fact,
she who had taken over my mother's place—as soon as the
first desires came upon me. I had always something to
trade for the service, for I needed only to ask Audris for an
old silk ribbon or take a heel of the fine bread or rich
cheese that appeared only on our table. Such small items
were sufficient; I knew I did not need to pay at all. A word
to the bailiff could have brought deep trouble to anyone
who displeased Sir Oliver's squire—but I never used that
weapon. Quite aside from the fact that Sir Oliver would
have been furious if he found I had misused my power in
such a way, I had too clear a memory of my mother's
troubles (despite being shielded by the presence of the
lord's bastard and my father's favor—such as it was) to
wish more trouble on any woman who needed to ply
Berta's trade.

I think I was a favorite with the whore too, partly
because I was a whore's son and partly because I was
young and not ugly. Whatever the reason, she taught me
ways to pleasure a woman so that she could receive from
me some measure of return for what she gave. I was
impatient at first, eager only for my own delight, but I
soon learned that to resist my satisfaction was to make it
more intense when it came. I do not think, though, even in
those early years when the body's demands are paramount,
that I was a lecher. And later, I was even less given to the
demands of the flesh—but to be honest, that may have
been because once I left Jernaeve, most of the women I
could afford, if I wished to use them often, I could not
stomach.

What drove me that night in London, though, was less a
need of the body than curiosity. I imagined that a whore in
a great city would be something strange and somehow
richer than the woman who plied that trade in Jernaeve.
Had I not been warned by a priest that the lips of a strange
woman drop as a honeycomb and her mouth was smoother
than oil? Having been told that such joys existed, was it
not natural that I should be eager to experience them?

Not being an utter looby, I realized that the price of
what I bought would be higher in London than at home,

but I had several items for trade. One of my perquisites as squire was to keep the horsehair I curried from our mounts, and since I was assiduous at such duties, I had a bag of the resilient hair beaten free of dirt. This was much favored for stuffing pallets or cushions. I had also the candle ends from the thick candles that Sir Bernard burned at night to ward off evil spirits. The candle ends were of a good length, no mere stubs, since the days were long and the nights short in the spring. In Jernaeve, I knew any of these would be a welcome gift, but here in London I took along one of the coins from the purse Audris had given me when I left Jernaeve—I knew enough not to take along the purse.

Clever as I thought myself, I was still skinned. My "pleasure" cost me my shirt as well as the other items, but in a way I received value for my payment. Because of my expectations, I chose the most exotic appearing of the women I encountered. In the uncertain light of flaring torches she looked a marvel—her eyes rimmed with black, her skin whiter than milk, her cheeks and lips a more brilliant color than those of any woman I had seen. I had no idea at that time that a woman could paint herself to change her appearance, and I followed her eagerly, expecting wonders, only to discover that she was less in every way than the whore of Jernaeve—even after I bribed her, knowing the way of whores, to show me some new twist in the play of love. And I discovered, too, once I had recovered from my disappointment, that there was only a shade of difference in my own pleasure and that difference rested only on the fact that I was fond of the woman in Jernaeve and cared nothing for the whore in London. Years later, if I could have found that whore I would have given her a round sum, for that lesson was worth far more than I paid her.

My other lesson came with being blooded in battle—a little more thoroughly than Sir Oliver had intended, I suspect. In fact, I am not sure the action at Bourg Thérould should be called a battle. There were no tens of thousands drawn up with brave banners flying and heralds riding to and fro crying defiance and shouting heroic lines to hearten their masters' men alternately with crying curses and imprecations at the enemy. Perhaps Bourg Thérould was no more than a skirmish. However, it was battle enough to me—it was my first and God knows it was a bloodier fight than many far greater battles.

I changed from boy to man that day. I was a boy when I waited to charge, lance in hand, thrilled to know that I would be aiming at a living man rather than a senseless quintain. Such are the young: I did not once think that if my aim was good a living man, against whom I had no spite, whom I did not even know, would be painfully hurt or die. I did not harm my first target. I was not heavy enough at fifteen to overset him, and either by luck or skill, I warded off his lance; but the second I struck true, and the dreadful scream as my lance thrust through mail and gambeson made me a man. Quintains do not scream.

I cried out too, in horror at what I had done. Could I have withdrawn, I might have run away, but I was attacked and by instinct defended myself. And then Sir Bernard was struck down. I did not know that he was dead, and it was my duty to defend him so I fought on. I did not even dare spew up the meal I had so gaily eaten that morning, though the screaming and stink of blood and excrement from the loosened bowels of the dying (or terrified) roiled my stomach. Instead I went away inside myself to some far place where all the stench and noise were very distant and could not touch me. I have sought and found that place many times since then, but I no longer wake up as I did the night after Bourg Thérould, sobbing bitterly.

I was utterly amazed, wondering about what I was weeping. When I caught my breath, I realized that the tent was free of my master's snores, and it all came back to me. I still am not sure why I wept, and I have given the matter some thought over the years. Oh, I was sorry that Sir Bernard was dead, but in those days the only person whose death could have wrung from me those racking tears and sobs was Audris's. Perhaps I wept for those who had died by *my* hand, or for all men who died in battle— but I think it was more for myself, because the innocent joy of boyhood in my skill in arms was lost.

Later in the day, though, I remembered how the leader

of our force and many others had praised me for my heroic
defense and I began to grow proud of what I had done. Is
it not this that makes war possible? That men forget so
easily their revulsion at inflicting pain and death on others
and recall only their pride in their own prowess?

After the battle, which broke the back of the rebellion
against the king, I was witness to the punishment of the
prisoners. I saw how men without influence were sen-
tenced to be maimed or blinded or killed, whereas one
such as Waleran de Meulan, who had been a leader of the
rebels against the king—although he had been raised like a
son in the king's own household—was only sent into
gentle imprisonment. One good effect of the fearful pun-
ishments exacted for rebellion was that I became less
discontent for a time with the quiet life in Jernaeve and
was glad to go home.

I was welcomed back with wild joy by Audris, and that,
too, sweetened the days of that summer—but I found also
that Audris and I had come to a parting in the ways of our
hearts. Out of love, she listened to my tales of war, but
she was horrified, gentle creature that she was, not excited. She did not even much relish my tales of London
and the foreign towns I had seen. It was the hills and
forests and the wild creatures that lived in them that she
loved, not close-packed houses filled with people or the
streets busy with trade. We did not love each other less,
but we had grown apart.

As if to compensate, I was closer to Sir Oliver for a
time than I had ever been before. I had brought with me a
sealed letter for him from the commander of the force,
which, I am sure, held high praise of my behavior in both
camp and field, and for the next few years Sir Oliver put
me to use fighting off raids by outlaws and Scots. That
first year I went with Sir Oliver to drive the raiders away
and follow them back and burn their villages. The next
two years I led a troop of my own, and was welcomed
warmly in the manors to which I brought relief and protection. In some of them I stayed the night or even a few
days, and more than once I was asked questions about
Audris that puzzled me.

At first I said nothing to Sir Oliver about these questions, fearing to bring trouble on my hosts, but their curiosity about Audris herself, and such matters as when she would be ripe to marry and whether Sir Oliver was soon planning to betroth her and to whom, remained in my mind. Then one afternoon while Sir Oliver and I were idly drinking ale before the high-burning fire of deep winter, before I thought, my mouth had disclosed what puzzled me.

In the next instant my blood froze in my veins, so strange was Sir Oliver's expression as he slowly lifted his head. He had been idly watching the flames in the fireplace as he grumbled; now, instead, he stared at me for a long moment in silence. Finally he said heavily, "I knew the time would come."

Pretending my heart was not leaping in my throat, I stared back at him. "If I have done wrong and should have told you about this sooner, I am sorry. I thought there was no harm intended, just a natural curiosity about Audris because she is so shy."

Sir Oliver sighed. "You have done no wrong. Still, you must leave Jernaeve. I cannot keep you anywhere on the lands. You are a danger to Audris."

"I?" I gasped, the shock of hearing so suddenly that I must leave my home being swallowed up in the far greater shock his last sentence gave me. "I a danger to Audris? I would die to protect her."

"I have no doubt of it," Sir Oliver said sadly, and then with a spurt of bitterness, "Damn your Fermain face! Why could you not look like your mother?"

This time I was so stupefied by astonishment that I could not find my voice at all and just gaped at him.

"Do you not see that the men beholden to Jernaeve might prefer a strong man they know to hold the lands, bastard though he be, to a frail maiden?" Sir Oliver went on after a moment, watching me all the while as if he would draw the thoughts inside my head out through my eyes.

He could have discerned nothing but astonishment and disbelief, because that was all I felt—but it is likely he could not tell what I was thinking at all. I had not that trust in people that allowed every emotion to play freely over

Audris's face, and it had long been my practice to hide what I felt.

"You cannot believe I would have any part in such a scheme," I protested when I could speak.

Sir Oliver shook his head. "Nonetheless, the longer you remain, the more men will compare you with Audris and the greater their discontent will grow. You must go."

Fear and desire warred in me. I knew that I no longer had a home, that I was to be cut off from Jernaeve forever and that was a fearful thing, but I also had a deep craving to go out into the world, where perhaps I could make a place for myself that did not depend on being my father's get on a whore. I also feared Audris's reaction to hearing I was leaving Jernaeve for good, and I dared not tell her the real reason. It would be a bitter brew indeed to make poor, loving Audris drink of, that because she was a frail woman I had become a threat to her possession of Jernaeve. A silly fear. Audris had always known me better than I knew myself, and she had seen my restlessness. She tried to hide her tears to spare me pain and only made me promise that I would never fail to send her letters.

Again, I was not cast out but sent with honor, with a fine horse of my own training and good arms and armor. In the spring, I went to serve Eustace Fitz-John, in Alnwick keep, as one of the captains of the men-at-arms. I had my seat among the other captains and the upper servants at the second table and respect from the common folk and men-at-arms; I had no need to feel that I had fallen. And, although the troop I was given to manage was small and all raw men, that was to be expected for one as young as I. I took great pleasure in training the men and polishing them, and in the small actions we were sent on they behaved well. The troop was enlarged and then enlarged again.

Before I realized it, two years had passed. Every few months a messenger came from Audris in Jernaeve with a letter of news about the keep and the family, and I sent a letter back with the man with my small news, but in 1126 I had matter of greater interest to tell, great enough to hire a messenger of my own to carry word to Jernaeve. King Henry's son-by-marriage, emperor of the Romans, had died, and his widow, Empress Matilda, had returned to her father. King Henry had been in Normandy all this time, but now he was coming back to England, bringing Matilda with him with the avowed purpose of forcing the barons to swear that they would take her for their queen when he died.

To my surprise, I was chosen to accompany Sir Eustace to the swearing. It was most interesting to see the seeming eagerness with which all men swore to uphold Matilda's right to the throne against all others in the king's presence. The greatest lords gave their oaths first. King David of Scotland swore to her first; after that there was nearly a quarrel between Robert, earl of Gloucester, the king's most beloved bastard, and Stephen of Blois, sister's son to the king and his favorite nephew, as to who should first swear fealty. Robert claimed the right of half brother; Stephen the right of sister's son.

I could not help wondering, considering what I had heard in Alnwick, on the road, and in the drinking houses, which of the three would betray her first, for Matilda, I could see, was not the kind of woman who could make a man *wish* to die for her. Out of the king's sight and hearing, it was clear that no one was happy with the idea that a woman would rule England.

CHAPTER 2

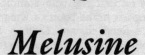

Melusine

I was the precious poppet, the dearest toy, the brightest ornament of the manor of Ulle. It is not often, I know, that the birth of a daughter is welcomed with cries of joy by her mother, let alone by her father, but my parents already had seven strong sons. It was plain enough why my mother was joyful about having a daughter; she had no other woman of her own kind to share her interests and burdens, but one might be surprised by my father's gladness and attention to me. He never said why, of course, and for a long time I did not know his treatment of me was different from that of other fathers so I did not ask. By the time I realized that I was cossetted and favored above most other daughters, there were good reasons for his favor and I was too busy and too content to think about it. Now that I look back, I would guess that my father was a man who needed the soft love of a woman, the fond flattery and the gentle bantering talk that only a woman can provide.

I do not mean to say that my father and mother lived unhappily together. They did not quarrel nor hate each other, but there was a cause of distrust between them. I know that grieved my mother, at least in later years, for she felt the cause was long gone—but she did not know my father as well as he knew himself. Thus, she could not understand the wariness he still felt toward her after so many years as husband and wife, and when she sickened it troubled her mind so much that she talked of it.

My father, Sir Malcolm of Ulle, was not born in Ulle. He had been liege man to Duncan, eldest son of King Malcolm of Scotland. When Malcolm was murdered and his brother, Donald Ban, came to power, Duncan fled to England and my father came with him. Papa learned the ways of the Normans in the court of King William Rufus and rode back to Scotland with Duncan when, with the English king's support, he drove his uncle from the throne. In less than a year, however, Duncan had been murdered too, and my father fled for his life to a distant cousin of his mother's who held the lands of Ulle. Three years later, Edgar, Duncan's half brother, drove Donald Ban from the throne, but though papa loved Scotland and still considered himself a Scot, he saw no reason to go back there. He was a younger son in a large family and had no heritage to claim. Edgar, the son of Malcolm's second wife, was not likely to offer much to his brother's man when he had so many of his own retainers to reward. And papa had made a place for himself in Ulle, for his cousin was a lazy, dissolute man who was delighted to let my father manage his estate. He had no heir and wanted none, quite content that papa should hold the lands after his death—if he could.

Mama did not know when papa's cousin died, but by 1104 when Henry, who had been king of England for four years, came on a progress to take fealty of those subjects who had not previously sworn to him, papa was holding Ulle. At that time, King Henry did not have the absolute power he came to wield over his subjects in later years, and he still needed to consider the opinions of his barons. So, because papa's neighbors liked him and his tenants had few complaints, King Henry decided not to try to drive him out of Ulle, even though he was Scots born and had no real legal right to the estate. On the other hand, King Henry did not trust papa—well, from what I have heard, he did not trust anyone very much—I mean that he trusted papa even less because of his Scots birth and his remaining love of that country.

Mama was the answer to that distrust. Her father was totally dependent on King Henry's favor, and mama was bidden to marry my father and to watch for signs of treason in him. If she sent warning, she would be rewarded and her children would be assured of the estate and of other favors from the king. If she did not send warning, not only would she and her children suffer the same fate as her husband but her father and mother and siblings would go with her to blinding or exile or death.

I remember crying out against so disgusting a charge and saying that I would not consent to be a spy against the man to whom I was united in wedlock. Mama's eyes had grown huge with the wasting of her face and body, and now, though she laughed at my childish protest, they glittered darkly with tears.

"A woman has no choice," she said. "Could I seize my sword and leave my home to make my own way? My father would have beaten me to death if I had set my will against that of the king."

"There are convents—" I began.

She laughed again. "Few that would take in a woman against the king's will and her family's will, but even if I had been a man, I would have been constrained to obey. My refusal would have meant disaster for my whole family. How could the king trust my father to hold lands and enforce order if he could not obtain obedience from his own family?"

"And why did papa agree?" I cried, for I was still young enough then to think my father the strongest and wisest man in the world, one who did not need to submit his will to any man.

"He had no right to Ulle," my mother replied. "He had no more choice than I, for if he refused so reasonable a request, no one would have blamed King Henry for being unwilling to enfeoff him."

So, in exchange for a charter for his lands, papa had to agree to take mama as his wife. Whether King Henry actually told my father what he had arranged, mama did not know, but papa was not stupid and he guessed.

I did not learn until much too late that my mother had been the victim of *two* clever men. Years after mama had told me her story, papa retold it, except he laughed—not at my mother's pain, I do not mean that. Papa was not a monster, and he had had his own grief to bear, for he had never dared to let himself show affection for mama or let her forget her purpose. It was King Henry at whom he laughed because the king had not seen the trap he was laying for himself—at least, that was the way my father saw the matter. To promise my mother that the lands would stay with her and her children if she gave warning of any treason intended by my father had freed him, papa said, to do as he pleased. When there was some contest between England and Scotland, where he felt his honor was engaged with the Scots, he planned to tell my mother to send her warning, which would ensure she and his children would be safe from retribution.

It happened that it did not matter. In all the years of King Henry's reign, there was peace between Scotland and England. I do not count the raiding by outlaws and by the lowland lairds, who sought to add to their thin fortunes with loot from England. Naturally, papa fought raiders with the same ferocity whether they were Scots or English or anyone else, just as any other landholder did. Besides, most of the raiding took place in the west, where, I now know, the land is richer. Thus, there was never any reason for mama to be torn between loyalty to her husband and fear of the king.

At the time my mother spoke to me of these matters, of course I did not know why my father had kept the memory of the purpose of their marriage always between them. I thought that wrong, but there were many reasons I never spoke of the matter to him. The most important was that when he saw mama was dying, he softened and became tender to her. I was afraid then to blame him for past coldness lest he be angry with mama for telling me of her long pain and withdraw the warmth he was at last offering. There were also selfish reasons: I adored my father and could hardly bear, even for my dying mother's sake, to make him angry. Least important, but still a real problem, was that I had little time or energy to spare for anything. As my mother weakened, more and more of the ordering of the household fell on my shoulders. I was only thirteen, and for fear a mistake would bring the servants' scorn on me and make them disobedient, I did too much myself and mulled over every order ten times before I dared give it.

I have not mentioned my grief at my mother's illness and death, partly because it has grown dim over the years that have passed and partly because that whole period was so filled with pain for me that I could hardly distinguish one grief from another. I know that such things are the will of God and God's reasons are beyond our understanding. So I am sinful and rebellious—I have been told that many times—but I still think it cruel and unfair that sorrows be heaped all of a sudden on the head of one who is unaccustomed to their weight. Sorrows, like any other burden, should come small at first and then larger, until one has gained the strength to bear them.

For me they did not come that way. From the day of my birth, I was petted and pampered, for my brothers might contest against each other but all of them scorned to fight a girl. As an infant and a young child, I was a toy, a beloved plaything, to all the men in my family. Not one came back from his fostering for a visit without bringing to me a new toy or, later, a new ribbon or lace or other ornament. To speak the truth, although I was tall and sturdily made, they all, my father also, watched over me so closely that I sometimes felt I would be smothered under their care. It seemed I could not turn around lest one cry out, "Be careful, you will grow dizzy and fall," nor walk a straight path lest another take my hand to be sure I would not trip and scrape my knee.

Among them, they would have made me unable to draw breath without help and spoiled my temper completely, except that even with seven coming and going, my brothers were rarely at home. Papa, too, was often away, and when he was not he was busy. Thus, my care and upbringing were in my mother's hands, and mama would have nothing to do with weakness and willfulness. She saw that my father and brothers would soon ruin me, and as soon as I could walk and talk, she set about teaching me not only all the womanly skills she had but that I was a real person, no weaker and no stupider than my brothers. If mama bade me carry a message for her and I said I was tired, she sent me five times over the route. If I wept without reason, she whipped me soundly to give me a reason. If I pouted and said a lesson was too hard, she set me two that were harder.

I learned quickly that I was strong enough and clever enough to do anything. And since I had learned that lesson from mama when I was very young, my menfolk's cossetting raised a demon of mischief in me. To say it plainly, I led them all round by their noses, and by setting one against the other and working on their fears for me, I induced them to teach me all kinds of unsuitable things. Papa was the one easiest to wheedle with tears; he taught me to ride a fat, placid pony because I wept and pleaded, but it did not take me long to transfer that knowledge to a swift, rangy mare called Vinaigre for her habit of biting. But she did not bite me, for I brought her sweets, and by the time papa learned what I had done, I managed her so well he was proud rather than angry.

Duncan, my eldest brother, taught me to shoot a bow. Malcolm, my second brother, taught me to handle a hawk. Donald, the third, was a great one for women, willing or not; he taught me to use a knife and other ways to defend myself against men. Andrew, who was pledged to the Church, taught me to read and write. Angus let me ride hunting with him—but he was only four years my elder and not as sure that I was as fragile as his older brothers believed. The two youngest, Magnus and Fergus, taught me nothing new, but I honed my skills against theirs and they knew I would not break.

So my life was full of joy, holy and unholy, until my thirteenth year. I was born in the spring, on May Day, and that day had always been a high festival for my family. If they could, my brothers came from wherever they were to join the celebration, and so five of them did in the year 1129. Five came and four, two with their wives and their children, died.

I was too sick myself to understand the calamity that had befallen us. When I learned of it, I wept for days and began to sicken again. I remember my father sitting beside me and trying to comfort me, begging me to eat, himself weeping, holding me in his arms all night long, rocking

me in the hope I would sleep. The kindness made me
worse, for I felt it to be my fault that so many had died.
All I could say, between sobs, was that they would still be
alive if they had not come to make me happy on my
birthday. Then mama came to sit with me for a little time,
begging my father to go and rest, but as soon as papa was
gone, she slapped me as hard as she could—not very hard,
for she was weak herself—and called me a selfish, thoughtless slut.

"You spoiled, self-indulgent monster," she hissed. "Do
you think your father does not grieve, nor I? What right
have you to add to our pain with your lamentations? If as
you say it is your fault your brothers are dead, is it not
your duty to comfort *us*? Your father has not slept in two
nights because of your selfishness. Will you be more
content when you have killed him too?"

The slap and the cruelty of her words stunned me. I was
silent for a minute or two, then cried that she was cruel
and heartless and I hated her, and wept more than ever—I
wonder if I wished she would beat me in the hope that the
punishment would lift away some part of my burden of
guilt. But she did not respond either to my tears or my
words, only sat staring into nothing with a face like a stone
mask of misery until my father's step could be heard
returning. Then her face changed and she went to him and
scolded with loving gentleness because he had come so
soon. He said she should be in her bed herself and that he
could not rest while I, his pearl of price, he called me, was
in danger.

My cot had been moved into mama's bedchamber so
that she could hear how I was cared for even while she lay
abed. The window was wide open in the mild spring day,
and the light from it fell full on papa's face as he stood in
the doorway. When I saw how sunken were his eyes, their
bright blue dimmed to watery grey, and how the skin hung
on the broad bones of his face, my mother's cruel words
rang in my head . . . and did not seem cruel but just. I *was*
a monster not to have seen how much I added to his
suffering while I indulged my own grief. From that moment I struggled to bury it, and I think I succeeded in

becoming a comfort to mama and papa. But I never celebrated my birthday again . . . never.

So my thirteenth year began and so it ended. Duncan
and Malcolm, with their wives and children, and Angus
and Fergus died in the first week of May. Andrew, who
had survived the disease, as had I, was granted the high
honor of accompanying his bishop on a trip to Rome; he
died there late in January. We did not learn of his death
until the end of April, and by then I had no more tears to
shed, for my mother had died only two weeks earlier. It
was the one mercy of that terrible year that my mother did
not need to hear of Andrew's death.

After that, the hand of God was lifted from us—but not
all the way and only for a time. Donald left his service
with King David of Scotland and came home, for he was
now the heir to Ulle. He had sworn he would never take a
wife, but now he agreed to marry to breed sons. Papa
chose the girl, far more with an eye to the sum she would
bring as dower than to her beauty or temper—papa was
sure that Donald was too hardened a sinner to be reformed
by any woman—and so Mildred's dower brought Thirl
manor and its lands into my family. And then a strange
thing happened: Although I cannot say Mildred was a
beauty, she had such charm that Donald was soon weaned
away from his pursuit of other women. Somehow she
satisfied him completely.

I cannot help but laugh at myself and my stupidity when
I think about Mildred. I was then so sure of my power
over men, not thinking that when I was neither sister nor
daughter my advantage might disappear, that I never asked
Mildred how she had conquered Donald. We were good
friends too, for Mildred was not jealous by nature and she
did not begrudge me my sister's share of Donald's love.
But mayhap it is as well I never learned, for I discovered
Mildred was not a Christian; although she went to Mass to
save trouble, she worshipped the old horned god. The
priest said it was that devil worship which brought our
final catastrophe upon us, but I do not believe it. Most of
the common folk worshipped as Mildred did and no ill
befell them. Besides, I loved Mildred and love her still.

The first years of Donald's marriage were good years.

Day by day the pain I hid and thought would never ease grew less. I learned to laugh again, and Mildred brought new life into our family. She and Donald lived in Thirl, not Ulle manor, but it was no great distance and we were together often. And at first when papa saw how Donald was changing and casting aside his wild ways, he was delighted with Mildred's power; so was I, and I never came to think differently for Donald was a very happy man. However, Mildred did not get with child, and as the years passed and no seed quickened in her womb, my father grew dissatisfied. I will say for papa that he tried everything to get an heir for Ulle before he said one word against Mildred. As soon as Magnus was knighted, my father found a wife for him.

I have been telling my tale as if the outside world did not touch me or Ulle, and in a way that is true. The country around Ulle is wild and mountainous and has little to attract those not bred to the place. Strangers fear the steep, rough tracks that climb from our narrow valleys over the high passes through the hills and creep around the edges of our deep tarns, but the valleys are sheltered and fertile and the tarns are full of fish. So, though we are not rich in gold and gems, there is food in plenty for the few people who live here. And, though we are few, the people are not weak or slavish. Every man must use bow and spear and long knife to protect himself and his family and beasts against the bear and wolf that roam the mountains, and our people do not fear to turn the same weapons against human enemies.

Still, we are not wholly free of affairs outside our own shire. I have told already how King Henry, as one small part of tightening his grip on England, summoned my father and arranged his marriage. Some years later, when King Edgar of Scotland died, King Henry helped Alexander, Edgar's half brother, succeed peacefully to the Scottish throne. Since papa agreed that Alexander had the right to rule, it caused no change in our lives—except for having to listen to papa grumble that it was not Henry's business to interfere, even if what he did was right. Papa felt the Scots should settle their own affairs, even if it meant they would fight and murder each other for years. Now, I do not know that I agree with him, although then I was too young to have any opinion.

Far more important to my family was that Prince David, Alexander's younger brother, became overlord of Cumbria. Papa went to his investiture and did homage to him and came back full of praise for the prince. I do not remember that, for I was only six when King Alexander died and David became king of Scotland. King Henry insisted that David relinquish the rule of Cumbria when he took the throne. I know this because papa constantly bewailed the loss of David as overlord. To me it was never entirely clear why he bewailed it, but a hint here and there implied that David had favored a fellow Scot, whereas an English overlord would be prejudiced against him.

For many years I thought that rather funny. I am of Ulle, not Scottish nor Norman nor English, and I could not understand why my father, who had lived at Ulle all except a few years at the very beginning of his life, did not feel the same. Moreover, after my mother's death I was responsible for tallying the dues that came in from our tenants and the smaller manors that papa had bought or established on unsettled lands near us and the dues that we sent to our overlord or to the king. Since there was no great difference no matter where the dues went, I could not believe we were worse treated than any other holder in the shire.

Later I learned the charters for the small manors papa had established at Wyth, Rydal, and Irthing, where he had settled an old friend, Sir Gerald, had been written and sealed by Prince David. Even then I saw no real reason for papa's complaints. We paid dues on those new manors, which would profit the overlord, whoever he might be. Though I kept the accounts, papa did not think women fit for understanding the intricacies of politics and did not discuss such matters with me, so I was left to believe he feared a new overlord would not honor the charters for spite. I did not realize there was more profit to enfeoffing a new man than in collecting rents faithfully paid.

Those manors papa founded kept us poor. Had he not diverted flocks and men from Ulle into the new lands, we could have established new villages in Ulle, enlarged our fishing fleet, and sold our produce, particularly the lake fish, which were in great demand. Sometimes I resented the draining away of our wealth, especially when I was young and was refused some bauble or a length of fine cloth or gold thread, but I soon realized why papa was so intent on those new manors. He loved his sons and would not send them out to make their own way as he had been sent with no land to come back to. And one of the manors, Wyth, was to be my dower.

Until King Henry died, all went well with us. We rejoiced heartily at the birth of the king's grandson in 1133 because, if the child lived, he would rule in his grandfather's place rather than Matilda, to whom the barons had been forced to swear. The king, though aging, seemed strong, the land was at peace, and our personal concern—who would hold Cumbria—seemed settled. To avoid giving offense to King David, who claimed Cumbria for his eldest son, or to Ranulf, earl of Chester, who claimed it because his father had once ruled it, King Henry would hold it as Crown land. And since no one could alienate Crown land except the king, papa believed that the new manors would be "old" and ours by long custom as well as by law before any question regarding them could be raised. Another son, Geoffrey, was born to Matilda in 1134, securing, as we thought, the succession.

Papa, who had been uneasy and grumbling ever since the swearing to Matilda, stopped talking about the probable horrors of being ruled by a woman—to which I had made no answer, although he tried my temper sorely. I often felt like recommending to him one of his own favorite maxims: Never cast away dross without a careful look; a jewel may be hidden within. But I had met Matilda when she came north with her father—not to Ulle, of course, but once in Carlisle and once in Richmond, and unfortunately, I thought papa was right, except for discounting *all* women. Besides, pert remarks, except in jest on light matters, are no way to manage a man, so I held my tongue.

So the year 1135 opened with contentment for us, which deepened into a hope for happiness as Magnus was wed to Winifred—both being willing and well satisfied with the match—and she got with child within the month. To ensure her comfort and safety, papa bade the young couple live with us at Ulle instead of at Rydal, which would eventually be their home, and built them their own small house within the walls. Winifred was happy, and though she was a simple soul and I could not feel for her what I felt for Mildred, we lived peaceably together. The crops were good that year and the fish plentiful. The priests are always mumbling about signs and portents, but they are all liars, I think. There were *no* signs that summer or autumn of 1135 that the long peace in which England had basked and grown rich was about to be shattered.

CHAPTER 3

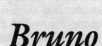

Bruno

I LIVED in Alnwick nearly ten more years before I had an answer to the question I had asked myself when I had gone with Sir Eustace to watch Stephen of Blois and Robert of Gloucester swear fealty to Matilda. I do not recall whether I remembered my curiosity about which man would first betray her when news of King Henry's death and Stephen's crowning as king came to Alnwick. However, I did not feel surprised when Sir Eustace, seemingly without giving a thought to the oath he himself had sworn to Matilda, greeted the news with pleasure and swore fealty to the new king. I *was* surprised when I heard that King David of Scotland had determined to abide by his oath to Matilda and had brought an army into Northumbria, demanding that each keep yield to him in Matilda's name, but that was because at that time I was not aware that King David had a strong claim to the lordship of Northumbria through his wife.

Since winter was well advanced, all the crops were in and the early slaughtering had been done so the keep was fully stocked. By that time I was master-at-arms in Alnwick, and I began with all speed to prepare to repel an assault or withstand a siege. All the war machines on the walls were tested, and stones for flinging by the trenchbuts, huge

arrows for the ballistas, were set ready. The fletchers were
set to making arrows and quarrels; the smiths to repairing
armor and making extra weapons; and the serfs to prepar-
ing long hooked poles for casting down ladders, carrying
sand and oil for heating and pouring down on our enemies,
and piling hides where they might be needed to protect
against fire.

We were ready when the Scots came, but it had been a
wasted effort. Sir Eustace had his terms of surrender all
ready to present to them. He would do homage to King
David as overlord of Northumbria and swear to support
Matilda if he was confirmed in his possession of Alnwick.
I could hardly believe my ears when he ordered me to
carry these terms to the leader of the Scots.

"Why should you propose terms to them?" I protested.
"There are no more than five or six hundred men out
there. Probably we can drive them away, but even if we
cannot, the Scots have no staying power. We can sit them
out."

"Fool!" he shouted. "Do you think this is all the army?
Norham was taken—"

"It is all the army that is here," I snapped back. "And
certainly not enough of an army to make me change my
mind about who would better rule England."

"Make *you* change your mind!" Sir Eustace bellowed.
"Who are you to throw your opinions in my teeth, whore's
son? You are my hired sword, and you are no longer even
that, since you refuse to obey my orders. Get to your
quarters and out of my sight. Get out!"

What he saw in my face turned his purple. After that, I
barely escaped with my horse and arms. I think I succeeded in riding out on Barbe because Sir Eustace was
either afraid or ashamed to order the men-at-arms I had led
to stop me. The Scots, having had so easy a conquest,
were too surprised to interfere when I galloped out and, I
guess, felt one man and one horse not worth pursuing. It
was not until I was well away and sure of freedom that I
began to wonder what to do with it.

Sir Oliver would surely blame me for throwing away my
livelihood. Doubtless he would think it was not my business what Sir Eustace did with Alnwick; *my* honor was in

no way involved. I began to wonder whether the real
reason that I had insulted Sir Eustace was because I was
bored and his refusal to fight had meant my boredom must
continue. The more I thought, the more dissatisfied I
became with my behavior and the less willing I became to
reach Jernaeve and face Sir Oliver despite an icy rain that
began to fall. I turned Barbe due west toward Wark,
telling myself that Sir Oliver must know of the coming of
the Scots already and that it would not matter if I slept the
night in Wark. It was only right to warn Sir Walter Espec's
castellan, too, I reasoned.

The fact that it was full dark by the time I topped a
small rise not far from Wark keep saved me. Though I was
half asleep, my hands instinctively pulled back the reins to
stop Barbe. It took a minute longer for my tired thoughts
to fix on what was wrong—and then I saw there was a
yellow glow beyond the shadow of the keep. I had been
looking straight ahead above the level of the ground on
which Wark's motte rose, seeing nothing in my weariness
and heartsickness, trusting Barbe to find safe footing as we
went. Now I looked down the slope to ground level and
saw the cause of the glow. Wark was ringed with camp-
fires. The keep was besieged!

Then, as I turned away southward, I nearly ran into a
troop of men who were not intent on raiding but seemed to
be searching for someone. I escaped partly because I knew
the territory from the years I had lived in Jernaeve and
fought for Sir Oliver and partly because, as tired as he
was, Barbe was a better horse than any the troop rode. Yet
Barbe was my greatest danger too. I might have escaped
more easily on foot, slipping through the woods while the
pursuers followed Barbe, for I was well within walking
distance of Jernaeve, but I never considered leaving him. I
loved my stallion; still, it was not that which bound me to
him. Barbe was a knight's destrier, and it was unlikely that
I could ever afford another if I should lose him. It was
only my fine sword and mail and Barbe—mostly Barbe—
that raised me above a common man-at-arms, and though
perhaps I should have overcome selfishness and considered
Jernaeve's danger more important than my horse, I did
not.

I need not dwell longer on the horrors of riding and hiding in the icy rain. For me, they shrank to insignificance in the warmth of the welcome I received from Audris. Sir Oliver said no word of blame over my leaving Alnwick and he was glad of my news, for he had heard nothing about the Scots being so near as Wark, but I could see he was troubled by my coming. For Audris—and for me also, though I tried to hide it—it was a pure and utter joy. Knowing that we must soon part again and that she was now a woman grown, I tried at first to keep a distance from her, but Audris was no more manageable now than she had been as a little girl. She had her own way— sweetly and with laughter, but her own way nonetheless. I have often wondered how many besides myself realize how stubborn and willful Audris is, and how successful in gaining her ends.

But that day I was only too glad that she succeeded in obtaining her desire. She insisted on taking me to her own chamber, to which Sir Oliver agreed at once; that surprised me at first, but I will credit Sir Oliver for never harboring any suspicion of the love between us nor wishing to lessen it. I realized later that he only wanted me out of the way, and in Audris's tower no one would see me, but at that time I thought I would burst with joy. My heart had been cold and still for more than twelve long years, for there was not one person beside Audris that cared for me or desired me to care.

And to complete my joy, nothing in the south tower had changed. Oh, Audris had grown a few inches since I last saw her, but only a few; she was still a tiny, faerylike creature with silver-gilt hair, the merriest laugh, and the kindest heart of any child born of woman. The loom standing by the window had grown a great deal more than Audris, and from the display of yarn it seemed that her weaving had become a serious business, but there was also a table on the other side of the window on which lay a heap of scrolls. Plainly Audris's abnormal taste for the written word had not faded.

To see the writings brought back to me how near I came to murdering Audris when she insisted I learn to read and write when she did. For what, I had asked, does a man of war need to know such arts? If Audris wanted to addle her brain with those mysteries, well and good, but why drag me into the morass also? How I suffered! Audris learned as she learned to weave, as a bird learns to fly. Though she was seven years younger than I, it seemed she need see a letter only once to know it forever, and in her little hand the quill flew over the page forming graceful symbols. My hand, already hard and callused with handling bow and sword, resisted. The ink sprayed from the quill, forming blots and streaks with no meaning; I broke the point ten times in each lesson from sheer clumsiness, and my brain was as clumsy as my hand. I learned at last, for my love was stronger than my rage, and the skill has proved useful to me. But I never took joy in it, and to this day I use a scribe unless what I must put on parchment is so dangerous or so near my heart that it is worth the effort to take quill in hand myself.

I blessed Sir Oliver again and again during that first quarter hour while Audris and her mute maid made me comfortable and in the next quarter hour did him a grave disservice, I fear. I did not intend it, but I could not help feeling concern because Audris was still unmarried. It may have been because we came near to quarreling over my belief that she must take a husband, and soon, that fixed it into Audris's mind and some months later led her into mischief. In the end, all was well, so I did no harm, but Audris gave Sir Oliver much grief, and I never meant that to be.

Even while we argued, my heart sang with joy. To be caring and cared for again was like a resurrection to me. It was the more bitter then that my joy was so short. The very next day Sir Oliver bade me ride south to tell King Stephen that most of Northumbria had fallen into King David's hands. That morning Sir William de Summerfield had come to the north wall of Jernaeve and commanded Sir Oliver to yield the keep to him in the name of Empress Matilda. I would have laughed in Summerfield's face; Sir Oliver, being wiser, answered softly—but the sense was the same. He would yield Jernaeve to no man or woman. Then, having made an open refusal of King David's terms, no matter how civilly, Sir Oliver realized he had placed himself by default in King Stephen's party, and he might as well make a virtue of a necessity by warning the king of the Scots' coming.

I knew why he chose me as messenger—to be rid of me the sooner, and that was for Audris's sake, not his own. Nonetheless, it hurt me. I needed to sun myself in the warmth of Audris's love, only realizing when I was touched by it again how cold and heavy my heart had been all the time I had no one to care for. I felt that if I were with her for a little while, I could carry away that warmth with me; and I did not think my lingering a few weeks could have endangered Audris's hold on Jernaeve. Moreover, I believed my strength in arms would be welcome if there should be an attack. I knew, too, that the probable fate of a bearer of ill tidings was to be made scapegoat for them. Sir Oliver knew that also, for his eyes fell before mine when I looked him in the face after he ordered me to go. He did not take back the order, but he did offer me a shelter from the utter helplessness of one without friends or family by telling me to seek Walter Espec's protection if I had need and say any kindness to me would be a favor to Sir Oliver.

Audris came down at dawn the next morning to see me on my way, carrying a magnificent hooded cloak—a dark, rich red, lined throughout with thick, soft fur—and a heavy purse. My first parting from her and the purse she had given me then, which weighed so heavy on my conscience, leapt into my mind. I had taken it then because I feared to expose to Sir Bernard, who was waiting for me, the fact that Audris had raided her uncle's strongbox. This time there was no Sir Bernard, and I got down from Barbe and hugged her and said, "You naughty girl, where did you come by such a cloak and such a purse?"

She hugged me back and laughed, though tears stood in her bright eyes. "Both are mine by right, the fruit of my weaving. None questions what I take from Jernaeve's coffers, for I put back ten times the value, at least."

I stroked the cloak, knowing that its richness would have far greater benefit than warmth alone among the people I would meet around the king, yet I was reluctant to take more from Audris. The purse I pushed aside. "I do not need that. My own is as heavy."

While I spoke, she had raised her arms, unpinned the clasp that held my cloak, and pushed it so that it fell to the ground. "There," she cried, "it is all muddied and you cannot wear it until it dries and is brushed clean."

I shook my head, but she had the other cloak around me and I saw she truly desired that I take it, so I kissed her forehead and agreed. Then I hugged her tight once more, caught the old cloak from the ground, and swung myself into the saddle, knowing we would both begin to weep in another moment. It was not until I stopped to eat a bite at midday that I found the purse tied to my own at my belt. That little devil's quick fingers had fastened it to me either while she diverted me with fond talk or when I embraced her that last time. As I have said before, it is seldom that Audris does not get her own way. I could not help chuckling as I undid it to stow it more securely, and it crackled when I touched it. There was a bit of parchment within that said: "Do not send it back, beloved brother. Use it for the scribes and messengers to bring me news. I can no longer send to you, for I cannot know where you will be, and I will be sick with worry if I have no letters."

Although I did not need it and would have sent news to Audris even if I went hungry for it, I would not send it back, I decided, smiling as I chewed my bread and cheese. Let her think she had bested me again, and when she had all but forgotten, I would find some rare trinket, something for a fairy princess, and send that instead. My spirits lightened after that. Audris's cloak was so warm around me that I felt enveloped in her love, and as if it was a shield for me, no ill came of the bad news I carried.

I am sure it was the glowing richness of the red cloak with dark fur in the torchlight that completed the impression made by my tall stallion, the silver glinting on the stock of my crossbow, the bluish sheen of the steel of my axhead, and the worn leather of the hilt of my sword. The sword, ax, bow, and horse named me soldier; the cloak named me rich. It needed the two together to open the small postern gate of Oxford in the middle of the night when I cried to the guards that I had a message for the king. But it was the king's own kindness that refrained from punishing the bearer of ill tidings and instead took that bearer into his service, into a place of great honor as a Squire of the Body.

When that place was offered me, I thought King Stephen was the equal of all the gods and heroes of legends. He looked the part, broad and well muscled of body, his face not of breathtaking beauty but handsome, framed in light brown hair, high of brow, with greyish blue eyes, a strong nose, and well-formed lips. But it was not the king's appearance that impressed me, it was his response to my birth. I had told him at once that I was no more than a whore's son trained in knightly skills by the charity of Sir Oliver, and he laughed and said it was all the better for him as I would give him my undivided loyalty.

He had that always—even if he did not always believe it, and even though I soon learned I had been mistaken in my first judgement. Not about the king's kindness; many of Stephen's troubles came from his generosity of heart, for he promised too lightly what he could not perform. Worse, for me, was that his sense of honor was not what I had learned from Sir Oliver. I learned to hold my tongue, but not before I came close, a few times, to prison or exile. Indeed, it was the king's kindness that saved me from his own wrath. Is it then any wonder that I loved Stephen and love him still?

It was the day I took service with the king that I met Hugh Licorne. I liked him at once, despite his strange face, and we soon became fast friends. I learned that he had been the first to bring news of King David's invasion, but it was my confirmation of the news that enabled King Stephen to set aside other demands upon him and take his army north to drive out the Scots. I had no chance then to show the king my abilities as a fighter. The Scots fled before us, and Stephen took the opportunity to prove himself a ruler wise, just, and of good will. Because I knew the land and the customs, I was able to help him and he showed his pleasure in me openly and told me more than once that he had been wise indeed to take me into his household.

Only one slight shadow marred those clear and sunny

weeks in my life—I can hear laughter for all know that Stephen made peace with David in Durham in February and that month is mostly wet and sometimes snowy and bitter cold in the northern shires. I do not recall the weather. I only know for *me* the skies were clear and the sun shone. After the treaty was sworn, Stephen made a progress around the keeps of the northern shires, and where he could do it without grave offense, he found husbands for heiresses and guardians for orphans among his own men. The little cloud I mentioned began to gather when I realized that Stephen intended to add Audris to the heiresses for whom he had found husbands.

The cloud was soon dissipated, however, when Audris called me "brother" before the king and flung herself into my arms as soon as she laid eyes on me, like the heedless creature she is. That made the king lose interest in getting her married because, Hugh told me to my horror, Stephen believed he could rule Jernaeve through me if necessary. But when my first distaste for the idea that I could be induced to take Jernaeve from Audris had passed, I became satisfied to allow the king his mistake. Should the situation ever arise, I thought, I could see Audris well married and happy and then find service elsewhere.

In any case, I need not have worried about that matter at all; Hugh and Audris settled it by themselves. All I saw, with a mild gladness, was that Audris took to Hugh, just as I had. She showed not a touch of her usual indifference to strangers but displayed to him her warmth, her laughter, and the sweetness of her nature, which is like a perfume that drowns the senses. I could see that poor Hugh *was* drowning, but I said nothing to him; he did not need me to tell him that an heiress like Audris was not for such as he—or so I thought. I did not speak to Audris about Hugh at all, assuming that her kindness to him was for my sake.

I am very glad I had not the smallest suspicion that Audris had found a new fixed purpose. My warnings would have changed nothing and added to the difficulties she and Hugh had to surmount—and would have been a grave mistake too, for I have never seen a better matched pair. Not that they married soon. It took them two years to bring their desires to fruition, but I knew nothing of that.

Audris, little devil that she is, never hinted of her purpose in any letter to me; and, although Hugh and I served together later that year at the siege of Exeter, he said nothing either. That was not to deceive me. At that time he had no idea that Audris desired him as he desired her, and anyway, we were both too taken up, first with the joy of fighting and then with the growing disaffection and tension among those who had just sworn to support the king.

I think Stephen hoped the yielding of Exeter would put a stop to any further rebellion and permit him to strengthen his grip on his throne and his barons. Exeter's lord, Brian de Redvers, was one of the very few who had not come to swear fealty and do homage to the king at the great Easter court of 1136. Although Stephen had pleasantly and without penalty pardoned those who had failed to come when summoned to his coronation in December 1135, he had made it clear he expected all to attend him at Easter. In the end, even Robert of Gloucester, Empress Matilda's half brother, had done homage. After Stephen had ordered Redvers to yield up the royal keep at Exeter, Redvers had offered to do homage but Stephen refused, delighted to have one man he could defeat and hold up as an example of the fruit of rebellion.

It is pointless now, so many years later, to describe the foolish mistakes made at Exeter. All I need say is that Robert of Gloucester's influence caused King Stephen to offer too-generous terms to Redvers to yield his keep. This caused a bitter quarrel between Stephen and his brother, the bishop of Winchester, during which the bishop said the one thing Stephen could not forgive—that he was like his father, a coward. In addition, I think the fact that the king seemed so fearful of offending Gloucester started William of Ypres thinking of being rid of Lord Robert once and for all, and that led to Ypres's attempt to assassinate Gloucester, which in the end caused the loss of Normandy.

I am sure that the king blamed the failure of our campaign in Normandy on Ypres and that Waleran de Meulan kept green both that memory and the insult Winchester had uttered. I did not like the strength of Waleran's influence. He was a fine soldier, but I could not forget how he had betrayed King Henry and he was too ambitious, too single-minded about his own advantage. I know that most of those who surrounded the king thought primarily of their own fortunes—and I, to my shame, was as guilty as any other—but Waleran was both short-sighted and arrogant, which often made his advice dangerous. However, I think it was Waleran who convinced Stephen to return to England to prepare a defense of the northern shires against a new invasion by the Scots.

He may have guessed the king would not be free to go himself and wished to defeat the Scots to raise himself still further in Stephen's esteem. The king had appointed Queen Maud as regent, but Waleran had no great opinion of women and may have assumed—what never occurred to me—that Roger, bishop of Salisbury, the king's justiciar, and the other high officials would ignore her and hold for the king's return all the business they dared not complete themselves.

Salisbury was well able to rule the nation for he had acted as regent for King Henry, but Stephen never had the same trust in him—I suppose because the bishop had been Henry's man and Stephen feared Salisbury hid a secret leaning to Matilda. And ignoring Maud as he did, which was made plain from the amount of business Salisbury had to present, angered the king. Stephen had all my sympathy. I, too, felt it was wrong for him to be bound to Westminster when he should be marching north to meet King David's offensive.

No loss came of Salisbury's insistence that Stephen attend to the acts and grants that had been pending for months. Waleran took the footmen of the king's army west into Cumbria and drove the Scots east into the arms of the Northumbrian barons, who did not love them. The king intended to follow in a few days with the mounted troops, but it was actually closer to three weeks before we were able to leave.

Fortunately there was little need for us as a fighting force. Waleran's swift advance through Cumbria forestalled any invasion or rebellion in that shire. When we met Waleran's army in southern Scotland, we learned that he had relieved a siege at Wark, discovering among those killed and taken prisoner a number of men from Cumbria.

That was enough for Stephen. Their service to David
against him, after swearing fealty to him in 1136, made
them open rebels. This was more than adequate cause for
the king to disseisin these men, or their heirs if the rebels
had died in the battle, and put loyal followers of his own
on their lands.

So we turned west, again harrying southern Scotland.
The memory of that action is dim. I know the purpose of
burning villages and taking the stored food and livestock,
but I cannot help being troubled by the agony of the poor
common folk as their homes are destroyed, their women
raped, their children carried off. I knew too that their
agony could only increase as they starved and froze and
sickened over the bitter months of winter.

I was greatly relieved when we turned south into Cumbria.
Here, we went slowly and Stephen forbade wanton destruction. His purpose was to visit each keep or great
manor and insist on a renewal of the homage and oath of
fealty given in 1136 from each man who had not joined
King David. From the adherents of those who had been
killed or captured in the force besieging Wark, the king
demanded total submission, offering them only life, the
clothing they were wearing, and their arms when they
went into exile. Even those poor terms were grasped at
eagerly; most often, worse befell helpless rebels, and the
king's army was large. None of the keeps or manors had
the smallest hope of withstanding it, so all yielded immediately except one, and that was taken in a single assault.

Strain as I will, I can remember nothing noteworthy
about taking the manor of Ulle. Oh, I remember that
Stephen named me to lead the attack. The king had taken
two small keeps in Normandy by assault and I fought at
his shoulder. Stephen was an exceptional fighter. It was a
thrill to fight beside him, and I had some compliments on
my own strength and skill. In fact, after the king and I had
almost been isolated from our party and trapped in the
bailey of the second keep, fighting back to back to save
ourselves from being dragged away as prisoners, Stephen
said something to me about knighting me. That came to
nothing—Stephen often forgot such promises—but he had
not forgotten my skill it seems, and he passed over his

greater lords and named me captain of the assault. No one objected. Little honor could be gained from winning so easy a contest, and the prize was not valuable. Ulle manor was not likely to hold rich loot. In any case, with the king present, the loot would be his to distribute. With one thing and another, my appointment was no cause for envy.

There was no cause for sharp memory either. All I do recall was a sense of surprise that those within Ulle had tried to resist; there were simply too few to defend the place. We were over the wall on the first rush, and I cannot remember that any of the king's men suffered a worse injury than a bruise. Then I ordered the gate be opened for Stephen. There was no keep. The halls within the manor compound were meant for living in, not for defense, so I did not fear for the king's safety. Still, I went ahead of him into the main hall after the ram had burst in the door. There was not a man in the place, and since all I saw was a group of wailing women clinging to one who seemed too petrified with fear even to cry, I left more hastily than I had entered. I thought that was the end of the matter, but it was not. Eight months later, the king bade me marry Melusine of Ulle.

CHAPTER 4

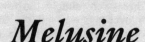

Melusine

BECAUSE LIFE HAD been smooth and pleasant—except for Mildred's barrenness—the shock to us was all the greater when Sir Gerald of Irthing returned from a journey to Carlisle with the news that King Henry had died in Normandy on the first of December; that his nephew, Stephen of Blois, had arrived in London less than two weeks later; that Stephen had been acclaimed king by the Londoners; and that Henry, bishop of Winchester—Stephen's brother— had convinced Roger, bishop of Salisbury, who was justiciar of England, to accept Stephen as king. All this might still have come to nothing, Sir Gerald went on, but Salisbury and Winchester together had talked William Pont de l'Arche into putting the royal treasure into Stephen's hands. Stephen now had the funds to pay the mercenary army his wife was sending in waves from Flanders, and the archbishop of Canterbury, with the bishop of London's approval, had hesitated no longer but had crowned Stephen king in Westminster on 22 December. Papa stood gaping like a netted fish, staring at Sir Gerald, and after a moment Magnus shrugged.

"So, all the better," he said indifferently. "We will not have Matilda as queen."

Papa turned his shocked gaze on Magnus. "But Stephen

swore," papa roared. "He *fought* for the right to swear to Matilda before Robert of Gloucester."

Magnus was the cleverest of my brothers, and not the sweetest. I did not always succeed in duping him, and when I did get my way, I was often left wondering whether he had been fooled or yielded because what I desired fit in with some private purpose of his own.

Now Magnus shrugged again and smiled. "That would be a clever move to make. After Stephen himself is forsworn, with the august approval of three bishops and an archbishop, how can any other man be troubled about violating that oath? It is no bad thing to have a clever king."

"It is no good thing to have a dishonorable king," papa rejoined. "I did not love Henry, but a man could trust his word once given. Who could trust the promise of a man who forswears himself apurpose?"

"Would you rather trust the promise of a woman?" Magnus asked, his lips twisting. "Do you think Matilda more likely to stand by her word than Stephen?"

I was annoyed. I cannot say I was above duplicity in dealing with my father and brothers when their misconceptions about me and protective instincts threatened my reason and freedom, but I have never broken a promise and I do not see why women should be thought less trustworthy than men.

"Why should you think Lady Matilda more likely to take what is ours from us? Is she not likely to abide more faithfully by her father's arrangements than a nephew who has already violated his oath?" I asked hotly, and, I admit, considering what I knew of Matilda's character, before I thought. And then, seeing how surprised the men looked, I realized they might have been considering the nebulous "good of the realm," which so often occupies men when they should be thinking of their own affairs, and I added, "I suppose you *are* talking about the possibility that Wyth, Rydal, and Irthing will be seized by the Crown and bestowed on others?"

My father put out his hand and stroked my cheek. "Neither is any trouble to concern you, pretty chick. You may be sure I will find a husband for you whose place is secure—but not tomorrow, eh, my love? You are needed here at Ulle, and we must see what comes of this usurper's claim to the throne before I choose a man.''

''Do not so glibly say 'usurper' of a king who has a fortune in hand to pay the army of mercenaries that support his claim,'' Magnus warned.

Turning from me, my father made some sharp remark in return, but I had lost interest in the discussion, which I knew would have no immediate result. I had heard everything Sir Gerald had to say, so I knew the facts, and I had noted papa's and Magnus's opinions, which I was certain would only become more fixed the longer they argued. Ulle breeds stubborn folk. If it should be necessary in the future for me to try to bring them together or to change some plan of action, I had the information I would need to reason or plead, speak or weep. I felt I could let my mind wander to a more personal topic—that of my marriage.

By Church law—a law made by men, of course—a girl may be married at twelve. I learned that listening to a priest who had come to propose a match for me with a neighbor well into his fifth decade, who still had no heir to his lands. This was just before I had begun my thirteenth year, and the priest's statement of the law was his reply to papa's protest that I was too young. In fact, I am sure papa was not thinking of my actual age—I was always his ''little baby girl,'' even long after I had topped the height of most of the common men—but it drew forth a lecture from the priest on the nature and duty of females. This so angered papa (not that he thought better of women in general but because *I* was the subject) that he roared, ''I have said my daughter is too young, and Church or no Church I am the master of my daughter's life.''

That fat slug of a priest, who had been eyeing me in such a way that I guessed who *he* intended should father our neighbor's heir, was terrified by papa's rage. He began to stammer compliments about how good a father papa was and to assure him that the purpose of the Church in fixing the age for marriage at twelve was to protect daughters of less kindly and considerate fathers from being married off at nine and ten, or even three and four, not to force marriages. At that point, mama, who did not believe in giving unnecessary offense or allowing anyone to realize how much value my father set on me, pointed out that she was not well and I was needed at Ulle.

There had been offers after that too, but my mother was dead by then and I *was* needed at Ulle. I suppose my father could have married again—had he done so I would have managed to induce him to find a husband for me. Once Ulle came under my sole rule and I had fitted my shoulders comfortably under that burden, I do not believe I could have tolerated any woman in authority over me. Even at fourteen or fifteen I was too much mistress to become maid again. But papa showed no interest in marriage for himself—not even after my brothers died. At the time I did not think about it, but now I wonder if he could have cared more for my mother than I believed. For my own part, I was content as mistress of Ulle and more relieved than sorry that papa did no more than say he had turned a suitor away or, more often, did not mention the offers to me at all.

After Magnus married Winifred, however, I noticed that papa began to talk about my marriage again, always with excuses for his delay in arranging for it. I knew he did not want to part with me but felt guilty about depriving me of my right to be a wife and mother. I could have soothed him with a few words, assuring him that I did not wish to marry, but . . . I was not sure. When I saw what was between Donald and Mildred, I could not help longing to taste that enchantment for myself; and when I saw Winifred's pride and contentment, I could not help wondering if something very important was not missing from my life. And so, when my father mentioned marriage to me, it was that I thought of rather than the effect Stephen's crowning would have. How could I have guessed that the one would make the other?

Not immediately, of course, although neither did life move on unchanged. Sir Gerald had brought the news about Stephen after Epiphany. Too soon after, a royal messenger demanded entrance at the gate of Ulle manor—but the messenger was from King David, not from King Stephen. The man gave us news first: that Carlisle had yielded to David in the name of Empress Matilda; then he

said that King David desired papa's pledge to support King
Henry's daughter against the usurper Stephen in her rightful claim to the throne of England. Papa would have given
his word then and there, but Magnus signalled urgently to
me, and I went forward and drew the messenger away,
cooing of women's concerns—that the man was cold and
tired, that he must be warmed and fed.

Instead of taking him to the guest house and seeing to
his comfort myself, however, I brought him to Winifred to
be cared for so I could go back to the hall. And just as I
feared, Magnus and papa were at each other, hammer and
tongs, papa swearing he would stand by his oath to Matilda and Magnus swearing that papa would ruin us by
opposing the power Stephen had mustered. Usually I did
not interfere between my father and my brothers when they
argued. They loved each other too well to do one another
any harm; in fact, mostly they seemed to enjoy a loud
quarrel. But they were all stubborn men, so sometimes, if
the matter seemed important, I would make peace between
them. Then, later, in my own way, I would bring one or
the other to see the case as *I* thought right.

This time I stood silent, though I was shivering with
inner cold. This time, I knew that tears and pleas would
not change papa's purpose, yet I felt sure it was Magnus
who had the right of the argument. He, like me, was of
Ulle and cared nothing whether we were ruled by Scot or
Norman so long as the overlord was just. What was foremost in Magnus's mind was the safety of our lands. Moreover, what he said was true; Cumbria had been subject to
the king of England since the time of the first William.
David had been my father's overlord, but only as a vassal
of the English Crown.

As if answering my thought, papa snarled, "I do not
swear to David as king of Scotland but to Matilda, who is
the rightful queen."

"She is too late with her claim," Magnus snapped in
reply. "No human hand can wipe the holy chrism from
Stephen's brow. Whether or not the archbishop of Canter-
bury was right or wrong in anointing him king and setting
Saint Edward's crown on his head is not ours to decide.
Stephen *is* king of England. Swearing faith to Matilda

cannot change that. It can only lose us our lands when Stephen comes to contest the Scots.''

"I swore—''

"You are absolved by the highest priests in England!'' Magnus shouted. "Did not they swear also? You do not want Matilda for queen, do you?''

My father shrugged. "What does it matter who rules England? David will be our overlord again if Matilda takes the throne. Queens even less than kings are likely to trouble us. There are no jewels here, no rich fabrics, and no reason to fear us, since we swore while she was the weaker—''

"And so you name us enemy to the stronger,'' Magnus interrupted furiously. "I tell you, Matilda will never hold the throne, and David will not hold the north. If he stopped with taking Cumbria, Stephen might ignore it since there would be no one—or almost no one—to protest David's rule. But David will strive to take Northumbria too, and they will resist and cry to Stephen for help. And Stephen will come to them. So early in his reign it would be disaster for him to refuse help to a vassal attacked by a foreign king.''

Papa growled a wordless, angry admission that Magnus was right and kicked a log protruding from the hearth, which sent sparks fountaining up toward the black beams of the roof. There was no chance of setting the high roof afire, but some of the embers that sprayed outward flew beyond the slabs of stone on which the fire was laid and smouldered among the dry rushes. I stamped out a few near my feet, and a manservant ran to kill the others. Papa stared morosely at the threads of smoke that rose and then were extinguished by the servant's feet.

"I have lived my whole life in the expectation that this summons would come,'' my father said at last. "I will not turn my back on it. And who knows,'' he added, shrugging again, "David may conquer.''

Magnus, enraged beyond speech, did not answer that but flung himself out of the hall. I heard him calling for his horse before a servant closed the door, which he had left standing open in his fury. Papa did not raise his eyes to follow Magnus nor to meet mine. That was the final proof that my fear was well founded, that papa knew he was doing wrong, and that King David could not be the victor. And he was not, of course. It happened just as Magnus had foreseen—King David invaded Northumbria and the barons of that shire cried for help. When King Stephen rushed north in strength to drive out the Scots, King David knew he was overmatched and yielded without a battle.

Nonetheless, no immediate evil came of papa's—to my mind—ill-placed loyalty. In fact, when papa returned to Ulle in March 1136, he brought with him several heavy gold armlets and a magnificent necklet of rubies and diamonds, as fine as anything I had seen Lady Matilda wear, and gave them to me. I smiled and thanked him and tried to look pleased, for to do otherwise would have hurt him, but inside I shuddered with horror. I knew the jewels were loot—one of the prime reasons that men so loved war—and I could not help but imagine them torn from the throat of some poor woman who might also have lost more of value than the ornament.

I was disgusted, too, that papa was so cheerful in the face of his liege lord David's defeat, thinking that his high spirits were the result of his gain, for he had brought home horses and armor and I think silver and gold coins as well as the jewels he gave to me, but I was wrong in that. As soon as Donald could be summoned and come from Thirl, papa explained why he was so pleased with what seemed a crushing blow to King David. We learned that the peace Stephen had offered was mild beyond any expectation. Far from seeking to punish David, Stephen had allowed him to keep control of Carlisle and some of the lands beholden to the keep. Unfortunately, Ulle and the new manors were not part of the lands ceded to David, but papa had appealed to King David to exchange our manors for some others near the coast so that he would be our overlord.

King David had agreed to grant papa's request, but I suppose he had no time to suggest the exchange to King Stephen because in April papa was summoned to come to Oxford to swear fealty to King Stephen. I was afraid that he would refuse, but when I mentioned my fear to Magnus he laughed and assured me that papa would go. The swearing would not affect the transfer of the lands if Stephen had no other reason to refuse; he could release papa from his oath at any time. I was glad for the reassurance, but somehow my uneasiness would not disperse. There seemed no reason for it; papa went to Oxford and returned home well pleased. The king had accepted his homage without a word about his joining King David and had uttered no threats or warnings. Stephen was a very easy-tempered man, papa said, but still some sense of foreboding clung to me. Once I tried to warn papa that the king's seeming indifference to his disloyalty might be a trap, but he laughed at me and told me not to trouble my pretty head about men's affairs and that in any case Stephen had gone to Normandy and would be no danger to us.

I do not know that I believed papa's easy assurances, since I knew that sooner or later Stephen would return; and it seems to me I once heard papa and my brothers talking about the possibility of King David invading Northumbria again while Stephen was gone, but I paid little attention because I had more serious worries closer to my heart. Mildred was growing more desperate by the day about her barrenness and, though Winifred was happy, that was only owing to her simplicity and lack of understanding. Even I, who had borne no child, knew she did not look as she should. Her feet and legs were all swollen and she had trouble breathing if she walked only from her quarters to the hall. The midwife was not at all happy about her. In the end, the midwife tried to bring on the babe before its time. She had felt it weakening—by then, Winifred realized something was wrong herself because the child no longer moved in her—but it would not come, and Winifred grew weaker and weaker and died, at last, poisoned by the dead child within her.

We all grieved but not, I am afraid, very deeply—not even Magnus, who agreed that papa should find him another wife as soon as Winifred was decently buried. Poor Winifred had been too sweet, too simple, too gentle to be other than a nothing in our violent, volatile family. Mildred and I shed the bitterest tears—alas, not for Winifred but for the loss of an heir to Ulle. Had Winifred borne a son, papa and Donald would have been content; both would be glad enough that Magnus's child inherit our lands just as both disliked the thought that any blood but ours should rule them. Winifred's death made Mildred's inability to get with child a larger and larger wound in her mind, though neither Donald nor papa reproached her.

She tried, I think, to convince Donald to repudiate her—she did not admit it to me, but Donald began to question me about what Mildred said about him and whether her eyes strayed to other men. I burned his ears for that before I realized what must have engendered his jealousy. I did not dare say what I thought to Mildred—for all the love between us, there was something fiercely private about Mildred that forbade me to tread where I was not invited, and she was years older than I—but I did speak to her and warned her that Donald felt she was discontent with him. How I have regretted that! How often have I wondered if putting on a smiling face for Donald drove her sickness inward harder and deeper until she became altogether desperate. If so, I murdered my beloved sister.

I thought though that her spirits had lifted when papa brought Catrin home for Magnus. If they had, so much the lower did they fall when less than a year later, in the summer of 1137, Catrin took a fever and died. I did not realize that at first. For myself, I was more relieved than grieved, for Catrin was shrewish and obstinate and thought she should rule Ulle because she was a son's wife rather than a mere daughter of the house. So I was not sorry to be rid of her without asking papa to banish her to the manor meant for Magnus—which would have meant that Magnus would have to spend at least part of his time alone with her and bear the brunt of her tongue.

It was after papa's offers for a girl from Keswick were turned away with weak excuses that he suggested Donald set Mildred aside. They quarreled bitterly, Donald with an intensity that bordered on true hate, the first time ever there was real bad feeling between my father and one of his sons. I made peace between them, but it was an uneasy peace, and Donald came seldom to Ulle after the quarrel. I went to Thirl when I could, but winter was drawing in and the track over the mountains was treacherous. In November storm followed storm; papa forbade me to try the passes, but remembering what had looked out of Mildred's eyes the last time I saw her, I rode out one day when it seemed to me the sun might pierce through the racing clouds. I did not reach Thirl. So great a blast of wind rushed down from the Black Crag that my mare was toppled from the path. God knows what saved us, for neither Vinaigre nor I was more than bruised, but I took warning.

Was it my lack of courage, my failure to dare enough for love that took Mildred's last hope from her? I must not believe that, as I must not believe coming to celebrate my birthday killed my brothers. I told myself over and over that one of them must have brought the sickness with him; it must be so, must it not? There was no sickness at Ulle until after they came. As for Mildred, even if I had got to her that day, would she not have fulfilled her dire purpose on another? I am torn apart anew as I think back on that time. Am I blackening my sister with the idea that she took her own life only to salve my own sick spirit because I was not brave enough to go forward that day?

Whatever is true, it is an abiding sorrow that I learned she had died the very day on which I had failed to ride to Thirl. Late the following afternoon, Donald came into Ulle with Mildred in his arms. Papa and I both ran to meet him, but such horror filled my spirit that I could barely force my limbs to move. I knew before I saw Donald's face that she was dead, even though she was tenderly wrapped in his cloak. There was no need to run for Mildred's sake ever again, but I forced myself forward, fearing that Donald would vent his anguish and bitterness on papa. But though my brother was half dead with searching and half crazed from finding Mildred drowned, he did not blame papa. Indeed, I realized in the next moment that he never suspected she had killed herself.

Perhaps I am wrong, but I saw things they did not. Once papa got him down from his horse, Donald told us in broken pieces, still clutching Mildred to him, how he had first found her horse grazing in a little valley where the Thirlwater met the land gently, and then found her drifting in the tarn not far away. There was mud on the horse's

legs and side, and Donald clearly thought the beast had
slipped up on the steep-sided hill and thrown Mildred. If
she had been stunned, she could have rolled into the tarn
and drowned. But when we at last coaxed him to let her be
laid out, I was the one who washed her and combed her
hair—and there was not a single mark or bruise on her
head or body.

I kept that to myself, of course. All we needed was for
the priest to hear a hint that Mildred had taken her own
life. He knew whom she worshipped and would have
grasped eagerly at any excuse to refuse her a grave in
consecrated ground. Mildred would not have minded; she
would have laughed, for all fertile earth was holy to her,
but Donald . . . It was really from Donald that I hid my
horror. I think if the idea that Mildred had deliberately
smeared her horse with mud and then walked into the tarn
had once crossed Donald's mind, he would have followed
her path. And papa was troubled enough already, for he
was, I suspected, in a way glad Mildred was dead—and,
perversely, that added to his grief for her.

Whatever papa's feelings, he knew by instinct what to
do for Donald—or was it by experience? He had suffered
when mama died. Did he remember what he had felt?
Still, papa had the lands and his children to force him to
put aside sorrow and Donald had nothing. He felt papa or
Magnus could carry on for him because, I think, he had
not won the land for himself as papa did nor had he been
bred to put Ulle before all else as Duncan, being eldest,
had been. When the first shock of loss had passed, papa
tried to reawaken Donald's interest in living by setting
tasks for him. My brother did what he was told out of
duty, but his spirit did not lighten, and when papa wished
to take him hunting or to engage him in any other light
sport, he refused. We were all sick with worry as well as
grief.

And then Waleran de Meulan passed through our lands.
Until that time, my mind had been so fixed on private
troubles that I had not taken in the news of the king's
return to England—if, indeed, papa had mentioned it. But
Waleran had come from Normandy with Stephen, and the
king had sent him to the northwest to drive King David's

men out of the lands that had been ceded to King David by treaty and make sure King David did not draw strength from our men or produce, thus breaking the treaty of 1136.

As I have said before, I did not care who was our overlord, but I conceived a hatred for Waleran de Meulan that I have never found reason to change. It was Waleran's pride and arrogance that drove papa to break his oath of fealty. No, that is not all the truth. Waleran's haughty threats against any man who sought to aid King David's war and his contemptuous dismissal of the "little" men whom he could break at will if they flouted his orders infuriated papa and made him speak unwisely. In my heart I knew the reason papa broke his oath was the light that came into Donald's dead eyes when papa roared that his oath to the king did not include swallowing insults from Waleran and that he would go join any force that would fight that braggart. I think papa was only in a rage, shouting the first words that came into his head, but Donald came to his feet with gleaming eyes and said, "Yes, let us thrust that fool's threats down his thick throat."

I am sure papa knew Donald did not care whom he fought or for what reason. Donald would as gladly have joined King Stephen's army. He just wanted to fight, I suppose against life itself for taking Mildred from him—or perhaps he wanted to die, not fight. I think it was that papa feared. I could see him swallow down his rage and shrug his shoulders in pretended indifference.

"Talk, just talk," he said. "I must look about and see what will be best to do. There is no sense in letting a loud cur drive us into a foolish action."

But the harm was done. The first smile I had seen since Mildred died appeared on Donald's face. "You are right about that," he agreed heartily. "We can have it both ways. You bide here, which will stop that fool from any chance of harming Ulle, and I will gather a force and join King David. He will remember me, even though I have been away all these years."

Papa knew what that meant. Donald would go no matter what he said. He glanced toward Magnus, who had been sitting beside me on a small bench near the fire. Magnus had not said a word beyond necessary remarks about food and such everyday matters since they had all returned from their meeting with Waleran. His dark eyes, much like mine and mama's—I think his nature was more like ours too, not so open and sudden as my red-haired papa and Donald—had been narrow with anger. It was clear that he liked Waleran no better than papa did. Donald, I think, had noticed neither the words nor the manner of the king's envoy, for he had been as turned inward when they returned as when they rode out; he had responded to the word fight, not to Waleran's insults. But Magnus, angry as he was, still believed Stephen would be the victor in the struggle with Henry's daughter Matilda and did not approve any action against the king or his man.

Nonetheless, when Donald jumped to his feet, Magnus said, "I do not take a blast of foul, hot air from the mouth of a head empty of all but arrogance as seriously as you, but I will go if you bid me." His eyes had moved to Donald and then back to papa as if to add that he would do his best to keep Donald safe.

"No," papa replied, though his long look at Magnus was like a caress. "I will go. I wish to go."

What papa said was true enough. I am sure he took considerable joy in the idea of fighting for King David, but there was more too. There was no way Magnus could control Donald. Magnus was the younger and Donald would either ignore or laugh at cautions or commands from him. Most likely papa had visions of Magnus flinging himself in front of Donald to protect him in an effort to keep his unspoken promise—and thus losing both sons. But papa was wrong about that. Magnus was more likely to hit Donald on the head from behind and drag him off to safety, which I thought was very sensible but which I know would never occur to papa (or if it did would horrify him).

Donald laughed in the old, reckless way, the way he had laughed before he married Mildred—before life began to have a deep meaning to him. Magnus frowned and I saw a ring mama had given papa glitter briefly in the firelight as his hand shook. Papa, who did not care for ornaments much, had put on the ring to please mama when she started to weaken with her last sickness and he had never taken it off. The flash of light seemed to pierce me and a coldness spread over me so that I shuddered.

"Why should either of you come?" Donald asked, his voice hard but light, almost gay. "I said King David will know me; likely he will take me back into his household, and from that place I am most likely to meet this Waleran directly. You are the one who gave oath to Stephen, father. If you are in Ulle, the king cannot call you traitor, and we will have our revenge and come scatheless away, too."

"Broken treaty, broken oath," papa said. "If Stephen had not sent his vicious dog to deprive the Scots king of what was given him by treaty, I would have no reason to leave my lands. Besides, when peace is made this time, I will no longer be Stephen's man, so Ulle is in no danger."

"If David wins," Magnus said dryly. "Loud-mouthed cur Waleran may be, but I looked about his camp and had a word with this man and that. Waleran is a soldier—and that is more than I can say for David. And remember, most of the best men David has hold English lands, much richer lands than those they hold in Scotland. Brus, for one, went north for love of David, but he also did fealty to Stephen for his English lands. I heard it said in Carlisle a year ago when David first planned to take back the north that Brus had begged him not to fight the English king and warned him that he would not be able to support any attack on Stephen."

Donald did not even stay to listen to this. He went off toward the bedchamber he had been sharing with papa (he dreamt, I think, and needed to be awakened and perhaps comforted), I suppose to look for his sword and armor. Papa's eyes followed him, and he shrugged again.

"Win or lose, Ulle is in no danger," he said, though he did not look at Magnus. "Stephen is not even with the army, and I doubt any man from these parts will carry tales to Waleran. And, since that haughty lord did not deign to distinguish such unimportant folk one from the other, I do not see how news of what I do can come to the English king."

I was surprised at first that Magnus made no sharp

answer to that. Jealousies and greed—and there were those who envied us the rich fishing and Ullswater and the new manors papa had bought or reclaimed from wasteland— can make men put aside insult from a haughty overlord and carry tales when they hope to profit. But this time Magnus held his tongue, and I understood it was because he knew papa was going less to support King David than to keep Donald from throwing away his life.

"Besides," papa said, now looking at Magnus, his mouth grim, "you had better find yourself a wife, since I have done so poorly."

I bit my lips to keep from crying out. I knew the chances of war because in neighboring manors fathers and brothers had been lost in battle, but I had not before looked deeply into that well of fear. Death's scythe had reaped differently in my family, and my father and brothers had come home laughing and scatheless each time they had fought. Now papa's thinned lips and hard voice renewed that pang of terror and spreading cold I had felt earlier. He had never looked like that when he went off to fight raiders or the first time he took up arms for the Scots king. This time, I felt, he thought he might not return.

Should I have pleaded and cajoled, wept until I made myself sick? Perhaps my sickness could have kept papa at home, but it would not have held Donald, and if he had died I think my father would never have forgiven me. In any case papa's next words made me doubt that I had read his grim look aright. He said, "I do not know when, or even whether, Donald will be willing to marry again, so it comes back to you. And I have been thinking that perhaps we have gone about this business the wrong way. It may be that the girls fear you abused your wives because you were not satisfied with my choices."

Magnus looked up, as if he were about to say something, but he did not speak and papa went on, "So, this time look about yourself to find a girl that pleases you. Then show her attention; get her mind set on you. Once the girl is willing, it will be easier to bring the father to terms. We should be back by the early planting."

Those last words comforted me a little. They came out easily, not as if papa were straining to reassure us, and so I was able to part from him without outward show of my heaviness of heart. I am glad of that, glad that he did not carry away a memory of me weeping, glad he never knew that his charge to Magnus to find a wife cost his son's life.

I think Magnus first chose Mary because she was a widow with two young sons and good property not too far from Ulle and needed no man's yea-say as to whom she would marry. I suppose by right she needed the approval of her overlord, but her lands—for she was living on her dower property, her husband having been a younger son— were north of Keswick in that part of Cumbria ceded by treaty to King David, so Magnus could count on approval . . . if King David was successful and Cumbria did not change hands.

I also know Magnus liked Mary's boys; he spoke of them more than of Mary at first, except to say she had a strong will and would take him, if he could win her favor, in spite of her husband's family and the new man they had chosen for her. After a few weeks though, he began to talk about Mary, and what he said about her gave me hope that she would be a sister I could love. I hoped, too, that Magnus would find the kind of joy that Donald had known and be enthralled by his wife.

I think it would have gone that way because one evening Magnus came home in a rage and told me that her husband's kin had come and threatened Mary, saying they would take her sons and the lands and thrust her into a convent—or worse—if she did not accept the man they had chosen for her. Magnus went more often and stayed longer after that, and I noticed he had provided a good coin dowry and sent away the girl he used—I was not supposed to know about that, but I had always kept an eye on my brothers' women.

Anyway I was not in the least worried when he did not return to the evening meal as he said he would on the fifth of January. It was the last of the twelve days, and Magnus had ridden over to give Mary twelve pearls as her twelfth-day gift. I was sure he intended to ask her to pledge to him that day and equally sure she would agree. In fact, I rejoiced when I sat down, later than usual, to eat alone because I thought Mary and Magnus must have been celebrating their betrothal so heartily that he forgot the time and had decided to stay rather than brave the bitter, icy roads as dusk was falling. I went to bed very happy that night, hoping that Magnus, who was growing a bit restive without a woman, would have come at last into a safe haven.

He was safer than I thought, safe for all time in God's arms. A shepherd who was out seeking a missing ewe found him lying in the road pierced by five arrows.

I think that was when I gave up hope. I did all the right things—set the huntsmen and tenants searching for any sign of the murderers, sent a messenger to Mary and several men to find King David's army and tell papa and Donald what had happened. I even rode to Keswick to put a complaint before the sheriff about my brother's murder and to testify to what he had told me of the threats of Mary's husband's kin. But I do not remember weeping for Magnus nor did I really expect that papa or Donald would ever come home. I am not even sure whether it was one week or two that passed between Magnus's death and the day that Tom, our bailiff, brought the news that King Stephen himself had set out from Carlisle with a huge army and was sweeping through Cumbria and taking every manor.

"I will not yield Ulle," I said, knowing that was what papa would have said.

"Lady, lady," Tom cried. "We could not even hold a keep against that army. Ulle is only a manor house. It is not meant to be defended against an army. Will you ask us to throw away our lives?"

The bailiff was loyal and I was sure he was not lying to me. I knew he had defended Ulle against raiders and fought bravely under papa's orders. If he said defense was useless, it probably was. Ulle would be taken, but I would not give it away. Papa would blame me for that. It would have to be taken by force, and I would not yield nor sign any writing nor give oath or pledge of any kind ceding my right. If the king had me killed, I would have done my best and would be free to join mama and my brothers— and papa too if what my heart said was true. But I did not really think the king would kill me, and as long as I lived I would have a right to Ulle. Papa would expect me to try to hold the land and, if I could not, get it back in some way sooner or later.

"No," I said, "I do not want you to throw away your lives. I want you to do nothing and say nothing. Move everything that can be moved into the caves. Sail the boats under the cliffs where they cannot be taken. Make no resistance to the king. If he takes Ulle, I do not think he will harm me. If he takes me away and sets a new master into Ulle, cheat him as much as is safe. Watch for my father and my brother so that they do not fall into any trap when they return."

I remember how Tom's eyes lighted at my words and the fervor in his voice when he said, "We will be watching for them, lady." But there was no answering light in my heart. I was only saying the words I knew papa would have expected me to say and acting as he would have wished me to act. There was no hope or expectation in me.

As the king's army drew closer and it became clear that Stephen would not, as some had hoped, pass east along the easier route south of the tarn and ignore Ulle, I called the manor folk together and told them they must leave and take with them into hiding all the valuables of the household. I bade them take not only the strongbox of money and jewelry, the two pieces of fine plate, and the few glass and silver goblets but all the stored food and stock, even the linens and feather beds and extra clothing. When Stephen took Ulle, he would find bare bones, and old bones at that, with all the marrow gone.

I had wanted to stay alone; the people wanted me to flee with them, but I explained that I must stay to maintain my father's claim to Ulle—I was wrong about all this, but I was ignorant because papa had never explained such matters to me, thinking women unable to understand, and the manor folk knew less than I did. But they would not hear of my staying alone, and they arranged among themselves that all the young men and women should go, leaving behind only a few old womenservants and the men of my father's retinue who had been ordered to protect Ulle in his absence.

I had no notion they meant to fight. Papa had only bade

them guard Ulle to salve their pride—had he feared an
attack he would never have gone, and Donald would have
stayed too, to fight for his own land. The men-at-arms
papa left behind were all too old or too crippled to go with
him. But they gave me no warning of their intention, and
when Stephen's army was sighted, one column winding
down the pass from Darkgate and another creeping along
the track by the tarn, the captain asked me to go inside the
main hall with the four women who had remained and bar
the door. I went without words, for he had already promised not to open the gates but to make the king's men force
them. I believed he wished to bargain for my safety—or,
perhaps, for his own.

So I went inside and sat down on papa's chair to wait,
and the women drew stools close around me. The windows
had already been shuttered, and the hall was lit only dimly
by the wan grey light that seeped down from the smoke
holes in the roof and the low-burning fire. I was not
conscious of the passing of time, but it could not have
been very long because we saw the army soon after dinner,
and when I heard the first stroke of the ram on the gate,
the light from the smoke holes had not grown dimmer. The
sound of the ram woke no fear in me; it was dulled by
distance and by the walls of the hall and the shutters on the
windows. To me the hollow thuds were much like those of
heavy clods of earth falling on a coffin—all too familiar to
my weary ears.

Then there was a crash. The women on the stools
around me set up a wail, and it took me a moment to hush
them. Only then did I hear the shouts and a faint clashing
of metal on metal and realize that those foolish old men
were fighting. I cannot imagine what they thought they
could accomplish, but perhaps they only wished to die
with honor instead of being driven out to beg for bread. At
the time I did not think of that. I jumped to my feet to run
out and stop them, but the women clung to me, weeping,
ignoring my commands to let me go. And the battle, if it is
not laughable to call it that, was over before I could free
myself. The clashing died away and what noise there was
of more men entering did not penetrate into the hall, but
soon the shouts began anew, this time in tones of rage as

the invaders saw the bare stables and outbuildings and realized the shell they had cracked was empty of meat.

Around me the women, who had been murmuring to me, fell silent, although they clung still tighter. I could feel their terror, and tendrils of it crept through the deadness in my soul until my heart could scarcely beat, so encased was it in the ice of fear. I had said the king would not hurt me, but what if he should torture me to discover where the wealth of Ulle was hidden? I could not tell him. I did not know where the manor folk had fled. There were caves and hollows in the hills that I had never seen or heard of. Or what if Stephen should throw me to his army as a scapegoat to be used by the men until I died?

A mailed fist thudded against the hall door and a single male voice, strong and clear, rose above the noisy confusion. A moment later the ram crashed against our last defense. I suppose it was fortunate that it took no more than a few blows to burst open the door and that I was frozen with terror. Had I not been, I would have disgraced myself by running about and shrieking as mindlessly as any frightened hen.

The splintering of the door loosed my women's tongues and they began to wail. One further blow and the door sprang open, letting in the soft light of a grey winter's day. It did not blind me, but it was bright to my dark-accustomed eyes, and my fear gave a sharp-edged, slow-moving quality to everything that happened.

First, a man in full mail with a bared sword in one hand and a raised knight's shield in the other leapt in and stepped sideways to put his back against the door, as if he expected the sealed hall was a trap. The shrieks of my women, augmented by his entry, drew his head to us. The light then fell full on his face—dark and . . . and hungry. I will never forget that face. I have reasons enough now to remember it, but at that moment terror seared the features and expression into my memory. He had lowered his shield when he saw only women and there was no nasal to the helmet he wore, so I could see clearly the large, black eyes, the high-bridged, aquiline nose, and the mouth—but that I did not see as I saw it later; then it was only a thin, grim line in a black-stubbled face. Simple as I was, I thought he was the king. I learned later that two men could hardly look more different—or be more different.

The difference in looks I discovered in the next moment when a second man came through the door. I knew at once the mistake I had made when I saw this man's armor, for his shield was beautifully painted and gilded, whereas the first man's was chipped and battered, and this man had a gold circlet affixed to his helmet. This was the king, but somehow I was less afraid. His face was obscured by the nasal of his helmet, but the eyes were mild, the mouth bland, and there was a fullness about the chin that robbed it of determination even though it was not weak. His expression, puzzled rather than angry, held none of the intensity of the first man's, who said a word to him softly and went out with an indifference that showed contempt and emphasized my powerlessness.

Others came in then, but with sheathed weapons; and as the king approached me, he put his own sword away and lifted off his helmet, handing it to a smaller man—perhaps it was a boy, a squire. "Be quiet!" he said to the women. "I will do you no harm." They obeyed him better than they would have obeyed me. He stopped about a yard away from us, his followers respectfully behind him, and asked, "Who are you?"

The question was plainly addressed to me, and I suddenly found that my tongue no longer cleaved to my mouth, bone-dry with fear. I answered quietly, "I am Lady Melusine of Ulle."

"Where is your brother Magnus?"

His voice was sharp now, still not hard, but my heart sank. I remembered how my father had said the king would know nothing about us, but papa had been wrong. It seemed that Stephen knew far more than papa had guessed. Still, nothing could hurt Magnus ever again, and my first terror worn away, the deadness in my soul had crept back, making me indifferent to my own fate.

"Magnus is dead," I said softly. "He was murdered on the road on his way home from his betrothal."

Shock, followed by sympathy, showed on the king's face, and it came into my mind that I might yet save Ulle with weakness where strength would not serve. So before

Stephen could speak I asked, "Why did you attack me? I have done no harm to anyone."

The little hope was crushed at once. A kind of spiteful stubbornness replaced the look of sympathy, and the king snarled, "Why did you seal your manor against me, against me, the king? You knew your father and brother were rebels, gone over to King David. Well, the lands are forfeit for that. I am done with forgiving rebellion. And you need not think any will dare oppose me. I have cleaned out this sewer of Scots lovers. Nor will there be any to lead uprisings. Your father and your brother are dead, killed at Wark in open rebellion."

I had known they were dead. I had known from the moment the shepherd brought Magnus home with frost crystals whitening his eyes that whatever curse had fallen on me on my thirteenth birthday would not lift until all I loved were destroyed. Still, to hear it said, no longer to be able to fight the knowledge, no longer to be able to cling to any shred of hope—that felled me. I must have fainted and perhaps I was unconscious for a long time and that reawakened the king's sympathy. I learned many months later that he had treated me with great kindness, but I have no memory of that nor of anything else that took place until the beginning of September. I must believe, little as I like it, that I was quite mad for nearly eight months.

CHAPTER 5

Bruno

"MY LORD, I do not want a wife, especially one I do not know, and I cannot provide for one."

Fortunately the king and I were private when the words burst from me, and he laughed at my reaction. "You know Lady Melusine. She has been one of the queen's ladies since you took her manor—Ulle. You must have seen her many times. She is the tall, dark lady to whom I often speak—a very beautiful woman, very quiet and gentle. Well, *I* think her gentle."

I called her to mind as soon as the king described her, but I did not think her beautiful—a big mare, good for heavy work like a peasant, not small and delicate like a great lady. And her face—all I could remember was the expression of terror that had twisted the features.

"But, my lord," I protested desperately, "you have disseisined her, and for excellent reasons. I heartily support your decision. Still, if I marry her, she will be reduced to a condition unfitting her birth."

"Nonsense," Stephen rejoined, still smiling. "If you take me for a fool, at least do not tell me so to my face." He chuckled at my visible consternation and took my hand, for I was standing before him. "Bruno, my Bruno, I know you have nothing—" The smile on his lips twisted.

"—and is that not your own fault for refusing bribes to whisper this and that in my ear?" Then his look softened again. "It is wrong that you be poor because you are honest. Moreover, although I am sure you think I had forgotten my promise to knight you, I have not forgotten. I did not wish to do it without some special reason. There are already some who look sidelong at you and call you 'favorite' under their breaths."

I knew at least one of those "some" who looked sidelong at me. As Waleran de Meulan increased his hold on the king, he grew more and more jealous of anyone Stephen loved, and Waleran knew I thought much of his advice wrong. He wished to be rid of me. Could this marriage be his way to send me away from the king?

To accuse him of it though would be a faster path to the same result, so all I said was, "I am sorry, my lord. Perhaps my manner has been at fault. I will take more care—"

Stephen waved that away. "I have been seeking an excuse to advance you, and I have found it in Melusine. For my purposes, she must be married, and to a man whose loyalty to me cannot be shaken. Thus, the marriage is a service to me, and will make it only reasonable for me to knight you and grant you a pension. But the pension will be for you, Bruno. Melusine will remain Maud's lady, so her food and much of her clothing will be provided. And since you will now be a Knight of the Body, you will still be lodged and fed at my expense."

Knight of the Body . . . then I would remain connected to the king, although not so intimately as I have been as squire. That thought pulled me this way and that: I would be safer if I was less close to the king, for I often rubbed him wrong by speaking my mind or reminding him of the queen's opinion when he did not want to hear; yet I loved him for his kindness to me and I owed him what little I could do to check his impulsive nature. Also, I wanted to be a knight. God knows I was far past the usual age for knighting and being a squire made those who did not know me look at and speak to me in a way that rubbed my soul. And a pension . . . But at the cost of a wife? I had a brief memory of Audris's face when she spoke of Hugh, and a heaviness came into my chest at the thought that I would never see a woman look at me like that.

"It is too great a favor, my lord," I said. "There must be many men who are more worthy."

"But I have chosen you," the king said, frowning now. "I trust you, Bruno, and I think you less likely than any other to allow your wife to make trouble for me."

I must have gaped at him like a fish out of water, for he shrugged as I echoed, "Make trouble?"

"I thought it would be sufficient to place her in a convent, but Maud will not hear of it. Lady Melusine's father was a man of influence in Cumbria, and I hear from the steward I sent to Ulle that the people are only waiting for a signal to rise up against me. If Ulle rebelled, it is possible the rest of Cumbria would follow."

"You think Lady Melusine would escape from a convent and return to Ulle to lead a rebellion?" My voice rose with incredulity.

"No, I do not," Stephen replied. "I have spoken to her many times, and I am sure she is a—a docile creature."

I wondered about that hesitation before the word docile, recalling also the way the king had said *he* thought Melusine was gentle, but I only nodded acceptance of his answer.

"But," the king went on, "she did try to leave us secretly when we were on progress in the north. I think the poor girl misses her old home. I doubt she ever left it before I took her with me to court. Yet as long as she is unmarried, I dare not allow her to go there even for a visit. There is too great a chance that a man of those parts—and I trust none of them for I think they all have a secret leaning toward David—might seize her and marry her. He could then claim her right to Ulle, and use my denial of that right to raise rebellion."

As he spoke Stephen's face showed only interest and his eyes were guileless. I knew him and believed he was telling the whole truth, or as much as he knew of it. But then he shifted slightly in his seat as if something had made him uncomfortable and added, "And Maud says Melusine is hiding something, but I cannot believe it."

That cast a different light on the matter. If Queen Maud said Lady Melusine was hiding something and it was the queen who had opposed placing the girl in a convent, her attempts to escape became more significant. Although it was no pleasant prospect, I felt it was my clear duty to marry her. The queen had an uncanny ability to sense any danger to her husband, so she was more likely to be right about Melusine than Stephen. My selfish desire for a marriage of caring and warmth must be put aside—not that I was losing much, since I doubt I could ever have made myself an acceptable suitor to any well-born woman.

"Very well, my lord," I said. "I will marry Lady Melusine when and where you say."

"You need not look as if I have just condemned you to torture."

Stephen looked decidedly irritated, and I realized that my expression must have been grim. "You have taken me by surprise," I replied. "I have never been responsible for any other person, and to be tied for life . . ."

The king reached out and grasped my arm, and grinned suddenly. "I understand. Now that I think back, I could not have looked much happier when Maud was proposed to me. I did not think she was an attractive woman." He laughed heartily. "What fools men are. If I had known the prize that was being given me, the joy she would bring me and the help, I would have spent the time between our betrothal and our marriage on my knees praying for her welfare. But you can have no quarrel with your lady's looks—ah, the pension."

"I had not even thought of that," I said indignantly. "You must know, my lord, that I have always found you over rather than under in generosity. As for beauty, I prefer my women small and fair, so we are in much the same case. I do not think my bride very attractive. I can only hope that fate will be as kind to me as to you. If my marriage brings me even a part of the happiness in yours, my lord, I will be blessed above most men."

A small frown formed on Stephen's brow and then quickly smoothed away, and he nodded in seeming satisfaction. "That is true, and my hope goes with yours. Maud and I thought that fifty marks a year while you are on duty at court and a hundred marks when you must live on your own means would be suitable."

I bowed deeply. "That is indeed generous."

I know neither my face nor voice betrayed my surprise and uneasiness at the amount of the pension the king was offering. It was too much—a knight's fee was twenty pounds a year, and out of that the knight must find food and shelter for himself and his horse. With all necessaries found for myself and my wife, and some clothing too, Stephen was offering more than a double knight's fee. Had such an offer been made by any other man, I would have suspected that the woman was not only a hunchbacked dwarf but a raving lunatic too. But I knew that Lady Melusine was normal in appearance and quiet and well behaved among Queen Maud's ladies. The overgenerosity had nothing to do with the lady; it was typical of Stephen.

The king was large of promise, poor in fulfillment. I was certain that as soon as the wedding service ended, Stephen would hand me a purse with the first quarter's payment of my pension. I might receive another quarter, but after that it would depend solely on the state of the king's purse. If it was full, the money would be given with a smile and a jest; if it was not, I would have the smile and excuses; if I persisted, anger would replace smiles—and the larger the sum that was owing the deeper the anger would be. It was a fault I feared deeply, not so much for its effect on me—if worse came to worst, I could always send my wife to Audris so she would not starve—but for the dissatisfactions it bred among the nobles.

As I came up from my bow, I could see that the king was dissatisfied by my guarded voice and expression. I was struck by remorse, for I knew how much pleasure Stephen took in making people happy—and he truly meant to fulfill his promises, I am sure. It would not have hurt me to bend my lips into a smile. Stephen was not much aware of other people's feelings and would never have known the smile was false. But I had no time to amend my mistake, for his next words again took me by surprise— only proving what a fool I am, for I should have realized what he must tell me.

"Then the day after tomorrow I will knight you, and in a week's time—let us say the first day of September, that will be an easy day to remember—we will have the wedding.''

I forgot completely the need to seem happy, as a wild protest rose to my lips. I managed to swallow it, but I could not command my voice and could do no more than bow again, and when I tried to speak, Stephen waved me off, saying petulantly that I should go gaze on my bride's beauty and find a better mood.

The remark about my bride I took to be an order, and I left the king's chamber to go to the queen's quarters, but I doubted that Melusine's appearance would do much to improve my mood. Although I knew better, I could not help but be irritated by the king's expectation that I would show joy over his proposal. Even if I had believed he would be faithful in payment, could he not realize that my heart would be heavy at the prospect of taking an unwilling bride? But then I thought of what Stephen had said, and I began to wonder whether Lady Melusine *was* unwilling. Some women are so trained to obedience that they seem to have no will at all. That idea did not make me much happier. I suppose it is better to have a placid, obedient wife than a bitter, unwilling one, but it woke no enthusiasm in me. The only great lady I knew well, my beloved Audris, was as willful and naughty as she was sweet and delicate, and I thought that a great part of any woman's charm. I always chose my whores from among those with saucy tongues.

The thought was double-edged. With a wife in my bed I would no longer need to use the whores. Not only would that save money, but Lady Melusine would, I hoped, be cleaner and sweeter smelling than a whore. On the other hand, the notion of a woman with the right to ask me about my comings and goings was not so pleasant, and I thought again with resentment of the king's great eagerness to bind me to this woman I did not even know.

In a moment I realized I was being unfair. There were good reasons for the king's haste. A knighting and a wedding would be a diversion for the small court gathered around Stephen at Winchester. For a little time each event would provide something to talk about besides the increasing number of men who were rebelling against the king. In

June, the attempt in Normandy to ambush Robert of Gloucester had borne bitter fruit despite the king's denials. Gloucester had sent envoys to Stephen to cry defiance—a formal renunciation of Gloucester's oath of fealty. Although it was no part of the defiance, the messengers had also carried the bad news that Gloucester had submitted Caen and Bayeux to Geoffrey of Anjou.

Many of Gloucester's English vassals had followed his lead, some because they were good and honorable men but more because they were discontent with what Stephen had given them, having hoped from his promises for much more. If Gloucester had come to England at once and united those men, I do not know what would have happened, but he had not. Each had cried defiance separately, and thus far, Stephen had put down each rebellion as it rose. But as defeat for each rebel was only followed by another's defiance, even those most firmly committed to the king were growing uneasy.

To make matters worse, King David had attacked and besieged Norham castle in June; for a time he had seemed stalled there, but through July and August the news had been very bad. Castle after castle had fallen to David, and the Scots had flooded down through Northumbria and Durham and were now threatening York. Yet Stephen did not dare go north to fight David lest the Scots' attack be only a feint to draw the king away so that Gloucester could come from Normandy after all and lead a unified rebellion. That would deprive Stephen of the rich and populous south—not to mention the ports through which Queen Maud's ships brought men and money from her lands.

Any diversion, even such small ones as a knighting of the king's squire and the marriage of one of the queen's ladies, would be welcome. I would have been in urgent need of diversion myself—little as I had to lose if Stephen were driven out of England—if I had not had a letter from Audris that past week, telling me she was safe in Jernaeve and Hugh was off to join Sir Walter Espec, who was gathering an army to defend the north. Audris's news had comforted me; foolish as it was, I felt that Hugh was doing my part as well as his own in defending the shire. I knew I could not go myself while trouble held the king in the south, but I did not worry about Jernaeve. The Scots might raid the lands and even take the lower bailey, but they would never take the mighty keep itself by assault or siege. If I knew Lady Eadyth, Jernaeve was stocked for a year or more and Audris would be safe.

Moreover, I thought, stopping abruptly in the middle of the hall, the diversion provided by my knighting and marriage would be especially absorbing because there would be meat enough for vicious gossip over the giving of a true-born lady to a whore's bastard. Then I started forward again, almost smiling. There might be talk, but as the king had said, there would be little envy. Stephen would be sure to describe his generosity to everyone—perhaps that was another fault, but most of the time I found the king's eagerness to be praised rather endearing. It would save me from making more enemies, since all who did not know already would soon learn that Lady Melusine's father had been disseisined and she had no dower.

On that thought I reached the top of the stair and entered the small anteroom to the queen's chambers. The page nodded to me and before I could ask for Lady Melusine called through the door, "The king's squire for the queen."

It was not worthwhile to make the boy feel a fool by correcting him. I knew Queen Maud would not be angry when I explained the mistake—she did not have that kind of haughty temper—and perhaps she would bring me to Lady Melusine and ease our first introduction to each other. Beneath that thought lay another. If this marriage was Stephen's idea and he had not discussed it with his wife, it was possible that Maud would oppose the union. With the queen on my side, I was certain that I could escape; but Maud's first words, after I bowed before the chair in which she sat and said I had no message from the king, dashed that hope.

"You have come to see Melusine, I suppose. That was kind, Bruno, but I think it would be better if you did not."

A bitter bile rose in my throat, but I think my voice was steady when I asked, "Is she so unwilling? Because I am a whore's son? Madam, if she—"

"No, no," Maud assured me. She had been slow to interrupt only because she had first risen from her chair to take my hand. "She is not unwilling at all. I have told her of the marriage and of your birth." The queen hesitated and smiled at me with a hint of apology in her eyes. "I had to tell her. You know what the court is like. She would have heard from others in a less pleasant way. But I was also able to explain why the king and I had chosen this marriage for her—that you were kind and would take her without any dowry and that you would surely find great advancement because you were a fine man and because of the deep love the king bears you, and of my own affection for you, Bruno."

"Thank you, madam."

I hope she understood the sincerity of those few words. I loved the king in spite of his faults, but I respected and admired the queen to the very depth of my soul. When not driven by her need to help and protect Stephen, she was both wise and kind. It was certain that she had used all of her considerable ability to persuade Lady Melusine that I was a prize of inestimable value, to make me acceptable rather than a hated necessity, which I would certainly have become if the queen had simply told Melusine that the marriage had been the king's order and could not be opposed.

"Then why," I continued, "should I not see Lady Melusine and tell her myself that though I take her by the king's command, I will do my best to be a kind husband?"

"A small precaution," Maud replied, going back to her chair. "You remember, do you not, that you were the first man into the hall at Ulle? If Melusine should recognize you, she might change her mind and try to refuse to marry."

"All the more reason for me to speak to her now—" I began.

"No," the queen interrupted, and her eyes now looked like bright black stones. "I tell you that will she, nill she, she will marry you within the week. I would prefer that I do not need to drag her bound and gagged to the altar, but I will do it if I must. The bishop of Winchester will marry you, and I will find witnesses to testify that she was willing. Stephen has too many troubles now for me to allow this girl to add even a small one, and the way to keep her from that is to have a husband loyal to the king.'' Then her expression became gentler. ''But that would be a dreadful beginning, and I do not want that for you, Bruno.''

''And if she recognizes me at the altar and cries out?'' I asked, my voice harsh although I tried to keep it quiet.

''I do not think she will notice then,'' Maud said. ''She will be confused and excited, and even if she does recognize you, I think she is too clever to try to protest. I have given much thought to this girl—no, woman. Maiden she is, girl she is not. For months she has tried to show herself as quiet and gentle, utterly obedient, but I sense that this is all a lie. It is what I said—a show put on to deceive us and make us trust her. There is much, much more to Lady Melusine than I have ever seen. And she is much beloved by the lords of Cumbria. The king has had inquiries about her health and well-being even from those most faithful to him.''

''But surely—''

The queen shook her head, cutting off what I would have said. ''The king and I are agreed that you are the only suitable man for our purpose. And, perhaps Melusine will not recognize you at all. If she does, you will soon be able to convince her that you were only doing your duty to your master. After all, you did her no harm. You did not, if I remember aright what Stephen said, even go near her.''

''That is true,'' I had to admit. ''And I left the hall at once. Lady Melusine was very frightened. It may be that she will not remember me.''

''I hope so,'' Maud said, ''but I do not wish to take any chances. And since you are to be knighted before the wedding, I can tell her that you were given no opportunity to come and speak with her. I see that you do not like this, Bruno, but the king believes, and I agree with him, that having given your oath to him, rich or poor, you will keep it to the death.''

''That is so, but there are other men as loyal,'' I said, and the queen, who was as sensitive to the feelings of others as Stephen was blind to them, no doubt heard the hint of resentment I could not keep from my voice.

Instead of growing angry, she smiled at me. "Be that as it may, there are other things that can change a man besides the desire for power and wealth. As many men have been bent—and broken—by women, though few men will admit it, as by other cravings. And Melusine is beautiful—and clever. I know that despite her long attempt to make me believe she is stupid." Maud put out her hand and touched mine in a kind of gentle apology, which puzzled me until she uttered the words, "Whore's son, you know more about women than any other man I know."

"I?"

My shocked expression as the word burst from me made the queen laugh. "Yes, you. I have seen how you look at the maidens of my court. Women have no hold on you."

I thought of the way a single tear sparkling on Audris's lashes could turn my bones to water and make me allow her anything she desired no matter how wrong or dangerous. But was that not because I remembered her as an infant, her little wet kisses the only show of love that had ever been mine? It was true that what made my shaft stand hard could not touch my will. Still, I knew there was a kind of weakness in me; what made my heart warm could make me foolish too.

"I know my place," I said, because if I tried to explain that I was not as hard to women as she thought, the queen would only believe it was another protest against this marriage.

She shook her head. "Many men know their place, but what is in their eyes is different than what is in yours. You are the right husband for Melusine. She will not be able to trick you or drive you into treason, and because you are the man you are, I believe she will come to value you as you deserve. Then you will be happy, although I know you now think Stephen and I are doing you a wrong."

I did not make a formal protest. The queen would have known it for a lie, and though I was truly willing to die for Stephen's sake, I had never expected to be asked to endure a life sentence of torment instead.

Before I could bow my acceptance, Maud got up and

moved closer to me, touching my hand again. "Bruno, if this marriage remains bitter to you, when the kingdom is firm in Stephen's hand, you may set your wife aside. We will help you, I promise."

I do not know what I said as I bowed and the queen nodded and gave me leave to go. It must have been thanks of some kind because I understood she meant well, but the notion was shocking to me, almost as horrible as the expectation of a wife who hated and scorned me. Perhaps I could set such a woman aside, but what if my hell were of my own making? What if Melusine *were* stupid, and the queen had misread her? Could I cast aside a simpleton who disgusted me when she was trying to please?

Those were not thoughts I wished to dwell on, and I reminded myself that I had something much better to think about. If I was to be knighted in two days, I must cleanse myself and prepare. For that I needed time, so I presented myself to the king again and asked for leave for that purpose. He was still annoyed with me, and for a moment I thought he would deny me. Then he looked amused, nodded, and waved me away. Perhaps he was thinking that such a serious attitude was not fitting for a man of my years, that bathing and confession and a night of vigil were only meant to impress a young man and I should know better. Or perhaps he was surprised that at any age the ceremonies of faith and dedication to the order of knighthood should be more than a formality to be overpassed if possible.

I did not care. From the time Sir Oliver had sent me away from Jernaeve, I had believed I would never have a chance to attain this goal. To me knighthood was a high honor, not mine by right of birth but an achievement. If that achievement was a little soiled by being tied to a marriage I did not desire, so much the more must I take care that my heart was clean and that my understanding of the purpose and duty of a knight was whole and perfect within itself, separated from outside matters.

I had no close friends, although there were those who liked me well enough to have helped me make ready if I had asked, but I did not desire help. Those I drank with and whored with were by nature light of heart and would have hurt me unawares by jests and teasing. So I was busy all that afternoon. First I had to arrange for a real bath in a tub in a private room, rather than a steaming and scouring in a bathhouse, then I needed a white gown to wear after my bath when I went to confession. It was fortunate we were in a cathedral town or I might have had trouble finding one on such short notice. My last errand was to arrange with a priest to hear my confession after vespers the next evening. After that I found a quiet corner and cleaned my sword and armor. I kept it sound and free of rust, of course, but to stand before God and His saints, the dull grease-clotted mail was not good enough. It took me until it was too dark to see that day and almost until dinnertime the next, but when I was finished the mail shone like silver, brighter than it had when Sir Oliver gave it to me.

I suppose I must have spoken to people and eaten and suchlike, but I remember nothing of that. I remember washing myself—with soap to be sure I was clean—and the odd thought, as I walked from the house where I had paid for the use of a chamber to the church, that I was glad it was summer or my feet would have been cold. I confessed that petty thought as I confessed my greater sins and my lack of faith in my doubts about my coming marriage. It was a long confession, for I was not usually overcareful in freeing myself of my sins. I heard my penance and rejoiced; I would perform it and be free. My heart was lighter, even when I thought of Melusine, as I changed into my armor and went to stand and pray through the night. I have no more to say of that. I do not wish to hold anything back in this telling of my life, but I have no words for what I thought and felt.

To my surprise and great joy, I was not without sponsors. William Martel, the king's steward, and Robert de Vere, his constable, separated from the group watching and came forward, one taking my sword and the other my helmet, so they could return them to me as first and second guarantors of my fitness for knighthood. And the queen, acting for the king, gave me a pair of gilded spurs as third guarantor. I was so happy, I could have floated up on to the dais, but I managed to keep my feet on the ground and even kneel.

The king looked down at me and I saw the mingled amusement and remaining touch of spite in his face. He meant to knock me off the dais to sprawl on the floor and I almost let him do it—almost, but when the blow from his fist came my pride would not yield and I braced myself. He rocked me, but I did not fall, and he laughed, his good humor restored as I sprang to my feet. He embraced me with good will, and called my name aloud, "Sir Bruno of Jernaeve, Knight of the Body, I greet you." I knew him, all his faults and weaknesses, but how could I help but love him nonetheless?

There was time to change out of my armor before dinner, but when I presented myself at the king's table and he had, as was customary because of my clumsiness at carving and presenting, excused me from serving, I noticed that Melusine was not among the queen's ladies. The king might have forgotten a small thing like that; the queen would not. I have no doubt it was Maud's doing too when, after dinner, the king summoned me and sent me off to Oxford with a letter for his castellan. Since I was given no verbal message that might need discretion, any messenger could have done the task as well.

I guessed at once that the purpose was to keep me out of the way; nonetheless when the castellan of Oxford confirmed my suspicion by telling me it would take him a day or two to find the answers the king desired, I was overwhelmed by a black loneliness. Although I had known the time for fulfillment could not be soon and my chances of success slim, I had nourished a dear dream ever since the king had taken me into his service. I had hoped that when England was firmly in Stephen's hand, I would be given some estate as a reward for loyalty. Then it would be possible for me, I dreamed, to take a wife—a woman who would be a pleasure to my eyes and heart and who would come willingly, even with joy, to my bed so that I would have a warm, caring companion with whom to share my life.

That dream was utterly destroyed. From the queen's eagerness to prevent Melusine and me from catching even a glimpse of each other, I had to assume that Maud had used the word "willing" to gloss over a sullen acquiescence to the king's command. Then, even if Melusine did not recognize me as the first invader of her hall and think of me with hatred, it seemed the best I could hope for was a cold indifference. One spot of warmth and light shone steady above the sea of black despair—Audris's love. To that I turned, purchasing parchment, quills, and ink and setting myself to pour out my anguish, writing in my own hand what I could never have spoken out loud to a scribe.

It was not the first time that I blessed my slow and awkward management of a quill. Before I had struggled through the first part of the tale, I had rehearsed my bitterness in my heart ten times over, not only that I must take an unwilling wife who was not to my taste but that I would in the end carry this burden without the ability to feed and clothe the woman, who must be as unhappy as I with the bargain. The fourth or fifth time that ran through my head, I finally understood what it meant.

If the king failed in payment of the pension he had promised, I might be brought to the point where no resource at all remained to me so that Melusine might need to live on Audris's charity some day. I did not need to add to my poor wife's bitterness by sending her to a place where she would be treated with cold courtesy, for I knew Audris would resent anyone she believed had made me unhappy. Thus, I realized that no hint of my reluctance to marry Melusine must stain the letter.

By then, thanks to God, the very thought of Audris's sympathy had soothed me and I began to think that patience and kindness might in the end win me what I hoped to have at first. I did not then believe that even fondness could make Melusine beautiful to my eyes, but that was a small matter. One hardly sees the physical form of those with whom one spends every day—there were some among my fellow squires I had once thought ugly, some beautiful, and now I did not notice the difference between them.

I cannot tell how often I wrote and rewrote that letter. I scraped clean that parchment so often that the surface became too rough and the ink spread from each letter into a blot no matter how carefully I wrote. Still, I never found the right words to explain my marriage. At last, every explanation seemed suspect to me, and when I got a fresh parchment, I wrote to Audris only that I had been knighted and that I had more important news for her which I would bring in person as soon as I could get leave to come to Jernaeve for a visit. And after all my effort, I could not find a messenger willing to carry my letter to Jernaeve. All had heard horror stories of the Scottish invasion, and I knew there was no purpose in arguing. I could send my letter with one of the king's messengers going to Newcastle.

Having talked, or rather written, myself into some concern for the poor woman whose dreams had no doubt also been shattered, I used the idle days in Oxford to have new shoes made and a fine gown of dark red, richly embroidered, as elegant as any nobleman's dress. Usually I dressed plainly, partly to spare my purse, partly because I was more comfortable in simple garments that freed me of the constant worry of soiling and spoiling, and partly so that no man could say that the king's favor was making me rich. In this case I thought it more important that Lady Melusine not be shamed or shocked at our wedding by a common appearance after all she had probably already borne from gossip about my birth.

CHAPTER 6

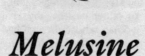

Melusine

MAD! I must have been mad, for by the king's and queens's orders, I was married—without a murmur of protest, I have been assured—to a man without name or property, a landless bastard who had no more to recommend him to me than that he was the favorite of my captors.

I do not remember being dressed; I do not remember the king leading me to the great doors of Winchester; I do not remember Henry, bishop of Winchester, speaking the words that bound me to Sir Bruno of Jernaeve; I do not remember the crowd of witnesses that watched my wedding, nor the celebration that followed it, nor being undressed and shown to my groom. Doubtless he was displayed to me too, but I must not have looked at him, which was taken for maidenly modesty, I suppose. I do not remember the chaff of jest that flew about, nor being led to the bed and placed into it with Bruno beside me.

All I remember is a piercing pain between my thighs and suddenly coming awake to see above me the face of the man who had burst in the doors of the hall at Ulle and turned away from my terror with such contempt. The shock deprived me of both speech and movement, and I did not fight him or even cry out in my pain. To me, no time had passed between the moment I dropped senseless before the king in my agony of grief and finding myself

impaled on the shaft of the invader of my home. I could
only believe that the king had thrown me to his army to be
used until I died, and that kind of death was a horror that
again deprived me of my senses.

I came to myself with screams bubbling in my throat,
with my hands curved into claws—and with nothing to
claw or scream about. I lay unmolested, a fine woven,
light woolen coverlet drawn up over my shoulders. For a
single instant my heart leapt with joy as I wondered if all
the horrors that had befallen me were no more than an evil
dream; in the next moment I felt the ache between my legs
and the stickiness on my thighs that told me my maidenhead had been reft from me and that the soft breathing to
my left was not a maid on a pallet but *that* man.

One man. A flood of relief lifted me on a wave crest
only to sink me into the trough with shame that I should
prefer to be an enemy's lemman to dying, even by torture.
And the shame brought back the face I had seen above
me—handsome in its lean, dark way, although I have
never found dark men to attract me—which bred more
shame. There had been no joy, no pleasure, not even a leer
of lust in that man's face. The hunger I remembered in his
expression was there, but it was not hunger for me. That
was a deep, abiding part of his nature. Overlying the
hunger was the hard mask of a man doing a distasteful
duty. But why should a man who did not want me take me
for his lemman?

Though the answer to that question—that one does not
refuse what a king offers, even if it is not what one
desires—came into my mind at once, I had no time to
consider it because a maelstrom of incongruities burst
upon me. A thin woolen coverlet was all that covered me,
the bed curtain was looped back, and by the light of the
night candle I could see a black rectangle of unshuttered
window—yet I was almost too warm. In the depths of
winter?

A faint shudder passed through me as I remembered
Magnus's frozen eyes. Yes, it had been winter when Magnus
was killed; I could not be mistaken about that. And it had
been no longer than a few weeks later when the king took
Ulle. But the light breeze that came from the open window

and stirred the bedcurtain near my head was heavy with
warmth and sweet with the scent of flowers, and the wall
into which the window was set was stone. This was not
Ulle, and winter was long gone.

I very nearly fainted again and for what seemed like a
long time I did not think at all. The first new question that
formed in my head after I realized that I had lived out the
winter and spring and most of the summer—instinct, not
thought, had picked out the scent of late-blooming plants—
was how long I had been the lemman of a man whose
name I did not know. I almost turned to look at him, to
confirm that I had really seen the face I thought, but the
slight movement of my hips recalled a shadow of my pain
and reminded me of the blood that had flowed. I had,
then, been a maiden until this night.

Screams of a different kind of terror tore my breast, but
I set my teeth against them. It is no light thing to realize
that more than half a year of one's life is gone without one
spark of memory to mark it, but to me it was a worse thing
to wake the man beside me. I could choke back my cries,
but my body would not be denied completely and I could
feel deep tremors starting inside me. Holding back my
shudders with the last of my will, I eased myself inch by
inch out of the bed. Once I felt the man stir, but he did not
turn toward me and I made good my escape.

A few steps took me to the door, but I was no longer
mad and I stopped. Where could I run, naked and blood
smeared? Clothing lay across two chests. I stepped softly
to that with the woman's garments, but I did not don them.
The cloth was richer than any I had ever worn, even for a
high celebration at Ulle, and the gown and tunic gleamed
with gold thread embroidery. Who had given me such
garments and why? Even if the king had decided to carry
me with his court—what could stone walls mean but a
royal keep?—as some kind of trophy of victory, such a
gown and tunic could not be everyday attire. That notion
joined and mingled with the soreness I felt on walking,
and it came to me what such fine clothing and the loss of
my maidenhead after so many months of captivity must
mean. Marriage!

"Come back to bed."

The deep voice brought a faint squeak of terror from me before I could close my mouth with my hands. I stood frozen, regretting that I had not pulled on the clothes and fled.

"Come back to bed," the man repeated. "You will take a chill standing there naked. The night is warm, but cold oozes from the stones. Come. I will not touch you again."

The tone was weary and sad, the words spoken slowly, as if to one who had great difficulty in understanding, like a very young child or . . . or a woman of feeble mind. That was when I first realized that the months missing from my life were missing because I had been mad. A protest rose to my lips, but I swallowed it down, wondering if I might not benefit from being still thought out of my mind. Then the bed leathers creaked and I knew that the man was making ready to rise and put me back to bed. I could not bear to look at him, so I came back before he could move and lay down. A moment later he started to turn toward me, and I shrank away instinctively before I could think whether that might anger him. If it did, he did not show it then for he came no closer.

I neither wished to sleep, fearing that despite his promise, he would take me again if I did, nor did I think I could sleep. I suppose that my shock and confusion had exhausted me, however, because I remember lying stiff and wary at one moment and, seemingly, the next, opening my eyes to see sunlight in the room. This time though I had no need to gather the small fragments of memory together. The man, fully clothed, stood by the window, looking out.

"Get up now, Melusine," he said. "You will want to dress before the king and queen come to see that you have been well and truly made a wife."

I realized that I must have been wakened by him saying my name, but he did not turn his head toward me as he spoke, only repeating, "Melusine, get up and dress now."

I stirred then, unable to bear the dull, patient repetition. As I got out of bed, I seethed with fury. What kind of a man, I asked myself, marries a madwoman, even at a king's command. Only the dregs of the earth—either a coward, shivering for the safety of his skin, or one so eaten up with greed that no act is too shameful if it will fill his purse. My eyes flicked from side to side seeking a weapon with which I could rid myself of this creature, but there was nothing, and I remembered that he had said the king and queen were coming. The king and queen? Then I was at court. But I had no time to think of that. I did not want to be found naked with blood-smeared thighs, and I hurried to the chest, laid the fine garments on the other, and opened it.

"Do you not wish to wash?" The slow words were a mocking insult. "There is time for washing, and I have poured water for you."

Still without turning, he pointed to a table on which stood a basin with a washing cloth and a drying cloth folded beside it. I hesitated a bare instant, unwilling to accept what seemed a kindness from the animal that had despoiled me, but I was disgusted to sickness by the dry stains on my legs, and I almost ran to the table. In stretching my hand for the washing cloth, I saw my nails were all filthy, and I shuddered, realizing that I had scratched at the smears during my sleep when they dried and began to itch. The reminder was of use though, for I washed my face first—I could not have borne to wash it with dirty, bloody water—and then my hands, only last cleaning my legs and the thick black curls that covered my woman's parts.

I could not even bear to leave the water in the basin, and I carried it to the pot to pour away, but the moment I saw the pot, of course, I felt an urgent need to relieve my bladder and bowels. Before that man? I threw a hate-filled look at him and saw that he was still staring out of the window. Then I realized he had not once looked at me—or if he had, it was no more than a brief glance. One can feel it when one is watched, I more than most because I had been so often annoyed by my father's and brothers' watchful eyes. So he found his bargain distasteful, did he, that clod who had accepted a madwoman or half-wit for profit?

While the thoughts coursed through my mind, I had used the pot. He must have heard—there are unmistakable sounds—and he made one small movement that almost caused me to leap up half finished. But he did not turn, only moved the shoulder he was leaning on the window frame. Nor did he speak again until I had selected clothing from the chest and pulled on my underclothes and tunic. When I thrust my arms through the sleeveless summer bliaut and settled it on my shoulders to show the proper amount of the embroidered neck of the tunic, he asked, "Shall I lace you up?"

I was too surprised to reply, partly by the keenness of his hearing, which had apparently told him to what stage my dressing had progressed, and partly by the offer itself. But it was necessary. The loose gown of a peasant woman can be simply pulled over the head. At Ulle I had a number of such gowns for work in the stillroom or the garden, but the fine bliauts of a lady laced tight to the body from hip to breast either at the back or the sides, and a maid was necessary. The absence of a woman to assist me was another shock. Who had helped me dress all these months—or had I been moping and mowing in a cage all this time, only drawn out to be married to this man? And married for what purpose? Ulle?

He turned and came to me before I could speak the bitter questions in my mind. I do not know what showed on my face in the instant before I made it blank; it did not matter because I do not think he even glanced at me. A surge of fury at his contempt followed. What right had he to be contemptuous of me? One does not deliberately go mad. It is no shame to be stricken by the hand of God or to be broken by sorrow. To my mind it was a far greater shame to fill one's purse or lickspittle by taking a mad wife. Nor did it soothe me that he knew well how to lace a lady's dress, drawing it just so in a way that did not furrow the cloth between the lace holes. So he was a womanizer too. Well, who else would take a mad wife but a man who used women so freely that a disgusting wife meant nothing.

"There," he said, turning me about and stepping back. "You look . . . ah . . . very handsome. Can you comb your hair or . . ."

I almost spat in his face, but my growing rage needed a fuller—a bloodier—satisfaction. I had no weapon now and knew I could not kill him even if I had. I remembered how he carried himself with sword and shield under the weight of his armor when he burst through the door of my hall, and I had been watching him since I woke. There was an easy, fluid grace to his movements that told me he was too strong and too quick to be taken by surprise . . . when he was awake. I would need to wait until he slept. And I would need to appear half-witted and harmless . . . and find a knife.

CHAPTER 7

Bruno

I COULD HAVE SPARED the effort to look as fine as the other noblemen. It would have made no difference if I had dressed in rags or come unshaven with my hair knotted in filthy tangles. All the thought and effort I had given to my appearance on my wedding day, to make myself as different as possible from the battle-stained person who had burst into the hall of Ulle, were wasted. Not once, from the time the queen brought her to the church door, did Melusine raise her head and look at me.

At first all I felt was relief. The thing that had haunted me at every odd moment all the time I was in Oxford, all the sleepless night before the wedding, and all the long day—for the king and queen had chosen that we be married just before vespers—was that Melusine would take one look at me and begin to scream. I knew the queen; the girl would be forced one way or another to go through with the marriage, but I did not know whether I could endure it, and it would ruin forever the small hope I had of bringing my wife to true acceptance.

I did nothing to draw her attention to me as Henry of Blois, bishop of Winchester, began the wedding service. But when I lifted her limp right hand to place the ring on her finger and even more when I had to lift her face to kiss her lips, I began to suspect that the queen had given Melusine some potion to keep her quiet. There was something wrong with her eyes—I cannot define what it was, only say that there seemed to be no soul behind them. I felt sad that Queen Maud thought it necessary because that implied that Melusine's objections had been stronger than sullen acquiescence; however, I was not angry. Better to deal with the screams and tears in private. The whole court had attended the wedding, I suppose by the king's request, and the last thing I needed was gossip among them about an unwilling bride.

The worst, the very worst, was taking the poor girl's maidenhead. The king and queen did not permit any long delay over the disrobing, cutting short the usual spate of bawdy jest and comment which had broken out as soon as Melusine's magnificent body was exposed. I have said before that I prefer women to be small and delicate, but no man could have found fault. Her skin was like pale, dull cream-colored satin; her breasts large and full but firm; her waist narrow; her hips broad and strong; her dark hair, glinting with red in the light of the torches, fell to her beautifully rounded buttocks. At another time and place I suppose I would have responded as any man to that lush invitation. On the day of my wedding, however, even that beautiful body could not arouse me, and my shaft was shriveled to nothing with disgust and dread. I have never been sure whether Melusine and I were hurried into our chamber, away from the guests, as soon as they acknowledged there could be no annulment for physical fault to conceal Melusine's condition or to conceal mine.

The queen herself helped Melusine into the high bed, and the king came and put his hand on my shoulder, saying, "Be gentle with her." He hesitated, glanced toward Maud and added, "But make her your wife beyond doubt or question."

Stephen's glance toward the queen saved me from utter consternation. If he had observed my distaste for himself, most of the other guests would have been equally aware, but that the queen had urged him to make sure I did not leave my bride a virgin did not surprise me. I thought of it nonetheless. A small cut could provide enough blood to give evidence of our mating and free me of the need to violate an unwilling woman. But I put the thought aside as Stephen and Maud went out. To do that would betray their trust.

The sounds from outside stopped suddenly, and I knew either the king or queen had shut the door. My first thought was that the drug must be wearing off—I was surprised that it had lasted so long—and the closed door was to conceal the shrieks of my bride. I shuddered, but when I glanced at Melusine she was sitting just as the queen had left her, apparently staring at her own fingers. My next thought was that it would be best to broach her while her senses were still dulled and that, drugged as she was, with her will weakened, her body might respond and make her ordeal easier or even a pleasure. With that in mind, I got into bed quickly and touched Melusine's shoulder. It was smooth and cool—too cool.

"Lie down," I said, and then, hoping to excuse what might seem a peremptory order, I added, "You are chilled."

For a long moment she did not respond, either to my touch or the words. Then, without lifting her head, she slid down and pulled the cover up. In that moment I became aware that her skin was soft and smooth and her hair and body had been scented with something sweet that was a delight to smell. The inviting odor gave me a spark of hope. If she had perfumed herself, was that not for me? Perhaps not. Perhaps that too was by the queen's order.

I suppose I should have said something more. Had she reacted in any way, I would have known what to say. As it was, I was afraid anything I said would be wrong. I lay down beside her and stroked her arm and hair—but she responded to that no more than to my first touch, lying with closed eyes. Her face could have been carved of stone for all the expression it had. I did think of trying to arouse her, but I dared not play the rough games that delighted the little whore of Alnwick, nor invade her private parts as I did with that girl and others to make her ready. Slaps and tickles can only be exchanged between those who are fond and trusting, and to place fingers or lips to Melusine's nether mouth without invitation would, to my mind, be worse than the forced coupling itself.

I am not sure why that notion was so fixed in my mind. It seemed to me that to couple by order would be equally unpleasant to both of us, but I would have had pleasure out of touching and fondling and if she was unwilling that was unfair. I was growing angry too over the sullen, passive resistance, over her stubborn refusal to recognize my presence at all. By the moment I grew more certain that it could not be all the result of the drug. No drug could keep its full power for so many hours, and I resented the fact that Melusine did not guess this was as hard for me as for her. That was foolish. Later I realized that most women think a man is always ready, but it was not so for me. I had never forced a woman in my life—I suppose because each time an opportunity arose I imagined Audris in the place of the terrified girl. But it did not occur to me then that Melusine could not know that.

The anger helped, although I still needed to handle myself to harden my shaft. That made me angrier, but it also led me to wet myself well with spittle to make entry easier. I did it for my own sake, not for Melusine's; later I was glad I had hurt her as little as possible. It troubled me that she did not move or open her eyes when I mounted her and thrust her legs apart with my knees, but I dared not stop for I knew I would never again nerve myself to broach her if I did not finish.

The full horror of what I was doing did not overwhelm me until, at my first really hard thrust, when I burst her maidenhead, I felt her stiffen to fight me off. That response, the fact that she had made any response, even a kind I did not desire, encouraged me to thrust twice or thrice more, since her passage was now well-slicked with blood and my motion must hurt her less, perhaps even give her pleasure. And then I realized she had gone too lax. This was not the stillness of submission or pleasure; the poor girl had lost her senses.

I could not continue. It was like having ado with a corpse, and I found it no sacrifice to withdraw without spilling my seed. I looked at Melusine, and the light of the night candle was enough to show me that she was breathing evenly. She would soon revive, I thought, and turned my back intending to sleep, but a fear that had passed glancingly through my mind a few times took a stronger hold on me. What if Melusine's behavior had not been caused by a drug? What if the queen was wrong and she was half-witted?

I felt the body beside me jerk and then lie stiffly still again. I knew I should turn and speak to her, but I could not bear to have my fear confirmed. If only she would rail at me, curse me, strike me—but she lay quiet without speech or movement. Later—I had almost drifted off to sleep despite my heartsickness—I felt her leaving the bed. I turned carefully, only enough to follow her with my eyes, hope rising again, but the poor creature only took a few steps toward the door, then a few more toward the chest on which her clothing lay. Then she stood still, as if she had not mind enough to understand where she was or what had befallen her. For a few minutes my sickness rose high in my throat so that I could not speak, but at last I forced myself to address her calmly, softly, slowly, so I would not frighten her and bade her to come back to bed.

As she had done before when I addressed her, at first she did not respond, seeming almost not to hear, but then she slowly did my bidding. Then I understood, and I had some ado not to burst into tears—I am not sure whether out of pity for her or for myself. Poor thing, poor thing, she was slow to obey not out of sullenness or reluctance but because it took her so long to understand what was said to her. I felt her settle beside me and began to turn to her, thinking to comfort her like a child, but she shrank away, and remembering that I had hurt her, I decided to let her be until her feeble mind lost that memory of hurt. Then, knowing the worst, beyond hope or doubt, I slept.

The morning began with a confirmation of my unhappy knowledge. Melusine had to be told everything—to wash, to dress. The only action she took without my order was to use the pot. Yet there were also little things that kept pricking me into doubt and hope. True, sometimes she seemed confused about the simplest matters, standing as if bewildered when I pointed out the water for washing, yet she had sense enough to put aside her elaborate wedding garments and seek for plainer ones inside the chest.

I began to see why the queen had not been willing

simply to thrust Melusine into a convent and forget her.
But I had no time to devise any way to test my doubts, for
Melusine was hardly dressed when the king and queen
came with other guests to witness the consummation of our
marriage. I do not know whether I could have faced
Stephen and Maud without resentment if that small thread
of doubt had not been woven into the blanket of sadness
and disappointment that covered me. As it was I could
barely keep myself from asking bitterly what I had done to
deserve a half-witted wife. But I suppose none of my
bitterness showed on my face. Maud looked well pleased
and smiled at me as she held up the blood-smeared sheet.

I am still not certain why the queen was so intent at that
time on having Melusine bound in marriage beyond any
doubt. Perhaps the rebellions and the Scots invasion made
her feel that one more trouble, even a small one, was
unbearable. Or perhaps she believed that if Melusine escaped and made her way back to her own property, the
lords of Cumbria would not only take her in and protect
her but rise in rage against Stephen. I saw her take the
sheet to store away, as if she might need proof that Melusine
was well and truly a wife, and then the king came and
struck me fondly, saying he had missed my service and I
should come with him.

I saw no more of Melusine that day. The king dined
privately with his brother Henry of Winchester and Roger,
bishop of Salisbury, and commanded me to take the dishes
at the door, as I had done as a squire when Stephen desired
privacy. I do not think I looked surprised or indignant—I
certainly did not feel either emotion—but a few minutes
later Stephen suddenly broke off what he was saying to the
bishop of Salisbury and beckoned to me.

"I forgot you were a Knight of the Body now," he said
contritely. "This service is not fit for you."

"My lord," I said, smiling—who could fail to forgive
him when it was so clear he meant no insult?—and, after
all, I had myself forgotten my new state, "any service you
ask of me is fitting."

But then Stephen began to draw me into the conversation. At first I was troubled, thinking that he was trying in
that way to make up to me for asking a squire's service of

me. Soon, however, I saw he was not thinking of me at all, except as an escape from a greater unease. What that was I could not tell; there seemed no special subject that the king wished to avoid. It was as if the very presence of his brother and Salisbury made him uncomfortable, even when they had nothing over which to quarrel.

That idea made *me* so uneasy that I did not give Melusine another thought all day. I knew that Roger of Salisbury had been Henry I's chancellor and justiciar, and with the assistance of his nephews (if they were nephews and not sons) Alexander, bishop of Lincoln, and Nigel, bishop of Ely, who was the king's treasurer, Salisbury still managed almost the entire government of the country. I do not know whether they were good and honest men, but I did know that the chancery and exchequer performed their business smoothly. They had accepted Stephen and I thought served him well. I was sorry about the coolness between the king and his brother, but that had existed since the end of the siege of Exeter. It would be worse if Stephen's anger was growing to involve Salisbury and his subordinates.

My concern was partly selfish. If Stephen now distrusted Salisbury and gave his offices to someone with little experience and ability, no doubt one of Waleran's family or friends, it was possible that revenue to the exchequer would fall. I had little doubt that the first expense to be cut would be the payment of pensions. But after the bishops left, I felt ashamed of my thoughts. It seemed that the king had really missed me, for he kept me close the whole day. We rode out after dinner, hawking, the king flying the superb bird he had been given at Jernaeve. Between the flights, Stephen talked, mostly of how he had frustrated any hope of Robert of Gloucester and Empress Matilda coming to England—but it was Queen Maud who had the largest hand in that.

When Walchelin Maminot, who held Dover, rebelled to give Gloucester a port of entry, the queen had bidden her ships from Boulogne to blockade Dover from the sea while she brought an army to besiege it from the land and forced Maminot to yield to her. Not that Stephen was trying to steal credit from his wife as so many men did; he valued her above anything on earth—or in heaven, for that matter.

It was only a careless form of speech, partly because he truly considered himself and Maud one body and one soul and partly because he was in high spirits. There had been no new uprisings, and all the south of England, except the far west, seemed to lie quiet in his hand.

I could not help thinking of the Scots swallowing up the north, but I held my tongue. I knew well by now the king's habit of setting aside unpleasant thoughts and dark prospects with an easy optimism. In this case, despite the pain I felt for my land, I could not blame him. It was impossible for Stephen to leave the rich, well-peopled south to drive the Scots away from a poor, barren shire. He had done so twice already, showing his good intentions toward Northumbria and Yorkshire, but times were more dangerous now. If the king took his army northward, there might be more rebellions. Then men who held other ports than Dover at which the earl of Gloucester and Empress Matilda might land could have second thoughts and welcome them ashore.

By the time I was free of service, it was dark. I fear my mind was so far from my marriage that I would have sought my old sleeping place had not the king dismissed me with a half-jesting apology for keeping me so long from the new delights of my marriage bed. I was fortunate that he turned away from me too quickly to notice the shudder I could not restrain at the memory his words called up. I thought of finding myself another place to sleep, but I could not leave the poor creature to whom I was married in doubt and perhaps fear—if she remembered me and the hurt she had suffered.

The door was open, but only the faint glow of the night light lit the chamber when I arrived. Melusine was already abed, either asleep or pretending to be so by the stillness of her body under the coverlet. I was glad of it, for it spared me the need to talk to her, and I undressed and lay down on my left side with my back to her, hoping that if she were only pretending my position would be sign enough that I would not trouble her.

Fortunately for me I was more accustomed to sleeping on my back or my right side and not at all accustomed to sharing my bed with anyone. Because I was not comfortable, I could not sleep, so after a time I turned gently to my back. Melusine gave no sign of being aware of my movement and I began to relax. Perhaps I was half asleep by then and my breathing changed its rhythm, but the presence of another in the bed kept me from letting go completely. A tiny shift in the sheet and mattress brought me more awake. Had the movement been swiftly over, I think I would have dismissed it and truly slept, but it was too slow and went on too long to be a natural shifting. I do not think I felt any suspicion, only a mild irritation because Melusine was not yet asleep and a sleepy reluctance to find words of reassurance. But suddenly the slow shifting changed to a swift lunge upright, and a shadow with a dully gleaming tip arced downward toward me.

CHAPTER 8

Melusine

THE NIGHT when I first regained my senses had been so full of terror and my waking moments so full of rage that my head had no room for memories or my heart for grief. Perhaps too I closed papa and my brothers out of my mind for fear of the agony remembering my loss would bring. I had played such tricks on myself in the past, when I was trying to forget what my thirteenth birthday had brought upon my family. That morning, although I did not deliberately refuse to think of my menfolk, I may have slipped into the old pattern out of hate and fear. I knew that my only chance for revenge would be lost if anyone suspected that I was no longer mad. Thus my entire attention was devoted to behaving as closely as I could to how I had acted before I recovered my wits.

Since no one seemed surprised when the queen brought me in among her ladies—and several who had not come to see the proof that my maidenhead had been wrested from me greeted me kindly—I assumed that there had been no need to confine me in the past. Beyond that I had no guide, but it seems that my hesitation to reply or act, bred out of the fear I would betray that I was in my right mind now, was considered normal for me. As soon as my terror of exposing myself was a little eased, I began to think where I could obtain a knife long enough, strong enough, and sharp enough to kill.

From Donald. Papa would not give me a long, sharp knife and Magnus would ask why. The unbidden answer was in my mind before I could guard against it, and with the thought came an involuntary bracing of my body as if to endure a physical pain. But there was no stabbing in my chest or throat so sharp as to stop my breath. There was only loneliness, the terrible knowledge that my menfolk would never again help me, cosset me, or interfere with me. In that great desolation, my resolve to kill the greedy cur that had married a mewling madwoman for favor and gold hardened for I had nothing to lose. The punishment for murder was death, and death would save me from being alone.

Perhaps I sobbed once or made some low sound of misery. I was not aware of it, but a woman came to me and led me to the queen. Clearly Maud had no idea that I was grieving for a loss more than half a year in the past. She thought only of my current state and tried to reassure me about the pain of coupling and explain that my husband was a kind man of the highest character and a great favorite of the king. I did not want to listen; I did not wish to hear good things about a man so venial that he would marry a madwoman for profit; I would not believe what she said.

All I felt was surprise that she should trouble herself to try to soothe me, but I saw the way she watched me as she spoke and guessed that she was suspicious of me. I could not guess why. What danger could one helpless prisoner be to the queen of England? My father and brothers were dead; they could not come to rescue me. And even if they had been alive, there was not the strength in Ulle or even all of Cumbria to challenge the king. Yet after Maud spoke to me and I was led away, it seemed to me that I was watched constantly by one or another of the queen's ladies when Maud was not herself among us.

That puzzle so teased my poor head that the sharp anguish caused by remembering my loss eased. Later, I was shocked when I realized how easily I had been di-

verted from a pain that should be consuming me. When I
thought of it, the pain was there, but put away in a corner
of my being, almost as if I had been aware my dear ones
were dead over the lost months of my madness and had
been grieving all that time. I was familiar with the separation of grief from ordinary life; I had lived with that buried
ache since my thirteenth year.

The fact that my life was not at all ordinary right now
also ·overlaid the pain. The queen's suspicion must have
something to do with Ulle and so did my marriage. I was
certain of that, for in myself I was only a young woman
without power or influence. Perhaps mama's relatives in
England . . . but we had lost touch with them after mama
died. Anyway, I was certain that papa had told me years
ago that mama's own brothers were dead and there were
only cousins, whom we never saw. It must be Ulle. If only
papa had explained to me what could give Ulle such
importance instead of telling me always that a beautiful
woman had no need to trouble herself with politics. What
value could a poor manor like Ulle have to a queen and
king who ruled a whole nation?

I had to keep pushing the puzzle out of my thoughts, for
it was leading me into senseless speculation that was di-
verting me from seeking a knife. Other things diverted me
too—a woman who stared at me for a moment, making me
so nervous that her words pierced my preoccupation. She
said, with a shake of her head to the friend seated near her
that it was a shame to give Bruno of Jernaeve a wife who
had not sense enough to appreciate a man with so little
interest in playing with women.

And the other laughed and said, "Did you try for him
too? I think a man whose mother was a whore might know
too much about women."

"Perhaps," the first admitted with a shrug; then her
tongue flicked out to touch her lips and her voice thick-
ened, "but I have heard he knows all the right things as
well as all the wrong ones."

They spoke low enough to keep what they were saying
from other ladies at a little distance but ignored me as if I
were a cushion or a bench, although I was too close to
miss a word. I kept my head down watching my fingers

and cursing them. Until that woman spoke it, I had not
known the man's name. Now I knew it was Bruno of
Jernaeve, and he became more a person, less a symbol of
the fall of Ulle and of greed without honor. I rose and
wandered about, touching this and lifting that, but without
much hope. The queen's quarters were not a good place to
find a weapon, there being little beyond embroidery needles and small, delicate eating knives available. I did not
need to steal one. I had my own eating knife, but the
short, narrow blade would have to be aimed too exactly. It
would not guarantee success to a hurried thrust in the dark.
What I needed was a wide, double-edged hunting knife.

I felt a fool as soon as I thought the words. That man
must have a hunting knife, and he was not wearing it this
morning. He had been dressed in plain, sober garments—
not the sort of clothing one would expect the son of a
whore to choose . . . Son of a whore. It was his name that
had first stuck in my mind, but now, as I tried to remember the details of his dress, those words came back. They
explained the hunger I had seen burned into his soul and
the greed that had driven him to accept marriage to a
madwoman. Pity stirred in me and I ground it down. It
was true that his mother's trade was no fault of his, but
someone had lifted him out of the dirt. He had the means
to gain an honorable livelihood. There was no need for
him to become the lickspittle of an usurper.

His knife would do if it was with his clothing and other
possessions, but I needed to get back to the chamber in
which we had slept to find it—and to free myself from the
women who watched me to steal it and hide it. A need to
piss came over me—from fear at the thought of what I
must do and what must follow that act, I suppose—but I
found that I knew where to go, although I could not
remember ever having used the privies. I wandered toward
the door, and I heard a voice call after me, "Where do you
go?"

I made no answer until she came after me and gripped
my arm, and then I said, "To piss."

The woman sighed and let me go, but she followed me
out of the queen's hall to the privies at the back. Nonetheless, after I relieved myself I did not go back to the

queen's hall but to the guesthouse chamber I had found myself in last night. I stood in the doorway at first simply letting my eyes wander about the room. Since my gaoler was behind me she could not see where I was looking; perhaps she thought my eyes were on the bed—still tumbled because I had no maid of my own, as I judged from the fact that no one had come to help me dress. I suddenly remembered how skillfully Bruno—no! that man; I would not think of him by name!—had laced my dress. Yet the gossiping women had said he was not a womanizer.

None of that matters, I told myself angrily, pulling my eyes away from the untidiness that grated on me, the cover half sliding to the floor and the pillows all awry on the bare mattress from which the queen herself had removed the sheet. That act made me seem a person of importance, but the lack of a maidservant surely showed that I was of no account at all—unless the queen, or the lady responsible for such matters as assigning a maid (I had not the faintest idea how so great a household was managed) had forgotten. Yet people of importance are not forgotten . . . and unimportant people are not watched.

My thoughts having come round full circle again, I barely restrained a cry of rage and forced myself instead to consider the knife I needed. I could see the chest holding my clothes from the doorway, but I had to step farther into the room and turn to see the man's possessions. My watchdog followed, and I heard her exclaim wordlessly—I assume when she saw the unmade bed—and step out again. I took two swift steps toward the chest, then froze as I heard the woman call to someone and bid that person watch the door and keep me within. And then the door closed.

I remember a strange sensation about my mouth and cheeks and then realized I was smiling. To be able to feel the difference told me how very, very long it had been since I last smiled—but what had I had to smile about? Now that I had purpose again, I could smile with satisfaction if not with joy. I was on my knees beside the chest, praying it was not locked, heaving it open before the prayer was finished, my fingers catching in the engraving on the lid. I barely stopped myself from grabbing garments and tossing them to the floor as I took in the neatness within. I had expected the same wild jumble that filled my father's and brothers' chests no matter how often I created order in them, but here every shirt and tunic and pair of braies was folded and in a place, even those that were worn and clumsily patched—no doubt by the hand of a man who had no woman to mend his clothes. Pity wrung me again; although I do not know why, there was a terrible feeling of loneliness in that inept patching and careful folding.

I drove the pity out, cursing instead the pinchpenny ways of the low born which made it needful for me to remove and replace the contents of the chest with care when I might be interrupted at any moment. Without more ado, I lifted out the fine gown that man had worn to the wedding, then a layer of plain sober tunics and chausses like those he had worn this morning, and finally came to a set of stained leather garments that must be hunting clothes. Beneath them lay what I sought.

The knife was long and strong with a wide, curved guard, and I had some trouble forcing it up my inner sleeve. It was sharp and keenly pointed too, and cut the cloth in several places as I shifted it around so it lay along the outside of my arm. Anyone who saw the sleeve would see what I had hidden there, but my long, wide outer sleeve would hide it, and it was heavy enough so that I could not forget it and expose it by accident. Having replaced the clothing, I closed the lid and could not help seeing that the carving that decorated the lid formed the word Bruno. I turned my eyes away and hurried back to stand where I had been when my watchdog went out. Not long after, she returned with a maid who carried a clean sheet. I did not stay to see the room put to rights, but went back to the queen's apartment.

The rest of the day was worse. I hardly had to pretend not to hear what was said to me or to be slow to understand. I could think of little else than what I must do this very night for the weight of the knife in my sleeve made my purpose real and did not allow my mind to wander from it. There were moments when I exulted: I would have my revenge for the violation of Ulle and of my body and cut away this favorite from the king, who had been papa's

enemy, as my papa and brother had been cut away from
me. But somehow my joy in revenge would not stay clean
and hard.

I was not much afraid, for all but my life had been reft
from me already—I had no family, no lands, even my
body was forfeit to my enemy—and a brief time of pain
would make me safe and rejoin me with my papa forever.
But somehow the contents of Bruno's chest—not a nameless enemy but a man called Bruno—kept rising before my
eyes. I saw again and again those patched and folded
garments, and tears prickled behind my eyes when I thought
that the hands that had taken such patient care would never
touch them again.

Still, the day passed and at least I was spared being
seated beside the man Bruno either at dinner or the evening meal. The queen dined in the great hall, but the king
did not, and the evening meal was served to the queen and
her ladies separately in the queen's hall. After I had choked
down what I could of it, I rose and walked toward the
door. As before, a lady pursued me, asking where I would
go, and I paused and thought and replied slowly, "To my
own chamber, to bed."

This reply caused great mirth and several crude jests
about how even the slow-witted had sense enough to learn
quickly the pleasure of the body and how I would no doubt
sleep less restlessly now that I had a husband. I should
have expected it, I suppose; I knew about wedding and
bedding and the sly teasing that accompanied them, but
my case was so different that the implication of what I had
said had not occurred to me. My head came up to snap
back a hot retort, but fortunately my glance caught the
queen's face, and I saw that the smile on her lips was not
mirrored in her eyes. She nodded as if in agreement with
the jests, but she also ordered the same woman who had
followed me before to go with me and find a maid to help
me undress and sit with me until I slept.

Perhaps the fact that I made my way to the chamber
unerringly and had stayed so quietly in the room earlier
gave the woman confidence. Whatever her reason, I could
see by the irritated downturn of her lips that she thought
the queen's precautions needless. In the hall outside the

queen's solar, she had beckoned a maid to follow us. She stopped outside the chamber, leaving me to myself while she instructed the maid, so I had time enough to move the knife from my sleeve and conceal it under my pillow. Once in the bed, I lay quietly, looking about for a time and then let my eyes close. Later, I turned to my side and thrust my hand beneath the pillow to grasp the hilt of the knife.

I think I did sleep for a while, for I do not know when the maid left. I came awake when the mattress sagged under the weight of another body, but I could not have been deep in sleep because I knew at once who it was and what I must do. Memory of pain, of the slickness of blood on my thighs, of the hard contempt on the face of the man who had violated me without joy or pleasure flooded me with hate. My hand tightened on the hilt of the knife, ready to draw it forth and kill the moment he mounted me—but he did not touch me at all. I suppose that should have been a relief; it was not. I hated him more, both for making me wait to kill and for the scorn that dismissed me as not desirable.

I did not move and neither did he, but I knew he was no more asleep than I. And as my heart pounded out the long, slow minutes, my rage against him grew, and I remembered tales of the old days when the most common way to gain lands was to kill the holder and his male heirs and marry a daughter of the blood. Perhaps this creature had urged the king to let him take Ulle because he had already murdered my father and brother. The longer I lay tense and still beside him, the more reasonable that seemed to me; and the more reasonable it seemed, the more eager I grew to draw out the knife and cut out his heart.

I fought against that desire, knowing that my chance of success would be much greater if the man was asleep, and at last he turned on his back and after a little while the sound of his breathing changed. Then I dared draw the knife from its hiding place, little by little, and little by little, inch by inch, free my knife hand of the covers, turn on my back, and move my left arm so that I could lift myself up in one single, swift motion and stab downward.

I do not know what mistake I made. Perhaps I drew a

deep breath before I thrust myself upright; perhaps I hesitated a tiny instant before I stabbed downward—although I had smothered it and buried it deep, there was a horror in me at the thought of killing. I was sure he was sound asleep when I moved. I know my left arm held down the coverlet so his right was imprisoned. And still, with all my precaution, I did not even prick him. As the knife swept down, when it was no more than a hairsbreadth from his throat, he put out his left hand and caught my wrist— without effort, without surprise, with the ease of a mother preventing the mischief of a baby—and laughed, *laughed!*

He did not even hurt me! He did not wrench my wrist or twist my arm. He was so strong that even though I was above him, pressing down, he simply raised my arm away from him and sat up—and laughed. And then he said the strangest thing: "Good evening, Lady Melusine. I am glad to meet you at last."

I gaped at him, too stunned to make a sound, and he shook his head and grinned at me. I could see his expression well enough, for my eyes were accustomed to the dark and the night candle was behind me so the light fell full on his face. I swear he looked delighted. A chill of terror rippled along my spine. All I could think was that he had been waiting for an excuse to beat me to death and now had it.

"It is too late to look at me like that, my lady," he said with a satisfied chuckle. "You never managed to convince the queen that you were an idiot, and your cleverness at obtaining and hiding a knife has given you away to me. I do not know the purpose of your game, but the game itself is now useless, so you may as well speak lies as act them. Come, give me the knife. I cannot let you keep it just now, and I do not wish to bruise you."

I blinked at the last words, and looked down at the knife, realizing that though he still held my wrist too firmly for me to move it, he also held it gently. But if he intended to beat me for trying to kill him, why should he worry about a bruise on my wrist? Could I use the knife to defend myself? As the question rose in my mind I realized I had instinctively been straining against his hold all the time and his hand had not even quivered. It seemed to me that he was the strongest man I had ever come across in my life, for I remembered that my brothers had never been able to control me so easily. Later it occurred to me that I had essayed no trial of strength against my brothers since we were all children, but at the time all I felt was that any idea of self-defense was hopeless. I allowed my hand to fall open, and watched him pick up the knife, raising my eyes to his face to seem unafraid.

His smile had disappeared, but he did not beat me or turn the knife on me. He released my wrist and got out of bed, asking in an easy, cheerful voice, "From whom did you take the knife, my lady? I must return it."

"It is yours," I said, beginning to wonder whether the king and queen had decided to marry a madwoman to a madman. I had a vague memory of Maud telling me that Bruno was a sweet-tempered man, but even the sweetest of tempers must resent being a target for murder.

"Very clever, my lady." He tossed the knife carelessly upon his chest and took a twig to the night candle to light the tapers on the stand where he had set the water for my washing in the morning. Then he turned toward me and nodded with what appeared to be real approval. "You saw that I did not wear hunting garb this morning and reasoned that I must have such a knife. Clever. Clever."

Clever? What was clever about reasoning out so simple a matter as the fact that any man had a hunting knife and if he was not wearing it, it must be with his possessions? Yet he seemed to be gloating over my ability. But surely he could not really take pleasure in being the victim of attempted murder? Was this a cruel game to ease my fear and thus make my suffering worse when he attacked me?

"So how will you punish me?" I burst out. I suppose my fear made my glare at him seem more virulent.

To my surprise, he dropped his eyes and repeated sadly, "Punish you? Not in any way. I know you have cause to hate me—or fear me. What you did was natural enough. I hope some day we can both forget this, or laugh over it."

Laugh over it? Laugh? What cause could I have to hate him or fear him? Because he burst into Ulle? But he had done me no harm except to look at me with contempt. Why should he look down as if ashamed over that? Perhaps it was not only that. Could the wild thought that he had been the one who killed papa and Donald be true? I should have felt a new welling of hatred, but all I felt was confusion, which was compounded as I stared at him by my awareness of his naked body.

He was still standing close to the candles and I could see the thick muscles on his arms and chest and, in a swift glance that I could not resist, even though it shamed me, on his strong thighs. Between them, the hair was so dark that his shaft showed pale. My eyes fled from that at once, but not so soon that I did not see that he seemed larger than my brothers, and as I looked up I saw that he was staring at me. I was sure he had noticed where I was looking, and I shrank back. He turned away at once, caught the knife up off the chest and opened it to draw out a coarse tunic, which he pulled on after dropping the knife in the chest. Now I think I may still have been a bit mad, because I had so much to fear yet what troubled me was that Bruno had no bedrobe.

"You need not be afraid," he said harshly. "I will not force you again." He hesitated and then went on, still with his back to me. "I am sorry for taking you against your will last night, but I had given my word to the king and queen that I would make you my wife beyond contest or doubt—you must have known what would result when you agreed to accept me as your husband."

"I never—" I began, and then fell silent.

Perhaps I *had* agreed to the marriage. I had no memory of it, but I had no memory of anything. Could I tell him that? Would he believe me? Recalling his words about my trying to convince the queen that I was an idiot, I doubted anything I said could shake his belief that I was playing some sly game. Besides, I did not want him to know of my weakness. He had turned to face me again and I met his eyes defiantly, not knowing what else to do.

"I want you to know," he said, "that I was no more eager for this marriage than you—"

"And how could *you* be forced to marry?" I interrupted bitterly.

"I was told you were dangerous and that it was my duty."

"Dangerous?" My voice squeaked in surprise, but it was fear that prevented me from laughing afterward, for Bruno's eyes flicked sidelong at the chest where lay the knife with which I had tried to kill him.

He merely shook his head and smiled, however, saying, "It is too late to pretend innocent frailty. You are a clever and beautiful woman, but I must warn you that I am not a man that can be led around by my rod. Neither beauty nor cleverness will turn me against the king and queen. I owe Stephen a great debt of gratitude and nothing will make me betray him."

He called me clever and beautiful, but I grew cold again. I was sure he was telling the truth when he said that passion had no hold on him. I remembered what the women in the queen's chamber had said about Bruno that morning: The whore's son knew too much about women, and surely I have never seen a man look at me with greater indifference. But underneath the hardness was that hunger. Whoever learned to satisfy that—if it could be satisfied—would be Bruno's master. I recoiled from the idea; it was more likely that whoever probed that hunger would be swallowed up.

"I am your prisoner?" I asked, my voice quivering in spite of my efforts to keep it steady as he came toward me.

"In a sense, I suppose you are," he said irritably. "I am pledged to make sure that you commit no act of treason against King Stephen, but I wish you would stop pretending to fear me." Then he sat himself on the bed and looked deliberately toward the chest. "I seem to be in more danger from you than you are from me," he went on, turning his eyes back to me. "I have told you already that I will do you no hurt. We are man and wife and must find a way to live together. I want to be able to sleep at night without expecting a knife in the back."

I could feel my blood rising into my face, but I made no reply. I knew I would never be able to nerve myself to try to kill him again, but why should I give him the ease of mind of admitting that?

"I have a proposal to make to you," he said, his face set like stone. "You know my state. I am a landless bastard, a whore's son. I desire an estate. Your condition is little better than mine, for you have been disseisined. Stephen holds your lands, and you have no hope of restoration because the queen knows you are an enemy. But I am close to the king and have some influence with him. It is not impossible that, in time, Stephen can be convinced to grant your lands to me. Understand, I will make sure you cannot raise rebellion against the king, but you will be able to live in the comfort of your own home among people you know. If you will make truce with me, I will promise to do my uttermost to have Ulle and whatever other lands belong to your estate restored to us.''

I do not know how long I sat staring at him. My first impulse was to spit in his face because what he said seemed to confirm that papa and Donald had died by his hand so he could marry the heiress to Ulle. But he had also said that he had been unwilling to take me as his wife. Which was the lie? And then I remembered that papa had married against his will to keep Ulle. Surely he would expect no less of me. And once at Ulle, it would be easy, so easy, to avenge papa's death. It would not even be necessary to shed any blood. Accidents were all too common in my part of the country even for those who knew the land. It would be very easy to arrange one for a man who was ignorant of the wild winds that came of a sudden down our mountains and swept men and horses off the narrow roads that hung above the deep tarns. And when my husband was dead, I would inherit his lands. Ulle would be mine again! My breath eased out and I lowered my eyes. Papa would approve of this truce. He would rest easy when Ulle was in my hands and his killer was dead.

Slowly I put out my hand. "Truce," I whispered.

CHAPTER 9

Bruno

THE GLITTER of the night candle on the knife blade gave me an instant's warning, and I caught Melusine's wrist just as the point touched my throat. It took all my strength to lift her arm away from me and to hold it until I could sit up. I suppose I should have been angry, but instead I was filled with a crazy joy because the queen had been right. I was not married to a witless lump of flesh. This woman might be a devil—indeed, she looked it with her big, black eyes wild and her hair disheveled as she strained to free her arm and plunge the knife into me—but I could fight a devil or come to terms with it.

The sickness that had pervaded my very soul all day was gone, and I could not help laughing for joy. I do not remember what I said first; it was silly and shocked her, but it served my purpose in letting me take the knife from her without hurting her. At first she tried to pretend idiocy again and then tried to make me believe she was terrified of me, but I soon showed her I could not be deceived by such pretense.

One thing I told Melusine most sincerely was that I was sorry for my rape the night of our wedding, that it was of necessity not of my will. I do not know whether she believed that because, when I got out of bed to light

candles so that we could talk, she had no doubt seen that
the sight of her had half roused me. I put on a tunic then,
so she would not be able to think she could judge my
thoughts by the swelling of my rod—and I warned her that
the desire to couple never warped my will. But I doubt she
believed that either; women never do—and I must admit
that with life and fire in her she was far more lovely than I
first thought her, although she was still a bigger, darker
mare than suited my taste.

Despite that and her dark coloring, which I never cared
for in a woman, she *was* lovely, and I had to remind
myself more than once that she had tried to stick a knife in
me. Nor from the way her eyes met mine would it be her
last attempt, and there is no way for a husband to shield
himself from his wife at all times. Clearly she felt her life
would be well lost if she could end mine, and if she had no
fear of retribution, unless I maimed her or locked her into
a dungeon, she would succeed sooner or later in killing
me.

I thought then that she remembered and hated me for
taking Ulle. I was the first man in, and she blamed me for
the loss of her lands. That was not reasonable, of course.
It was the king who had ordered the taking of the manor,
and if I had not led the attack some other man would have
done so. Ulle would have been reft from her in any case. I
almost said that, after telling her that I wanted to be able to
sleep at night without fearing a knife in the back, but I
stopped myself in time, hoping she would not notice the
sheen of sweat that burst out on me when I realized how
serious a mistake I had nearly made.

As a flash of lightning over a battlefield will etch each
detail, everything had been made clear to me. I suddenly
knew why I was the man Queen Maud had decided must
be Melusine's husband, the *only* suitable man. I had been
chosen *because* I was the focus of Melusine's hate, because as long as she had me to hate, the queen hoped she
would not turn that hate on the king. But why had the
queen not simply done away with Melusine if she thought
her so dangerous? Partly, I guessed, because Stephen had
become fond of the girl, would not believe ill of her, and
would be angry if harm came to her, and, of course, partly

because Maud was not *sure* Melusine was dangerous. Had Maud hoped that if Melusine attacked me I would kill her in a rage or while defending myself? If so, she had misjudged me. Despite my liking and admiration for the queen, I knew that she was not in the least scrupulous when Stephen's good was at stake, and I would not do her dirty work for her.

And then, as swiftly as I had seen the problem, I saw the solution. If Melusine hated me because she blamed me for the loss of Ulle, could we not live in peace if I promised to do my best to get Ulle back for her? But why should I? I could not admit that my purpose was to cool her hatred for the king lest it set ideas into her head and make hatred a prize to cling to against all reason.

While all these thoughts flickered through my head, my eyes had rested on Melusine's face. The flush of color that had come into her cheeks when I said we were man and wife and must learn to live together still lingered and reminded me of another reason she might hate me. A lady born might resent being forced into marriage with a whore's landless son—and she would certainly believe that he would use that marriage as a basis to win lands of his own.

I had to phrase my proposal carefully, pointing out that she had no chance at all to regain her lands without me, and that I could only serve that purpose because I was a favorite with the king. Thus, I hoped I had made clear that Stephen and I were both necessary to her purpose and must not be targets for her spite. In fairness, I warned her that, if I were successful in getting Ulle regranted, I would not permit her to use those lands for treasonous activity—but I was not really worried about that. Women are not much interested in political matters unless they affect them directly.

I was very pleased by the length of time Melusine took to think over what I had said. Had she leapt at the offer without thought, I would have had grave doubts of her understanding and seriously accepting the proposal. But she thought for several long minutes, her eyes fixed on my face as if she hoped to pierce through and see what was written in my mind, and only slowly stretched out her hand to me, saying softly, "Truce."

I felt she meant it, and I took her hand. "We will both

benefit by peace," I told her, "but I must remind you that
to achieve this purpose will take time. I hope you do not
expect me to ask tomorrow and be granted the lands the
next day."

"I am not a fool," she said, and then blushed hotly.

I laughed, knowing she had remembered that she had
deliberately been acting the fool. "You have got yourself
into the stew by pretending to be an idiot," I remarked,
not sorry to rub a little salt in the wound. Perhaps she
would be more careful of the lies she acted in the future,
but the pretense was now as awkward for me as for her, so
I went on, "Can you think of a way to climb out of the
pot? I will be glad to help in any way I can, since I do not
want everyone laughing at me for being married to a
half-wit."

"There are more who would envy you than laugh," she
said with a wry twist to her full lips. Her voice was deep
for a woman, without the lilting quality that made Audris's
speech so charming.

I thought that over because in a way she was right. Most
men seemed to prefer silly women—even the king, although he had come to value his wife highly. I too valued
a clever woman who could talk to me and even in certain
matters advise me because Audris had been such a one,
and during my early life I had no other friend or person to
love, man or woman. And now that Hugh had married
Audris I was again without a heart that belonged only to
me.

I was glad for Hugh and Audris, but a pang of regret
stabbed me and I released Melusine's hand, which I had
been holding absently since we swore truce with each
other. How I wished she had offered me that hand in trust
and affection instead of as a thin bridge over a river of
hate. But I would not despair. We had a great interest in
common, and that might easily be a foundation on which
trust and affection might some day be built. For the present, it was fortunate that my notion of what was best in
womankind seemed to fit with hers, if I had read that
scornful turn of the mouth aright.

"I am not one who cares for stupid women," I said. "I
wish to be able to approach my wife and be seen to talk

with her with pleasure when the king takes his ease with
the queen.''

Her eyes, which had been on the hand I had been
holding and then released, rose to study my face. She
looked startled and then very thoughtful and at last said
slowly, ''I suppose I could pretend to have been sad and
fearful and thus guarded my every word so that I seemed
dull. And now that the worst has befallen me I could
pretend that it is not so bad as I expected so my fear could
wear off slowly.''

I was not too well pleased with her remark that she
could *pretend* the worst was not as bad as she expected. It
seemed a poor return for all the effort I had made to soothe
her, but then I reminded myself that she believed she had
cause to hate me while I had none—except her unwillingness to marry me—to dislike her. Still, I said to her, rather
sharply, ''I hope that pretense will include civility to me in
public.''

''Yes,'' she replied, ''of course. If you are to have any
chance to retrieve my lands, I must seem reconciled to my
fate.'' Then she frowned and added thoughtfully, ''We
will need to balance carefully between seeming content
with each other and waking suspicions in the queen that
you are growing enamored of me. It would be better if I
seemed to come to you and seek your attention.''

Clever, I thought—not as I had thought earlier when the
fact that she could think at all was a blessing like a shower
of gold to me—but with some caution. Melusine not only
had a quick mind but also did not allow herself to be
diverted from a purpose by foolish considerations of pride.
It could not be easy for her to seem to pursue a whore's
son, but she was willing to put the greater purpose ahead
of the pinpricks she must know the queen's ladies would
inflict on her. However, a clever woman sometimes thought
she was the only one of her kind, and the queen would be
watching.

''It would be better,'' I agreed, ''but remember that
your pretense of stupidity did not work on the queen, and
she may see through this new pretense with equal ease if
you do not take care.''

She stared at me for an instant, and then uttered a

strange, brief bark of laughter which seemed to startle her as much as it did me; then she shuddered. "I will take care," she said, and lay down and pulled the blanket up over her shoulders as if fear had chilled her.

I almost reached out to touch her comfortingly, for if I had been the queen's enemy and trying to deceive her I would have been sorely afraid, but I remembered that Melusine might take such a gesture as a threat and changed the movement of my hand to pushing myself up off the bed so I could snuff the candles. Having removed my tunic and dropped it on my chest, I returned to the bed.

The effect of lying naked beside Melusine was irritating, even though I was not touching her. All the time we had been talking, my eyes had rested with indifference on her face and full breasts, bare except for the veiling of dark hair that fell over her shoulders. Now that her body and features were hidden from me, I was suddenly achingly aware of them and I felt a warmth and filling in my loins.

I could not force an unwilling woman, but I regretted that I had spoken in such terms as to preclude any attempt to make her willing—or had I? Could the same carrot that had led her—I hoped—to give up any notion of murdering me be used to induce her to agree to our coupling?

"There is one more thing I must say before we sleep," I remarked, trying to sound completely indifferent. "I promised not to force coupling on you, and I will keep my word, but you should consider that a child would be a good reason for the king to enfeoff me with Ulle. Stephen is fond of children and I could make a good case pleading that my child not be deprived of the security of a home and lands. If you feel this is reasonable and are willing, I will do my best to make the coupling as easy for you as I can." I could feel a very faint movement, not as if Melusine had shifted her body but as if she had stiffened, and I said quickly to forestall a flat negative, "You need not answer now. Take time to consider. I am in no hurry."

Then her body did shift; she turned her back to me with a hasty flop that would have betokened bad temper in any of my usual bed partners. Bad temper? I reviewed my hasty and thoughtless words and grinned to myself in the dark. Who would have thought it? I would have assumed that the disinterest of a whore's son would have provided the well-born Lady Melusine with relief, but apparently great lady and common whore agreed on one thing: Neither liked to find *any* man indifferent to her.

The revelation restored my good humor, although it made it no easier to convince my standing man that he would find no soft, warm haven this night. Partly to induce him to lie down and partly because I did not really trust the truce with Melusine enough to sleep yet, I thought over what I had so hastily promised to pacify my wife. I had not lied to her; I would indeed do my best to convince the king to grant me Melusine's heritage. The only untruth was the implication that Stephen might possibly enfeoff me with those lands.

Was it really so unlikely? The more I thought about it the more I thought that what I had said only to obtain a breathing space in which to tame Melusine might be the best possible solution to a number of problems. The first of those was the strong possibility that Stephen would fail to pay the pension he had promised, which was all I had to support my wife. From what I had seen of Cumbria, the income from Melusine's estates would come to considerably less than the pension. The land was able to provide a subsistence to those who lived on it but little more than that. Yet for me, a secure subsistence based on lands of my own was far more desirable than a rich pension—even assuming it was paid with reasonable regularity.

For the king there would be a profit far greater than relief from payment of the pension or the guilt of not paying it. Although Stephen had disseisined those knights and barons who had been actively disloyal during the winter invasion of England, all knew that Cumbria remained a hotbed of disaffection. It seemed to me it would add greatly to the peace and stability of the shire to enfeoff a man loyal to Stephen but married to a native Cumbrian. To disseisin men and place stewards on their estates had no ring of finality. If Stephen were defeated, those lands could be returned to their original holders with no more than the stroke of a pen and the pressure of a seal. But once a new man was settled on the estate, particularly one

married into the legitimate line, it would take a war to
restore the property to the man who had been disseisined.

Holding Ulle in my own right, I would serve as an
example of the evil result of rebellion as well as furnish
Stephen with a voice in the councils of Cumbria—and I
would be well placed to deal out further lessons to the
rebellious barony if they intended to welcome David and
his Scots again. But thinking of the Scots sent a sharp
pang of anxiety through me. By the last news Stephen had,
David had swallowed up all of Northumbria and was
driving south toward York, where Hugh's foster father
Archbishop Thurstan was gathering an army to oppose
him. Had they met? Who had triumphed? Had Hugh been
hurt in the battle? If he had been wounded or killed, I
would have to go to Audris to give her what comfort I
could.

Then I remembered that I had never sent her the letter I
had written while I was in Oxford. That could be amended
easily; I would send it with the next messenger to go
north. But now I realized I had too lightly ignored how
much of a hold David might have on the countryside. My
heart sank farther as I thought Audris might need my help
and I not know of it. I had better ask the king for leave and
go myself to make sure all was well with Audris. But if I
asked Stephen for leave because of the Scottish threat in
the north he would be hurt and angry thinking I was slyly
reproving him for not helping.

As I cast around for some other excuse to offer Stephen,
a small and very ladylike snore sounded in my ear. Melusine,
about whom I had forgotten completely and who had
nothing at all to fear from knives in the back, had fallen
fast asleep. For one instant I was so enraged by the
contrast in our conditions—mine filled with unhappy anxiety and hers one of relaxation and confidence—that I was
sorely tempted to shove her out of bed and dump her onto
the floor. In the next I forgave her, for I had found the
perfect excuse to give the king: I wished to take my wife
north to introduce her to my "family." I breathed a deep
sigh as another soft, delicate snore preceded a shift of
Melusine's body, an easy, boneless kind of turning that

guaranteed sleep. Tomorrow I would speak to the king about leave, I thought, and let my eyes close at last.

I did receive permission from the king to go north the next day, but as matters fell out, I did not need to ask for it. When I came on duty, Stephen had not yet come from his bedchamber into the hall, and when he did Waleran de Meulan was with him. I do not know whether Mass had been said in the king's bedchamber, but I did not think so, and they did not go to the chapel so I missed Mass also. That did not trouble me for myself, but I wondered whether it was a chance occurrence or whether it marked another step in the king's estrangement from the Church. Stephen smiled at me but did not speak and sat down at once at the single table set for him to break his fast, gesturing to Waleran to join him. Their expressions roused a cautious watchfulness in me. The king looked uneasy and stubborn and Waleran's face carried a muted triumph.

The morning meal was never formal, and on a fine day like this most people took their food out of doors; but there was food in the hall for those who wished to wait there on the chance that Stephen would notice them and beckon them to him. Naturally, the great lords did not bother to come; they had more direct methods of approaching the king. There were few gentlemen in the hall this morning, and those did not come closer when they saw Stephen was already engaged.

I stood back somewhat behind Waleran's position, directing the squires to carry dishes to the table but moving as little as I could myself, for stillness confers a kind of invisibility. Waleran did not like me—not, I think, for any personal reason but because of the trust in me Stephen showed. I believe that Waleran did not want the king to love or trust anyone except those tied by blood or interest to himself.

I could not help thinking as I watched Stephen's ease and confidence with Waleran how different he had been with his own brother and the bishop of Salisbury the previous day, and I felt it was wrong. I did not desire that Henry of Winchester rule the king, but I did not want Stephen to be ruled by Waleran de Meulan either. I remembered how Waleran had betrayed King Henry, who had loved him as tenderly as a son, and I feared Waleran was more interested in his own wealth and power than the good of the king or the realm.

The way Stephen and Waleran looked at each other told me that Waleran had convinced the king to do something that others might not approve, and I wanted to know what it was. Waleran was not likely to speak openly about what he felt was so confidential it should be urged only in the king's bedchamber, but Stephen was prone to hints and significant glances about a subject that was occupying his mind. Although Waleran's influence was growing steadily stronger, I could sometimes interfere in small ways by making the king see certain of Waleran's suggestions in a different light.

I learned nothing, Waleran having cleverly diverted the talk at the table to a new hawk he had given the king. Their discussion of the bird's strength and agility, which it seemed they were planning to test later in the day, was interrupted only by a page who came running to announce that a messenger from Archbishop Thurstan had arrived and was on his way to the hall. In his eagerness Stephen jumped to his feet and went down the hall—and I went also, my heart suddenly pounding in my breast.

"God has saved us!" the messenger cried as he crossed the threshold and saw Stephen. "The Scots carpet the field of Northallerton like cut rushes, and those who survive flee north in disorder. King David's army is no more."

"Well come!" Stephen responded, clapping the young priest on the shoulder. "You are most well come. I am sure God has shown His favor because of the blessed Thurstan's piety. And now that threat in the north is lifted from us, we will have peace in the land. Come, sit with me and tell me all the news."

Stephen led the priest back and I followed close on their heels, forgetting all about Waleran's purpose in my anxiety about Hugh, who I was sure had been in that battle. But it was through the news of what became known as the Battle of the Standard—the rallying point for those loyal to King Stephen had been a standard of saints' pennons and a pyx prepared and blessed by Archbishop Thurstan—that I

learned what Waleran had convinced Stephen to do and
was given leave to go north.

The battle had been described between bites of bread
and cheese and pasty and gulps of ale, which the king
urged on the priest, who had obviously been present on the
hill where the standard was set. Then the priest told Stephen that William d'Aumale had organized the pursuit of
the Scots and intended to take back those castles that had
fallen into David's hands. Suddenly, Waleran, who had
been listening with great interest, leaning forward with an
elbow on the table, sat up and touched Stephen's shoulder.

"Aumale should be rewarded, my lord," he said. "It
seems to me, that it would be most fitting to award him the
earldom of York. He is already in good repute with the
local barons, familiar with the shire, and engaged in protecting it. Would it not seem reasonable to give the authority over the north into such loyal and skillful hands?
Perhaps he could be invested at the same time as you
assign Worcester to me and Bedford to Hugh and give
formal recognition to Gilbert as earl of Pembroke."

For a moment I was distracted from my fear for Hugh.
If I had heard aright, a good portion of the great nobles of
England would be members of Waleran's family. Robert,
Waleran's twin, was already earl of Leicester; William de
Warenne, Waleran's half brother, was earl of Surrey; Roger
Beaumont, his first cousin doubly tied in blood by being
married to his half sister, was earl of Warwick. Now three
more were to be belted as earls: Waleran himself would
hold Worcester; the Hugh he spoke of was the youngest
of the three full-blooded Beaumont brothers and had been
called the Pauper because there had been no lands to give
him—he would be a pauper no longer but the earl of
Bedford; and Gilbert de Clare, married to Waleran's full-
blood sister, would gain full title to what he had long
claimed and be earl of Pembroke. No wonder Waleran and
the king felt privacy was needed.

I knew at once, however, that this matter was beyond
my touch and my judgement. I feared the elevation of so
many Beaumonts would increase the dissatisfaction of other
noble families, but they might not take it amiss. Anything
I said on such a subject would be presumptuous. Doubtless

Waleran was advancing his family because he expected
they would support him, but there was no guarantee of
that. I knew that Waleran's twin brother, Robert of Leicester,
had taken no part in Waleran's rebellion against King
Henry. Moreover, Robert was respected by all for his
sober judgement, and William de Warenne was well liked
too. From all I knew and could guess, there was as much
likelihood of evil resulting from refusing to elevate Waleran's
candidates as from agreeing to do it, and I could see no
good in my interference.

The king, filled with enthusiasm by the good news,
nodded eagerly at Waleran but turned back to the priest at
once to ask if there was anything else he wished to say. I
do not know that he had, but he had lowered his eyes
thoughtfully when he heard Waleran's proposal, and now
shook his head at Stephen's question as if he wished to
have time alone to think. Assured that the messenger's
budget was emptied, Stephen took a rich ring from his
finger to reward the bringer of glad tidings and told him
that he might go and rest.

That wiped all thought of the ennoblement of Beaumonts from my mind. I could not leave the king and could
not be sure of finding the priest again. "My lord," I cried,
"may I beg a few words with this messenger?"

"Most certainly," Stephen replied kindly, "but he can
have no news of Jernaeve or your sister."

"I know, my lord, but my friend Hugh Licorne, who
was Archbishop Thurstan's foster child, must have been in
the battle." I turned to the priest. "Do you know Hugh
Licorne?"

"I do, but I have no word of him." He smiled at me.
"That must be good. Sir Hugh was one of the leaders
under Sir Walter Espec, and I spoke to Sir Walter. I am
certain that if any harm had come to Sir Hugh, Sir Walter
would have sent the news to my lord the archbishop."

I drew a deep breath of relief and thanked him most
fervently. Each time I thought of how Audris's light had
been dimmed just by separation from Hugh when she
knew him to be safe and well, my terror increased about
her reaction to his death. As it turned out, the priest was
wrong and my relief premature, but since Hugh recovered

I was grateful for the mistake. I would have torn my heart out with worry to no purpose at all had I known the truth.

The priest rose, bowed slightly to the king, and left the table. As I backed away a few steps to make room, Waleran raised a hand to stop me from going farther and said to the king, "My lord, this is a day on which all things must go well. I was just wondering where we would find a man to carry your message to Aumale—and here he is. You are from the north, are you not, Bruno?"

Stephen gave me no chance to reply, laughing at what seemed to me great presumption on Waleran's part, but he did say, "You are very free in disposing of my favorite servant. Surely I can send a message back with the priest or find someone else to carry my gratitude to those who defended the realm."

"I beg pardon, my lord," Waleran said, "it is not that I wish to rob you of Bruno's service, but you know the priest's first loyalty is to the archbishop. He will go to his master before he goes to Aumale, so the offer of the earldom will seem to have come through Thurstan's influence instead of direct from the goodness of your heart." He shrugged. "You know I am glad of the victory over the Scots, but I could wish it had not been handed to us by a prince of the Church."

"I do not think we need worry about Archbishop Thurstan," Stephen replied. "He is a most pious man who would not overstep the bounds of his spiritual office."

"Only because he is too old and too sick," Waleran remarked sourly. "He was not so meek in King Henry's time. But we are losing the point of who should go north with your thanks and rewards. Not the priest—I agree with you there."

My lifelong training held my face straight, but I did not know whether I felt more like laughing or crying at the way Waleran had turned *his* objection to employing the priest as a messenger into Stephen's idea. Then the import of what they had said sank into me, and I could hardly believe my ears. Stephen had never been ardently religious, which I counted a virtue I must admit, but it was strange to hear him speak of a churchman overstepping the bounds of spiritual office. Churchmen had always held

high temporal places, partly because of their ability to read
and write and speak in Latin, whereby they could commu-
nicate with others nearly everywhere in the world, and
partly because of their knowledge of God's law and man's.
Nearly every high office in England was held by a
churchman—chancellor, treasurer, justiciar. Did Stephen
mean to change that and appoint . . . whom? I felt blank
and lost. Who could take the place of Salisbury and his
nephews without causing great disruption in the government?

Waleran had not stopped speaking while these ideas
about the place of the Church in the affairs of the realm
were running through my head, and part of my mind had
heard him. "My lord," he had said, grinning as if he were
joking, "you know what will happen if we send someone
strange to that part of the country. He will lose himself a
dozen times over in trying to follow Aumale and take ten
times as long even when he knows where he should go by
keeping to the great roads instead of taking the forest
paths." Then he grew more sober and pointed out seriously, "I would never have come to Wark in time if I had
not had men native to Northumbria with me."

The king frowned at this, clearly having dismissed the
idea of using the priest as his messenger and considering
seriously whom he could send. He glanced at me once or
twice as Waleran added a few additional points that made
me an ideal messenger, one being the fact that I was a
Knight of the Body and thus might be considered a more
personal envoy, another that I would know better what to
say, since I knew many of the men to whom I would bring
the king's thanks. I said nothing. I assumed Waleran was
trying to be rid of me so that he could more easily learn if
any objected to the great advancement of his family, but I
did not feel that I was responsible for protecting the interests of every man who spoke to the king. What was more,
I had come to understand that it would not be as easy to
obtain leave as I had originally thought, so I welcomed
Waleran's interference.

Many of Stephen's Knights and Squires of the Body
served in rotation, having homes and families and sometimes estates that needed their attention. Since I knew Sir
Oliver preferred I stay away from Jernaeve, I had seldom

asked for leave, and Stephen had grown accustomed to having me with him. But Stephen himself had given me a great responsibility other than my service to him. And though I loved him, I could repose no trust in his continued payment of my pension—particularly if he were about to cause violent disorder in the exchequer by dismissing those who had long managed it. I had to make Melusine known to Audris so she would have a haven if my purse failed or, worse, rebellion was fanned to flames again.

I had not been following the discussion closely, but I knew Stephen, out of kindness, would ask my preference and I was ready when he said, "Well, Bruno, what do you think?"

"I would be sorry to leave you if you need me, my lord," I answered, "but I think as Lord Waleran does that I would be a suitable messenger. I know my way about Yorkshire and Northumbria, and though I would not go so far as to say I *know* William d'Aumale, Walter Espec, and the others, I am acquainted with some and know the others by repute. I think I could express to each your sentiments in such a way that he would be pleased with your thanks and gratitude. I also have a personal reason to wish to go, if you will forgive me for letting such matters intrude. I greatly desire to make my wife known to Lady Audris of Jernaeve, so this journey could accomplish two purposes and I will not need to ask leave again."

Stephen first seemed surprised at my answer; I suppose he expected me to say I preferred to stay with him, as I had in the past, but my mention of Jernaeve brought a nod. Although I am certain the king no longer had any doubts of Sir Oliver's loyalty, since Jernaeve had not been on the list of places that had yielded to King David and were to be objects of Aumale's attention, perhaps he still thought I could hold the keep for him if Sir Oliver died. That was now totally out of the question because Audris had a husband, but I did not think anyone had sent the king news of Audris's marriage to Hugh—I certainly had said nothing about it because I knew Sir Oliver had disapproved. And I was not about to say anything that might lessen my chances of taking Melusine to Jernaeve; Hugh was as loyal as I to

the king, so it could not matter to Stephen who held
Jernaeve.

"Hmmm, yes," the king said, as he nodded, his expression suddenly thoughtful, as I had hoped. "It has been a
long time since you were last at Jernaeve. It would be a
good idea to see how they weathered the invasion. You
might ride around the country there while your sister and
your wife come to know each other. I will give you a
purse so you can offer help to those who have suffered
damage from the Scots." Then his handsome face looked
worried. "Your sister will not be jealous of your wife, will
she?"

"No, indeed," I hastened to assure him, avoiding any
comment on his notion that I could—or would—ride about
and visit those beholden to Jernaeve to ingratiate myself
with them. Sometimes the flexibility of Stephen's notions
of honor distressed me, even though I had tried to make
my peace with myself on that subject.

"Audris will be very happy to learn I am married to so
well born and lovely a woman as Lady Melusine," I went
on, thinking wryly and with some amusement that what I
said would be true only so long as I did not tell her how
the marriage was forced on me and that Melusine had tried
to murder me. But I did not intend to make Audris unhappy with the true tale. "I am more concerned with how
to resist her invitation to stay with her than that she will
not welcome us," I added more truthfully.

My attention had been on Stephen, and I had not noticed
that Waleran was looking at me as if I had grown two
heads. "Do you mean to tell me you are known and
welcome in Jernaeve?" he asked.

Surprise at his vehemence made me hesitate, and it was
the king who answered, smiling. "He is the holder's
brother."

"Sir Oliver's *brother*?" Waleran repeated, clearly at a
loss to connect the king's statement with what he knew of
my history, but with a kind of recognition.

Stephen laughed. "No, the holder of Jernaeve is Lady
Audris, not Sir Oliver. Bruno is Lady Audris's half brother,
and much beloved of the lady."

"I do not remember any Lady Audris when Sir Oliver

grudgingly allowed me and my two chief captains a night's lodging and made my troops camp beyond the gates," Waleran said angrily. "We had come to protect him from the Scots and he treated us like an invading army."

"Sir Oliver is very cautious and very devoted to his niece," I said, biting the inside of my lip so I would not laugh at Waleran's indignation.

The man must think everyone but him an idiot. Jernaeve needed no protection from the Scots or anyone else *outside* the gates. No more than Sir Oliver would I have allowed so good a soldier and so ambitious a man to bring troops into Jernaeve. But Waleran was a bad enemy to have, so I tried to soothe him. "Lady Audris is very shy of strangers," I explained. "My lord the king will tell you that she had to be summoned specially when he himself visited Jernaeve. And I am sure the welcome you were offered was not meant to seem grudging. Sir Oliver is naturally brusque of manner. As for excluding your troops, he was only following old custom."

The words came smoothly, and I thought wryly that I must be learning to be a courtier at last. I had told a whole series of untruths without uttering one lie. I do not know whether I salved the hurt done Waleran's pride by Sir Oliver's treatment. Actually, I doubt he was even thinking about what I said although he eyed me speculatively as I spoke, and he did not answer me at all, turning to the king instead.

"By all means, my lord," Waleran urged, "if you have a key that will fit in the lock of Jernaeve, let it turn the lock often so that it will turn easily if you ever need a way in."

A very clever man was Waleran and yet he was very stupid too. I tried not to like or dislike any of the king's intimates, but Waleran would make an enemy of me in the end despite my will. However, although I could not like the manner in which he spoke or his implication, Waleran's last remark brought the king to the decision I desired.

Stephen sighed and shrugged and said, "I do not want to lose you for too long, Bruno, but you can take time to let your wife and your sister become true sisters. Perhaps if she can feel she has a family again, that will ease Lady

Melusine's sorrow. Poor gentle creature that she is, I am sure Lady Audris will learn to love her.''

A vivid memory of Melusine's lips drawn back from her teeth as the knife in her hand flashed down toward my neck made me bite my lips to keep from laughing at the king's description. Audris would not love Melusine for trying to kill me—but she would never know of it—and she would love her better for a high spirit than for being a poor, gentle creature. But it was not being taken into the bosom of a family that would ease Melusine's ''poor'' heart. It was the restoration of her lands . . . Then I suddenly saw how I might induce Melusine to be on her best behavior on this journey and in addition gain some idea about whether she simply wanted the lands or was, as the queen feared, a rebel at heart.

CHAPTER 10

Melusine

ONE WOULD THINK that sleep would be hard to find after trying to kill the man sharing the bed. I certainly did not expect to sleep, since I only half believed that he would take no revenge for what I had done. I was utterly furious with him too for the obvious indifference he felt toward me. Men accounted me a highly desirable woman. Many had sought me in marriage. Papa had told me that some offered to take me without any dowry other than his friendship—and this boor to whom I had been married casually threw away the right to my body. Yet sleep I did, hard and fast, before I had even been able to enjoy my rage and hate.

More surprising still, I was not pursued through the night by evil dreams. I dreamt of Ulle, and of the promise to return I had given so indifferently. But the first idea that came into my mind when I woke was to wonder in whose bed I was sleeping. I do not mean that I had slipped into madness again. I remembered perfectly where I was and what had happened, but great beds with fine curtains and bedding are no common matter; they are costly and might be the whole of a poor knight's dower to his daughter. I also remembered that Bruno was poor. Whence then had come this great bed, finer than my mother's and father's?

Surely from the king's or queen's favor—so Bruno had not
lied about being a favorite.

Then I realized I was alone in the bed. Fool man, I
thought, how am I to dress myself? Must I go with laces
undone . . . Before the thought was complete, I saw movement and a young girl rose from where she had been
sitting on my chest and came toward the bed. She was thin
and clad in little more than rags and she was shaking with
fright, but she spoke to me in fair French, explaining that
Bruno had sent her to help me dress this one day.

"But who are you?" I insisted, realizing that despite her
ability to speak our language she could not be a servant to
any of the queen's ladies. The tattered clothing made it
unlikely, and her manner to me—a deference that I had
discovered none of the maids would show the woman they
thought a half-wit—confirmed my guess.

She hesitated and then shrugged. "Bruno said I must
speak the truth, so I will. My name is Edna, and I am a
whore who can no longer ply her trade. I hope you will not
be angry. Bruno found this service for me out of pity; he
said you would see that I was fed."

For a moment I just stared, so consumed with fury that I
could not speak, but the girl certainly looked as if she
needed a meal, and my rage began to fade into puzzle-
ment. "Do you know how to lace a lady's gown?" I
asked, mostly because my mind was reeling with so many
questions that I could not decide which to ask first and so
asked the least important.

"Yes, my lady. I . . . served in a place where gentlemen were entertained and fine gowns were worn."

"Were you Bruno's whore?" was my next question,
and I was far more surprised when the words came out
than was the girl. Why should I care whether or not she
was?

"I lay with him once or twice," she admitted, looking
at the floor, "but he did not come often to the place where
I worked, only when he was with a group of friends.
Please do not hurt me. He said you would not care . . ."

Her voice was steady, but she was trembling even more
and her face was wet. "Why should I hurt you?" I remarked. "If I were angry, I would be angry at Bruno and

he, not you, would suffer for that. And since I must have a maid right now, I will use you.''

I looked at her hands as I said that, expecting to have to tell her not only to wash but how to do it—but they were clean, even the nails, which were pared smooth. And the rags she wore looked dirty because they were stained beyond cleaning, but they did not smell. I began to think about what had seemed to me at first to be a deep insult—or an incredible stupidity—and I began to laugh.

Edna drew a deep breath. ''Shall I help you out of bed, my lady? The washing water is ready. Shall I get the pot?''

''The pot. I can get out of bed myself.''

We did not exchange many more words. The questions I wanted answered could only be answered by Bruno. It occurred to me that he might not have expected me to question the girl. Perhaps the wife of a great nobleman would not have done so, taking for granted the service offered. If I had not asked, I could not have been offended, for Edna was a good maid. Still, she said Bruno had told her to speak the truth, so perhaps he *did* want me to know she was a whore, and one he had used.

I was still puzzling my head about Bruno and Edna when I came into the queen's hall to break my fast, and it is just as well I was full of my own problems. I was only slightly aware of excited voices and a sense of jubilation among the women. Then suddenly I felt the queen's eyes on me, and I looked up quickly and caught her staring. She smiled at me when our eyes met and then looked away, but it was warning enough that the excited talk somehow concerned me. Still, it took me several minutes, listening to a snatch of talk here and there as I gathered up bread, cheese, and wine, before the pieces of statements and exclamations I heard came together into the news that King David had suffered a great and bloody defeat at a place called Northallerton.

What the queen had been seeking in my face, I did not know. All that could have been there was a vast, empty indifference. Once I had felt King Stephen to be my worst enemy because his henchmen had angered my father and set papa's feet on the road to war that led to his death, but

the fierce rage like the worst bitterness of my grief seemed
to have been swallowed up in those lost months. Now I no
longer had anything to hate or fear. Everyone I loved was
dead already, so no battle, whether it brought victory or
defeat, had meaning for me.

Perhaps a better daughter than I would have grieved
over the loss suffered by the king her father supported, but
I had never been wedded to my father's political beliefs
and now I loathed equally all kings and all causes. Why
should I love King David? Had he not started the war that
caused papa's and Donald's deaths—and Magnus's too, in
my opinion—and for such a cause! For the right of Matilda
to rule, curse her pride and greed. And King Stephen had
taken Ulle from me—though *I* was innocent of any crime.

I found a place to sit and took an angry, hungry bite
from my bread and cheese, paused in shock, and then went
on chewing slowly. Should I be hungry, I wondered, as I
took a sip of wine? In a sense my father and brothers were
newly dead, but the grief I felt was distant, muted. I felt
more anger at the stupid kings and their quarrels than I felt
sorrow. Perhaps I had been grieving in all those months I
could not remember, and the sorrow had worn thin as it
had for my other losses. Even when my mind spoke my
menfolk's names, no fierce pangs ravaged me; there was
only that distant ache of loneliness, only the dimming of
all brightness in life as I remembered that there were none
left in the world for me to care for and none to care for
me.

Yet the dull uncaring could no longer smother me. One
bright, sharp point of hope existed now. I could recover
Ulle . . . through Bruno . . . but nothing in life is perfect
and perhaps I would not need to endure him long after the
lands were mine. That sensation of being watched with
which I was so familiar stiffened the little hairs along my
arms. This time I did not catch the queen's eyes on me,
but still I knew that favorite of the king or not, the
recovery of Ulle would not be so easy as Bruno implied.
Or was that only to pacify me?

I did not know how much influence the queen had—
some women were less considered than a horse or a dog,
but Maud did not have the look or manner of those. She

was neither meek nor a tyrant but had an assured, easy manner with her women and the gentlemen who served her. But whatever her power with her husband, the suspicion the queen felt for me could only increase the difficulty of convincing the king to regrant the lands. And Bruno had not lied about Maud's suspicion. A queen does not so closely examine the face of a nothing without kin or property, so there was something she feared I could do to hurt her. Somehow I would have to prove I was no threat.

Proving innocence is no simple thing, particularly when the crime—beyond so general an idea as treason—is unknown. Nonetheless, I found myself biting and chewing with enthusiasm, noting that the manchet bread was lighter and finer than what we made at Ulle and the cheese of a more subtle flavor.

"It is good to see you eating so eagerly."

I looked up and met Maud's small dark eyes, bright as polished onyx. My muscles tensed to rise, but she gestured negation at me and seated herself at the end of the bench I was on. Her look demanded an answer, although she had not asked a question, and I said, "The fear that has choked me for so long is less."

I had responded almost without thinking, not realizing until the words were out of my mouth that I was following the path I had suggested to Bruno for escaping my role of half-wit. I could swear the queen was startled by my answer, or perhaps by the fact that I had answered at all, and so swiftly. But her mind was on its own path, and she raised her brows.

"You are cleverer than that, Melusine," she snapped. "You will never convince me that you feared King David's victory."

"King David's victory?" I repeated blankly. "But did I not hear that he was defeated?"

"You did," Maud replied, staring at me hard. "I am asking why that should make you rejoice."

"I do not rejoice," I said. "I do not care. Whatever you think, I never cared."

"You have grown quick and saucy of tongue all of a sudden," the queen murmured, as though she had sprung a trap.

I shrugged. "I have said before, that the worst has befallen me already. I have nothing left to fear, so my thoughts no longer plod over and over the same trace, shutting out all else."

Maud looked indignant. "What fear, since you say you did not fear for King David's success? What did you expect? Did you think me such a monster—and Stephen? My husband has spent more time trying to soothe you and win a smile from you than he has ever spent on any other lady."

That was news to me, of course, but I lowered my eyes to my food and replied, "One cannot be rude to a king, but it could not ease my mind that my mistress's husband showed me more favor than another."

A warm chuckle burst from the queen. "Child," she said, "were you afraid I would be jealous? Or that Stephen had an impure motive? Why did you not speak?"

"I feared everything," I muttered, but I could not help liking her better because of the way she laughed at me.

It surprised me too. An older woman and one who could never have been a beauty generally is jealous when her husband pays attention to a much younger, handsomer woman—and even if my new husband found it easy to turn aside from me in scorn, I know my beauty is greater than Queen Maud's. Of course some women so abhorred their men that they loved and cherished their husbands' lemmen, but there was nothing bitter in the confident chuckle Maud had uttered, and her look was of amusement, that of a woman very sure of her man.

Thoughts are swift, but I found that one cannot allow one's mind to wander even for an instant in a conversation with the queen. "And now that you have a husband you fear nothing?" she asked in so smooth and uncaring a tone that I almost slipped into the trap and cried that a man forced on a woman without even her knowledge is no true husband.

Fortunately, I recalled my purpose in time and also remembered that Maud had spoken well of Bruno the morning after my marriage. So I kept my eyes down and shrugged and answered with what I hoped was the right mixture of sullen acceptance and relief, "I suppose I was afraid you would give me to someone even worse. I cannot say I am happy to be the wife of a whore's son with nothing but his sword to advance him, but he has not been unkind.''

"And he will not be, if you do not *call* him whore's son and drive him to it," Maud said. "I swear that if I hear those words again, I will make you bitterly sorry you spoke them. Bruno is not at fault for his mother's trade. Come, look at me. I wish you to see that I speak the truth.''

The color rose in my cheeks as I lifted my head, but not with shame or anger as the queen doubtless thought. My reasons for disliking my husband had nothing whatsoever to do with his birth, and the flush marked a little thrill of pleasure at my success in leading Maud to believe what I wanted her to believe. Now let her think I was easily cowed also.

"I do not blame him," I muttered, "and my honor, will I nill I, is tied to his. You may be sure I will not missay him to any other nor invite a beating by waking his wrath.''

Maud sighed. "I doubt he would beat you for speaking the truth—Bruno is honest and honorable to a fault, and such a nature has advantages—but you will lose all chance of winning his love if you show you scorn him. Oh, I know you do not now think that is of value because you are all the more foolish for being all too clever, but I tell you that there is no greater happiness on earth than a good marriage." She shook her head and sighed again. "It is a pity that most clever women are so stupid. Never mind what you think. Hold your tongue for fear of me, if for no other reason. Bruno is a good man and I do not want him hurt. I will give you another warning, which no doubt you will also scorn. Bruno is the *king's* man, and nothing you can do will change that. If you do not torment him to be disloyal, your life with him will be sweet.''

"It may be short too, if he spends all his time in the king's wars," I snapped before I thought.

To my astonishment, the queen winced as though I had slapped her, tears flooded her eyes, and she closed them. My hand went out and touched hers before I could stop myself as I realized that if she loved her husband, as what she had said to me about marriage implied, her fears must be even deeper and more dreadful than mine had been before all cause for fear was reft from me. I snatched my hand back and clutched my cup, which I lifted to my lips before her eyes opened, but I knew she had felt the touch. She said no more, rising and walking away, and I finished my meal, trying to lock her words out of my mind by thinking of the whore Bruno had sent to wait on me and my promise to see that she was fed.

This I managed by carrying down a good portion from the ladies' table. It would have to serve as the girl's dinner too, since I could scarcely ask a place for her among the castle servants while she was dressed in rags that would be scorned by the dog boys. I wondered what I would say to any queen's lady who followed me, but none did. I suppose responsibility for watching me was now Bruno's, or else he had told the queen that I had taken the bait of the restoration of my lands and would be quiet and obedient.

A flicker of rage touched me at that thought, but I was not nearly as clever or stupid as the queen believed. I had time to discover whether that offer was only a trap. Besides, I scarcely knew where I was or how to reach Ulle, and what I had thought the first day I recovered my wits was still true. I would be a greater danger than a help to my people if I fled to them.

When I returned to the queen's hall, there was so loud a sound of talk and so great a crowd that I paused in the doorway. A single glance showed me that the chamber was full of men as well as women, and I sidled in carefully and soon saw a small open space near the hearth where the queen was talking to a richly garbed man that could only be the king. He was tall and fair, very handsome, and his face was familiar to me. I put that memory aside to think about later because I was struck so forcibly by the look of pleasure Stephen wore while speaking to the queen, holding her hand in his and looking down at her. His expression caused a strange stirring within me and brought Maud's words about the joy of a happy marriage back to my mind. Her face, too, was changed. Nothing could make her features beautiful; nonetheless, there was a kind of beauty in her.

I had no time to see more because Bruno touched my arm to draw my attention. He looked at me with anxiety, and I raised my brows and stared back haughtily, thinking he was concerned about my reaction to discovering he had sent a whore to serve me.

"I hope you said nothing to make the queen more uneasy about your loyalty," he said softly, drawing me closer to him so that I could hear. "I am sorry I did not send word of David's defeat to you so that you would be warned and have time to collect yourself, but it was impossible for me to get away from the king at first. By the time I could have left him, I was sure you had already heard."

It was just as well Bruno's apology was so long winded for it gave me time to reorient my thinking and to reconsider expressing my exasperation too. "I said to the queen exactly what I am about to say to you." I spoke as softly as he and I made no effort to escape from the arm that was encircling my waist, but I did not try to hide the sharp edge of irritation in my voice either. "I do not care whether King David was defeated or victorious and never did care."

The anxiety cleared from Bruno's face, and the arm around me tightened a trifle. "She will not believe you, but it was the best thing to say. I—"

"Do *you* believe me?" I interrupted him because I was annoyed and wondered whether he would lie and say he did.

A slow smile curved his lips and lit his dark eyes. There was a kind of contagious mischief in that expression that made me smile back and almost forget the whore.

"Should I not?" he countered, then smiled more broadly and added, "I think I do believe you—but I will not tell you why since that will make you cross and I want you in a good temper. I have news for you. I hope you will think it good news."

"I am sure to think it the worst news in the world after that introduction," I said, but I could not keep an angry look on my face. My lips quivered upward, tempted to laughter by the teasing.

"Why then, I will not tell my news at all," Bruno remarked loftily.

That drew a gasp of indignation from me as I saw the trap into which I had fallen. "Why did you go to all that trouble *not* to tell me something that you could simply have kept to yourself in the first place?" I asked angrily.

Bruno opened his eyes wide in a patently false astonishment. "What? And have you hear from someone else of the king's order, then blame me for not telling you now so that you seemed neglected by your husband and the last to learn from him what you should be first to know?"

I burst out laughing. I could not help it. The open admission of his maneuver was too comical to resist at the moment, although I knew I would be furious later. All I could do was take a small revenge by asking, "Did you say that in the most confusing manner and the largest number of words possible apurpose, or is that the way you talk all the time? If so, I will know that the king and queen have visited upon me the worst cruelty they could imagine by condemning me to a lifetime of listening to you."

"How do I know how I talk? Ones does not listen to oneself talk," Bruno pointed out gravely. "Half the men in this court would have hung themselves years ago if they did."

Despite my desire to choke him, I crowed with laughter again and then was startled to feel the arm that had been holding me drop away. Bruno stiffened and stepped to the side. Almost, I cried out that I was sorry I had offended him and moved toward him, although I had not the faintest idea what in my laugh could have made him angry. I bit back the words and checked the movement as I saw his eyes were looking past my shoulder at someone behind me. I turned, and there were the king and queen. Stephen was smiling broadly at us; the queen was smiling too, but the curve of her lips was not mirrored in her eyes.

"My dear Lady Melusine," the king said, "that is the first time I have heard you laugh in all the months I have known you. I have wished you happy already at your wedding, but it is a great easing of my heart to see—"

"The first step in that direction," Maud interrupted smoothly. "I beg you, my heart, do not speak of happiness yet lest an evil ear be cocked to catch your words. Recall that they have not yet had *time* to quarrel. In a year, you may praise them for being happy. Now is too soon."

Stephen patted his wife's shoulder. "Very well, I will say no more, but you are always too fearful of expecting a happy future, Maud. Surely you can see that these young people are well-suited."

"I hope they are." Maud's voice was warm while her eyes were on her husband. "We would be monsters if we planned a marriage for those we knew to be ill-suited."

Then she looked at Bruno and me, and there was no more to be seen in her eyes than in small black stones. It took all my strength not to shrink back into the protection of Bruno's arm, and I flushed with the realization of how much comfort his embrace had given me. Yet he had withdrawn from me the moment the king and queen came near. To show them he did not wish to be coupled with a rebel? The question gave me a feeling of hollowness, and I was ashamed of myself. Where were my vaunted courage and independence? I had always thought myself able to stand alone, but was that only because in the back of my mind I knew my father and brothers would support me?

Shame made me stiffen my back. Perhaps Bruno saw that for he was a step behind me and could not have read my face. He put his hand on my shoulder, and it was then I noticed that the queen's expressionless eyes had shifted to him. If Bruno was disturbed, there was no response to that concern in the hand that held me. It was warm and steady, gently linking us, and his voice was amused when he replied lightly to the queen's remark, "I beg your pardon for contradicting you, madam—not to say we are ill-suited and that you knew it—but we have already quarreled. Somehow people always have time for a quarrel."

"May all your quarrels end in laughter," Stephen said, and put his arm around the queen and drew her away.

"I wish you had not played the fool for so long," Bruno said when they were gone. "She is very suspicious of you."

"I was not—" I began angrily, about to deny that I had

"played the fool," and then realized that was useless and changed it to "I could not think what else to do. I am very sorry if you are soiled with my dirt," I added coldly.

"And so you should be," Bruno replied equably, dropping his hand to my arm and turning me toward him, "because if I were, your purpose would become impossible to gain. But you need not worry that the queen suspects me of disloyalty. Within or without reason, my life is pledged to the king, and she herself has done me such favors that no service I do her can free me of obligation."

"Well, she certainly looked at you strangely for someone who harbors no doubts or suspicions," I answered tartly.

"Did she?" Bruno looked puzzled and then shrugged easily. "No doubt I will learn soon enough what troubled her—if she was thinking of me at all. It is not easy to read the queen."

He drew me toward the door then, and I saw that everyone was going to the great hall. At dinner, all the talk that came in snatches through Bruno's conversation was about the great victory at Northallerton. But Bruno seemed to be trying to shield me from this, seating me beside him at the end of a table among the lesser knights and keeping most of my attention with a merry explanation of why he was never chosen to serve the king like the other Knights of the Body. Despite the fact that I was annoyed by his apprehension that I would betray some anger or hurt at the slights to King David, I was amused by his tale.

Besides, I was glad to be sitting with him rather than among the queen's ladies. Now that the queen knew I was awake and alert, I dared not continue to pretend to be an idiot among them. I was certain that would make Maud even more suspicious of me. Yet to burst out suddenly into my natural behavior would doubtless make all the other ladies hate me. They would think, as the queen did, that I had been shamming and had made fools of them or, perhaps, heard secrets I should not, as I had heard the previous day that Bruno was little inclined to play with even willing women. Perhaps I should not have cared that the women would dislike me, but I would have to spend nearly all my waking hours with them. I did not know if I could endure to be shunned and despised by all.

I was glad of a respite from the problem and enjoyed my dinner, thinking when the meal was over and the king rose to leave the table, that I could put off dealing with the queen's ladies a little longer. I would go and walk in the garden and possibly explore the keep so I would not be lost if any need came to find my way alone. Bruno had risen too and pushed our end of the bench back so that I could step out easily, and I smiled at him and nodded my thanks automatically. He glanced quickly at the king, who was saying a few last words to Maud but already looking toward the entrance to his closet where several men waited.

"I must go," he said, "but will you take what food you can to Edna? And if you can find her anything to wear better than what she has on, I will be grateful to you and replace with new whatever you give her."

I had forgotten all about the girl so that Bruno's words were a shock. And I was all the more furious because he was gone before I could find my voice and ask him how he had dared to send a whore to wait on me. I would have liked to spite him by refusing what he asked, but I recalled the girl's eyes when I brought her the bread and cheese remaining from the morning meal. I had seen eyes like that before—thank God not often—in the rare years that not only crops failed but fish and game were also hard to find. No matter how angry I was with Bruno, I could not deny the girl whatever food I could bring. She could take away what she could not eat, and for a day or two, at least, her belly would not cramp with hunger.

I glanced around and saw a servant with an alms basket and beckoned him to me. He showed no surprise when I asked for the basket, just gave it to me and went off—I suppose to get another. I had been a little concerned that at the king's table the custom might be different, but I had taken the chance because I knew that even at such great places as Carlisle and Richmond it was quite usual for noble ladies to gather up the scraps and bring them with their own hands to the beggars at the gate.

While I piled the basket high, putting at the bottom whatever I thought least likely to spoil, I tried to think what I could give Edna to wear. A chill passed through me as I realized that I had not the slightest notion of what was in my chest, aside from my wedding dress and the clothes on my back. It is not pleasant to remember that you were truly mad. Most of the time, even when I thought of the queen's suspicion of me and how her ladies would react to the change in my manner, I almost believed what Maud thought was true—that I had been pretending. So when I came to my chamber, I was glad to see Edna there, glad to be able to talk to her and use the excuse that Bruno had told me to give her a gown to turn out the chest with her help and see what was there.

It was a relief to find that everything that had been mine in Ulle had been sent with me. I suppose the old maids that had stayed with me to face the invaders had packed my things. Even my riding dress and the rough gowns I wore to work in the garden and the storehouses were there, and at the very bottom, my sewing basket, with needles and pins and thread and my scissors. I might have dissolved in tears, remembering that most of my sewing had been the mending of my menfolk's clothes, but I was distracted from that grief by the need to do something about the gown I had offered Edna. She was half my size and I had to laugh when she put it on. It was more like a tent than a garment.

I was much surprised to learn that she could not sew. She had been so deft in helping me dress that I thought she had all a maid's skills. But her fingers were nimble, and when I cut off a wide swathe of the skirt and showed her how to thread the needle and set stitches, she folded and hemmed quite well enough for that rough wool gown. There were things I had to show her, of course, and that was excuse enough to stay in the chamber, away from the other women. I could not say I had been teaching my maid to sew, but it would be natural that, newly married, I examined and altered my gowns.

Pleased with this notion, which could protect me for several days, I smiled when Edna asked in a timid, shaking voice, "What shall I do with this piece of cloth, madam?" Her fingers caressed the rough length of wool— the gown had been the most worn and stained of my gardening clothes, faded a dull brown from what had been, if I remembered, a rich maroon. The new color had the advantage that the earth stains hardly showed.

"Would you like to keep it?" I asked in return.

"If it is not asking too much," she faltered. "I could use it as a shawl. The weather will turn cold soon."

She was so thin I thought that she might feel cold when my body was glad of a breeze. "Take it then."

"Must I go now?"

Because I did not know what to answer, I almost lost my temper with her—but it was Bruno at whom I was angry, not poor Edna. And the thought of Bruno reminded me that I could not undress without help. His help? The idea terrified me. I did not then know why, although I soon learned, but I said quickly, "No, stay here. I may need you at bed time. You may practice your sewing by hemming the length of cloth where it was cut. Sewing is a useful skill."

She thanked me with pathetic gratitude so that I first wondered whether she had no place to go, but she was too clean for Bruno to have picked her off the street. Then I remembered a glimpse of dark bruises on her legs—I had turned away to give her privacy to change to my gown when I realized she wore nothing under her outer rags and had seen no more of her body. Now I thought she must be mistreated wherever she lived. I was tempted to ask whether she would like to remain with me and be my maid, but I held back the words. I would say nothing to her until I had discovered Bruno's reason for selecting such a servant.

Nothing happened during the rest of the afternoon to move that purpose from my mind, and I intended to get some satisfaction from making Bruno ashamed of himself, although I had to admit that Edna had some extra skills in service that made me think again of keeping her with me. She found some twine, for example, and strung it through my tunic and bliaut so she could hang them in front of the window to air. And she brushed my hair as no one had ever done, touching the scalp just enough to make it feel clean and fresh without scraping painfully and stroking so evenly that I almost fell asleep on the stool.

I suppose I was tired by the strains of the day. I remem-

ber only telling Edna to leave all the bedcurtains tied back.
Then, I suppose I slept as soon as I was stretched out in
the bed, but I was no longer so shocked and exhausted that
I could not wake easily. A bump against the bed brought
my eyes open.

"Edna, if you cannot be still—" I began to say irritably, and realized the bump was on the other side. Edna
was gone, and I sat up and glared at Bruno, who had
knocked against the bedpost.

"Sorry," he said. "I just doused the candles and I'm
still light blind."

"Well, you can just light them again and find somewhere else to sleep," I snapped. "How *dare* you send
your whore to wait on me."

He stopped where he was, naked, one hand still on the
bedpost to guide himself around the corner of the bed. The
previous night I had seen only the power of his body;
tonight I was able to pick out details—the triangle of black
hair on his chest, pale scars on shoulder, arm, and hip that
contrasted with skin that was dark even in the dim light. I
could see such details because the wick on the night candle
was high, and wakened from sleep as I was, my eyes were
already adjusted. Gazing at him, I felt again the strange
terror that had gripped me earlier when I thought of him
undressing me, but it was like no fear I had ever known
before. I was not cold and clammy but too warm, and my
insides shook in a strange way.

"So you did know what Edna was," Bruno said, coming forward again. "I thought when I came in the morning
and found her still here that you had not bothered to ask."

He got into the bed as if I had not just bade him to find
a place elsewhere, and I could not speak because I knew
my voice would break.

"It is useless to pretend to be angry with me after being
so kind to her," he went on, turning toward me and
grinning.

"Why should I be unkind to the girl?" I got out,
although I could not keep my voice completely steady.
"She cannot help what she is. She scarcely looks to be
happy in her work or able to deny any order given her. It

was you who insulted me by setting your lemman to wait on me, not her.''

"No!" Bruno exclaimed, putting his hand out to take mine. I shuddered, and he withdrew it, his face creased with anxiety. "I swear I meant no insult to you, Melusine. I swear I did not. Good God, Edna is not my woman. I may have lain with her once, but I had forgotten all about it until you said it.''

I looked at the hand Bruno had been reaching for and saw that it was turned palm up to clasp his. "Then why did you send her?" I asked, staring down at my hand and wondering if it had been lying that way all the time. But that was impossible; it was too uncomfortable. I must have responded without knowing it when he reached toward me.

"If that is not the silliest question I have ever heard it comes near it," Bruno said irritably. "You know I must be in attendance on the king at dawn. Where the devil did you think I was going to find a woman who knew something of maid's work, was reasonably clean, and spoke French an hour before dawn? Did you expect me to wake the queen or one of her ladies to ask to borrow a maid at that hour? And do not tell me that I should have thought of it before," he snarled, his voice growing louder. "I had more to think of than who would help you dress yesterday.''

It was a logical answer and delivered with no attempt to charm me. I could not doubt that the reasons Bruno had given me for thinking of a whore were true, after all an unmarried man would not often have been attended by a woman in other circumstances. "But why Edna?" I asked. "Why your whore rather than another?" I could have bit my tongue as soon as the words were out of my mouth. He would think I was jealous.

"I have said already that she is not my woman." Bruno merely sounded bored, perhaps slightly annoyed. "I assure you that however ill you think of me, I would never permit any woman in my keeping to be starved or to dress in rags. I went to that house because it is the best in this town and the women are all clean and know French. I took Edna because when she opened the door to me she begged me for something to eat. I was sorry for her, and I also thought she would not be likely to missay you or walk out on you."

"Missay me?" I repeated. "Would such a woman dare?"

Bruno smiled. "From that house, it is possible. Some of those women have powerful protectors. They judge me a poor knight—which I am—and do not regard me with much awe. So my wife might be given scant courtesy." Then he sighed. "I thought when Edna told me what had happened to her, that she might continue to serve as your maid. Of course, if you do not like her, I will have to find another woman, but—"

"I do not dislike Edna," I interrupted, feeling quite exasperated, "but I cannot have a practicing whore as my maid—even you must see that."

"But Edna cannot ply that trade any longer," Bruno stated. "That is why she is starving and in rags. Did she not tell you that? The girl is a half-wit. No wonder you were so angry with me."

My hand flew to hide my mouth, and then, realizing that the gesture had betrayed me I said the words it had instinctively held back. "She did tell me. I just did not think of it until now."

"It was too much fun being furious, I suppose." The mischievous grin that had made me smile back earlier did not have the same effect now, and Bruno shook his head as I opened my mouth to protest. "I will leave it to you to settle with Edna whether you wish to keep her or not, but I hope you will. You see, I do not want any royal servants waiting on you. A servant loyal to someone other than her own mistress can twist what is perfectly innocent into something else to win pay or praise. I want no twisted tales of you carried back to the queen. Perhaps your maid will be questioned, but if she answers with the truth we will have nothing to fear."

"If Edna truly can be chaste—or at least as chaste as any other maid—I will keep her."

"Settle it with her," he repeated. "I bade her sleep in the hall outside and come to you again in the morning. Now I have something much more important to talk about than maids. The king has ordered me to carry certain messages north for him and has given me leave to take you with me.''

For a moment I looked at him, probably open-mouthed with surprise, then swallowed and croaked, ''Go with you? But why?''

Bruno looked back at me, trying, I think, to make out my expression in the dim light of the night candle. ''Do you not wish to go?'' he asked, his voice carefully flat.

''Oh, yes,'' I cried. ''Indeed I do, and it cannot be soon enough for me, but I do not understand why—''

''I warn you,'' he said, ''that if you try to escape me and run home as you did before—''

''No, no,'' I gasped. ''I—'' I was about to say that I was not such a fool, but what he said implied that I *had* tried to get away before, and I knew he would not believe my denials. ''I have come to understand that that would be a very foolish thing to do, that it could only make trouble for my people.''

''I hope you are speaking the truth, but you seem so very eager—''

''Only because I wish to get away from the queen's ladies.'' I explained how I was caught between increasing Maud's suspicion of me and making the other women look foolish and dislike me. ''If I am gone from them for some time, it will be easier to change my ways. I—I am tired of being thought a half-wit.'' That was true, even if I had only endured it for a few days rather than many months.

Bruno laughed, but I thought, though I could not truly see, that his eyes still watched me warily. All he said was, ''I am not surprised.''

''But I still do not understand why the king should allow a messenger to take a woman with him,'' I said hurriedly. I needed no more lectures on why it was unwise to play sly games.

''It is a special case,'' Bruno told me, pulling up a pillow behind him and relaxing against it. ''There is no need for special haste in delivering these messages, so the speed at which I travel is not important. Moreover the journey will take us close to Jernaeve, where I was born and bred. The king was kind enough to yield to my desire to introduce you to the people there who have been very kind to me and cared for me.''

"But I thought . . ." I hesitated, not knowing how to ask a question without hurting him.

"You thought a whore's bastard was born and raised in a ditch? How do you think I came by my skills and accoutrements?''

"I thought nothing of the sort," I riposted sharply, angry that he thought the worst when I had been trying to spare him. "I thought you had quarreled with your family and were not welcome among them.''

"There has been no quarrel, and I am sure I will be welcome in Jernaeve now." He paused as if to weed out of his future words certain matters, then said, "Sir Oliver— and I must tell you that I am *not* Sir Oliver's get, no matter that we resemble each other—who was warden of Jernaeve for many years, holding the right of his niece, Lady Audris . . .'' He paused again, wondering I think whether to add something, but continued with what was clearly the main thread of his story. "Sir Oliver sent me away from Jernaeve because he was afraid the holders of smaller estates sworn to Jernaeve would prefer me to Lady Audris. I went willingly, for I love Audris above my life, above the salvation of my soul. But she is married now, to Sir Hugh Licorne—''

"Licorne—a unicorn?" I interrupted, not caring but driven to say anything to hear no more about his love for this Lady Audris. Despite the fact that our union had been forced upon him, how dared he lament another woman's marriage to his wife.

He chuckled and I realized at once what a fool I was. If Sir Oliver was Lady Audris's uncle and Bruno was not his son but yet resembled him, Audris must be at least Bruno's first cousin—if not his half sister. The easy chuckle told me there was no deep hurt connected with Lady Audris's marriage, and no anger at my interruption, but I suspected that Bruno was not given to telling this story and I wanted very much to hear it.

I touched his hand. "Forgive me, I did not mean to interrupt you. You must believe that I am deeply interested in this matter.''

Still smiling, he patted with his other hand, mine, which had remained resting on his. That senseless fear started up in me again, but this time I fought it, ignoring the crazy trembling inside me and fighting to keep my breathing from going short. I would not withdraw my hand and anger him for a senseless fear. In God's name, what had I to fear from Bruno?

"Everyone is startled by Hugh's surname," he said, "but Archbishop Thurstan is the one who named him and he must have had a reason. I do not think the archbishop is a fanciful man. Nor can I remember that Hugh told me the reason. Perhaps he did not know. I cannot imagine myself questioning Archbishop Thurstan about why he did anything. But the point is that Hugh is perfectly fitted in every way to hold Jernaeve and has the full right of husband of the holder, so I cannot be a threat to Lady Audris's right and I am sure I will be a welcome guest."

"Naturally, I will be very happy to meet your f-friends, but—"

I faltered a bit over the word, unsure of whether to say family but very aware that Bruno had been specially careful to make no such claim. And I was angered for him, believing that he was despised among the people in Jernaeve and that he was taking me to them to show that he now had importance in the world and had been given a noblewoman to wife. That made me ashamed of him for the first time, and I was about to urge him to have more pride when he interrupted me.

"I can see that you are wondering at my desire to drag you hundreds of miles into the wilderness of Northumbria over lands devastated by war," he said, smiling again. "I am not mad. I have a good reason, and one that will please you, I think, for taking you north. The king has given me two months leave, which I have permission to stretch to three at need. There will be time enough for us to visit Ulle."

"Ulle?" I gasped. "You will take me to Ulle?"

"If you make yourself pleasant to those at Jernaeve and give me no reason to think that you will do anything to spite the king or lessen his power over your lands . . ."

I knew Bruno went on speaking and my eyes were fixed

on his face, but I neither saw nor heard. A cold horror had overtaken me. Could I go back to Ulle, to those halls and chambers haunted by my brothers and father? Bruno had spoken about getting back the lands, but that had been a thing in the distant future. I suppose I had believed that it would be years before I need see another man seated in my father's chair, other hands than those of my brothers' holding cups at a high table. I heard a strange sound, like the whimpering of a small lost beast, and suddenly there were warm arms around me and a man's smell in my nostrils as I was pressed against his chest, and a deep voice crying, "Melusine, Melusine, what is wrong?"

All my life I had been comforted by men. My mother loved me, but she felt I got petting enough, and when I was hurt or frightened, it was always papa or my brothers who held me and begged me to tell them what was wrong and kissed away my tears. I clung to that broad warm chest, to the man-smell that meant safety and comfort, and sobbed out my hurt.

CHAPTER 11

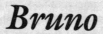

Bruno

I HAD GOOD REASON to believe, as did the queen, that Melusine had been pretending to be half-witted for some purpose of her own. After all, she had almost succeeded in sticking my own hunting knife into me. But as I sat looking down at her after she had at long last cried herself to sleep, I began to wonder if perhaps she had not intended to deceive anyone but had been living in some world of her own because she could no longer bear her grief in this one. I was shaken to my core with pity for the child within the grown woman, who still believed she had murdered a good part of her family just because they had come to celebrate her birthday. And that clinging memory of the ice crystals whitening her murdered brother's eyes—I shuddered at it myself.

Had I known the burden Melusine carried, I would have been more careful in introducing the subject of taking her home. I had thought that she would be overjoyed and my only problem would be keeping her at Jernaeve until I had finished the king's errands. Now I did not know what to do. I had told her that there was no need to go to Ulle, but I do not think she heard or understood me. And if we did not go now, I was not sure when I would be able to get leave again and I was eager to look over what had been Melusine's property.

I had been totally indifferent to everything except the immediate problem of taking the manor when I was there with the king's army. I had no idea I would ever have any special interest in Cumbria. When I thought of the grant of lands I might some day receive as a reward for loyal service, I always thought of lands in Northumbria. And it was always a thing very far in the future so I did not, like many of those who expected favors from the king, look at every keep and manor he took with an eye to asking for it. Thus, Ulle and the area in which it lay were only dimly remembered. I had intended, with Melusine as a guide, to examine her lands to see if there was some great source of wealth in them. I did not think there would be, nor that I would discover any strategic reason I had missed when we passed through for the king to hold those lands in his own hand. But I had to be sure before I approached the subject of reclaiming Melusine's estate.

She was still sobbing in her sleep, so I stroked her hair and she grew quieter. One good thing about her tears and terror was that they had cooled my lust. When she had accused me of setting my whore to serve her as an insult, I had barely held myself back from proving that I was as hungry for her as for any whore—and perhaps a little more. She might be too big and too dark with features too strongly marked for my taste, but she had been a sweet-smelling armful when I held her in the queen's hall, and the way she laughed when I teased her had sent waves of heat through me. I had to let go of her and step away lest my rising lust show openly.

Even though I felt no desire now—poor Melusine was too much like a hurt child to think of coupling this night—I wished I had not so lightly given my oath not to demand my marital rights. Tomorrow it would not be easy to lie in this bed with her without some relief, and the next day would be harder yet. Perhaps I could find some reason to leave before the week the king had set for our departure. Once on the road, separate pallets or camp beds would keep us well apart and I might have time to slake my thirst on some girl without Melusine's knowledge. Or, would it be better if she suspected? Had her anger about Edna been more than that of a dog who keeps an ox from his manger out of pure spite? She had been angry when I showed myself indifferent to her charms even soon after she had tried to kill me.

A wicked notion came to me then. Perhaps I would ask her permission. I could flatter her at the same time by saying she was so beautiful and desirable that I was finding it hard to keep my promise not to couple with her. I considered that as I slid down to lie flat, enjoying my memory of how her dark eyes seemed almost to show a flicker of red when she was angry at me in the queen's hall, and how laughter had overcome her anger. A quick temper, but not a sour or stubborn one, thank God. The king and queen might not have done so ill for me as I thought at first—unless Melusine, who I was now sure did not remember that I had been the man who ''took'' Ulle, suddenly recalled it.

That brought my mind back to Melusine's violent reaction to my offer to take her home. I turned my head but could not see her face, which was nearly buried in the pillow. Her breathing was quiet now, not troubled even by the little hiccups that follow prolonged weeping. I sighed and closed my eyes. I would not force her if every mention of the place drove her into a frenzy of grief and fear—if it did, what would be the use of trying to reclaim the property? But only time would tell. If she did not broach the subject herself, I would try again in a day or two after she had time to grow accustomed to the idea.

Since Melusine was still asleep when I had to leave, my duty requiring me to be in the king's outer chamber before he woke, I could do no more than tell Edna that Melusine should ask the queen to send for me if she needed me. I hope she did not need me, because I was away from Winchester soon after the king broke his fast. Stephen's spirits had been so elated by the defeat of the Scots that he cast aside all business and took those of his court that favored the sport off on a great hunt. Being in attendance as Knight of the Body, I had no choice but to go.

That solved—for a little while anyway—my troubles with sleeping beside Melusine. We were away three nights, two spent in hunting lodges and one in Alresford. I was not on duty that night, so I sought out a woman—a thing I doubt I would have done had my appetite not been whetted by my wife. Not that I had forgotten my little plan for inciting Melusine's jealousy, but it was safe to seek relief in a town miles from Winchester without asking permission. I paid to keep the woman with me all night and used her well, striving to leech all the hot spirits out of my body. And so I learned from a whore a second lesson I would never forget: Using the whore of London taught me that pleasure increases with caring, not with beauty; using the whore of Alresford taught me that the act of futtering does not reduce desire. The moment I laid eyes on Melusine, I was as ready as I had ever been.

If she had tried to find me and been angry at my absence, she had forgotten or put the anger aside. She seemed glad to see me; her dark eyes were bright when they found me, and she took my arm and clung to it as we all, huntsmen and stay-at-homes alike, trooped into the great hall to eat a much elaborated evening meal. For this meal there was no formality or precedence. Except for the king and queen on the dais, everyone seized food from the trays as they were borne about or set down and found seats where they could. The heads of the greatest kills were brought in—one of the boars was the king's but another, even larger, was mine—and Melusine smiled at me, glowing with pride, and joined the shouts of approval before asking, "Were you hurt?" Clearly she knew that wild boars were not easy to kill, and it warmed my heart that she should ask about my safety.

"A little bruised," I replied. "I went over and the devil stepped on me before I finished him."

"I will look to it later," she said calmly.

I was strangely torn between relief and disappointment. I certainly did not want Melusine to express concern for me too openly before the whole court; to draw the eyes of others always makes me feel hot and desire to hide my face. But if she cared, would she not have sounded more anxious or tried to drag me away at once to make sure the hurt was not dangerous as Audris would have done? *I* knew I was telling the truth and had no more than a few bruises, but how could she know? Before I thought, I voiced the question, and Melusine laughed.

"Because I am not likely to misjudge a man's health no matter what he says. You rode here and were steady on your feet when you dismounted and you are eating well and with good appetite, so no great harm can have been done. I saw your color and the way you moved. I was only nine or ten years of age when I began to tend bruises and sew up rents in the hides of my bro—"

Her voice quivered and stopped, and she closed her eyes. I took her hand and said, "Melusine. Melusine, do not—"

She opened her eyes again. All the brightness was gone, but there were no tears. "You need not fear that I will fall to weeping again. I am sorry if I was a burden to you Monday last. You took me by surprise, and—"

"You were no burden," I said quickly, cutting her off. "Never mind that. Tell me instead what you decided to do about Edna and how you have managed with the queen's ladies?"

She shook her head, and her full lips twitched, but she told me that she had decided to keep Edna, at least until we left, because she had been able to tell the queen that I had given her a fool for a maid and use Edna as an excuse to spend nearly all her time in her own chamber. I think she was annoyed with me for believing she would say too much in public, but I would rather have her annoyed than take the chance that word of my plan to visit Ulle would get back to the king or queen and I might be forbidden to take Melusine into Cumbria. I would have tried to pacify her, but I had no chance. The parade of the kills had signalled the end of the meal. Before Melusine could finish her tale, several men who had not accompanied the hunt came to congratulate me on my kill and stayed . . . to talk to Melusine.

She certainly knew how to please men, what to say to them to set them at ease, to draw smiles, and to manage the talk so that no one man had more than his proper share of her attention or the general conversation. I was more silent than I should have been; Melusine had to draw forth my voice more than once and I saw that the other men were looking at me and smiling. They would roast me well later and spread the word that I was jealous—but, odd though it may seem, I was not jealous.

I was glad to see Melusine's eyes gradually brighten as the talk and attention eased her grief. Perhaps I am not a jealous man, but it was also clear to me that Melusine was not trifling with the men around her; there was nothing in her manner to rouse a man's lust—unless the man was one of those who thought her beautiful, and even then I thought it unlikely for any to be tempted. I myself felt none of that hot rush of desire that had flooded over me several days ago in the queen's hall and in our bedchamber or even when she greeted me on arrival.

Rather than being jealous, I was stunned by her skill. I had seen no woman but the queen so able to control a group of men, and the queen was older and, when she wished, could enwrap men in a motherly warmth. As that realization came to my mind, I understood at once how Melusine pleased without stimulating. She was . . . sisterly. I recalled her desperate weeping as she recounted the roll of her losses; well, she had practice enough in being sisterly with seven brothers. But I also remembered that I had responded to her as a woman whenever we talked alone. Had her manner to me been different? If so, was that difference deliberate?

The very notion started a new rise of heat, and I forced myself to pay attention to the talk and participate in it more, meanwhile rising from the eating bench myself and moving Melusine away from the table. It was not long after that when the king and queen left the hall, and I could begin maneuvering our small group slowly down the hall toward the outer door. I made no haste, but Richard de Camville, a clever devil and a pleasant drinking companion (now that Audris was safe from him), became aware of what I had done when our slow progress stopped.

"That is a most tactful hint, Bruno," he said, chuckling and directing the attention of the other men to the guest-house across the yard. "But tactful or not, my friends, I fear we are being told that we are not wanted."

"Clever man," I remarked. "I knew I could count on you to save me. Gentlemen, Camville is seeing to the heart of the matter as he always does. You are not wanted. I have better company for this time of night.''

Although Melusine responded easily to the teasing comments made on parting by the other men, I sensed that what I had said had startled her and was making her uneasy. To shift the subject from what she feared without renewing my promise not to urge coupling on her, I said the first thing that came into my head, which was that I did want to talk of our journey north—I did not say to Ulle, fearing to set her grieving again—but that I did not wish to discuss it where a report of our plans might come to the ears of the king or queen. As I spoke, I could see the tension go out of her, and when I had finished she nodded.

''I am not a fool,'' she said shortly, but without anger, and then, in the same indifferent voice added, ''Take off your clothes and let me look at you.''

I gaped at her, associating what she said only with the jesting remarks I had made to rid us of our companions. I could not believe I had been mistaken in her almost fearful reaction, and this flat-voiced invitation was scarcely seductive, but a hope sprang up in me that despite her fear she wished to be fully my wife. Fortunately, I was frozen for a moment in the conflict of hope and disbelief, and Melusine cocked her head questioningly.

''I have seen you naked before,'' she remarked. ''There is no need to be coy.''

There was something in her voice that warned me that I had somehow misunderstood her, but my head was bemused by my rod, which had risen to attention, and I could only ask, ''Then why do you want to look at me?''

Melusine had started to turn toward the door, but she stopped and stared at me over her shoulder, frowning. ''To see if your bruises need salving. Do you not remember I said I would look at them later?''

My disappointment was profound but too mingled with amusement at how desire could wipe out of my mind what did not feed it to allow my rigid shaft to shrink. In the past I had tried to hide from Melusine the fact that she excited me. This time I thought it best to let her see my desire and show her too that I was not a slave to it, so I stripped off my clothes without more ado. She stood watching me as if she had forgotten that she had started to turn away, the puzzled frown still on her face; but that looked as if she had forgotten the expression too. When I was naked I found she had turned back to face me fully, and I smiled at her.

"The bruises need no salving," I said softly, "but you are very welcome to look at them—or any other part of me."

I saw her eyes flash down and widen, and she backed a step away.

"I will not pretend that I do not desire you, Melusine," I went on. "But you need not fear I will force you either. I am the master of Monsieur Jehan de la Tête Rouge—" I tapped the red head that had pushed its way through the foreskin so she could not mistake of what I spoke, "—not he of me."

There was a moment's silence, then Melusine swallowed hard and stepped forward, her full lips thinned and her round chin jutting. "Then hold Monsieur hard back, for I think myself a better judge of hurts than you."

"He is as hard back as he will go," I protested in a slightly choked voice, and then began to laugh.

"Perhaps those are the wrong words," Melusine said stiffly. "I know little of such matters."

That made me laugh even more, and she regarded me warily but continued to walk toward me, and when she was close enough, laid a hand on my black and blue ribs. I could feel her fingers tremble, but her hand was warm, not cold with fear, and she peeped downward once or twice while she felt my ribs. That was enough encouragement to keep my shaft hard and to tempt me to advance my cause. I leaned forward and kissed the bridge of her nose, which was all I could reach, her head being bent. She leapt back like a startled doe.

"You promised—" she gasped, her voice trembling more than her fingers.

"Only not to force you," I pointed out. "I never said I would not try to make you willing. And you need not look at me as if I were threatening you with torture."

Indignation chased the fear from her face. "I am not afraid of pain," she said, much more steadily, and then, her voice shaking again, "I agreed to a truce, not to a true marriage."

"As for pain, I do not think I would hurt you if you were willing—or, at worst, only a little and for a short time. As for marriage—will you or nill you, Melusine," I reminded her, "we are truly married. For better or for worse, I am your husband. I would prefer that it be better between us."

She swallowed hard again. "It may be better for you if we couple. I do not think it would be better for me."

I shrugged. The talk and my inner knowledge that she was not yet ready to yield to me had reduced the urgency of my desire, but I was not looking forward to lying beside her without satisfaction for three more nights, or even one more. "Do you think you can be ready to leave tomorrow?" I asked as I got into bed. "Last Monday the king said we were to go in a week, but if the letters I am to carry have been written, I cannot see why we should not leave sooner."

The tense alertness of a creature poised to flee relaxed, and Melusine sounded more natural, even tart. "If you will tell me how much to take and how you intend it to be carried, I can be ready in a few hours."

"What do you mean, how much to take?"

"Is the bed ours?" Melusine countered reasonably. "The bedding?"

"Good God, I never thought of them," I admitted, drawing Melusine's pillows to me so I could prop myself upright. "I think they are only lent by the king and queen. I will ask."

She made a moue of distaste, which made me wonder whether she hated Maud and Stephen so much that it offended her to lie in a bed they owned, but her next remark offered a different interpretation for the expression. "I hope they are lent, but we still have the chests, which must go in a cart and that will make for slow travel. And—and I do not wish to sit in a cart like baggage."

The last sentence was almost a plea. "You ride?" I asked, feeling blank.

I realized I had never thought of all the difficulties when I asked Stephen for permission to take Melusine with me. One thing I had not considered was how to get her to Jernaeve. I could not take her pillion on Barbe; he was not

accustomed and was too nervous a horse to take a chance.
But to give her the freedom of riding a horse of her own
might be a temptation too great for a woman's promise.

"Yes, yes I do," she said eagerly, and then, as if she
had read the doubt in my face, "and I will not try to run
away. I swear I will not." In her earnestness she came to
the bed and put out her hand, as she had when she had
sworn truce.

"Very well, you shall ride," I agreed, glad to make it
seem that I was doing her a favor.

In reality I could see no other way of getting to Jernaeve,
doing the king's business, and still finding time to visit
Ulle. But even if Melusine rode well, that still left the
problem of what to do with those things that could not be
taken with us. In the past, my baggage had always gone
with the king's, and before I came to court I never had
more than could be carried in a blanket roll behind Barbe's
saddle.

"But we will not be able to leave tomorrow," I went
on. "I will have to make arrangements to store the chests
and whatever else we do not take. There is no chance the
king will remain here long, and I do not wish to burden
anyone with the responsibility for our possessions."

Melusine nodded. "It is better to have a home to which
possessions can be sent and faithful servants who will see
that they arrive safely."

Our eyes met. "As soon as I can," I agreed and then,
cautiously, "if you can bear to live there."

I had taken Melusine's hand when she promised not to
flee from me and she had not withdrawn it. Now her grip
tightened on mine, and I drew her closer and put an arm
around her.

"I do not know." Her voice quavered, but she steadied
it. "I think about it often, and it seems to grow less
painful. When we are there, if I cannot bear it . . ." She
buried her face in my shoulder. "I do not know what I will
do. Papa would be so angry . . ."

I did not make any direct reply. What could I say except
that her father was dead and would not care at all—and
that might hurt her more than believing he did care. I
stroked her hair for a minute and then bade her softly to

make ready for bed, turning her gently so I could untie and unlace her bliaut. She pulled away before I was quite finished, thanking me in a choked voice and saying she could finish for herself, and all but ran to the other side of the room. I was puzzled by Melusine's change of mood, for she had come into my arms herself, and I had made no sexual gesture that could frighten her. Still, I knew she could not be pushed further that day, so I tossed her pillows back to her side of the bed and lay down with my back to her to give her privacy to finish undressing.

It was as well that I had realized I would have too much to do to leave the following day. When I arrived in the king's antechamber at dawn, there were already petitioners waiting, each pressing to be heard first, if not by right of earliest arrival then by right of the urgency of their business. And long before the king was ready to see anyone at all, the bishops of Winchester and Salisbury came in, both with sour downturned mouths. To give Stephen a little warning, I remarked after I told him they were waiting, that perhaps we should not have spent quite so much time in the chase, but he seemed at first not to want to understand, laughing and clapping me on the shoulder.

"I am delighted that your wife already finds your presence so necessary to her that she quarrels with you over your absence," he said, and then I saw he understood very well because he added, "My ministers do not have the same excuse but seem to feel the same way—or say they feel the same way while they urge me to give them the power to rule my country without me altogether."

My chest tightened with anxiety. That sounded as if Stephen suspected Winchester and Salisbury of wishing to overthrow his rule. I could not be sure about Salisbury, but it could not be true of Winchester; he was Stephen's brother.

"It is not that they wish to restrict your pleasure," I offered, trying to seem unaware of the direction the king's remark pointed. "The bishops fear, because of the recent troubles, that you might be drawn away again to defend your throne before necessary business is done. I am sure that if you explained carefully that they can trust the queen—"

"They do not wish to trust Maud," Stephen said in a peculiar voice. "They want the power themselves, so they look for problems, not solutions."

He was, I thought, partly resentful and partly uncertain, and I would have been hard put to find an answer that would not have deepened his resentment. All I could think was that King Henry had trusted Salisbury to rule England for many years at a time and few had complained of the bishop's management—and that answer would only have made Stephen angrier. Fortunately he did not wait for me to speak, gesturing irritably during his last few words for me to bring Salisbury and Winchester in.

I was surprised to see that Stephen had smoothed the anger from his face in the few minutes it took me to fetch the bishops into his bedchamber, and he greeted them with a jest about trying to escape a scolding for running away from his duties by seeing them before he was truly awake. Both smiled at once, making me wonder if their sour looks had been owing to expectations of an unpleasant greeting rather than irritation with Stephen for hunting. It might be, I thought, recalling that stiff, uncomfortable dinner the day after my wedding. Winchester pressed the king's shoulder gently, saying that Stephen deserved a few days rest. But Salisbury, although he looked quite benign, remarked that King Henry had loved the hunt also and found it restored the balance of his mind.

I held my breath until Stephen replied. Considering his earlier mood, I feared he might become angry at what I took to be a subtle reprimand. But the king only agreed and said blandly that he supposed he might have inherited much from his uncle and then smilingly asked why they had rushed to see him before he broke his fast if they had not come because great numbers of pressing affairs had arisen in the few days of his absence.

"One affair is pressing enough," Salisbury said. "I would like to send a royal messenger to King David this very morning with terms for a treaty."

"It was David who was defeated," Stephen remarked, suddenly standing, turning his back, and throwing off his bedrobe. A squire leapt forward, holding out a pair of chausses and another came with a shirt. "Why should I

hurry to send terms to him? That would seem as if I
doubted Aumale's ability to take back the royal castles
from David's men." His voice was muffled as he drew on
his clothing.

"I am sure King David will not think you doubt Aumale,"
Winchester said. "He will believe that you wish to save
fruitless bloodshed on both parts. Stephen, I know David.
You will have more leverage with him if he believes a
treaty will save his men's lives than—"

"Save their lives for what?" Stephen interrupted bitterly, turning to face his brother, his hair tousled from
pulling his shirt down. "So David can gather them and
bring them down on me again? Let them die. When he is
too weak to fight, he will sign what I want him to sign as
meekly as he did for King Henry."

Winchester looked shocked. "But our men will die
too," he protested uncertainly.

"I am sorry for that," Stephen replied, gesturing away
the squire who was trying to slip under his arm and tie his
shirt at the neck without interfering with the conversation,
"but David's losses are more important than mine in the
north." He paused and then went on, his voice sharp with
exasperation, "Henry, do you not see that I cannot call a
levy on the northern shires as long as David is strong so
that losses among those men do not weaken me. God
knows, I wish they were at peace and not dying, but—"

"Then let us at least try," Winchester urged. "I tell
you, I know David. If he can be brought to sign a treaty
and swear he will no longer support Matilda's cause, he
will keep that treaty."

"Perhaps." Stephen shrugged.

"My lord, there is another reason for offering a treaty
now," Salisbury put in before Winchester could insist
again that King David was a man who kept his oaths. "We
hope, as you do, that Robert of Gloucester will not be able
to find entry into England and that the unrest caused by his
defiance is at an end, but if rebellion should burst out
again, there will be far less chance of bringing King David
to an agreement favorable to us."

Stephen laughed, and my heart sank. I desired peace in
the north more fervently than the bishops. Northumbria

was my home; it was men I had fought with in Alnwick and Jernaeve who would die, and innocents, like a little whore I knew in Alnwick village, who might be destroyed by the fighting. For my own sake, I had hoped the king would listen to Winchester, though I knew from a military point of view that the bishop's argument was not convincing.

What Salisbury had said was entirely different. So far, it was true that Gloucester had shown little desire to act in his sister's cause, but that could change. It was also true that the rebels against Stephen had not joined forces and had been easily suppressed. That, too, could change. And if, God forbid, Gloucester should find a way into England and rally the rebels into a powerful, coordinated force, King David would surely refuse to sign an unfavorable treaty. There would be too great a chance to win back all he had lost with Gloucester's help.

My worst fears were confirmed when the king made an obscene gesture and cried, "Gloucester? Aumale will have time to clean out Northumbria and take half of Scotland before Gloucester can make up his mind what to do."

"Do not be too sure of that, my lord," Salisbury warned. "Now that he is in company with Geoffrey of Anjou, he may be spurred to action. Anjou is a man of firm decision, and he has a fluent tongue and convincing manner that could arouse Gloucester. And Anjou has very good reasons to foment trouble in England. If you are at war here, you would be unable to fight him in Normandy."

"Nothing will stir Gloucester," Stephen scoffed. "Even if he should try to come, Maud's ships will stop him in the channel. And should they miss, the coast is closed to him. Morever, I have taken the heart out of the men who might have rallied to him if he had come earlier."

When I heard that, I knew the king's easy optimism and perhaps his remaining anger because his brother had accused him once of carrying his father's cowardice were blinding him to the truth of Salisbury's warnings. The more they argued, the more stubborn Stephen would become, I feared, and my fear was realized. The argument continued for some time longer, the bishops yielding only when Stephen finally lost his good humor and roared that he would not be driven into an appearance of weakness. I had not dared intrude, but when I opened the door to let them leave, I followed them out into the great hall.

"My lords," I said, "if you would allow me a word?"

"What is it, Bruno?" Winchester asked kindly, although his lips were set in a thin line.

"If you would bring this matter of the treaty to the queen's attention . . ." I let my voice drift, unable to say too much, but I hoped the bishops had seen, as I had, Stephen's special deference to Maud's opinion. "Women always desire peace," I added hopefully.

"Women have not the brains of lice," Salisbury snarled, and pressed on past me.

Winchester tried to smile and shook his head. "Maud is too bound to Stephen's desires," he said and went on past me too.

They were both wrong, I thought, but I could do no more except hope that Stephen would be right. I tried to put the matter out of my mind, but later in the morning when a page came and asked me to attend the queen I hoped that Winchester, who knew Maud well, had spoken to her after all. Even if Maud was angry that I had dared to interfere and had summoned me to remonstrate with me, she would still think about the advantages of making peace with King David now. And if she thought that best, I believed she would be able to change Stephen's mind.

Only the lesser petitioners were left by the time the queen's page arrived, and it would matter less if one of them were offended, so I went up to the king and asked him if I could go to the queen before dinner. He gave permission at once, but he did not meet my eyes or make any teasing remarks, which surprised me a little. I was surprised again when the page told me to follow him, for the child knew I was familiar with the queen's apartments. However, he led me out and into the garden, where I found Maud walking alone among the strong-scented herbs.

"Madam?" She turned at my voice. I bowed, and she watched me. It seemed she was angry, but I had acted for what I thought was the best and I withstood her gaze without flinching or changing color.

"Melusine has told me you intend to take her north with you. Is this true?"

I was so surprised by this total change from the subject I expected her to broach that I must have stared blankly for a minute, and Maud repeated her question sharply.

"Yes," I replied, still too off balance to do more than confirm that Melusine would go.

"I thought you would have more sense," the queen snapped. "Has the woman turned your head already?"

By then my wits had come back. "I do not think so," I answered honestly. "It was not Melusine's idea to travel with me. She did not know I had been chosen to carry the king's thanks to Espec and Aumale and the others and was greatly surprised when I told her that I had begged and received the king's permission to take her."

Maud examined my face as if her eyes could scrape away the layers of skin and flesh and come to grips with my soul. I tried to soften the impassive mask I had worn since childhood, first to hide fear from my father and later to hide weakness from anyone so I would not invite hurt. I wanted Maud to read me, to know I was telling the truth, that the desire that had wakened in me for Melusine had not and could not ever shake my loyalty to Stephen and her.

"Why?" the queen asked.

"I wished to make her known to my . . . to Lady Audris at Jernaeve." I hesitated a moment and then decided that I must speak honestly and without regard to giving some offense. "I have no land, madam, no source of income but the king's favor. If circumstances should press on my lord so bitterly that he is forced to tighten his purse and you should no longer be able to keep Melusine, I would have no means of caring for my wife. In such a case or if I should die in the king's service, I could send her to Jernaeve, where she would be safe and comfortable. Her future will no longer burden my soul, and I will be able to continue my service to the king without regard to anything beyond my oath of loyalty."

"And so you could send her whether or not she was known," Maud replied coldly, staring at me. "I know Lady Audris is your sister and fond enough of you to welcome your wife known or unknown to her."

I stared back. "Yes, madam, Audris would welcome

her for my sake, but how would Melusine feel, knowing herself to be an object of charity and thrust into a strange place without introduction to the people or having any idea what they feel about me. She is my *wife*," I said, "not a dog to be sent from kennel to kennel without knowledge or explanation. I must live with her for the rest of my life, and my life will be far sweeter if I can make her happy and bind her to me so that she obeys me willingly. Making her hate me can serve no one's purpose, for if she hates me, will she not hate you and King Stephen more for tying her to me?"

At that the queen's eyes dropped and she walked ahead silently for a few minutes, gesturing me to walk with her. "Of course it is true that it would be best if she does not hate you," she agreed with a sigh. "One of the reasons Stephen and I settled on you for her husband was that we knew you would be kind to her. But Melusine troubles me." She sighed again. "I have never known anyone before who could play a part so faultlessly for so long. Such desperate determination implies an equally great cause, and I cannot see what that cause could be except a full-scale rebellion in Cumbria. And this would be the worst time, the very worst time for such a rising. The rebels may be quiet, but they are still rebels at heart. All they need is the rising of a whole shire; they would fly to arms again and the Scots would fly to support their dear friends in Cumbria, and—" Her voice shook and she stopped speaking, no longer looking at me but staring ahead into a bleak future.

I listened in growing delight, realizing that Maud had been building great castles of plots on a foundation of the wet sand of fear. Not that I dismissed completely either her projection of the damage a rising in Cumbria could do or her suspicions of Melusine. I simply did not believe it would be possible for anyone, particularly a woman, to wake rebellion in Cumbria after the winnowing the king had given that shire in the beginning of the year. As to Melusine, it was indeed possible that she had been playing a part to accomplish a purpose—but I was reasonably sure that purpose had great significance only to Melusine herself.

I could not tell the queen of Melusine's attempt to kill

me because, prejudiced as she was, Maud might demand that my poor wife be punished. Yet that attempt on my life was one good proof that Melusine had no larger purpose in any of her actions than an ultimate escape from fear and despair. She must have known that, had it been successful, my murder would result in her own death and thus in the failure of any political move connected with her presence in Cumbria. Thus, had she had a political object in mind, she would not have tried to kill me. Nor were her actions since we had made a truce enough of a single piece for a person with a fixed and overwhelming purpose.

With all of this evidence in Melusine's favor, I still could not ignore the queen's fears. Maud was too keen a judge of people for me to follow my own opinion. However, I did not agree that the solution was to mew up Melusine. Eventually I would come to hate her from the constant tension of needing to be her keeper. Better to bring her to Cumbria and test her so that any doubts of her purpose could be resolved.

"I assure you, madam," I said, stepping around in front of the queen so that she had to stop and look at me, "that Melusine will raise no rebellions in Cumbria. I will kill her if I must," I promised grimly, "and I will swear that by any oath you desire."

It was an easy enough promise to make. I was very sure that Melusine's purposes were all personal—perhaps only finding a little peace and happiness for herself after her losses and sorrows, perhaps winning back her estate. However, if I was wrong, I would keep my word to the queen, for a creature able to manage so deep a deception was surely a creature of the devil and better removed from this world.

CHAPTER 12

Melusine

FOR SOME MINUTES after I woke the morning after Bruno told me he would take me to Ulle, I continued to lie with closed eyes listening intently. I could not remember exactly what I had said and done, but I knew I had given way completely to my grief. Bruno—my husband—had been as good and gentle to me as papa . . . No! No, I must not allow myself to think of him as good and gentle. What if he had killed papa and Donald?

There was a faint sound of breathing in the room, but no movement. Could Bruno be sitting and watching me? What would I say to him? Could a man who had killed my father and brother show such concern for me? Yes, of course he could if he wanted Ulle and a peaceful life, and he had told me outright that was what he wanted. Tears stung behind my closed lids. I would have to thank him as coldly as I could and then send him away.

When I had conquered the tears, I opened my eyes, but it was only Edna sitting on the chest and staring out of the window. By nature every creature flees pain, so I fled from the problem my husband's kindness created to the much simpler problem of what to do about Edna. Having used the pot and washed—she having served me most deftly and in silence, although I could feel her look at me whenever I was turned away—I said to her when she began to dress me that Bruno had told me she could no longer practice her trade and asked her why.

"I got with child and could not birth it," she replied, her eyes staring past me into nothing. "Three days I screamed and it could not come. I was dying. They thought they could save the child, so they cut it out of me. Somehow I lived and it died, but if I get with child again, I *will* die."

"Do you mean to tell me that the—the place you work permitted you to refuse?"

"No, madam." She looked at me and a smile I never hope to see on another face twisted her lips. "They 'persuaded' me until I agreed, but I could not. When a man came to me, I fought. I could not help myself."

"I should think they would have cast you out then. Yet Bruno found you there."

"I served as maid to the others and cooked and cleaned. Also—" Edna looked away again. "There are a few men, not many but a few, who only take pleasure in forcing a woman. They kept me for those."

I recalled the bruises I had seen on her and felt sickness well up in me, but I also knew that women bred to Edna's trade were also bred to deception and dishonesty. I knew the bruises could be dyed into the skin with plant juices and the emaciation be deliberate, but I could not make myself send her back—and she was a skillful maid who was clean, spoke French, and could not have any loyalty to anyone in the court except myself and Bruno.

All the while we talked, Edna had continued to slip garments over my head. By the time I admitted to myself that I must keep her, because even the smallest chance that the tale she told me was true was too great, she had finished lacing my bliaut. I sat down on the chest carved with Bruno's name and gestured her toward the other.

"Do you wish to stay with me as my maid?"

Edna began to sob aloud. The first day she had wept, but silently. Now she slipped from the chest and crawled to my feet and bent and kissed them. I grasped her arm and jerked her upright.

"Do not use such extravagant gestures to me," I said.

"My people are faithful to death, but they do not grovel. I take it that you do wish to be my servant?" Still unable to speak for sobbing, she nodded vigorously. "Very well, I will accept you on terms. You will be fed and fed well, and I will see that you have decent clothing fit for all weathers—that is all I promise. Perhaps Sir Bruno will find a coin for you now and again, but we are not wealthy people. For your part, your duties will be much what you have done already—to clean our clothes and make the bed and suchlike—except that you will need to learn to sew and perhaps embroider. You are too old to learn to spin or weave."

She still crouched before me, struggling to master her sobbing, and gasped out, "I will do anything, learn anything if only I may stay with you. Only be a little patient with me. Do not cast me out for—"

"The only thing I will cast you out for is stealing or lying to myself or Sir Bruno. I know stealing is the custom of your trade and you do not think it to be wrong, but I will not suffer it. I am not talking only of your stealing from me or Bruno. In fact, I think you would not be so foolish as that, but if you steal anything at all from anyone at all, I will cast you *naked* into the road wherever we are. And for lying also—but only for lying to me or to Sir Bruno. One cannot be a servant in court without lying to others; only do not be so fanciful that you are caught in your lies."

I could not help smiling as I said that, and Edna wiped the tears from her face and timidly smiled back. "Madam," she whispered, "we were not allowed to steal. Great lords came to that place, and had one missed a ring or a coin, the punishment might have been death or maiming for all of us. But I am very good at lying."

"Good. Remember your lessons then, for the punishment here will be no less great, and you will bear it alone. But as to lying, we must begin that at once. For my own reasons, I wish to avoid the queen's ladies as much as possible. Therefore, I will tell the queen that Sir Bruno has burdened me with a singularly stupid and clumsy maid whom I must train as if she were a dog." I nodded. "Your bruises may be useful. You might show a few of the smaller ones to some of the other maidservants to prove you have been punished for stupidity. Since you say you know well how to lie, I will leave it to you to explain where Bruno found you and why you speak French. But be sure to tell one tale and hold fast to it, since you will live with the other servants and many will repeat the tale to their ladies.''

I sounded more confident than I actually felt because I had no idea how a servant was recognized and given the right to eat at table and a place to sleep in this great place. Therefore I had no choice but to explain my problem to the queen, and I was by no means sure Maud would agree to my having a maid who was not in her service. Nor was I at all certain what I should say if she questioned me about the journey north Bruno had mentioned. North was all I allowed myself to think, but in me there was a terrible longing for the place I dared not name, a terrible longing and an equally terrible fear.

After I had taken my morning meal to the darkest corner I could find, I watched for a moment when the queen was alone and approached her. She seemed surprised that I should willingly open a conversation with her but did not mention my going to Jernaeve, which made me suspect she did not know. Remembering how she had had me watched and that Bruno had said I had tried to escape in the past, I pushed my knowledge of our journey to the back of my mind and spoke of Edna as if I expected to remain with the court.

Maud smiled with her lips—I think to hide what she was thinking because I could get no impression of any kind of feeling—but she only said, ''Of course you must have a maid of your own if your husband is willing to pay for her,'' and then told me which of her gentlemen managed meals and quarters for her ladies' maidservants.

I remembered then that when papa went to swear fealty to Stephen—that was before Mildred died—he had complained that a charge had been levied on him for food and lodging for his grooms and horses, grumbling about the mean-fisted hospitality of English kings compared to the treatment of guests at the Scottish court when he was a young man. I had not thought of Edna costing anything beyond what worn out garments I chose to give her because when I went with papa to Carlisle or Richmond we had lodged in a private house, our servants with us. A small qualm of conscience passed through me, for I knew Bruno had little and a maid might be a burden on his purse, but I said nothing of that to the queen, who might think I was begging to be spared the expense.

In addition, Maud's near disinterest in whether my maid was one of her own servants reminded me that the queen was probably sure she could discover anything she needed to know from a maid whether or not the woman was in her service. I was not certain that Maud would be as successful in penetrating the practiced lies of a whore as she thought; nonetheless, I would take no chances and tell Edna to be very careful of the queen and speak only the truth to her—unless I bade her profess ignorance.

The idea coursing through my head had made me slow to reply, and Maud tapped my arm with an impatient finger, bidding me sharply not to play slow-witted again. I begged pardon, assuring her I had no intention of doing so, and then presented my excuse for remaining much of the time in my own chamber. This time, Maud raised her brows as she looked at me, and I found myself blushing.

"That is not true, madam," I admitted. "Edna cannot sew, but otherwise she is a most deft maid. I do wish to teach her to sew, but—but I really desire to hide myself from your ladies." Stumblingly, I confessed that I could not bear to be treated like an idiot any longer but feared their rage if they should come to believe I had been mocking them by pretending to be foolish.

The queen's expression was very strange as she listened, but she only said, "Very well. You have had no duties in the months you have been with me, so you will cause me no inconvenience if you absent yourself for a few days. However, you cannot hide forever."

"I thought I would change little by little," I said, "as if—" I could feel myself blushing again. "—as if marriage had wakened me."

"Very well," the queen repeated, both face and voice completely devoid of expression now. "You may go."

At dinner I learned that the king had gone hunting,

taking with him the servants on duty, which meant that
Bruno had gone too. It was a great relief to me, for I hated
the thought of seeming ungracious and ungrateful for his
kindness, and yet I dared not let myself accept it. Too late
I discovered that sitting alone in my chamber was no better
than being treated like an idiot. I had never been bored at
Ulle; usually there was too much to do, and a few idle
moments were a blessed relief.

There were things I could have done; Bruno needed a
nightrobe and in court a woman always needs clothing and
pretty new embroidered girdles or sleeve cuffs, but I had
no cloth or fine embroidery thread and nothing with which
to purchase any. It had not occurred to me to ask Bruno
for money, and I would not have done so even if the idea
had come to me. I knew he did not trust me and might
think I wanted the coin for some secret evil purpose. I
could not imagine what evil I could accomplish in a place
where I knew no one but a few women who all thought me
a fool. Yet it troubled me that he should not trust me, and
I knew if he refused me I could never feel the same toward
him. I remember putting my hands to my head when I
thought that and wondering what I meant.

Before the second day ended, I considered going to the
queen and asking for duties to be assigned to me, but I
dared not do that lest she use my new employment as a
reason to forbid my accompanying Bruno when he went
north. Altogether, he was too often in my mind over the
three very long, dull days that passed. In fact, I began to
long for what I had at first feared, and when Edna came
flying from the hall to tell me that the hunt had been
sighted nearing the castle, I forgot all my doubts about my
husband. I ran out into the bailey to meet the returning
huntsmen and greeted Bruno with delight, my heart warm
with having a man of my own to welcome.

And I must say that he made all too easy what had
burdened my spirit for the days he had been gone. Our talk
had been so pleasant and I was so excited by the huge boar
Bruno had killed, that I mentioned my brothers while I
was assuring him I was a good physician. The pang of
grief I felt when I remembered that I would never heal any
of them again made me close my eyes and catch my

breath. Again Bruno offered comfort, but I was not overcome as I had been on Monday night, and I assured him I would not let that happen again. I still had no idea how to avoid thanking him for comforting me, then and now, but before I could say anything he changed the subject to Edna.

That effectively quenched any gratitude I felt in an icy rage, but I had to swallow my renewed suspicion quickly. If I displayed it, Bruno would have reason to think me jealous—and what reason could I have? Should not an unwilling wife be grateful that her husband vented his lust on another woman? I swallowed down any expression of my rage to salve my pride; still, if I discovered that the tale Edna had told me had been concocted between her and Bruno so that he might have his whore at hand, I would . . . I had no idea what I would do, but I promised myself that neither of them would find it pleasant.

Fortunately, my rage was diverted by the arrival of a group of gentlemen who had not accompanied the hunt and wished to compliment Bruno on having made one of the greatest kills. He made nothing of it, turning the feat into a jest and making them laugh with a tale of how he tripped on his own feet in his eagerness to cut the beast's throat and was trampled for his clumsiness. I could see that he is of that kind of man who can never bear to be too much noticed—Andrew and Fergus were like that and Magnus too, but for a different reason—and before I considered what I was doing I had drawn the talk away, just as I had always done for them.

Once I began to talk to Bruno's friends, I forgot how angry I had been. It was very pleasant to be part of a group of men talking about such things as we all enjoyed—hunting in general and the use and care of the hawks and horses and dogs that were so much a part of that sport. I drew from each man his special knowledge and opinions, from Bruno some remarks on the training and flying of the great hawks of the north, but he was shy at first. Later he talked more freely—it was the training of horses that sparked his deepest interest—but all the time, without my noticing at all, he had been edging us to the door closest to the guesthouse. I was near speechless when he drove off the other gentlemen with a jest about desiring only my company at this hour of the evening, and led me in.

I could not refuse to go with Bruno without making myself ridiculous, but I entered the chamber prepared to defend myself, to resist as well as I could any attempt on Bruno's part to void his promise and force me to couple. Instead of seizing me, however, he began to talk about the journey north and his fear that if the king or queen were reminded too often of our going by courtiers' gossip, they might place restrictions on our route of travel. I understood that he was trying to warn me to say nothing of his plan to take me to Ulle without mentioning the place—and realized with surprise that I had thought of going there without horror, although there was still pain. So I said as shortly as I could that I was not a fool and changed the subject to the bruises he had received when he killed the boar.

The man is a devil! His face—if one is diverted from the hunger that lies under every other expression—is open and innocent; his dark eyes are sometimes wary but more often soft with kindness or bright with laughter. Bruno was not handsome to my eyes, not with the brilliant beauty of my red-haired, blue-eyed father and brothers. He was more like Magnus—that should have warned me; laughing or caressing, Magnus's clever mind always held firm to its own purposes. But I never thought of Magnus.

Despite the warning I had had in overhearing Maud's ladies speak of Bruno's knowledge of women and despite his open admission, in my presence, of his intention to the men he had dismissed from our company, I was beguiled completely. Only an accident saved me from falling headlong into the trap of lust that he set. He set? Or did I set that trap myself and Bruno only sprang it? It was I who bade him take off his clothes; he only used my own pride—but is that not the devil's favorite weapon?—to draw me to him, even after I saw his staff upright, its head bare in lust. I had never before seen a man so, but I knew what it was and what it meant from what rutting male beasts exposed.

Only Bruno is no beast; he is a clever devil. He would not let me put from my mind what I had seen, but fixed my attention on that standing rod, taking away any fearfulness I might have felt by making me want to laugh. Monsieur Jehan de la Tête Rouge, indeed! And talking of that part of him as if it were an independent personage with feelings and desires separate from his own. So instead of running to hide myself and being revolted by that swollen shaft, I actually came closer, finding Monsieur amusing. I felt again that warmth and trembling within me—perhaps I even knew then that it was desire, not fear—but I was too curious to be warned, so curious I had to press my hand on Bruno's ribs to keep myself from reaching down to touch Monsieur de la Tête Rouge.

Devil! Bruno knew what I felt, I am sure of it, and he bent and kissed my nose. It was a disarming caress, full of warmth and tenderness; it was also papa's favorite affectionate gesture when I was close, brushing dirt from his clothes or looking at something he was holding. Had it not been for that, Bruno would have had me then and there. As it was, the web he had been weaving around me broke and I jumped away.

Devil! He knew enough not to pursue me and to call again on my pride to smother my fear—not of him but of my own rising passion. Like a fool, I stood up to him, answering roundly the excuses he made for tempting me. Thus I let him beguile me again, for he set aside the issue of our coupling, as if he had been defeated, and then, while my pride still blinded me, he challenged my usefulness as a woman, asking, as if with contempt, whether I could make ready for our journey in one day.

In pointing out those things he had overlooked, or seemed to have overlooked—and in my joy at his promise that I could ride a horse of my own rather than being jounced in a cart like a servant girl—I all but forgot how he had made me want him. Without thinking, I ran to him for comfort when fear of finding more pain than I could bear at Ulle struck me. I thought the unruly ideas he had planted in my head were gone—until he began to unlace my gown. There was no hint of Monsieur's desire in what he did, but that wicked warm trembling began in me again. This time I had strength enough to flee—and that devil turned his back on me and was fast asleep before I had lit the night candle and snuffed the others.

It took all my strength, after I had lain awake some while, still warm, still wanting, to refrain from putting my foot in the middle of his back and shoving him out of the bed. I thought about it with longing, imagining his rude awakening, his shout of surprise and perhaps pain if he landed on his bruised side. I even began to believe it would be worth the beating he would undoubtedly give me—but what if instead of beating me, that devil understood. If he kissed my mouth, which papa never did, would I have sense and strength to flee him again or would I yield to the curiosity of my treacherous body?

Desperately, I tried to stop thinking about that infuriating man and fixed my mind on the problems of our journey. The diversion became preeminent when it suddenly occurred to me that more trouble would arise from keeping the trip north a secret than from telling Maud about it. It was possible that the queen would forbid my going altogether or forbid Bruno to take me to Ulle, but I did not think so. For the first, I doubted she would openly forbid anything for which the king's permission had been obtained. As to going to Ulle, I was quite certain it would not enter her mind that Bruno would consider taking me there, so it was unlikely she would forbid it. On the other side of the coin was the picture the queen would see if she heard of that journey by accident—a black picture of my deceitfulness.

I intended to speak to Bruno about this notion, to ask him what I was to do about Edna to whom I had promised service only this morning, whether he wanted me to arrange for carting or storage, how to do so, and a million other details, but of course he was gone by the time I woke. I do not know what annoyed me more—Bruno's ability to slip away without a sound or a quiver of the mattress or my own stupidity in forgetting to tell him to wake me when he woke. I suppose I looked like a thundercloud when I went to the queen's hall to break my fast, although I was not aware of it until Maud crooked a finger at me and gestured to the lady with her to leave us alone.

"You are much more amusing now that you have—so to speak—come into our world," the queen said, smiling at me as I made a small bow. "Certainly you do not trouble to wear a courtier's face. Tell me, Melusine, who or what has displeased you?''

"I am more worried than displeased, madam," I replied, cursing myself for my carelessness and wishing I had the player's skill with which Maud credited me.

I dared not even lick my lips, although my mouth had dried with nervousness. I no longer had the choice of discussing with Bruno whether it would be better to tell the queen. I must speak now or not tell her at all.

"Bruno told me last night that he is to carry a message north for the king and that I am to go with him," I went on, trying to keep the frown on my face unchanged so that Maud would not read my anxiety.

"And you do not wish to go?" Maud asked without inflection.

"Oh yes," I cried, "I do wish to go, but I am sure I must beg leave of you, madam, and I can give you no further explanation. Bruno told me no more than I have already repeated."

The queen looked at me with no more expression than there had been in her voice. There was no way to judge whether she believed what I had said, although in a way it was true since Bruno had not explained the king's purpose.

"I hope you will grant me leave," I went on. "Since I have no duties, I am sure my absence would cause you no hardship—" I glanced quickly over my shoulder and lowered my voice to be sure I would not be overheard, "—and being away would solve my problem with your ladies. I suppose most of those attending you now will leave and others, who do not know me, will come before we return—Bruno said he had leave for two months. But even if I am wrong about that, surely the ladies will forget so small and unimportant a matter as my behavior or understand that the travel and excitement had changed me."

"What a clever girl you are, Melusine," Maud remarked so blandly that a chill ran up my spine. "I find you much more interesting than most other women."

"Please let me go, madam," I whispered. "I am sure you will find me more interesting still when I do not need to hide myself for most of the day."

"Oh . . ." The queen drew out the sound until, though soft, it rang with irony. "So you intend to return?"

I stared at her, blank with fear and then asked, "Where else have I to go?" The question brought a brief look of surprise to Maud's face, and wildly seeking any topic that would keep her from asking me a direct question about Ulle, I blurted out, "And I do not know what is mine to take. I have several grand gowns in my chest that are new. Are those to be returned to you, madam? The bed, I am sure, was lent, but is it to stay in that chamber or should it be packed away? And do I need a tally to mark that I have returned what was lent?"

"The gowns are yours," Maud snapped. "Two were given to you by Stephen to make you less sad, and your wedding gown was my gift. Why do you continue to pretend that you do not remember?"

"I do not pretend, madam," I said seriously. "I do not know why I do not remember. Perhaps I did not listen properly because I was thinking about my sorrows, or perhaps I did not want court gowns because I did not want to be at court."

"Whatever you are, you are certainly not a flatterer," Maud remarked, her brief flash of temper replaced with wry amusement.

"Would you believe me if I said I was overjoyed to come into your service—or your care?" I asked quietly. "It would be foolish for me to pretend that. Yet, madam, now that my bitterness is a little eased, I can see that you and the king have tried to be kind."

"I am glad your bitterness is eased," Maud's smile, as so often was the case, did not reflect in her eyes. "I must suppose that is Bruno's doing."

To my horror I felt myself blushing, but I would not look away and seem ashamed. "He is not a man I would have chosen for myself," I said firmly, hoping she would recognize the truth when she heard it for once, "but he is not cruel or ungenerous. Since it is too late to hope for better I must be content with him and make as good a marriage as I can. So will you give me leave to travel with him?"

"I will tell you tomorrow or send a message if you need to know sooner."

There was a slightly troubled look on the queen's face, but I did not think it had anything to do with me, and she continued to be withdrawn into her own thoughts as she told me that I did not need tallies for the bed or bedclothes and gave permission—unasked—for me to go and begin sorting and packing as soon as I had broken my fast.

I was sick with worry all the rest of the day, but I had no chance to confess what I had done and warn Bruno because he did not sit with me at dinner. And when I told him at the evening meal, explaining my reasons for telling the queen, he only nodded and said he was sure Maud would give me leave.

"I am so glad you are sure," I said somewhat spitefully, remembering how unpleasant my interview with her had been. "Now will you please tell me what you want done with the chests—and with Edna. You told me to take her as a maid, so I did, but I am sure she cannot ride. Do you want me to store everything or to hire a cart—"

"Oh, bless you, Melusine," he cried, "if you will see about the hiring of a cart and a couple of men to drive it and guard it, I will somehow find time to get a horse and saddle for you." Then he looked at me hard and said in a somewhat lower voice, "I do not wish to ask the king for time to go into the town when my service will be withdrawn from him altogether so soon."

"But—" I began, about to protest that Bruno had misunderstood me. Then I hesitated, knowing that if Magnus had given me such a look, it would have some important meaning and I suppose inside me something woke to alertness so that small incidents stuck firmly in my mind. There was no immediate threat, however, and my attention jumped back to the fact that I knew nothing of the town, that I was not sure the queen would give permission for me to run about in it, and that I had not the faintest idea how to go about hiring a cart and men anyway because at Ulle I had owned the carts and the men had been servants in the household.

"Oh, of course, you will need money," Bruno said, seeming to associate my unfinished remark with the wrong uncertainty. His hand fumbled in his belt, but he was no longer looking at me and he did not look down for his

purse either. He had glanced at the king's table when he
spoke of not having time to go into the town, and his eyes
stayed fixed there, following a gentleman, most gorgeously
attired, who was crossing behind the queen.

Bruno pushed a purse into my hand, and rose to his feet.
We had not finished eating, but I felt his movement had
more to do with the gentleman he was watching, who now
bent over the king's shoulder and said something that
made Stephen laugh. The queen looked up at him too. It
seemed to me that she had cast a quick glance at her other
table companion, who I knew was the king's brother,
before she smiled at the gorgeous gentleman. I thought
Bruno, who was standing beside me, still closing my hand
around his purse, had seen the glance Maud gave the
bishop of Winchester and stiffened, and a faint curiosity
about what it all meant stirred in me. In the next moment I
dismissed the matter. I had my own troubles to occupy
me. I had no idea of how I was to accomplish what Bruno
thought I had suggested.

Absently, my eyes went back to the king's table and I
wondered if I had imagined all those quick looks and
tensions. The bishop had apparently been included in the
jest that made Stephen laugh, for he was laughing too
now, and Bruno, also smiling, was talking to Camville. As
I watched, the royal party rose, having also finished eating. The king walked toward his private apartment with
the gorgeous gentleman's hand on his arm, while the
queen stood talking to the bishop a moment longer. When
they parted, I saw the bishop look at the doorway through
which the king had disappeared. For some reason, he
looked lonely—a ridiculous idea when applied to a man of
such wealth and power—but I had got to my feet and
started toward him before I realized how silly such a
notion was.

My next notion was audacious rather than silly. The
bishop of Winchester virtually owned the town. Who would
be more able than he, or one of his servants, to help me?
So instead of turning aside, I continued toward him as
quickly as I could. Winchester almost walked past me, and
if I had been able to absorb his expression before I spoke,
I would have held my tongue. However, the words, "My

lord bishop, a moment, please,'' were out of my mouth before I realized that Winchester's whole face looked frozen. I began to back away, but he had stopped and turned toward me, staring at me somewhat blindly. To continue to back away now that I had his attention would be stupid as well as rude, so I dropped a deep curtsey.

Winchester's expression softened into a smile. ''You are the new married lady—Sir Bruno's wife.''

''I am Lady Melusine of Ulle,'' I replied, somewhat tartly I fear, as I rose from my bow. I had little taste for becoming a mere appendage to any man, even my husband.

Although the smile remained on Winchester's lips, his eyes now looked wary. ''Life is as God directs,'' he warned.

I realized immediately that my denial of Bruno's name made the bishop believe I had accosted him to complain about my forced marriage and was at a loss for what to say. I would not say I was content, and I could not say outright that I knew complaining to him would be useless because he was only the king's and queen's tool. Then I was glad the thought had not leapt unbidden from my lips—as sometimes happened with me, spoiled as I was by my loving father and brothers, who would defend me even when I was wrong and not punish me themselves—because the bishop added, very kindly, ''But if I can help you I will.''

Dismissing my ugly thoughts, I admitted ruefully, ''I do not think the favor I will ask is the kind one can request of God, and I am afraid it is a great presumption to ask it of you, my lord, but I hope you will at least direct me to whom I should speak.''

''Any favor can be asked of God,'' the bishop murmured in automatic response, but curiosity had almost replaced the wariness in his face.

''My lord,'' I said, laughing, ''I will gladly pray for a horse and cart and some men to drive it and guard it and my maidservant if you think that is the best way to obtain them, but I do hope you can suggest some more direct and practical method because I need them very soon.''

''A horse and cart,'' Winchester repeated, blank with astonishment.

"I hope I have not offended you, my lord," I said quickly, fearing that he had the kind of pride that regarded as an insult being asked about any common matter.

A burst of laughter followed. "No, no, my dear, you have not offended me," he assured me, "but I feared you were about to . . . to pose some weighty problem to me and—" He uttered a small sigh, then smiled. "Well, let me say I am glad your trouble is so simple."

"Not to me, my lord," I pointed out, smiling too. "My husband, who is bound to close attendance on the king, has bidden me find cart, horse, and men—no, he said nothing about the horse, so possibly he means to obtain the horse himself, but—"

"The horse and cart are for Sir Bruno?" Astonishment again raised Winchester's voice.

"I am so sorry," I exclaimed, "I began in the middle of the tale and have confused everything. Please allow me to begin at the beginning—if you have time to listen, my lord?"

"This tale I must hear whether I have time or not," he replied, grinning.

"It is not nearly so interesting as I have made it seem, I fear," I said. "Simply, the king has ordered Sir Bruno to carry certain messages north and has given his permission for me to go also—"

"North? Bruno is carrying—" His voice had been above normal with surprise, and he checked it abruptly and spoke lower. "Is Bruno carrying messages to Scotland?" He looked eager and excited.

"He told me nothing of the messages, my lord," I answered carefully, "but I do not think he expects to go into Scotland. He intended, I know, to bring me to the people who raised him in Jernaeve keep. That is in Northumbria."

I realized that I had been foolish beyond measure. In a court everything has ten meanings more than should be conveyed by simple words. God alone knew what Winchester had read into what I had said. My slow, careful words and direct gaze at least caused his expression of eager expectation to be replaced by puzzled thoughtfulness.

"Ah, yes," he murmured, "you said you were to go

also and needed a horse and cart. The messages, then, cannot be very urgent if Bruno is to go no faster than you do in the cart."

"I ride, and I will cause no delay to Bruno's business," I told him, and then was furious with myself, pride having again driven me to speak before I thought. "But I think you judge correctly that no urgency attends the messages," I added, hoping to retrieve my second mistake. "Bruno is given two months leave."

Winchester nodded understanding, smiling and seeming more at ease although still very thoughtful. "That is why the cart is needed."

"Yes, my lord," I agreed. "Since the court will move on before we can return, we must take our possessions with us, and also my maidservant, who cannot ride."

"And when do you leave?" he asked.

"On Monday, I believe, my lord," I replied.

"Very well, Lady Melusine," Winchester said, "a cart will be ready early Monday. And you may tell Bruno that I am very happy to be able to be of help, and will be happy to serve him in any way I can in the future."

He smiled at me again and turned away. I was appalled, but I could not say a word for my throat had closed with fear. Apparently Winchester believed Bruno had sent me to him. I had no idea what I had done for good or ill, and I was left in that state until the morning we left because Bruno did not come to bed that night nor the next.

Saturday night I was half mad, terrified one moment and raging the next. The terror came first when Bruno did not come at his usual time. I was seized by the idea that Bruno was being questioned about my unwise disclosure and perhaps would be punished for it. But as the hours passed, I knew he could not have been detained so long and rage overwhelmed fear and regret. I became certain Bruno had made some assignation with Edna because I had not yielded to him the night before.

On Sunday morning I learned that Bruno had not slept with Edna, wherever else he had been. I spoke to the woman in charge myself and discovered that Edna could not have left the maids' lodging in the bailey that night. One of the women had been taken ill and two nuns had sat up with her all night. Then of course my fear returned, to be supplanted by rage again when I saw Bruno at dinner in his proper place among the Knights of the Body. He smiled at me, and lifted his hands, palm up, in a gesture of helplessness. That did not amend my temper much since I felt he could have sent a message and saved me a great deal of grief and fear. My resentment was only increased when I glimpsed him later, after the evening meal, in the doorway of the king's private apartment giving instructions to a page.

Because I had not slept at all on Saturday night and had been too busy Sunday separating what Bruno and I could carry on our horses and what must go by cart, I slept so fast on Sunday night I would not have known that Bruno had not come to bed if he had not confessed indirectly by bursting into our chamber after Prime on Monday, crying in a breath, "I am sorry to be so late. Can you help me arm?"

Haste combined with that question leaves no time for scolding, recrimination, or counter-questions. I sprang toward him, catching his belt as he opened it and flinging it on the bed, bringing his arming tunic as he lifted off the one he was wearing, holding his mail so that he could slide into it with ease, and bringing back belt and sword to be buckled on.

Only then did I say, "I do not know where your shield and helmet are. Bruno, what danger threatens?"

"My shield and helmet are in the stable with Barbe, and if we do not leave at once, we may never get away," he said, and went out before I could speak again.

CHAPTER 13

Bruno

I HAD NO IDEA that I had frightened Melusine nearly out of her wits when I demanded my armor and rushed out, sending two servingmen in to carry out our belongings. Nor did I realize that she would misinterpret my saying that we had to leave at once to mean that the king was furious and about to arrest me or had exiled me with only hours to escape. How could I guess she would be so silly? Had I not told her more than once that I was one of Stephen's favorites? Indeed, it was his fondness for me—or, at least, his conviction that I was more discreet than any of his other servants that nearly overset all my plans.

After I had killed that damned boar on the hunt, the king had said, half-jestingly, that I was too good a companion in sport to use as a messenger. I reminded him that it was not only to be a messenger but to bring Melusine to Jernaeve that I was going, and he said no more about keeping me, but a more serious threat to my leaving arose on Saturday afternoon. At first the canon, who had come from Canterbury, seemed to have nothing to do with me. The archbishop of Canterbury, that William de Corbeil who had anointed Stephen as king, had died less than a year later, in November 1136, and the canon had come to

petition that Canterbury should be permitted to elect an
archbishop when the papal legate should arrive.

I paid little attention, knowing that the king would put
off any election as long as he could because the revenues
of the see went to the Crown as long as there was no
bishop. Stephen spouted all the usual soothing words,
promising that he would obey the papal legate, who would
undoubtedly have directions from the pope about many
matters. It was only when the interview was over and I
heard the king suggest that the canon go quietly to Netley
Abbey rather than stay in Winchester's great house by the
cathedral so that "no undue pressure be placed on the free
canons of Canterbury" that my ears sprang to attention.
Next, while the canon was being served a farewell cup of
wine before his short journey, Stephen drew me aside and
bade me take him to the east gate, where he could board
the boat that had brought him. It would be best, Stephen
said softly, that he speak to no one on the way.

When I returned and was able to report that no attention
at all had been paid to the canon—and I had watched the
boat out of sight on the river—Stephen took a ring from
his hand, pressed it into mine, and said he could not spare
me, that he would find someone else to carry his thanks
and rewards north. I knew he meant only I could be trusted
to be secret, and I dared not protest again that I would
rather have leave than a ring, no matter how rich. Then I
wondered whether my own selfish desires were making me
blind to any real danger a loose mouth could do the king. I
thought of that for the rest of the afternoon, but I could not
see that anything the worst blabbermouth could have said
could be dangerous, which brought me to the sad conclusion that Stephen had a guilty conscience and was seeing
monsters that did not exist in dark corners.

That was why I felt free to catch Waleran in the king's
chamber after the evening meal and tell him that my leave
was cancelled. Possibly he was the cause of Stephen's
guilty conscience, but I knew it would take more power
than I had to raise doubts of Waleran's motives or good
sense at this time, so my presence could do no good.
Waleran wanted to be rid of me and I wanted to be gone;
all I felt was relief when having asked Stephen jovially

why I was not already gone north and hearing that I was not to go, he somehow managed to talk the king into changing his mind again.

Perhaps I should have been glad that Stephen felt he needed me so much, but I was not. I had seen others, closer and dearer, fall from favor. Because they were rich and powerful already and the king was not a vicious man who would strip everything from those he no longer trusted, they had lost little more than the ability to grow still richer and more powerful. But if the king should dismiss me, there was only the gutter of the common mercenary below. More than ever I wanted Melusine to be known and loved in Jernaeve and I wanted to see her lands and learn whether I could cozen the king into giving them to me.

I was like a man strung by the thumbs all Saturday night and Sunday. It made me a little easier in my mind that the king demanded that I sleep in the outer chamber both Saturday and Sunday night so that I could be summoned quickly if he needed me. Perhaps he thought I would feel deprived of the "service" of my wife as he felt deprived of my service, but I was doubly glad. For one thing, I hoped the king would work off his spite—sometimes he was spiteful, but the fit never lasted long. And anyway I got two good nights sleep away from temptation.

Still, I could not relax all day Sunday because Stephen grumbled all the time he was giving me my instructions and signing the writs that named the rewards for each of the principal men who had fought at Northallerton. And between attending to the king's business, I had my own to finish. I had already obtained extra blankets that we could use for camping out if we could not find a hostel and had discovered that Melusine had a horse and saddle, but I had to arrange that our traveling gear be brought from storage to the stable to be loaded and arrange with the queen's groom to bring Melusine's mount to the king's stable. I have forgotten all the small things, but Sunday was no day of rest for me.

Monday morning was worse, however. Stephen sent me on an errand to Robert de Vere that any page could have run, and when I reminded him that I had hoped to be on the road north as soon as Melusine had broken her fast, he shrugged and said it did not matter whether I left that day or another. Then I knew that although he would not openly oppose Waleran's desire to be rid of me, he intended to keep me from day to day as long as he could.

Robert de Vere, the king's constable, did not keep me waiting as he might have kept a page, so my errand was dispatched more quickly than the king expected. And Vere liked me, I think—he had stood sponsor to me at my knighting—and was no fool. He said nothing to me about Stephen's reluctance to grant leave to those he liked—Vere knew I was supposed to go from Stephen's grumbling about it—but he accompanied me back to the king and when Stephen dismissed me, Vere blandly wished me a good journey and said he would bid me fare well now as he did not expect to see me again for some time. I fled the king's chamber as if hounds were on my trail. If Vere could keep Stephen busy until I had left Winchester, Stephen might be angry but I doubted he would send after me and I was certain he would forget all about me while I was gone and welcome me back gladly. The king could be spiteful, but he did not carry a grudge.

What I had forgotten when I told Melusine that we must hurry and leave was that she knew nothing of all this. I assumed too that in eight months with the court, no matter how absorbed she had been in her own grief, she would have learned how changeable Stephen was and that one must seize an opportunity when it occurs. Of course, I also did not know that she had any private reason to be fearful.

I gave all my attention to seeing the small cart loaded so there would be room for Edna and the chests would not break loose and crush her. Then I rolled four extra blankets around the bundles of necessary clothing and other items we would need for the journey, since we would soon outdistance the cart. Inside Melusine's roll I could feel the shape of a small pan, and I blessed her silently for being a woman who knew the uncertainties of travel. From the corner of my eye I saw her take the rein of her mare from the groom, but I was busy giving directions to the driver of the cart and the two guards and seeing them past the inner gate.

When I hurried back, Melusine handed me my saddlebags bulging full and I slung them over Barbe without really looking at her. And even when I lifted her to the saddle and she said softly, "You have found Vinaigre for me," I hardly glanced at her but mounted Barbe and urged him forward. By then I knew there was no need for haste. If the king had decided to recall me, he would have done so at once. The only reason I can think of for feeling the devil was at my heels was that I was very weary of court life, very weary of the need to balance between offending great men or hurting small ones and protecting the king from their importunities, very weary of seeing a man I loved for his kindness and generosity act weakly, sometimes even dishonorably, under the influence of others. Until freedom was promised me and then nearly snatched away, I had not realized how desperately I needed to be free to speak my mind without fearing an unguarded word might do great harm.

The need to flee was so strong that I kicked Barbe into a fast trot as soon as I was sure Melusine was steady in the saddle. We soon passed the cart, and I paused only briefly at the gate to describe it and bid the guards let it pass. Then we were out on the road and Barbe's trot soon lengthened to a canter. I had no need to look back, for the thin head of Melusine's mare with her wicked white-rimmed eye held steady at my knee.

I know now that Melusine loves her dearly, but Vinaigre is a cursed beast if ever there was one. After we had ridden quite some time, the mare still did not need all her strength and speed to keep up with Barbe; she was sure-footed enough to turn her head midstride and nip my thigh. My hauberk kept me from any bruise and I smacked her nose, but she did not slow or miss a step, only rolled that eye until I was sure she was laughing at me, and I laughed back good and hard.

"Are we safe then, Bruno?" Melusine's voice was tight with fear, and I reined Barbe in to a walk, and when we were side by side turned my head to look at her.

"Safer than most travelers," I replied soothingly, noticing that my wife's face was white and strained. "The roads are not what they were in King Henry's time, but I do not think any outlaws would bother attacking us. I am well but not richly armed and you are dressed plainly.''

Astonishment replaced fear on her face. "Outlaws?" she echoed. "I thought we were fleeing the king!"

"Good lord!" I exclaimed. "Whatever gave you such a notion?"

"You gave me the notion," she snapped. "You said if we did not leave at once, we might not be able to go at all. What did you mean, if the king is not angry?"

"Just the opposite," I confessed. "Stephen seemed to feel that he could not do without my service. I am sorry to have frightened you, but why should you think I had suddenly fallen from favor so completely that escape was necessary?"

She did not answer at once, and then explained how she had obtained the cart and guards. "I thought, because of what the bishop of Winchester said about thanking you and being willing to serve you at any time, that my telling him of our journey had exposed some secret. And when you did not come back to our chamber to sleep or send me a message, I feared the king had learned of my indiscretion and lost his trust in you.''

I let her finish her tale without questions, but it woke all my uneasiness about the strain between the king and the bishops again. I must have been frowning too because Melusine added, "Then what I did *was* stupid and dangerous. I am very sorry. I could not avoid the queen, but I could have—"

"No, no." I smiled and reached out to pat her hand, which was tense on the mare's rein. "There was no harm in your telling Winchester, at least none to you or to me, and if there had been it would have been my fault for not telling you to hold the news secret. That is what is so strange. It was not a secret. God knows, Stephen was groaning and complaining to all his gentlemen that I asked for leave at the worst time. Why then did Winchester not know?''

"You asked for leave?" Melusine repeated. "But did you not tell me that Stephen ordered you to carry messages north?''

"I did. And, I swear to you, so it was, but the king

remembers things in his own way. It was Waleran de Meulan who convinced the king to send me——"

"Waleran de Meulan," Melusine gasped, her eyes growing large with an emotion I could not read. "What have you to do with him?"

"As little as I can," I replied, "but unfortunately a great deal. Waleran is Stephen's closest friend and advisor, so there is no way I can avoid him—and it is my duty not to do so."

"You are not Waleran's man, are you?"

"No. I am the king's man, and the queen's, but there is no conflict in that double loyalty, for the queen desires only the king's good."

I answered promptly and forcefully, and I watched her because the question had been asked with such intensity. Melusine's interest implied some connection between her and Waleran, but that was ridiculous and impossible—unless he had stopped at Ulle and some bond had been formed then? She had looked away so I could not read her face, but her knuckles, which had been white with the force of her grip, began to regain their ordinary color and she turned her head toward me again.

"Then why should Waleran influence the king's decision to send you north?" she asked.

I could not tell whether the question was asked out of simple curiosity or was a clever diversion to prevent me from thinking about her interest in Meulan. "He thinks that it will be easier for him to learn what the king says and does in private if I am not on duty in the chamber," I told her. "And the surest way to keep me from being on duty when matters that might be dangerous to Waleran are discussed is to have me gone from the court entirely."

Nothing showed in Melusine's face but bright-eyed interest as she asked, "If Waleran is, as you say, the king's dearest friend and advisor, why does he feel he must watch Stephen so closely?"

"The king has had other close friends and advisors who have lost their influence," I said slowly, not certain of how much it was safe or wise to tell her. "I will say, in the king's favor, that in both cases those men had said or done something that was truly offensive. However, I am not sure Waleran understands this. He is no monument of loyalty himself." I explained how he had betrayed King Henry, and she listened without any change of expression.

"I see." She nodded. "Being untrustworthy himself, he cannot trust others, so he sent you away to be able to buy information from one or another of the knights and squires who attend the king. Then he would know who speaks against him and exactly what accusation was made so he can counter it without even seeming to know he was accused. Yes, that is all very well, but why now? Why not six months ago or six months hence?"

For a moment I sat staring at her. I had been overjoyed when I learned that Melusine was not a half-wit, but I had not really connected that with the queen's insistence that she was exceptionally clever until this moment. I had a sudden uncomfortable memory of the queen's warning about falling into her power. But it was ridiculous to ignore a sensible question. There was no thread in this that could be woven into a rope that would tie me to Matilda's cause.

"Six months ago we were in the field and only a fool would speak against Waleran's influence there. He is a fine soldier. He is certainly too good a soldier to want to deprive the king of a loyal companion to support him when fighting is to be done. That answers why he did not wish to be rid of me six months in the past."

When I said that Waleran was a fine soldier, Melusine turned her head away again, but she bent to pull and flatten the loose end of the stirrup strap, so I could not be certain whether hiding her face was deliberate. That strap could have loosened during the canter and finally worked itself into an irritating loop. She had looked back at me wearing the same look of interest without too much intensity by the time I finished.

"And as to six months in the future," she remarked tartly, "once rid of you now, perhaps he hopes an accident or fate will remove you permanently. Never mind that. I thought from what you said that it was not easy to get the king to send you, so perhaps the king had more cause than usual to need a discreet servant. Or did I misunderstand?"

"No, you did not misunderstand, but when the subject

was first broached, a week ago, Stephen was not particularly unwilling to part with me. He was eager for me to renew my ties in Jernaeve—I must speak to you about that some time and explain, but it can wait. It was only after the canon from Canterbury came on Saturday that Stephen suddenly changed his mind. And you are right about something else. Waleran must have been desperate to be rid of me, for on Saturday night, after Stephen decided that he could not spare me, Jernaeve or no Jernaeve, Waleran took great trouble to get the king to let me go.''

"A canon from Canterbury? Does that somehow fit with Winchester's ignorance of the messages you carry?"

"Not the messages. They have nothing to do with the Church. They are only Stephen's thanks to such men as William d'Aumale and Walter Espec for holding back the Scots.''

But even as I said the words I remembered how Waleran had prevented Stephen from using the priest to carry the messages so that none who received the rewards should think they came through the archbishop of York's recommendation.

"Not the messages," I repeated slowly, "yet I am beginning to be afraid that through Waleran's influence something is being planned against the Church—no, not the Church but against Salisbury, Lincoln, and Ely." Instinctively I stopped Barbe to turn him.

"Are we going back?" Melusine cried.

I sat still for a breath or two, conscience struggling with desire, until reason intervened. My distrust of Waleran was making me see wrong where there might be right. I knew that Salisbury and his nephews did their work efficiently, but was I so sure that they were loyal to Stephen? They had violated the oath they had given King Henry to support Matilda—of course, Stephen had violated the oath also, but it seemed to me that when a man of the Church swore he should be bound more straitly than a common man. Besides, from all I had seen and heard—although it was many years ago—I did not want Matilda for a queen. And it was not only Waleran who would have better information about what Stephen intended. If anyone around the king could be bought, the bishops could buy as well as Waleran.

Turning Barbe's head north again, I said to Melusine, "We will not go back."

"Thank God for that," she sighed. "For you to thrust yourself between Waleran and the bishops is asking to be ground small between the upper and nether millstone."

"It is not that," I protested. "If I thought I could do good for my master or for the realm, I would do it. I dare not try to interfere because I do not know what is right and what is wrong." I told her then about the coldness between the king and his brother Winchester and how that coldness seemed to be spreading to Salisbury, Ely, and Lincoln, who were the highest officials of the realm.

"And I have no doubt that Waleran de Meulan is doing everything he can to make cold colder," Melusine mused when I was done. She was looking between Vinaigre's ears, and I wondered whether she approved or disapproved of Waleran's activity. Then she shook her head and turned to me again. "If I had known this, of course I would not have gone near Winchester."

"You think Waleran a better advisor than the king's brother?" I asked, doing my best to sound indifferent.

"How could I know such a thing?" she countered, not really answering my question. "What I do know," she went on, "is that safety lies in being attached to neither party. I was a fool. I should have gone to the queen with my questions about the cart or found some other way to deal with the matter. It was just . . . when the king went into his chamber without inviting Winchester, I had the strangest feeling that the bishop was . . . lonely. Is that not the silliest—"

"Not so silly," I interrupted. "I am not sure the emotion you read was loneliness, but it might be. I think that Winchester greatly regrets the quarrel that hurt the king and wishes to amend the rift between them. But that Stephen should go to be private with Waleran without calling Winchester to join them might easily arouse strong feelings other than loneliness in the bishop."

There was a long moment of silence. Melusine stared at me, but I do not think she saw *me*. She was remembering something else she had seen. Then she drew a deep breath, as one does when coming to terms with some unpleasant thought, and she saw me again, grimaced, and said, "I see that I spoke at just the wrong time, but I wonder what Winchester thought I was hinting at? And why was he so excited about your carrying messages to the Scots?"

I told her about Salisbury's suggestion that Stephen press King David for a treaty but did not say why. It seemed unwise to discuss the probability of future rebellions with the daughter of a rebel. "I suppose," I ended, "that Winchester hoped the king had changed his mind and decided to send a proposal. I am a Knight of the Body and would be considered a confidential servant; on the other hand, I am no great lord and could arrive at the Scots court and see King David privately, so if the idea of a treaty were refused, the matter might remain secret. It would have been a good plan, something old King Henry might have done, but Stephen is not subtle."

"Do you wish for a treaty?" Melusine asked.

"Yes." I shrugged. "But my reasons are selfish. Northumbria is my home, and it is Northumbria that is first ravaged in any war with the Scots. I am not sure that the bishops were right."

Then I fell silent because those last words were more a tribute to my loyalty to Stephen than to reason. I had none of the king's easy optimism. I could not believe that all rebellion had been quashed; neither could I believe that Robert of Gloucester would delay much longer in coming to England. Of course, if Queen Maud's ships took him prisoner or drowned him in the narrow sea, all might be well; however, if he escaped and found a landing place in England, his vassals would fly to arms again and there would be much less reason for David to accept reasonable terms of treaty.

"This is a lovely day for travel," Melusine said lightly, after riding beside me in silence for a time. "When we see a pleasant place, we can stop to eat. I have food and a little wine in the saddlebags."

"Again, bless you," I exclaimed. "I had completely forgot that the saddlebags on Barbe carry much less palatable stuff. Parchments and wax are poor stuff for filling a belly, however good these may be for the spirit."

I laughed, but I was most sincerely grateful to Melusine for so quickly leaving a subject that must have been of deep interest to her. A firm treaty with David would mean—or, at least, should mean—no support or encouragement for rebels in Cumbria, and that might make it easier to recover her land there. Yet Melusine had put aside her questions as soon as she saw the subject made me uncomfortable. I glanced at her, but her eyes were bright and her lips curved in amusement at my remark about parchment and wax. She was a very pleasant companion; I realized with a sense of surprise that for me Melusine was as easy to be with as Audris. Once more I reminded myself that Maud had been right about how extraordinarily clever Melusine was; and she might be right about her intention of ensorcelling me into an obedient slave. I almost wished, as she made some counter-jest about the food, that she would whine and complain or pick a quarrel.

To my dismay, I found myself liking my wife better and better with every day's travel—and that owed nothing at all to my physical desire for her. Except on one night I suffered no temptation, and on that night I was so tired that Sir Jehan could hardly lift his head and was easily discouraged. For the first four nights, we lodged in the hostels of either abbeys or convents, and both holy houses separated even married male and female travelers, lest they be desecrated by carnal congress, I suppose. The fifth day was wet, not a downpour, but a constant drizzle that annoyed without soaking. We had the choice of stopping too early to lodge in York and getting out of the wet or riding on to Ripon, which I thought we could reach before dark.

I offered the choice to Melusine, who said at once she wished to ride forward despite the rain. She seemed so eager to leave York, where we could have found comfortable lodgings, that I wondered whether she did not wish to stay near Archbishop Thurstan, who had created the army that defeated King David. Later, when it was growing really dark and I realized we had missed the side lane to

Ripon, I wondered if Melusine had distracted me apurpose by her lively conversation from watching for it because she hoped to reach Richmond. That was one of the keeps from which she had tried to escape and it was possible she had friends there. But when that thought came into my mind and I said we should make camp, Melusine displayed no reluctance to stop. And she was so cheerful as we made the best of cold, damp food and huddled together under damp blankets that I blamed myself for imagining she had any evil intent.

Indeed, I began to believe she had spoken the truth when she told me she did not wish to escape, that to run to her people could only do them harm. Certainly she made no attempt to escape, then or earlier when I gave her freedom—although not so much as she thought she had—to buy in the markets of towns we passed. Nor did she go from me that night, which she could have done for I slept very deeply. That worried me too. I should not have slept so soundly. No matter how tired I have been from march or battle, when there was reason to be watchful I have rested lightly, ready to wake at a twitch or a whisper. To let myself sleep like the dead meant that deep inside I trusted Melusine. Yet I *knew* it was wrong to trust her.

In the morning, she was no less cheerful—making nothing of relieving her bladder and bowels behind a thin screen of brush and casting about until she found a wild apple tree from which she brought back a skirt full of fruit to add to the even damper bread and cheese that remained. Apples were also offered to Vinaigre and to Barbe, after she asked if he were allowed to have them. So much sweetness and light did nothing to ease my mind. I was sure any other woman in the world would have been hissing and spitting.

As she helped me squeeze out as much wet as we could from the two sodden blankets we had hung from the limb of a tree to keep off the rain, my unease made me question her, disguising my purpose in flattery of her hardiness to discomfort. After looking at me in what seemed like honest amazement, she laughed most heartily at the notion that she would be deterred from doing anything by "a little mist in the air."

"When we come to Ulle," she said, still laughing, "you will see what rain and wind are."

But then the laughter caught in her throat and she looked stricken and turned away. It was not fear or horror this time though. Something to do with rain and wind in Ulle had reminded her of an unpleasant idea? experience?

We stayed that night at Durham, and the next day came to Jernaeve early in the afternoon. I do not remember much beyond the warmth of our greeting because after that I was told of Sir Oliver's death. I had not known how much I loved him until I learned he was gone forever. I do not think I had ever suffered such grief and such regret. In the past, after the battle of Bourg Thérould, I had wept bitterly for the loss of my boyhood, but that was nothing compared with the scorching of my soul when I realized I could never tell Sir Oliver that I understood what he had done for me, that I had never touched him or kissed him in love in all the years he had cared for me. Only then did I understand that he could have cast me out naked and that instead he had given me a father's care, provided for me as a loving parent would provide for a younger son.

It was worse for me because I could not speak of my grief to Audris or to Hugh. Hugh was still weak from a fever that had come from many small wounds and nearly killed him. And what I saw in his face when Audris told me of her uncle's death reminded me that he feared daily to hear the same news about his foster father, Archbishop Thurstan, who was an old man and very weak. To speak to Hugh of grief and regrets over the death of the man who had been, though I had never recognized it until too late, the only father I had, would come too close to his own fears and be cruel in his weakened state.

And Audris was already suffering too much for me to add the weight of my sorrow to hers. When she told me, her voice choked with sobs and she wept with a racking bitterness I had never before heard from that happy soul. Later, I learned that seeing me had unloosed the sorrow that she had not permitted herself to feel earlier—at first, because immediately after her uncle's death she needed to show herself confident to enhearten the men in Jernaeve to withstand the Scots, and after the Scots had fled all of her mind and will had been given to nursing Hugh, who had come to break the siege of Jernaeve with fresh wounds received in the Battle of the Standard.

I comforted her as well as I could when each word she said was a twist of the knife in my own heart. My eyes burned with tears I would not let her see when she sobbed of her ingratitude, her failure to show her love, her cruelty to Sir Oliver in running away to Hugh. Yet compared with Audris, I was a monster. She had been a joy to Sir Oliver just for her elfin ways and had, in the end, kissed him and teased him and displayed her love even if she did not speak often of it. She had not gone to Hugh to hurt her uncle but to save him the hurt of losing Jernaeve. And I—even in my own heart—I had not appreciated Sir Oliver's kindness to me. I had *blamed* him for "keeping me back," and later resented being sent away even though I *wanted* to go.

At last I diverted Audris by telling her that I must leave the next day. I could have taken some days of rest, but I could not bear to stay in Jernaeve until I had grown a little accustomed to my loss. Much as I loved Hugh, a rage rose in me when I saw him sit in Sir Oliver's great chair. In crying out against the briefness of my visit, Audris's self-blame was quenched, and I made her happy again by telling her that I would leave Melusine with her as a guarantee of my return. She lit with joy; however deep Audris's grief, it did not cloud her spirit for long. I know most of the joy was for the assurance that I would return, but some was for Melusine's company. I had seen the approval in Audris's face when I brought Melusine to her and they had almost at once laughed together, I do not remember about what but it was easy, happy laughter that promised a true bond between them.

Somehow I survived the evening meal and a few hours more, for it was important that Hugh know all I could tell him about the court and the outlook for King Stephen's future. I held back nothing, not even my doubts of the king's fixity of purpose—which Hugh knew because he had been at Exeter—or the doubtful wisdom of rejecting Winchester and Ypres in favor of Meulan. There were things I could say in words to Hugh's face that I would never dare tell a scribe to write and might even hesitate to write myself, lest the letter fall into other hands. But when I had passed the essential news, I could bear no more. All the time I had been talking, I was holding back tears because I would never bring such news to Sir Oliver again.

It was fortunate that Hugh was still not strong, and Audris thought it was my consideration for him when I said I was tired and would like to go to bed because I needed to make an early start in the morning. She might also have thought I was eager to lie with Melusine—or used that to silence Hugh when he wanted to draw out the talk—because she made crude and obvious jests as she showed us to the chamber Lady Eadyth had made ready. Audris may have the pale, transparent looks of an angel, but as I have always known, there is nothing else angelic about her.

To save Melusine the need for explanations that might turn Audris against her when I was away, I roused myself to respond to the jests as if all were as usual for wedded folk between Melusine and myself. The effort distracted me from realizing that Audris had led us into the north tower chamber, Sir Oliver's and Lady Eadyth's old place. Before I could protest, Audris assured me that she had not put Lady Eadyth out, that her aunt had preferred to move to a wall chamber. Thus the north tower had become the best place to put guests. It had had several occupants already—Hugh's great-uncle, Ralph Ruthsson, and Walter Espec, who had come for two days to see for himself how Hugh was so he could carry the news to Archbishop Thurstan, who was praying himself sick.

To my surprise, being in that chamber did not trouble me—and I realized that was probably the only place in all Jernaeve that I did not associate with Sir Oliver. I do not think I had ever been there in my life, certainly not in my father's time and not later because a bedchamber is much more a woman's than a man's. Sir Oliver came into the bedchamber only to sleep or get children, both acts that were none of my business. He truly lived in the hall, in the armory, in the stables, and that life I had shared with him; it was that life I mourned, that life I could not bear to see others, even others dearly loved, usurp.

Then Melusine laid a hand gently on my arm; I turned and saw tears in her eyes, and I understood what she had felt when I told her I would take her to Ulle.

"I know now," I said. "I will not make you go to Ulle. I will not sit in your father's chair, as Hugh sits in Sir Oliver's."

And she put her arms around my neck and laid her head on my shoulder. "Hush," she murmured, "you are too hurt to think now. Let me help you undress."

When we lay together in the dark—it was cool enough so far north to close the bedcurtains against the small light of the night candle—she said softly, "Time heals, at least a little."

"It cannot heal me." My voice cracked, but I had to confess to someone. "He was all the father I ever had—only out of the goodness of his heart. I had no claim on him. And I never thanked him, never, not once."

She slid an arm under my neck and drew me to her. "One does not thank those one loves. They understand without."

Then I wept, and she wept too, and the pain in my chest and throat grew a little easier so that I began to drift toward sleep. It was not until I woke in the morning and looked down at her and saw the stain of dried tears on her cheeks that I remembered my promise to the queen.

CHAPTER 14

Melusine

NEVER DID a journey begin so ill for me and turn to so great a pleasure. Once Bruno had explained that we were not fleeing for our lives and I had got over wishing to kick him for frightening me out of my wits—I had a little satisfaction in that Vinaigre had nipped him already—I was like a prisoner set free. If Bruno had been married to me to be my gaoler—as he had admitted—he was the strangest gaoler ever set as guard.

A gaoler wishes his prisoner helpless physically and beaten in spirit. Bruno did nothing to curtail my liberty and seemed to delight in making me happy. He did not take back the purse he had given me to pay for cart and guards; he let me wander through the markets in the towns we passed and buy food to replace what we ate on the road; he urged me to buy for myself such small items as caught my eye—a pincushion with pins, which had somehow been left out of my sewing things, a net for my hair because mine had caught on a twig and been torn; from his own purse he paid for a veil that I admired because I shook my head and said I had veils enough when he bade me buy it.

Most important of all, he did not try to keep me in ignorance, which is very strange for a gaoler, who should hope that ignorance will make his prisoner more helpless. Several times I had the odd thought that papa, who loved me, was more eager to keep me in his power than this man, who had said it was his purpose to control me. Bruno answered any question I asked. I knew that sometimes he held back something from me, but that was because he did not trust me—which I did not like, but it was reasonable enough. He did not demean me by saying that he would protect me and I need not worry my beautiful head about wars and politics.

To me it seemed sensible to explain. After all, Bruno knew we would have to return to court and I was less likely to say the wrong thing to the wrong person if I knew what was going on. What was remarkable was that Bruno apparently agreed that explanation was safe and sensible. Most other men would only have shouted at me, or perhaps beaten me, for what would have been a serious mistake in blabbing all to Winchester and ordered me to keep my mouth shut in the future—regardless of the fact that it is impossible for a lesser lady to keep her mouth shut when she is bidden to speak by some higher noble.

All this kept me so interested that I hardly noticed the miles march by. Not that I would have complained no matter what pace Bruno set. He was so good to me, more considerate than was at all necessary—imagine asking if I wanted to break our journey just because of a little drizzle; I had ridden with papa in downpours and raging storms if he decided he wished to be at some particular place. Papa might have worried about my being wet and chilled, but he never asked *me* if I minded.

That night Bruno apologized to me for missing the turnoff to Ripon as he hung blankets to keep off the wet and said not a word of blame—yet it was my fault we missed the road as much as his. And, seeing me eye the tiny shelter with doubt—I doubted it would keep us dry, not the small size that would push us into each others arms—he promised again that he would not force me when he wrapped me and himself together for warmth. I almost wished he had. I often wished he would be harsh and cruel now that we were alone and he need put on no face for others. I was coming to *like* him too much—quite aside from the craving of my body for his.

By the last two days of our journey, I felt in so great danger of my affection being fixed on this man as well as my lust that I could not ride long enough or fast enough to end our being alone together. I am afraid that my eagerness to come to Jernaeve, where I knew there would be others, made Bruno somewhat suspicious. He asked for no explanation however, and I offered none, but I sighed with relief when we came to the top of a rise and Bruno pulled Barbe to a halt and pointed a little northwest.

"Jernaeve," he said.

Familiarity must have made clear to him what was little more than a distant cliff face above a sparkling river to me. Or a different kind of familiarity blinded me, for God knows Cumbria has more than its share of high cliffs bulging over rivers and lakes and no one would bother to build a fortress there. We build in the valleys, close to the little land we have that is suitable for crops.

Even as we came closer I could see only stone, no sign of palisade or path or hall. It was only when we came right up to the bank of the river that I realized not all of the cliff was natural. Involuntarily I pulled Vinaigre to a halt and sat staring upward, suddenly aware of the two mighty towers and the wall of dressed stone that must have added thirty feet to the height. Now I understood better what Bruno had been telling me of the power and importance of Jernaeve, sitting astride one road that ran from Scotland to England and only a little more than one league from another, more important, highway. I did not like that threatening fist of rock crowned by that mighty bastion.

"Who built it?" I breathed.

"The first Fermain, I suppose," Bruno replied, but without much interest.

To him Jernaeve was a natural thing, a place he had always known. It did not look to him as it did to me, a lair for giants created by sorcerous arts. Bruno had smiled when he glanced up, a fond affectionate smile, such as one gives an old friend. There was no awe in his face, only a great eagerness—not for the place itself, I guessed, but for what was within.

Until that moment I had given no thought at all during our journey to those who held Jernaeve. I knew Northumbria was more fertile and less mountainous than my own Cumbria, but I also knew it was harsh and desolate compared with the south of England. Thus, I had assumed the people of Jernaeve were much like those I knew at home. Now I recalled the way Bruno had spoken of introducing me to those who had been kind to him and cared for him, not claiming them as family, and I remembered my shame and anger for his lack of pride in desiring to display his new status as the husband of a gentlewoman. I blushed for him, but it was too late to speak. He was already easing Barbe down into a deep and dangerous ford.

It was fortunate that Vinaigre was accustomed to our own rushing streams and sure of foot. We emerged unscathed only wet to the thighs, and I was furious that Bruno rode straight to the gate. I did not wish to be presented to these proud people looking like a beggar maid, stained and muddied. I had a fine gown in my blanket roll. I could have changed in the shelter of the lower wall. But I could not hold on to anger, for awe overmastered me again when we were admitted.

War had taken a toll of the lower grounds. Buildings had been burnt and were being repaired and restored, but I had little time to look about. The gate guard summoned his captain, and that man bowed as he bid Bruno welcome and said we might go up to the keep. I almost forgot my rage and shame in marveling as the horses climbed that road, winding back and forth to the upper gates. The upper bailey was untouched; I was not surprised that this keep had not been taken. Cattle lowed in the pens, dogs barked in the kennels, the sound of hammer on iron came faintly from a smithy I could not see. Before I could place any sound, Bruno was off Barbe, handing his rein to a groom who came running from the stable to our left, and he had turned to lift me down. I was barely on my feet when a small form flew across the bailey and flung itself on Bruno with such force that he staggered backward.

"Bruno! Brother! Dearling!"

The voice was high and sweet. I thought her a girl child before I turned to look, but even from the back the laced bliaut showed her to be a full-formed woman. She hung on Bruno's neck and kissed his cheeks and his lips, then flung back her head to see his face. He crushed her to him, released her, hugged her again, murmuring, "Audris. Audris. I knew you would be safe." And as he looked into her face, for the first time there was utter content in his. That deep hunger I had first seen when he burst in the door of the hall at Ulle and underlay every other expression was gone.

Wonder was what I felt at first. I had assumed that a whore's bastard would hunger for riches or for power and that no gain of either or both would ever satisfy him, for what is lost at birth can never be fulfilled. But I had been wrong, as far wrong as I could be. What Bruno starved for was love, to be cared for and caring.

When the meaning of that revelation burst on me, I was frozen in place with fear. Perhaps I had been more terrified when the ram burst in the door of Ulle's hall or when I first woke from my long madness and found Bruno mounted and thrusting into me, but that fear was for my body and this was for my everlasting soul. I saw how this man could be bent and broken, made into a puppet to do my will. I need not murder his body to get revenge; I could destroy his soul instead.

Perhaps if the embrace Bruno and his sister were sharing had lasted another moment, jealousy would have been added to the ferment inside me. But I had barely recovered from the shock my revelation had brought when Bruno turned Audris so she saw me.

"Here is the surprise I promised you, dearling," he said. "This is Melusine, my wife."

"Oh, how beautiful she is! How lucky you are, Bruno!" Audris exclaimed, and flew to me.

I say flew because I know no other way to describe Audris's movement. It was so quick and so light that her feet hardly seemed to touch the ground. When she was still, as she was in the next moment, having taken my hands to look smiling into my face, she was a tiny creature, not at all beautiful because she was so blond that she seemed altogether faded. Yet there was something about her that called aloud to my heart—was it that her eyes, so

pale as to be colorless, sparkled so brightly, that the barely
tinted lips curved up at the corners as if laughter always
lived in her, or simply the overflowing warmth and natural
joy of her greeting to Bruno.

Certainly that last must have had a large part in my
response because, as I pressed her hands in mine, I offered
no conventional greeting but asked, "Why do you call
Bruno brother? He speaks of you always as Lady Audris."

"Bruno is an idiot!" she exclaimed, glancing over her
shoulder with a smile that could have melted the ice cap on
a mountain in winter. "He is always mumbling and mowing about his unworthy mother. Who cares a fig for his
mother? I cannot even remember her, she died so long
ago. He is my father's son, my brother, who cared for me
every day of my life—"

"Your father did not recognize me, Audris—"

She let go of me and silenced him with a kiss, crying,
"Hush! I will hear no more of it, and if you *once* call me
lady, I will—I will pour honey in your hair!"

We all three burst out laughing, but even as I laughed
my eyes filled with tears. The threat was so clear an echo
of a childhood spent together in perfect security that it not
only assured me that Audris had told me the truth about
the value she set on Bruno but also brought back to me my
squabbles with my younger brothers. Audris had turned
back to me, I suppose with an invitation to come within on
her lips, but instead she took my hand again and whispered, "Oh, Melusine, I have hurt you."

"No, no," I stammered, "not you. Memories, only
memories."

And Bruno was beside me, his arm around my waist.
"She has much to grieve for," he said softly to Audris.
"And it cannot be amended."

"Then I will overlay the hurt a little with a sweet
poultice—I will show you my son," Audris said, glanced
at Bruno, and tightened the grip of her small warm hand
on mine. "But not at once," she went on, smiling. "My
aunt says I am a featherhead—" Her voice checked and
her eyes widened. "Oh bless me, I will be scolded again. I
never stayed to listen to the end of the guard's tale and
learn that Bruno had brought another guest. As soon as I

heard his name, I went running—" She sighed and shrugged.
"Well, it will not be the first time."

Bruno laughed. "Nor the last neither, if I know you.
Poor Lady Eadyth, how hard she tried to teach you the
skills and duties of a lady."

"I had rather climb for hawks or weave," Audris retorted. "What good would come of my knowing Lady
Eadyth's skills? I could never practice them without taking
from her a great pride and pleasure. Do not be so silly,
Bruno. Now come within, you are both all wet. My aunt
will have dry clothes for you, and bath water heating, and
all measure of guestly greeting."

My pain had disappeared completely as I listened to this
exchange. I suppose that was its purpose but I never
thought of that. "You climb for hawks?" I gasped.

Bruno groaned and Audris laughed this time. "He taught
me when we were children and he is still blaming himself
for it, but Jernaeve has the most and the finest hawks in
any shire in the land. Come, love," she soothed, looking
around me at Bruno. "There is no danger for me any
more. Hugh goes with me and I tie a rope to me so I
cannot fall."

"Hugh goes with you?" Bruno repeated in a stunned
voice, and I looked with great admiration on that little lady
who had so bewitched her husband that he assisted her in
doing what would bring on a fit in most husbands.

"Not right now," she said as we entered the forebuilding,
broke our grip on each other, and began to climb the stair
to the hall entrance. "And do not begin to scold him about
it, for he agrees with you from the heart and is not a whit
more able to resist. Besides, he is still weak from his
sickness after the battle."

"Sickness!" Bruno exclaimed, stopping on the stair.
"But the priest said he had not been hurt—"

"Go up," Audris urged. "He is better now, so there is
no sense in worrying."

I had no time then to marvel at the great hall, which was
as large as that of Richmond—and might have been even
stronger—because near the door was waiting the ugliest
man I had ever seen in my life. His hair was so red that it
glowed, even in the dim light of the hall; his eyes were so

far apart that I wondered if he saw two images; his nose was an eagle's beak; his long, narrow chin jutted too far forward—and then he smiled, and I forgot everything except that his eyes were a beautiful, luminous blue and he was welcoming me with a rare warmth.

The welcome, of course, was not for me at all; it was for Bruno, whom he clasped in his arms and kissed. And Bruno returned the embrace, but gingerly, as if he feared to do hurt by too tight a grip. Then he pushed away and scanned Hugh's face anxiously—for I realized this must be Hugh Licorne, Audris's husband—and urged him back toward the great hearth, where a fire burned low, and benches were set.

I have always been very partial to red-headed men, finding them more attractive no matter what their features than dark men like Bruno. However, I must admit that Hugh was an exception. Seeing him side by side with Bruno made me aware that, dark or light, my husband was a handsome man. I glanced sidelong at Audris, wondering how she had felt about Hugh's face when she first saw it, but the silly question slipped from my mind. All laughter had fled from her eyes and their brilliance was shadowed by remembered pain and fear.

In the next moment it was gone and she had called out merrily to halt Bruno's questions about what had befallen his friend. "One moment only," she cried, laughing. "I know there can be no longer stay before you plunge into a blow by blow explanation of the battle, but Hugh *must* greet Melusine. This is Bruno's wife, Hugh."

Two long strides brought Hugh back, and he bowed over my lifted hand and kissed it. "This is the most wonderful surprise!" he exclaimed. "I wondered what on earth Bruno could have meant, saying he had been knighted and was bringing us a surprise. Knowing Bruno—he has the strongest penchant for picking up ugly creatures and nurturing them; after all, he bade Audris love me—I had not expected anything so beautiful."

"That is quite enough," Audris put in, grinning. "I know I am half a loaf compared with Melusine—"

"Ah," Hugh murmured, running his eyes over her so deliberately that they might have been hands and I felt myself blushing, "but it is the half I like best, so I will keep it, never fear, and keep it warm too so it never goes stale."

"Is it not beautiful," Audris said, turning to me, "to have so dedicated a lecher for a husband. I never have the slightest fear that he will take another woman. At night I keep him hard at work, and in the daytime he is far too tired to manage more than his duties in the keep."

"In the name of God, Audris," Bruno protested, "Melusine is not yet accustomed to your humors. Let her test the water a little at a time. Do not throw her into the river all at once."

"But that is the best way," Audris countered. "Did you not take me beyond my depth to teach me to swim?"

"Not unless I was there to hold you up," Bruno said, innocently and unwisely, forgetting the original subject.

Audris widened her eyes. "I have no objection to you holding up Melusine. Often it is better so." She giggled. "But then I think Hugh has the better part. Half a loaf is lighter."

"Audris!" Bruno roared.

My face must have been redder than uncooked beef, but I could not help a little choke of laughter as Audris raised her eyes to heaven and sighed. What she would have said next I cannot guess, because just then a tall woman came toward us, her eyes fixed on me with a slight frown.

"Aunt," Audris said, smiling brilliantly, "this is Lady Melusine, Bruno's wife. She is the surprise he wrote about in his letter. Is it not wonderful?"

"I am very happy to meet you, Lady Melusine," Eadyth responded. The frown smoothed away, and I had an instant to wonder whether she had thought Bruno had brought his lemman with him before she added, "Audris, you take Lady Melusine into my chamber, where I told the servants to bring the bath because the fire was already lit there. Perhaps one of my gowns will fit—"

"I have dry and more . . . suitable clothing in my saddle roll," I suggested.

"So much the better," Eadyth said, nodding. "You will be more comfortable in your own clothes. I will have everything brought to the chamber for you, and send a maid, and have more water heated, and perhaps something extra prepared for the evening meal—''

''Never mind the maid, aunt,'' Audris interrupted. ''I will help Melusine bathe.''

''Help or hinder?'' Eadyth asked tartly. ''Remember that Bruno is also wet and cold—''

''Yes, aunt, we will be quick,'' Audris promised, leading me away.

''You are very patient,'' I said. ''Does it not tease you that she treats you like a child—and a silly one at that?''

Audris's twinkling eyes glanced up at me and her lips curled in a mischievous grin. ''I am accustomed,'' she said. ''And it suits me in many ways. She lifts the whole burden of woman's work in Jernaeve from my shoulders, and our paths do not often cross. When I am not in my own chamber weaving, I work in the garden or ride out into the hills—that is, I used to do so. Of late, I have been too busy with Hugh and Eric—oh, Eric is my son, a little more than three months old, and Hugh—'' The shadow I had seen earlier again darkened her eyes as she said, ''—Hugh nearly died and I was busy nursing him.'' Then the shadow was gone and she smiled anew, adding, ''But it comes to the same thing. Aunt Eadyth cares for the keep and I am free to care for what is important to me.''

Her moods were like quicksilver and she spoke lightly of her aunt, but I remembered what she had said in the bailey about taking from Eadyth her pride and her pleasure in caring for Jernaeve. My heart warmed to Audris as I considered how clever she was and how kind. Nor did she suffer from leaving matters in her aunt's hands, I thought, considering the order and decency in the hall we had just quitted. And Eadyth did not stint herself either, I decided, as we entered the small chamber carved out of the thick wall of the keep. It was lit by tapers—the room had no smell of torch smoke so the tapers were not only for a guest—and had a small fireplace, with a slit in the stone wall above to draw out the smoke, not that there was much, for the wood that was burning was well dried. There was a cot, narrow but with a well-plumped mattress on the wall facing me and two large chests along the wall to my right. A chair—a real chair with back and arms—

had been pushed aside to make room for the oval wooden tub.

I do not remember exactly what we talked about, while the servingmen filled the tub. Then Audris helped me unlace my riding dress, after which she ran out and came back with a handful of herbs to cast into the bath water just as I rid myself of my undergarments. From that we came to talk of wild herbs, and I found myself telling her about my life in Ulle. I stopped midway, catching my breath over a stab of grief, and she cupped my face with her hands but did not ask a question or offer a word of sympathy. It was exactly the right thing, for between weariness and the many shocks and surprises coming to Jernaeve had brought, all the horrors of my life since Ulle was taken would have poured out of me. I could not have endured that in my present state. I think I would have begun to scream or slipped back into madness.

How Audris knew, I cannot guess, but she said, "Oh, herbs. I had better make a confession to you and explain, since I hope you will stay with us for a time. There are those who call me witch—but I am not, I swear it." And went on to tell me about her knowledge of medicines and then about her weaving certain pictures that seemed to tell the future.

I did not make any direct answer, other than to say I did not hold to the common fears on such subjects. But I thought to myself, for I felt close to Audris already, that it seemed my fate to love those who, like Mildred, were looked upon askance by others.

Although I would have liked to soak until the water grew cool, I did not linger in the bath, remembering that Bruno would need to wash also and that it would soon be time for the evening meal. As soon as a maidservant brought in my clean clothes, I dried myself and dressed and we went out into the hall again. Bruno and Hugh were still talking about the Scottish invasion, but when we drew close, Bruno stopped mid-question and looked up and around as if he had suddenly become aware of how much time had passed and missed something.

"Where is Sir Oliver?" he asked.

There was a dead, breath-held silence, and then Audris

said in a trembling voice, "He is dead, Bruno. He was wounded in defending the lower wall. I tried to save him." Her voice shook more and more, tears began to flow, and she wailed between sobs, "I did! I did! I tried to save him!"

Hugh had started to rise, but Bruno had already gathered Audris into his arms, by habit patting her and soothing her while his eyes sought Hugh's and he repeated in a voice totally without emphasis or inflection, "Dead? Sir Oliver is dead?"

Hugh opened his mouth, perhaps to explain, but Audris's voice rose in that thin, pitiful wail. "I did try to save him. Why could I not save *him,* when I healed so many others?"

"Of course you tried, dearling," Bruno said. "You loved him. He knew. All knew how you loved him."

"Did he know, Bruno?" Audris pleaded, lifting her face to his. "Did he know? I never told him, or only once or twice, and I went away to Hugh and hurt him so much—so much. He thought . . . he said . . . I did not trust him."

Bruno had lowered his eyes to his sister's face, but I do not think he saw her—for the first and only time in his life. "But you came back. You trusted your life and your son's to him in the time of greatest danger. He was angry, no doubt, but I am sure all was well between you before the battle. He never could resist you, Audris. You had a smile and a fond word. He knew you loved him."

There was something terribly wrong with Bruno. It was not only that he was shocked and surprised to hear of Sir Oliver's death. Something deep inside had been broken. He was saying all the right things, but he might have been a body raised from the dead and made to talk for all the life that was in him. We all felt it: Hugh looked agonized and was wringing his big hands helplessly. Audris was fighting a battle with her grief and hysteria, and though I had lost much, much more than she, still I was sorry for her. It must be dreadful indeed to have a loved one die under one's own ministering hands and wonder forever if you had done too much or not enough.

I too had reacted to Bruno's state; instinctively, I came forward and put a hand on his arm. I do not know if he noticed—he did not turn or glance at me—but he began to speak again, shaking Audris very gently. "Love, love, do not weep any more. You know that if Sir Oliver could have chosen the death he desired it would have been to die defending Jernaeve. Now, love, I must leave early tomorrow to carry the king's messages. Will you weep away the few hours I have to spend with you?"

Gasps of protest broke Audris's sobs, and in a little while smiles replaced the gasps when Bruno admitted that he had only spoken about tomorrow itself and the week or so it would take him to find the recipients and deliver the king's messages. He would leave me in Jernaeve, if I were willing and welcome—upon which Audris flew to me and embraced me and begged me to stay, promising she would not be so dismal another time and offering so many, and so ridiculous, inducements, that an anchorite would have agreed with laughter.

While Audris was busy convincing me to stay, Hugh drew Bruno down on the bench beside him again and asked, "What messages do you bear, and to whom—unless it is a secret matter?" Hugh looked worried, and Bruno shook his head and began to explain about Stephen's thanks to those who had withstood the Scots and the secondary purpose under the honor offered Aumale.

Audris sat beside me, casting only one brief, worried glance toward Bruno. She seemed contented that he was talking easily to Hugh, and I felt surprised that one so sensitive to my moods and so loving to her brother should not notice that all was not well with him. Later, I realized that she was so accustomed to Bruno being the strong one who protected her that she had believed his distress was over the violence of her grief. Her will and attention were all to hide any further expression of it.

Also, Audris did not seem in the least interested in overhearing what the men said. Mostly to keep the subject away from her uncle and Bruno's reaction to the news of his death—Bruno's face was still without any expression, although he was telling Hugh about the elevation to the peerage of many of Waleran de Meulan's relatives—I asked whether her husband preferred that women did not listen or speak on political matters. Audris smiled and shook her head.

"I am sure Hugh would not care, but why should I wish it?" she remarked easily. "Hugh tells me what is important for me to know. But if you like we can join the men and listen. Are you interested in affairs of state?"

"I have no choice," I replied dryly. "But I have no need to listen; Bruno has already told me about the messages. I—" I hesitated, on the verge of pouring out the whole tale of my lost lands, my lost family. But this was not the time, not while we were all balanced on a knife edge of grief. Instead, I went on, "I am one of the queen's ladies. At court if I say the wrong word or smile at the wrong person at the wrong time I could bring great trouble upon myself and Bruno."

Audris shuddered. "That life is not for me. What is in my head spills out of my mouth. Do you wish to go back to court? You could stay here, safe with us."

"I wish I could," I sighed, "but Bruno is tied to the king, and—and I am suspected of being a rebel. If I did not return, the queen might blame Bruno for letting me escape her watchful eye."

"Are you a rebel?"

Audris's question held only a touch of surprise and mild interest, and when I shook my head and said that for all I cared a pox could take all three—King Stephen, King David, and Empress Matilda—she nodded but then shuddered again and said, "If only there would be no war, no more war, I would not care if an ape ruled."

Before I could agree, Lady Eadyth appeared and hustled Bruno away, and we talked of small, light matters until he came from her chamber in dry clothes. Then we had our evening meal. Another lady joined us, introduced as Hugh's Aunt Marie. She was very quiet, looking always at Hugh if she ventured any remark, though he smiled at her each time without fail. The talk was of local matters, the fear of famine owing to the ravaging of the Scots and what could or should be done to ease it and when, if ever, recompense could be expected for the outlay.

Then I went to Audris's chamber with her to see her babe. I was shocked by the ugliness of the maid who was caring for him and to learn that she was mute, but I soon saw the woman's devotion. And then I forgot her as Audris began to tell me of her childhood and Bruno's while she nursed Eric. The tale made clear to me the bond between her and Bruno and that there were things I must never confess—like my attempt to kill him—but there was nothing in what she said that explained how he had felt about Sir Oliver. I began to hope that I had misread Bruno, rather than Audris, and that only the shock of the news had turned him to stone. Only when we came down to join the men again, I knew at once that he felt even worse.

As soon as he saw me, Bruno broke off his talk with Hugh and reminded him that he wished to make an early start the next morning. He said also that I must be very tired and that he was tired too and wished to go to bed. I do not know why neither Audris nor Hugh seemed to see that Bruno only wished to escape. Perhaps they did understand and hoped to lighten his heart, but Hugh responded that an early bedtime was most suitable to his needs also— with such lascivious looks at his wife as made very clear what those needs were—and Audris began to make jests that brought blood to my face. There was fear mingled in with that blush—God help me, of desire, not shame—but Bruno did not betray my refusal to couple. He replied so cleverly that without saying yea or nay he made them believe all was well between us. The kindness, when I knew he was on the rack—and the suggestion, too—set off in me that warm trembling that I had learned to dread.

It died as swiftly as it had risen, as soon as the door closed and I raised my eyes to Bruno's face. I suppose, because of the jests, I had expected to see his face as it had been that night in Winchester when he first made me recognize my lust for him. Instead, I saw such desolation, such a depth of pain, that I reached for him. When I touched him, tears came into his eyes and he told me that he would not take me to Ulle and force me to watch another man sit in papa's chair.

I took him in my arms. I could not resist the need to comfort the agony that echoed mine—but I no longer felt that first piercing pain. I would hate seeing Stephen's warden in papa's place, but I could bear it, knowing it would not be forever. There was another thought, far more disturbing because it was *not* painful, that crept into my head as I soothed Bruno with meaningless words and helped him to undress and get into bed. Bruno in papa's chair?

Not painful? Was I so far gone in shame that I could be content to smile as Bruno, who might have killed my father and my brother, drank from papa's cup at papa's table? And then Bruno spoke again into the dark in a breaking voice of how Sir Oliver had been the only father he had ever known and how he had never given him one word of love or even thanks. My breath caught in sympathy for his suffering. That sorrow at least I had never needed to know, for all of us, except poor mama, took and gave freely words and gestures of love. I took Bruno in my arms again and wept for him. It was not treachery to papa and my brothers, I told myself. I was not giving way to love for their enemy. I was only making him love me. If I could fill his craving for love, there was nothing he would not do for me.

Bruno rode out the next morning, accompanied by five good men-at-arms who would give him dignity as well as be able to stand by him if they should meet any bands of Scots as he rode after Aumale. I was at once comforted by his having the men and made anxious by his need for them. Not that I cared if he were hurt or killed, I told myself, not at all, but God knew what second husband might be forced upon me; perhaps one that would not want to get Ulle from the king.

He was gone two weeks, and during that time the busy life of Jernaeve keep closed over and enveloped me. I was no guest, no stranger. Whore's son Bruno might be, but even to Lady Eadyth, who was the only one, I believe, who ever thought of him in those terms, he was part of Jernaeve, and I, who they assumed was part of him, must also be one with the place. When I could be useful, and all were busy in some measure in repairing the damage the Scots had done, my task was assigned without any question as to whether I would be willing. That was assumed, and it was most comfortable and comforting to me. I was at home, as I had been in Mildred's manor.

I realized soon that warm enfolding was owing to Audris's acceptance. Lady Eadyth went to and fro and gave orders concerning women's work, Hugh ordered and inspected those tasks men were wont to do, but the life of the keep flowed around and around one still center—Audris. When that had sunk deep into me, I grew cold at the thought that she might learn how I refused her brother, but I had underestimated Audris. I suppose I had shown some sign of my uneasiness, and on the third or fourth day—I remember it was pouring rain and I had naught to do—I was sitting in Audris's tower, watching her weave.

"I do not expect all to be smooth as oil between you and Bruno," Audris said suddenly. "I saw that it was not only shyness that made you blush when I teased you because Bruno wished to go early to bed. Have patience. You will find peace, and joy too, I think, in the fullness of time. I do not blame you for your doubts and angers. It was different for me and Hugh. We loved before we wed. That cannot have been true for you and Bruno."

"It could have been," I replied slowly, "but it was not." I recalled how it had actually happened, but I would speak no ill of Bruno to his sister. She would not believe me anyway. "I was with the queen some eight months, and part of that time Bruno was there too, with the king. We may have met. We may even have spoken to each other. If we did, I do not remember. One day I was told that the king had ordered we be married and we were."

"Bruno agreed to that?" Audris was clearly puzzled. "It is not like him."

I laughed. "I told you the queen believes me to be a rebel. I do not know why, but she seems to fear that I can do some harm. Bruno married me to protect the king. He believed it to be his duty."

"Ah, that sounds right for Bruno, but not flattering to you. Lovely as you are, I can see that you might hold a small grudge." Audris smiled. "But you, why did you agree?"

We were both at peace then, but the question, lightly asked and showing no awareness of my helplessness, set off a wave of bitterness in me. I told her—everything except how I had tried to kill her brother and my fear that he was the one who had taken my last two, my dearest, from me. Audris never said a word, nor did she ever show whether or not she believed I had been mad, but midway in my tale she left the loom and took her babe into her arms. And when I was done she gave the child to me, still without a word. He was so soft and warm. I had held Eric before, but not when I felt that blood should flow from my eyes instead of tears. I cannot describe the comfort and the terror I felt, for I was well aware how few babes lived to be men and women. Yet despite my fear of new loss and pain, a craving came into me for a child, a craving so strong that it pushed out all other feeling, even my grief.

It was then that I recalled that Bruno had said a child would be a strong reason for the king to grant Ulle to us, and I began to reconsider my refusal to couple with him. After all, what did it matter who the father was? I knew papa had not cared which of his sons sired the heir to Ulle nor on what woman the child was sired, so long as his grandchild would hold the lands. Well, my child would carry papa's blood as well as that of my brothers. Moreover, the more I considered the matter the more clear it became to me that I was not as young as most girls are when they marry so I could ill afford to wait much longer. Also, if the king granted Ulle to Bruno and Bruno died—I made myself think those three words despite my reluctance—would not the king disseisin me as he had done before? Me, yes; Bruno's child, no.

Such were the reasons that came and went in my head over the next ten days. The ideas did not come all together as they are written, but in bits and pieces, so perhaps I really did not see where they were leading . . . or would not let myself see. I am not sure about that. What I am sure about is the effect Audris's relationship to Hugh was having on me. By their manner and words to one another, they stripped away every ugly implication I had ever heard given to lust. Whether they tossed crude jests at each other or touched in tenderness or simply looked, the joy of his manhood and her womanhood was plain as the light of a torch in a small, dark room. They understood each other;

they shared all things large and small; but whether it was Audris telling Hugh of Eric's little ways or Hugh speaking to Audris of a necessary purchase of cattle, the red warmth of their passion underlit each word and gesture.

They were more open about the joy their bodies gave them than Mildred and Donald had been—at least, more open before me—but it was the same magic as I had seen in my own dear ones. I had desired to know it then—that was why I had never told papa that I did not wish to marry, although I knew he wanted me to say it—and I desired it again now. But now I need only reach out my hand and take what had been forbidden fruit before I had a husband. Yet if I found the magic and took it into my heart, was that not treachery to my dead? On the other hand, if I could not find the treasure with Bruno, that would free me from him completely. So, was it not reasonable to try that path of escape from my desire for him since I could find no other way?

If this reasoning does not seem at all reasonable, I must agree, but I was in a ferment that was not conducive to clear thinking. Each time Hugh cupped Audris's breast in his hand, mine swelled and tingled; his lips on her nape as she bent over Eric's cradle, caused a crawling up and down my spine. Other gestures made me fight to sit still without squirming. Fortunately, Audris and Hugh were so absorbed in each other that I believe they were totally unaware they were torturing me. Of course, I masked my response as well as I could, and Eadyth and Marie, if they noticed at all were either indifferent or repelled, but I barely restrained myself from dragging Bruno off to bed as soon as he rode in, and I did kiss him in greeting more warmly than was my habit.

His smile, startled and doubtful, presented me with a problem I had not considered in all my thinking. How was I to show Bruno I had changed my mind? I would choke if I tried to tell him in words. I could not! I would rather go celibate to my grave.

I am afraid that although I may have seemed to listen with interest to Bruno's report on Aumale's campaign and the reactions of the men to whom he had carried Stephen's thanks and rewards, I learned very little from what he said.

I remained in this quandary without the shadow of an idea all afternoon, appalled to discover that although I knew myriad ways to soothe quarrels among men, winkle secrets out of them, and induce them to agree to my notions of what was right in household and, sometimes, even political matters, I had not the faintest idea of how to lead a man into coupling with me. A few times I touched Bruno, stroking the back of his arm where Hugh and Audris would not see, but he pushed his leg against me impatiently, so I moved away. I suppose it was too soon to try to signal my willingness, but even later when I tried again in different ways, Bruno seemed too immersed in his political talk to be bothered with me—and the more I thought about how to get his attention, the greater my desire became.

It was only after the evening meal and after the two older ladies had withdrawn from where we still sat near the fire, for the evenings were growing chill as October advanced, that I realized the topic of conversation had changed. I was startled into attention by an explosion, half laughter and half exasperated expletive, from Hugh.

"No," he went on, "I mean yes, of course my Christian name is Hugh, but it is also the name of my family. My father was Kenorn of Heugh—a place not far from here. So Heugh and its manors are mine as well as Ruthsson and Trewick and some smaller farms. Well, Ruthsson is really my Uncle Ralph's, but he has neither the will nor the desire to manage the land and rule the people. I am embarrassed by riches, in land if not in anything else."

Bruno laughed. "A pleasant embarrassment."

The laugh was not forced and now that I had been dragged from my purely selfish concern, I recalled Bruno's misery when he left Jernaeve. It cannot have healed any more than my wounds were healed, but like mine his no longer bled unless they were touched. I realized too that Audris must have heard and remembered every word I said, even the few I expended on my first horror at the idea of seeing some stranger in my father's place. Unlike our first evening, Hugh sat with us on the benches. Sir Oliver's chair had been set aside on the dais, so there was nothing to remind Bruno every moment of his loss and he was at ease.

"Pleasant or not, it is an embarrassment," Hugh replied. "Ruthsson is not much of a problem. A really good bailiff to oversee the land is all that will be needed for a few years. Once the place begins to pay, I might go on with the work my grandfather started and build a real keep there, but that is for the future. Heugh is different. That is a strong place. Not like Jernaeve, but still stone built and as strong as Alnwick. There I need a man I can trust. Would you take it on, Bruno?"

I had almost drifted back to my private problem, but my attention was renewed by that last question.

"I?" Bruno was clearly distressed, thinking he had been asked to do a service by his friend. "Hugh, you know I cannot, at least not for longer than a month. I am now Knight of the Body to the king. I must return to my service before Christmas."

"I did not mean tomorrow," Hugh said. "I have a man there now who can defend the place, and it is close enough for me to ride over for a day or two to deal with the people on the land. But Pierre is a mercenary, and I do not want him to begin to think Heugh is his. Can you not tell Stephen that your sister's husband has offered you vassalage—"

"Vassalage!"

Bruno's eyes flew to me, and I knew at once that he was asking me whether I still feared to return to Ulle. Vassalage was a far different matter than holding a keep as castellan. A vassal held the land as his own and that land could be inherited by his children. If Bruno held Heugh as a vassal, we would be secure and free of dependency on the king and queen. But in the brief moment that our eyes locked, I saw Ulle nestled in the small valley carved out above the tarn; I saw Ullswater, dancing and sparkling in the sunshine, grey and sullen under a drift of rain, dark and deadly under a swathe of white mist.

"Ulle—" I whispered.

Bruno shook his head and looked from Hugh to Audris with such love that my throat ached. "So good you are to me, to rob your own child for my sake. I cannot take—"

"Nonsense!" Audris exclaimed. "Eric will have more than enough, and the others I hope will follow him also. Besides," she added, a touch of bitterness in her voice, "all that land seems to bring now is a need to defend it with blood."

"There is another reason also," Bruno said. "Did not Melusine tell you she was disseisined of lands in Cumbria? I have good hope of convincing the king to enfeoff me with those lands. What Stephen did was just, but *Melusine* was not at fault, and I will vouch for her future loyalty. What is more, the lands add little or nothing to the king's income, so I hope—"

"It is not impossible," Hugh agreed. "Old King Henry would never disgorge anything, particularly land swallowed for what he called treason." Hugh must have caught some flicker of movement that marked my unease, and he smiled at me. "I am passing no judgement, Melusine; what old Henry called treason might be anything from trying to overthrow the throne to sneezing at the wrong time, if you had something he wanted."

"But Stephen is different," Bruno pointed out. "He is generous at heart, and nothing pleases him as much as giving and making others happy."

Hugh sighed. "I know. He gave far too much in that last treaty with the Scots. Let us hope he does not give *more* away in this one, if one is proposed. Well, you must do what is best for you, Bruno, but remember the offer for you to be vassal at Heugh stands. Whenever you desire the place, you need only deliver to me . . . what is it? Oh yes, the token is three speckled chicken feathers tied to a poniard and an eel."

"Does the eel have to be fresh?" Bruno asked with spurious solemnity. "That might cause a problem. A pickled eel might be had at any time, but a fresh one—"

I thought that levity very wrong after Hugh's great generosity, and I pinched Bruno low on the back, where my hand would not be seen moving, to urge him to say one word of thanks at least.

Hugh jumped up and hit Bruno fondly in the head. "Go to bed!" he ordered. "I think you have pickled brains."

Bruno rose and took my hand with such alacrity that I

could only imagine some signal had passed between him and Hugh that I had not noticed. Surprise allowed my body to get up and follow my husband while my brain still sat on the bench wondering what had happened. It was still wondering when Bruno slammed the tower door shut with his heel and caught me into his arms and kissed me. In fact, I do not think my brain got off that bench and came up to join me until far too late. By then my body had been free for too long to be recaptured by sober thought.

CHAPTER 15

Bruno

I DID the king's business well enough, but it does not take much diplomacy to convince a man to accept thanks and a reward. That was fortunate because my mind was not undivided. In truth, I felt as if my head were full of separate parts: one part grieved over my stupidity and ingratitude to Sir Oliver; another rejoiced over Melusine's kindness to me; a third examined that joy with suspicion; a fourth tried to gather information on what was left of the Scots' resistance and whether Aumale was strong enough to wipe this out without the help of those from Yorkshire who had already left his force to attend their own affairs or were about to leave; and a last small fragment spoke to each man for whom I had a message of the king's pleasure in his strength and devotion and of the king's desire to see him at court and thank him in person.

As the number and importance of those to whom I must speak with diminished—naturally, I saw Aumale first, Espec next, and so on in order of precedence although it doubled or tripled the distance I had to ride—the first three concerns loomed larger and larger. In the beginning the injustice I had done Sir Oliver overshadowed all other thoughts, but each time that grief came into my mind I also recalled Melusine's tender sympathy. By the time my errands were done, the two hung in even balance, my reluctance to return to Jernaeve and face the piercing reminders of Sir Oliver just equal to my eagerness to see Melusine again.

The greeting I received overset that balance completely. After the hunt, Melusine had come to me with an outstretched hand and a warm smile, but in Jernaeve I found arms around my neck and a kiss that was a very distant cousin, indeed, to a kiss of peace. To my shame I must admit that any thought of Sir Oliver flew right out of my head. All that remained in it was a need to discover the meaning of that kiss. My earliest apprehension, that Melusine had somehow offended Audris—although how she could do that without hitting her with a stick or dropping Eric on his head I could not imagine—and made herself unwelcome and thus unhappy, was cast aside almost as it struck me. The laughter and comments showed Melusine to have earned love, making herself part of the family in Jernaeve.

There were then only two alternatives: Melusine's desire for me, or for a man in general, which I had seen partly wakened the night I returned from the hunt, had been again aroused—by my absence?—and she was so innocent and ignorant of men other than fathers and brothers that she did not herself understand the kiss she had bestowed on me. The other alternative, less pleasant, was that every move Melusine had made since our marriage had been planned, and she was a succubus straight out of hell.

The second alternative I dismissed—not completely, but enough so it would not influence how I intended to act. There was nothing I could do about the evil in her, if there was any, until she tried to use her power on me. So long as I was aware that evil might be intended, I could enjoy what was offered. It was much like using a strange whore in a large town. If you were not aware of the tricks that could be played, you might lose your purse and even your life to the girl or the men who owned her; however, with adequate precautions, she would work hard to provide you with pleasure.

Before the afternoon and evening had passed, I could cheerfully have murdered Melusine. She followed that kiss with more go and stop signals than the most practiced flirt among the queen's ladies had used to tempt me. One moment Melusine slid a hand down the back of my arm; the next, when I moved my thigh to touch hers, she moved sharply away from me. Then she would listen to me, frowning in thought while I spoke of the places the Scots still held as if she were measuring King David's chances to advance again. Only when I glanced at her to see her reaction to my words, I would notice her eyes had slid from my face to my lap. And yet there was no sly invitation in her eyes; she looked worried. I do not now remember everything, only that I was so bemused by Melusine's teasing that I did not understand when Hugh, out of the goodness of his heart and Audris's, offered me a true livelihood as vassal of Heugh.

First I thought he wanted me as castellan, and I was sorry I could not oblige him, but then he made it plain that he and Audris were prepared to rob their own children to provide for me. I hesitated only an instant, glancing at Melusine; I heard her whisper "Ulle," and could only hope she meant that she still wanted the lands. I could not steal from Hugh to provide for Melusine no matter how much she made me wish to protect her. If Melusine could not abide Ulle, we could rebuild or live on one of the lesser estates; if I could not get Ulle back and could not support her, she would have to live here in Jernaeve.

I had guessed right with regard to Melusine's desire for Ulle though, because she pressed herself against me when Hugh and I were talking of the possibility of regaining the lands. Hugh thought he had hurt her by mentioning her father's treason, but when I had spoken of it in the past she had only stared me down, so I think she wished to show she was pleased with my refusal of Heugh. But when I made a jest about the vassal's token to turn the subject, Melusine began to tease again and pinched me on the buttock.

Perhaps Hugh saw her hand move or I was not quick enough in hiding my expression, but he ordered us off to bed. At that moment I think I was more grateful to him for that than for the offer of Heugh. I admit I expected another shift to coldness, a protest that it was too early for bed or some resistance when I took her hand to lead her up, but she came at once, without a word, and in the time it took to cross the hall and climb the stair, I decided that I would bandy no more words or cautious gestures with her. As we entered the chamber, I saw some servant had lit tapers so we would not be in the dark, and I pushed the door closed with my foot, took her in my arms, and kissed her with all the passion pent up in me.

Since I had never before kissed an innocent woman, I had no idea what to expect—except that she might try to fight her way free of me. But Melusine did not resist at all. When I first put my mouth to hers, her eyes opened wide, and her arms hung limp; then her eyes closed and one hand stole up my arm to clutch my sleeve. A little later the other slid over my back and around my neck. Her lips were still, but as her eyes closed I could feel them grow fuller and a touch more moist. Her grip on me tightened too, so I took the chance of relaxing my hold with one arm and stroking her back, gradually moving my hand until the fingers were caressing one side of her breast. Her lips parted then, and I let my tongue, just the tip, slip between them.

Then I had a stroke of luck. Her bliaut was laced on the side where my hand touched her breast. It was not difficult to pull out the bow and begin to loosen the tie while I touched her,. but that was as far as I could go without breaking our kiss. I was hard and ready—I had been in that state and at some pains to conceal it more than once this day—and I gave a thought to pushing her back onto the bed, lifting her skirt, dropping my chausses, and having at her. In five minutes I would be content—and Melusine might be so disgusted that I would lose her forever. So I withdrew my tongue and lightened the pressure of my lips on hers, lifted them, kissed the corner of her mouth and then her chin.

Slowly, her eyes opened and she drew her head back so she could see me. "Oh, thank you," she whispered. "How did you know? I did not know how to tell you."

I almost pushed her away. After the skilled hot and cold teasing she had administered all afternoon, the words pretending innocence and ignorance seemed a crude contrivance, but my standing man throbbed and pleaded in his silent way and I decided to content him and at the same time to teach Melusine a lesson. When I was done with her, she would crave me more than I craved her. So instead of answering her directly, I turned her within my arm and drew her toward the bed, kissing her neck and stroking the inside of her palm with my forefinger.

Near the bed she held back and I thought that I *would* force her if she began to play no-I-cannot games with me now. As to that, I had misjudged her; she only asked, as simply as a child, if she should help me undress first or undress first herself. That made me a little less angry because I knew she had been a virgin when I first had her and whatever her intentions toward me or her knowledge of teasing a man, it was likely that she had never done more than tease in the safety of company. Perhaps she was not sure what to do.

"Let us make a game of it," I murmured, nipping her earlobe and breathing softly into her ear. "I will take off your clothes and you take off mine at the same time."

She giggled softly. "But we will get all entangled."

Her dark eyes were so bright that in this moment they shone more lucently than light ones. "That is our purpose after all," I told her, laughing also but watching her.

Melusine blushed. It was not as obvious as the red flush of a blond woman, but it had a subtle loveliness. The color came up under her dark skin, turning it softly rosy, like a rich fruit. I leaned forward and bit her gently, catching the musky scent of an excited woman mingled with something sweet—a rich fruit indeed.

When my teeth scraped lightly across her jaw, one of Melusine's hands rose and wavered about. I took it in mine and laid it on my belt buckle. The leather was soft; I had put aside my swordbelt when I took off my armor. She made quick work of undoing it, using no gesture, even one that might be thought an accident, to arouse me. It was just as well. I needed no encouragement.

I took longer over undoing the ornamental knots of her girdle, brushing her lower belly with my fingers as I unwove the silken cords. She closed her eyes again, standing with my belt hanging awkwardly from her hand; I had to push it from her fingers and she did not seem to notice when it fell to the floor.

So it went. As I laid her hand on each garment, Melusine took off my clothes without an unnecessary touch, seeming only half aware of what she was doing even when my upper body was bare. But I took no offense. It was clear that she was totally enwrapped in the feelings of her own body, and I had no difficulty believing that these were all new to her and that the long breaths and short ones, the little shivers and quick gasps were all true signs of what she felt. That gave me so much pleasure, for with a whore it is impossible to tell how much of their response is true delight and how much is art, that I came near to spilling my seed without any help.

I stiffened and drew a deep breath and then thought it was purposeless to torment myself with holding back. I had a long row to hoe before I could plunge my spade into Melusine's earth and plant seed there. Let her bring me on by touch; I would still be lively enough before I had her ready. So I pulled the tie of my chausses and set her hands on my hips. I knew she would have to kneel to pull off the feet—I had already slid my feet out of my shoes—and I had a hand under her chin to lift her head as soon as my feet were bare. Her face was only inches from my private parts, and she stiffened in surprise, perhaps in fear, for from so close an engorged rod might look huge.

"That is my standing man, Melusine," I said softly, one hand on her hair. "You know his name. You must not fear him, for he loves you and only wishes for your pleasure. Come, make friends."

She chuckled, and the stiffness went out of her, but she did not raise her eyes to my face, seeming fascinated by what she already saw. "How make friends?" she asked.

"He is not very clever," I admitted. "There is no brain in that red head. He loves to be stroked—but only if that gives pleasure to the doer."

Now I took my hand from Melusine's head so that she would feel no constraint to kneel longer, but she did not rise. She put out a finger and ran it from the head of my shaft to the base and back again. As is wont to happen, Sir Jehan bucked. Melusine jerked her hand away, then giggled, and stroked me again. I touched her cheek, slid my hand under her hair, and tickled her ear. She drew two fingers up me, scraping gently with her nails, and then again. It was enough. I gasped as my liquor spilled, and Melusine sprang up, crying, "No, no."

It was no mighty spill, nor was it accompanied by such thrills of pleasure as wring groans from a man and leave him breathless, which was my intent. I was able to catch Melusine before she moved away and draw her to me, murmuring, "Hush, you have lost nothing."

"But you have spilled the milk that makes a child," she cried, pulling away a little. "I thought you knew. I want a baby."

I had to swallow to hold back laughter. Now I understood the excuse Melusine had given herself for changing her mind about coupling with me. Not that I thought the excuse a false one—I had seen her dandling Eric and hugging and kissing him too—but it was plain she wanted more than the poke or two it takes to make a child. I had no intention of shocking her with the truth, however, and all I said was, "There is plenty more where that came from."

She blinked and looked away, color coming up under her skin again, more strongly than at first. "Yes, of course," she said. "I did not mean . . . I only meant . . ."

It would never do to grin like an idiot. She only meant she did not want to wait. The idea brought a stir to Sir Jehan, who had been drooping, and to encourage him to stand tall again as well as to save Melusine from having to find an end to her sentence, I caught her tight to me and kissed her again.

"We will start on that baby very soon," I murmured into her ear. "Silly woman, I spilled apurpose so that I should be able to show you how great a pleasure it is to create a child."

I do not think she believed me, perhaps because Sir Jehan was still leaning wearily against my thigh, but she did not push me away when I began to stroke her hip and thigh with one hand while pressing her against me with the other, moving my chest gently from side to side so that the cloth of her shift slipped back and forth across her nipples. I could feel them thrusting forward, pressing against me, and as I stroked upward I caught the shift in my hand and pulled it off. The cloth caught against the hard, rich-brown buds that topped her full breasts, and she cried out, lifting a hand to protect them. But I had bent and caught one in my mouth, cupping my hand over the other, before her hand reached so high.

She cried out again then, the hand she had lifted pushing against my shoulder for a moment while the other gripped my buttocks and pulled me tighter. In the next instant, she caught at my head to pull it closer, abandoned that movement, and tangled her fingers in my hair. I could feel her shaking, her legs trembling against mine so that I was afraid she would fall. Carefully, I backed her the few steps to the bed and, supporting her with one arm, pushed her back until she was lying down. I was hard and ready again; now she had to be so wild she would not notice any pain of stretching when I entered her.

I raised my lips from her breast to kiss her mouth, but continued to tease her nipples with one hand while I caressed her nether mouth with my other. She moaned and bucked, trying to force my hand into her, and when my fingers were wet with her woman's dew, I mounted her at last. Her need drove her to learn the rhythm of love easily, and she soon cried and shuddered in a climax of joy. I did not withdraw, but I let her rest, only moving enough to keep myself ready, then began again.

We lay late abed in the morning. Although I had wakened at my usual time, I was glad to take advantage of having no duties. I was very curious to know what Melusine would do and say. Not much later, I became aware that she had wakened also, but when I turned my eyes to her—barely shifting my head so that she should not notice me watching—I saw that her eyes were still closed. She was pretending sleep—out of shame? Before I had done with her during the night, she had rubbed herself against me and finally pleaded with me in words for release.

I was amused, knowing she had not expected to need to confront me immediately. Usually I was gone to my duties before she woke. For a few moments more, I lay quietly, wondering if she would give up her pretense, but then I thought it would be stupid if my teasing turned shame into bitterness and taught her to resent her pleasure in me. To be honest, I had never had such joy before myself. Even the first violent burstings of my manhood were nothing compared with what Melusine had given me. I had planned out of spite for the way she had teased me to make her crave me; probably I had succeeded, but I wondered if I had not trapped myself as much as her. I could die of thirst if she became so angry as to close her well to me.

"May I wish you a good morning, Melusine?" I said, turning to her openly. "God knows, I wish you nothing but good, morning, noon, and eventide for all of your life."

Her big eyes opened promptly, and she looked at me seriously for a moment, then smiled wryly. "You may wish me good, but I cannot yet judge what you have done me. Of one thing I am sure, not every woman has such an experience in coupling."

"I hope not," I replied, feigning indignation. "I was instructed by artists, not allowed, as most men are, to follow their brute instincts. Would you rather I disgusted you and caused you pain?"

Melusine had begun to smile at my jesting answer, but before I finished, her eyes slid away from mine, and her voice was uncertain when she said, "No, of course not."

Thinking she had suddenly realized who I meant when I said "artists" and that she might now object violently to my use of whores—she had been jealous over poor Edna—I stroked her cheek and murmured, "You need not fear I will be unfaithful. You content me more than any such woman ever could."

She looked up then and laughed. "And I save you both sin and expense too."

"Fool that I am, I never thought of that!" I exclaimed, smiling back at her. "But so you do. You are triply precious."

"And you," she retorted, suddenly thrusting back the covers and swinging her legs out of bed, "are as skilled with your tongue as with your shaft. Did you learn that from artists too?"

"God witness me, no!" I swore. "No one has ever accused me of oversmooth speech before. Who would bother seeking sweet words for a whore?'' While I spoke, she had pulled the pot from beneath the bed and squatted above it. The sound of her water flowing sparked in me an ardent need for similar relief, and I exclaimed that she should hurry.

"There is the window." Melusine giggled. "Easy for you; impossible for me."

I was up on the chest before she finished speaking, sending a golden arc of liquid sparkling through the air. "Not impossible," I remarked judicially, "but a tight squeeze, I agree. But I do not think you could fall out, and what a view from below."

Melusine laughed again, but did not answer, and I glanced at her over my shoulder to see if I had offended her. Her expression truly surprised me, for the remains of laughter mingled with a worried frown, which seemed a very odd response to so light and silly a jest. In the next moment she had drawn on her bedrobe and was gone to open the door and call down the stair for Edna while I came down from my perch. When she turned back to me, she looked only pleasant and mildly intent on her business, which was choosing clothing for me from my chest.

"The cart arrived," I said.

"Two days ago," she answered. "They had very good weather, only enough drizzle to keep down the dust and keep the horse cool. I sent the men and cart back to Winchester yesterday. I hope I did right. Audris said she would lend us another cart if we needed it, and if . . . if you do mean to go to Ulle—"

"Indeed I do—if *you* are willing, Melusine."

She was tying one sleeve of my shirt, her head bent to her task so that I could only see her temple and the curve of her cheek. I put my free hand over hers and captured them. She looked up.

"Yes, I am willing."

"If you cannot bear it, we will go away—perhaps to one of the other manors, where your memories will not be so sharp."

Melusine was silent for a moment, looking down again at our clasped hands. "Perhaps that would be best in any case," she said slowly. "If the king's bailiff is at Ulle, will he not send Stephen word that you were there and I also?''

Was this a test of my loyalty? Or was she already urging me to take the first small step into concealment and lying that would lead in the end to open treachery? I could lay a trap for her, but the innocent fall into traps as often as do the guilty, and I wanted no deception on my part. I would make her understand that even after a night of love I would never forget, even while her closeness woke in me faint echoes of that delight, my loyalty to Stephen stood firm.

''I would expect him to do so,'' I remarked sharply. ''I am not trying to hide our presence. That would be treachery. In fact, if the bailiff does not inform the king of our visit, I will tell him myself.''

She blinked with surprise. ''But you bade me not talk of it, lest we be forbidden—''

''Certainly, I did not wish to be forbidden beforehand because of the queen's conviction that you will create some kind of disaster if you return to Ulle. I *know* you will not cause trouble.'' I put all the threat I was capable of into that statement, and Melusine flung up her head and stared at me, wide-eyed. But though I had decided not to deceive her, there was no harm in offering honest honey to sweeten the threat, so I went on, ''In fact, part of my proof that it would be safe to enfeoff me with your lands will be this visit—the evidence I can present, with the bailiff to support my word, of how you greeted your people and soothed them so that the land would be quiet under the king's hand. Do you understand me, Melusine?''

''Have my people not been obedient?'' she asked in a thin, fearful voice. ''I bade them be quiet.''

''Did you?'' I asked, unsure whether to be surprised or assume she was lying.

''Yes, I did,'' she assured me anxiously, and then her lips thinned with anger. ''Not for fear or for the king's sake but for theirs. I did not wish them to be tormented or killed. What do they care who rules? They care for their fields and their herds and their boats.''

''And you, Melusine? For what do you care?''

''I care to have my lands back, and no longer be a beggar picking up crumbs from the queen's table!''

There was passion enough in that, her eyes flashing with
rage, and I nodded acceptance. I thought the reply was
honest; I *prayed* it was honest. I could not bear to think of
what I had promised to do if Melusine tried to stir up
rebellion in Cumbria. For a moment as I looked at her,
bending to pick up my tunic, I felt I must find an excuse
and not go to Ulle so that she would have no chance to
show the evil that was in her. But even as the beauty I had
never before seen in her face tugged at me, I knew I could
not live that way. I had warned her over and over. I must
take her to Ulle and test her with fire.

It was easy to think, not so easy to do. To tell the truth,
I seized eagerly on every excuse offered to linger in Jernaeve
and put off that test, but I only increased my pain. Each
day made Melusine more precious to me. She and Audris
were so different and yet their joy in each other's company
was clear; little as I knew of such matters, it was plain
from Lady Eadyth's approval that Melusine was a house-
holder of knowledge and high standards; and the nights
and early mornings . . . I understood at last why lust was
numbered high among the deadly sins.

At last I set the morrow, a few days before the start of
November as the time to leave. The weather was already
turning cold and rainy, and Melusine said if we did not go
soon, the high passes between Ulle and the other smaller
manors would be blocked with snow. Because we had
been talking of the journey to Ulle from time to time, all
was planned. The chests were to stay at Jernaeve; what we
would need for Ulle would come with us in travel baskets
on two packhorses. With us also would come Edna, riding
pillion—we had her practicing each day we lingered—behind
one of my new men-at-arms. I had three: Fechin, Cormi,
and Merwyn; they had come to me to ask if I would take
them the day before Hugh planned to select a few men to
act as guards and messengers.

After a moment of astonishment, both at the way the
servants and men-at-arms knew what no one had yet told
them and at these men's eagerness to join me—for I knew
Hugh to be a good master—I recognized them; they were
older now, but all three had served with me when Sir
Oliver had sent me to France as Sir Bernard's squire. I

explained that I was not offering an easy duty, that they would not be idling at court but serving mostly as messengers, riding back to Jernaeve in all weathers from all parts of England.

Fechin, the eldest, must have been near forty, but he grinned at me. "If I be goin' to see new things," he said, "I better be at it now, before it be too late." Then he looked down and scrubbed at the earth with one foot. "We be old friends, we three, and no women nor young to bind us. Sir Hugh, he be a good man, but—but it be strange wi'out Sir Oliver. We'ul be easier wi' you."

The others nodded soberly, and tears came to my eyes. I realized suddenly that since I had returned, Audris and Hugh had concealed any signs that Hugh was now lord of Jernaeve. At meals or in the evening, we all sat together on benches; Lady Eadyth ruled the household as she had always done; in the work of rebuilding, Hugh and I gave the orders—but all that riding up and down and helping the men lift and fit and pull out burnt stumps was young men's work and we would have done that even if Sir Oliver was still alive; it was as if he was away, up by the northern wall or visiting another keep. Nonetheless, I understood what Fechin meant. I swallowed the tightness in my throat and said I would have them gladly, if Hugh agreed.

There was no trouble about that, of course, and we set off for Ulle on the twenty-eighth day of October. It was a bright morning, the air crisp enough to nip nose and cheeks into rosiness but not sharp enough to bite, and the sun lay warm on our backs without dazzling our eyes as we rode west after fording the river. There was a smell of smoke in the air as we neared the village that was beholden to Jernaeve, but it had no acrid taint of destruction. This was the pleasant, homely smell of wood fires, bringing thoughts of warmth and ease. As we passed through I did see signs of the ravages of the Scots—the pale wood of the doors on some houses marked the recent replacement of older doors smashed in; there was new thatch on some roofs and burns scarred some walls.

I noticed too that a few of the places had not been repaired. Likely the menfolk of those had been killed, unless their skills had been needed in Jernaeve and they had been summoned to pay their due of labor in the keep. But the few folk who were at work in the village waved at us cheerfully, and Merwyn called out to one man to tell another that he would be gone for a while. A laughing, jesting answer was returned, showing that under Hugh as under Sir Oliver the villagers and the men-at-arms were on good terms. I was glad Sir Oliver's discipline had held and the men of the keep had not taken advantage of Hugh's sickness and single-minded devotion to the restoration of Jernaeve to ill-use the common folk. Briefly I was annoyed with myself for forgetting to ride down and make sure all was well, but fortunately no harm had been done.

When the river turned north, we angled northwest across the rising ground toward the road that ran just south of the great wall. It was easy riding because the land was grazing common, not wooded, but when we had almost reached the crest, Melusine exclaimed in surprise. I had half drawn my sword and my men were gazing around in utter astonishment for any threat before I realized that Melusine was looking far down the valley to where an eight-ox plow was breaking the sod of a fallow field for the planting of winter wheat.

"Now what do you find so startling about the field?" I asked.

"The field!" she exclaimed. "It looks to me like a whole shire. It goes on forever."

I stared at her, puzzled. The fields of Northumbria were small compared with those plowed in the fertile south. Melusine must have seen those expanses, checkered with their different crops, many times when she rode out with the queen. Yet surely her expression of amazement was a result of true surprise; she could not at this point in our marriage believe it worthwhile to raise again the subject of whether she had been playing an idiot during her first months with the court—or could she? In any case, I would not join her game if that was her purpose.

"If you think so," I replied, "the fields of Ulle must be very small indeed."

"Compared with these, yes," she agreed at once. "I cannot remember ever seeing eight oxen on a plow. Two are what we use most often, sometimes four to break new land.''

"The soil is light then?"

"I do not know," she replied, looking at me with lifted brows. "I never looked to the farms, except to mark down the yield and lord's share and suchlike. I had my own garden, of course, for herbs and spices, but—"

"But a manor garden does not grow grain for bread or peas and beans sufficient to last the winter," I interrupted. "Did you buy corn? And with what?"

"There are fewer people so we often do have enough," Melusine said absently, her mind clearly elsewhere. Then she added, seemingly reluctantly, "And we have the where-withal to trade—or did have before the king came and drove all the people away."

I needed a moment before I could answer. "You have tripped into your own snare," I remarked coldly. "I was with the king's force when we came down through Cumbria and there was strict order against looting or misusing the people where there was no resistance. In the north, there was some trouble, and those who made it were punished. But I know no one was driven away from Ulle. There was no one there to drive away."

"The people fled in fear," she answered insolently, looking right into my eyes.

"By your order?" I asked.

"Yes," she said with a slow smile of calm defiance. "I had to stay. I knew I could not hold Ulle, but I was not going to *give* it away. Anything taken by force—and more so from a helpless woman—is an outrage than can be appealed to a just lord."

"A just lord? King David?" My voice rose, but she still met my eyes.

"If he had the power to give me Ulle—yes!" Then she shrugged. "Since he has not, I will take it back from Stephen's hands as gladly."

To hear that last sentence was a distinct relief, and I remembered now that when we came into Ulle it was empty. The common folk had not fled in a last minute panic with what they could carry. Everything of value had been taken from the manor as well as from the very small village outside the walls. So her admission that she had given the order for the people to go was probably true, but that tale did not sit well with what she had said to me some days ago about ordering the folk to submit and obey the king's warden.

"You cannot have it both ways," I snarled. "Either you bade your people go or you bade them be quiet and obey the king's warden. Which is the lie, Melusine?"

She smiled at me, which did *not* ease my heart. "Do not be foolish. Why should both not be true? My people fled the army, but when that was gone, why should they not return? It was the dead of winter, and that hardship would be worse to bear than the harsh treatment of the warden. They could always go back to the hills in the spring if they were used too cruelly."

I have never hit a woman—except a few gentle slaps on Audris's hands or bottom when she was a babe—but I came near it in that moment. What Melusine said might be the literal truth, but something in the way she said it made it into a lie. I was too angry to say more, and rode ahead for a time, but no matter how I turned the matter in my mind, I could see no present political purpose for either lying or defiance. There was no war in Cumbria now, no Scottish troops that could be victualled or supported by Melusine's people nor any of Stephen's men, except the guards living in Ulle itself, to be harmed.

Then it occurred to me that Melusine might still fear what she had done in the past could bring punishment on her. I thought of those men Stephen had disseisined and exiled with their wives and families. If any had appealed to her, arms, comforts, and supplies might have been carried to them by those she had ordered to "run away." But that was near a year past now and did not matter to me. All I cared about was what Melusine would do in the future.

However much the matter worried me, it did not weigh at all on Melusine's conscience. She was in high spirits, and I must confess teased me back into good humor by her unaffected appreciation of a landscape that most southrons find too wild and barren. Only when we came near Carlisle she grew silent, sad too, I think, but she said nothing.

To spare her, I did not seek lodging at the castle but sent Merwyn ahead to find a decent place that would take us in for the night. I would not have troubled her that night, but she clung to me, so I loved her until she was weary—I too—so she would sleep.

The next day I would have followed the path the army took, west to the coast road, then inland and north again, knowing no other. But when I set off toward the west, Melusine called me back, asking in surprise whether I did not wish to go to Ulle and then telling me there was a shorter way. It would take three days to go the long way round, she said—I knew that was true because it had taken the army more than a week—but we could be in Ulle before dusk if we followed her. There had been something strange in her look and manner from the time we woke this morning. Until she spoke of a quicker way to Ulle, I had believed she was tormented by sad memories. Now I had doubts. Still, I could not believe she would be so foolish as to try either to escape me or to lead us into some ambush, so I agreed to go her way; however, I was prepared for trouble, and I warned my men that we would be going into wild and dangerous country.

At first there was little difference between the old road to Penrith and the one we had followed from Jernaeve. Some distance past the town, though, as we topped a rise of ground, Cormi called out to me in a voice that held a note of fear. My hand was on my sword hilt before my eyes followed his pointing hand, but I knew he would not fear men, and then Merwyn, who was closer muttered, "Faery!"

"Faery?"

Certainly it was a ring, clear of brush and smoothly grassed as if scythed with care, but the faery were little folk, and this ring was some twenty yards across, with a ditch and fosse. However, I doubted that ditch and fosse were for defense. For one thing, though far too deep and high to be the work of the little folk, they were surely not sufficient to protect defenders; for another, I could see the top of the raised mound of earth, and that had never held post holes for a palisade. Moreover, I could see that there was an inviting path of smooth green turf leading into the ring.

"I do not know." It was Melusine who answered my doubting question. "But I have passed it many times and have come to no harm."

Her voice was flat, as if she had no interest in the strange place, but I thought she knew more of it than she wished to say.

"This is Lady Melusine's country," I said to the men, "and she says this place is not dangerous—"

"No, I did not say that," she interrupted. "I know one can pass it in daylight in safety," she went on. "But that is all I know. I would not want any to come to harm from thinking I give more assurance than I do."

That made me wonder if Melusine was deliberately warning us away because this was a meeting place for the rebels. I looked at it again as we came down the hill and almost laughed aloud at my silliness. What right-minded man would come to so strange a place, even to plot mischief when he could meet his friends by his own fireside or in some wholesome wood or field with less chance of being seen. Melusine must be speaking the truth about the ring, even if she was not telling all she knew.

As we came down, the ring was hidden by the trees that bordered the road. We passed it warily, kicking the horses into a canter, but we did not hold the pace long. Melusine, who seemed somewhat amused by our caution—the first lightening in her somber mood that day—soon called to us to turn back. She had stopped Vinaigre by the opening to a narrow track that I had thought a game trail. It led southwest into what seemed a stark wilderness. Before we had ridden half a mile, the track met and followed a small river. By then it was clear this was no game trail. Low branches had been lopped back to make a wide enough passage for pack animals and brush had been cleared, but I saw that the track had not been used often this year; there was new growth that had not been cut. Melusine saw it too, but what she thought of it I could not tell. Her face was closed—dark and sad again.

Though narrow, the track was clear and easy to follow, and we rode along for near an hour with no surprises until

on a low rise it opened out into a small meadow. My
breath caught at the beauty of the scene below us. Melusine
had stopped beside me, and I heard a faint sound—a sob? I
put out a hand blindly to pat hers, but I could not tear my
eyes from the landscape. A long lake gleaming silver
under the lightly cloudy sky stretched away into the distance, bordered by steep hills that folded into each other,
green with forest close at hand and shading into blue and
purple in the distance. Aside from a few sheep grazing the
meadow, four very small houses, and what looked like a
stable and fenced yard for horses down near the water,
there was no sign of man's hand in this wilderness. To the
east of the lake, however, I was not sure the mountain
came directly down to the water. Though the bank rose
steeply, there might be a fold of land behind that could
hold an arable valley. But if the track we rode on began
again to the east, behind the few dwellings, there was no
sign of it.

There was not much sign that the road continued south
along the west side of the lake either, but Melusine confi-
dently trotted Vinaigre across the north edge of the valley
and then down toward the lake. I almost called out, thinking she was about to plunge into the water, when she
turned right sharply and disappeared. Since there was no
splash, I followed calmly enough, only to find myself
perched on a trail not much wider than Barbe's barrel and
hanging over the lake. The drop was not much at this
point, perhaps four or five feet, but ahead I could see a
few brown and grey splotches where the track was not
edged with trees and they were a hundred feet or more
high.

Fechin, seeing where my eyes were directed, uttered a
snort. "We be needin' spiders, not horses, to get up
there."

Melusine was already well ahead, so I could only shrug
and touch Barbe gently with my heels. He started willingly, by which I guessed the track must feel solid and
steady to him. "Do not look down," I called back over
my shoulder. "Watch the horse ahead and the trail itself
for holes or loose stones."

I began to follow Melusine's rapidly disappearing back,

and then had to shout to her to stop. That devil of a mare instead started a fast trot, which Melusine did not check, but I could not follow. Cormi had just called to me that Edna was in trouble. I cursed Melusine fluently as I backed Barbe a few steps to a spot wide enough to turn him. She could not get far nor elude me for long, but I was sick inside with fear that she had taken the first chance she had to escape.

I cursed Edna too, although she, poor creature, did not deserve it. Truthfully, I had been much surprised by how cheerfully she had accepted the discomforts of the long trip, how attached she seemed to Melusine, and her stoic endurance on this ride. She had only had a few hours of practice to accustom her to being perched on a horse, and we had ridden nearly forty miles from Jernaeve to Carlisle. When she dismounted at our lodging the night before, Melusine noticed how stiff Edna was and asked me to send a man to buy a liniment to rub on her sore muscles. She was better although still uncomfortable when she came to help Melusine dress in the morning, but she made no complaint when Fechin lifted her to Merwyn's saddle pad nor later when she was shifted to Cormi's to rest Merwyn's horse. I thought she might have grown faint from pain and weariness, but it was the sight of the road winding up on the cliffs that had frightened her so much she nearly fell off.

"Let me walk," Edna sobbed, when I asked if she could go forward after a short rest. "I will follow faithfully. I will run to keep up, but I cannot bear to sit up so high and look into nothing."

"My lord—" Fechin began, and then stopped suddenly, his eyes going past my shoulder.

I turned sharply to see Melusine coming back toward us at a sharp trot, and I had to grit my teeth to keep from shouting aloud with joy. My wife—the word was sweet in my mouth, although I did not utter it—my wife had not used the length of rope I had given her to hang herself.

Fechin shook his head and looked back at me. "Your lady makes us look fools," he went on, "but we'uld all be easier on our feet goin' up there."

Apparently Melusine had heard him, because she cried, "Oh! Do forgive me."

She sounded truly contrite and, oddly, somewhat embarrassed, and put out her hand to me, which I took and pressed warmly. If it had not been for the men, I would have kissed her; in fact, so great was my relief that my passion stirred, and if I could, I would have dismounted both of us and played mare and stallion without the help of Vinaigre and Barbe. Melusine must have seen that in my face—I hope no one else did—because she found a small smile for me.

"I . . . my mind has been on . . . on other things," she said. "I forgot your men were not accustomed to our roads. This road is perfectly safe, all sound, but the men can walk if they like. Ulle is less than three leagues and they cannot get lost." She looked at Fechin and smiled. "You need only keep to the road that follows the lake. There are only four tracks that turn off and they go directly away from the water."

The men dismounted with sighs of relief, and I turned Barbe and followed Melusine. This time she did not allow Vinaigre to go faster than a walk and I was close behind. Farther on, the road curved a little inward where the land was flatter and widened so I could ride abreast.

"You did not include me in the invitation to walk," I remarked. "But I wish you to know, I am quaking in my stirrups and hope you will keep a sober pace."

Cleverly, she looked at Barbe, not at me. The horse showed no nervousness—and he was a nervous horse—so she could assume I felt none. "I did not think you would let me go alone," she said, "and I certainly do not wish to walk all that way."

"Is there some reason I should not let you go alone?" I asked.

There was a brief silence, then Melusine said softly, "I am sorry I did not come back at once when you called. I was angry when you bade me to stop until I saw that something was wrong. I thought you believed I was running away. I would not do that. I have given my word."

"Did it not occur to you that there might be other

reasons I did not want you to go alone? You are dear to me, Melusine, and this is wild country—''

"Not to me," she interrupted, smiling. "There are no outlaws here"—the smile disappeared abruptly—"or were none. Perhaps good men have been driven into outlawry since I have been gone, but none of them would harm me."

"If good men have been made outlaw, I am sorry for it, and the king will be sorry also," I told her. "That was not Stephen's intention, and if I see the people are ill-used, I will do my best to amend it."

She shifted in her saddle restlessly, which surprised me. It was almost as if what I said made her uncomfortable because she did not want me to show interest in or sympathy for her people. That raised a new specter in my mind. The queen had wanted Melusine married so that no Cumbrian lord with a loyalty to David could seize her, marry her, and claim Ulle through her. Just now it had come to me that a widow would serve as well as an unmarried maid for that purpose. I suppose I was staring at her. I do not know what was in my face, but Melusine suddenly turned her head away from me, and as she did I thought I saw tears in her eyes. That only added to the puzzle, but I could think of no way to approach any solution to it, and I was thankful that the trail narrowed as we began to climb again and she pulled ahead.

I soon began to think my doubts were foolish. There was no reason for Melusine to want another husband. Her eagerness to couple and her transports in the marriage bed were genuine, of that I was certain. If she intended to be rid of me, why should she have made our marriage complete in Jernaeve? Surely if she wished to replace me with another man, she could have refused me a little longer. And God knew this homecoming must be bitter as gall to her. There were reasons enough for tears. By the time we came to the next space open enough to ride side-by-side, I had put the doubt aside and was only troubled about how Melusine would endure actually coming into Ulle. But that, like the road, was easier than I expected—except for a few breathtaking stretches.

The worst part of the road was the traverse of Stybarrow

Crag. For over a quarter of a mile, the track hung over the water, too narrow over that whole length to turn a horse. One man could hold off a whole army—if he did not tire. On the other hand, archers, so dangerous in most wild and wooded country, would be of little use because the hill bulged out above the road and there were few places where a shot could be angled correctly. My mind was on the impossibility of bringing an army along that road, and I must have pulled back on the reins with surprise because Barbe stopped suddenly. Around a curve below the rise on which Barbe stood, where I expected to see more wilderness, there was a tame and cozy demesne farm—for dolls.

I looked down at the tiny fields, each one not more than half or quarter of an acre—with the same surprise that Melusine expressed a day earlier on seeing the eight-ox plow working near Jernaeve. One could be fooled into thinking the fields were miles away and small with distance, except that below us, close to the edge of the lake, was a substantial, man-sized walled manor. That I recognized! Ulle!

Now my eyes flew to Melusine, but she had not stopped as I had. I could see her head turn from side to side, sweeping the fields and then the lake. I hoped she was not suffering too much; if she had turned to me I would have comforted her as best I could, but in a way it was a relief that she did not. I did not know what to say. I did not even know whether what she saw was the same or different from when she had been mistress of Ulle. I remembered now that the ground had been covered with snow when I led Stephen's forces into Ulle; that was why those tiny fields had not stuck in my memory.

All I could do was increase Barbe's pace so that I could ride beside her. Once I touched her hand, but she did not look at me and I made no further gestures. We met only one man, trudging along the track that bordered the fields with a faggot of sticks on his back. He looked up and gaped for a moment, then backed to the side of the road, staring.

"A good day to you, Tom," Melusine said. "I have come for a visit. I hope all has gone well with you these months I have been away."

"None so well," the man replied, glancing at me before he added, "none so ill either, my lady."

"This is my husband, Sir Bruno of Jernaeve," Melusine said, then nodded and rode on.

"Good day to you," I said, and rode on also.

There had been first gladness and then disappointment in the man's face after his first shock had passed. So much was easy to see, but I put that aside to think about later, my greatest concern being with Melusine as we drew nearer the manor. At least the gate was open and unguarded, which meant there had been no trouble with the local people. That was a relief, but I was surprised that Melusine's arrival caused no more than a few curious looks. The only armed man inside the walls stared at me open-mouthed before he hailed a manservant to take our horses and said he would inform the steward that guests had arrived.

I dismounted and hurried to lift Melusine down. Her face was a mask, but there was horror in her eyes. "Where are the old servants?" she whispered.

"Melusine!" I exclaimed. "Those who were here when the king came were still here when he left. You know they were unharmed, even those silly old men who tried to hold us off."

She shook her head. "Where are they now?"

"I do not know, my dear, but I will find out," I said, turning to face a man who cried a hearty greeting as he came, but keeping my arm around Melusine's waist.

"Well come!" he exclaimed. "I am Sir Giles de Montalbe. I have not seen a new face in months. You are well come indeed in this empty end of the world."

"It is not an empty end of the world to us, Sir Giles," I said. "I am Sir Bruno of Jernaeve, Knight of the Body to King Stephen, but I am on leave and my coming here has nothing to do with the king. This is Lady Melusine of Ulle, my wife, and I have brought her here because she was sick with longing for her home. I hope you do not mind."

"I would not mind if you were Satan, bringing Judas with you," Sir Giles said explosively. "And if your lady wife and you would like to stay for good and can get me permission to leave, I will be overjoyed."

There was bitterness in his voice and disappointment and anger in his face, and Melusine drew a gasping breath and cried, "Where are the old servants?"

"Gone," Sir Giles replied in a snarl.

"Dead?" I could hear the edge of hysteria in Melusine's voice and her body stiffened.

"How would I know?"

The rigidity of Melusine's body eased, and she said, "You mean they ran away?"

"I mean that when I came here there were the hall and outbuildings of the manor, sixteen of the twenty men-at-arms with their captain that the king had left to hold the manor, and *nothing* else. And only twelve of the sixteen men left could bear arms. The men had been hunting to feed themselves, and in two months three were killed by falls and another five had been seriously injured, and the captain had a broken leg. The bailiff sent by the king was also dead—he drowned while fishing, and one of the men-at-arms with him."

Now Melusine was wholly relaxed against my arm. "This is dangerous country," she said. "I was born here, and I have been overturned in the lake and blown off the trail near Black Crag—" She nodded northwest toward a glowering hulk of mountain that darkened the horizon. "I am sorry about the servants though. Would you like me to ask among the village people where they have gone and if they would be willing to come back?"

"Willing?" Sir Giles almost choked on rage. "They have no right to will. They—"

"Forgive me, Sir Giles," Melusine interrupted. "The servants in Ulle were all free. There were no slaves or bound serfs in Ulle." She smiled at him. "We were never rich enough to buy slaves, and they would have been useless for anything except household work or work on the demesne farm—which as you see is not large. As to trying to bind the native born into serfdom, how could we keep them if they wished to run into the hills and hide? It is more practical in Ulle to have free tenants who work willingly."

"Work?" Again Sir Giles's voice rose with rage. "Who works in Ulle? They are all idlers."

"Let us go in, Sir Giles," I interposed before Melusine could answer. "We have been on the road since sunrise and I am sharp-set. I know we have missed dinner—"

"Good God, forgive me," Sir Giles exclaimed. "I have forgotten my manners and am growing as savage as the country. Do come in and I will see what there is to eat."

He led us in, and I made sure to enter the hall first and cross to the firepit, leaving Melusine to hesitate at the doorway as she glanced around the room. I hoped the familiar hall would not be too much for her to bear, but I thought it less important to offer comfort than to keep her from seeing me in the doorway in armor, as she must have seen me the day Ulle was taken. But perhaps she would not have noticed me at all; she seemed far more smugly satisfied than distraught as she looked around the room, and her lips were twitching, not down but upward. I suspected it was laughter, not tears, she was trying to control.

Melusine's expression made me look about also. I cannot say I remembered the hall the day I burst in behind the ram. It had been dark, with all the shutters closed and barred, and my attention had been fixed on the wailing women. All I could remember was a chair of state behind Melusine. I had assumed there were other furnishings fitting for a gentleman's hall. What I saw now would have better suited a hunting lodge where men shelter for a night or two rather than a manor where men lived—three rough benches and a stool flanking the firepit, a trestle table of splintery planks on the dais, and that was all. I could not see behind the wall screen at the back of the dais, but I doubted that the bed in which Melusine and her brothers had been conceived still stood there.

Had everything in Ulle been looted by Stephen's army? Then I remembered that though there had been little of value, except furs, in any of the Cumbrian estates the king had taken—a few silver coins, some goblets and plate, and stores of food—in Ulle there had been nothing, nothing at all. Yes, that was why Stephen had left one of the minor clerks of his household to be bailiff and ferret out why Ulle was bare bones. But the bailiff had died. I glanced at Melusine, but she only looked politely bland now, as if she were entering a stranger's hall and were determined not to notice anything out of the ordinary.

Melusine maintained that bland indifference while we ate and through the afternoon and evening, making no reply to Sir Giles's angry complaints. He had been made steward, he told us, through the favor of the bishop of Ely and had assumed that there would be some profit to be made from the estate. Instead, he had found a desert. The people of the village had come back after the soldiers and their captain departed, he said, and they had planted the fields and made the furnishings—he laughed bitterly on the word—for his hall. Then he shrugged. At least they were quiet he admitted; though they were stupid and lazy beyond any serfs he had dealt with, they did not protest the double and triple tithings he made of produce, fish, and game.

How had her family lived, he asked Melusine. They needed little, Melusine replied; they were simple people, content to hunt and fish and eat the black bread and flat cakes from the rye and barley their thin soil would grow, to wear the rough wool woven from the fleece of their few, hardy sheep. Sir Giles came close to howling with rage, snarling that there was not enough, even of such things, to keep him alive, let alone a large family—and Melusine shrugged and said sweetly that she was sorry, she knew no more than she had told him.

I knew she was—not lying, for I had seen the gowns in her chest and it was plain which the queen had given her, but I had also seen her fine ivory comb set with small jewels, a silver thimble, and other such luxuries. She had once told me, too, that they had the wherewithal to trade. So she was not telling all the truth. Nonetheless, I held my tongue, pretending I did not understand what Melusine was doing until we were lying together, not in a bed but on straw-stuffed pallets in a little house in which Melusine asked to lodge, saying it had been built for her sister-by-marriage, who had died in childbirth.

Edna was at the far end of the single room, but she slept like one dead after the exhaustion and terror of her jour-

ney. I doubted she could be wakened by screams and kicks
and knew she would not hear our quiet voices. I took
Melusine gently by the ear and shook her head.

"Well?" I asked.

"I am well," she replied. "It looked so different, like
any other hall in Cumbria. I could not see papa—"

"Melusine," I murmured dulcetly, "I have never beaten
a woman in my life and I think it very wrong for the strong
to be cruel to the weak, but I am coming close to forgetting the rules that have guided me through life."

"What good do you think beating me will do?" she
asked, and I could feel the movement of her cheek that
meant she was smiling. "I can tell you nothing. I admit
I bade the people to take away and hide whatever was in
Ulle, but I do not know who took what or where it was
taken. I *think* the people would bring back what they
carried away if I asked them to do so." She hesitated, then
went on in a voice that was no longer light and teasing.
"But I would gladly be beaten to death before I would
give that order so that Sir Giles could sleep in my father's
bed."

"The king has the right—" I began.

"To sleep in papa's bed?" Her voice was small and
sad. "He would never get it. You heard Sir Giles say he
looked for a profit. Bruno, I swear to you that the full
yield from Ulle—there was none yet from any of the other
manors; we gave to them—would not pay one knight in
the king's service. Perhaps it would be worth being angry
with me if the king were able to buy a knight with the
blood drained from Ulle, but Stephen would never receive
a single silver penny—and you know it."

My hand had loosened from her ear—the hopeless sadness in her voice tore at my heart—and she turned her
head and kissed me when she finished speaking. I made no
answer because I did not know what to say. By strict rule,
Sir Giles's dishonesty was not my business; the full dues
of Ulle should go to him and he be responsible for what
happened thereafter. But I knew what Melusine said was
true. The king would not benefit no matter what was
squeezed from Ulle, and my loyalty was to the king.

Melusine was shivering a little. The cold struck up from

the earth floor through the thin pallets, so I pulled her to lie closer. She came quickly and so eagerly that she ended lying more atop me than beside me, and she kissed me again and stroked my shoulder and arm, running her hand down and up and then down again, only this time over my chest and belly and hip until she found the traitor who was never angry with her. Somewhere at the back of my mind I suspected that it was not pleasure alone that Melusine was seeking as she stroked my shaft, but I did not care. Pleasure first; I could think about why tomorrow.

CHAPTER 16

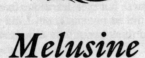

Melusine

To SEE A MAN lost to himself in passion was a revelation to me—not that I noticed the first few times Bruno and I coupled. In the beginning I was too lost myself to care what he felt, and he came into control of himself afterward faster than I—I suppose because he was much more accustomed to the violent pleasure. I think also, looking back, that in the beginning he was so eager that I be fulfilled, or rather, sated, that he somehow suppressed his own release. Whore's son that he was, Bruno knew every trick that could be played with the body.

At first I was appalled, for he taught me to crave that pleasure as I craved food and drink, and I feared I was trapped into a kind of slavery where he could control me by my longing. But when he saw that I desired him, he also let me see that he was as much my slave as I was his. That lifted my fear, until I realized that devil had played another trick on me. To see his eyes glaze, to hear him sigh and moan, only excited me to greater transports, tying the knot of my pleasure tighter around my neck.

I had begun to fear that there would be no way to free myself from my passion except to give some trusted servant in Ulle a sign that would cause Bruno to trip over a rock and plunge down a mountainside or fish too eagerly and fall overboard. However, that first night in Ulle, I used Bruno's weapon against him. With a few reasonable words and many touches and kisses, I diverted his mind from the disappearance of the revenues of Ulle and bound him to the notion that the poorer Ulle seemed to be the more likely Stephen would be to enfeoff him.

Poor Sir Giles. He was so stupid, I almost came to like him despite his greed. Later I learned it was not sheer stupidity, although he *was* stupid, but a complete lack of understanding of our countryside. Sir Giles came from the wide, flat fields of Norfolk and found it easy to believe nothing would grow among our steep hills. He really thought the demesne farm was all the cultivated land we had, and it was very easy to keep him from the hidden valleys where our grain was grown and the folds in the hills where our flocks were grazed. He did not even seem to realize that the people in the village were not creeping around in the last stages of starvation, which they should have been considering what he left to them after taking his share. But the people of Cumbria are lean and hard; perhaps the folk of Norfolk are fuller fleshed, and Sir Giles thought those of Ulle were thin from hunger. Bruno was not so fooled. I saw the way he looked at the folk and raised his brows to see them so sturdy. But I touched his face and pleaded with my eyes—and he said nothing to Sir Giles.

I was grateful to Sir Giles also for keeping Bruno busy for a few hours the day after we arrived. It was a grey, windy day, but not raining, and I was able to slip out to walk by the lake—where I was hidden from sight in a small hollow screened by brush after a five-minute walk. I knew Tom Bailiff would be watching for me; he was, and was with me soon after I could not be seen. Fortunately Bruno and I met him on the road, since I had expected to be able to send a servant to bring him to me and none of the old servants was at the manor.

Tom Bailiff told me that the servants had crept out and fled and were now in Wyth serving Sir Gerald, who had held Irthing from papa. I gasped with hope when I heard that, but Tom shook his head before I could ask or really feel any pain of disappointment, and I knew that Sir

Gerald had confirmed Donald's and papa's deaths. Tom did not say that, only told me that Sir Gerald had returned, more dead than alive, in the spring of the year, and that, as I had bidden them, they had hidden him in Wyth, fearing if he went to Irthing he would be recognized by someone more interested in the king's favor than in old friendship.

I praised Tom and promised reward and said that he must set a watch so that the next time I was free he could bring me the true tally sticks of what had been harvested from the fields. We could then decide which animals should be slaughtered and salted for food, which driven to market, and what to do with the spring wool that had not been used.

I told him that I would remit a tithe of lord's share because of the trouble and losses engendered by harvesting, slaughtering, fishing, and doing all other tasks in secret. The folk could keep that tithe as it was if they wished, but the stores from Ulle that had been hidden and this year's lord's share were to be sold in Penrith or Kendal. The coins were to be sent to Beric, at Wyth. However, as reward for his faithfulness and that of the other folk, the cloth, wool, and fleeces should be distributed. He could keep a second bailiff's share. The remainder could be sold or used by those folk who must stay in the caves or mountain shelters.

Although I thought my offer generous, Tom did not look too pleased, and I said sharply that he should not be unwise enough to think his service was worth more and even less should he believe he could keep it all. This he vehemently denied, but I felt the temptation would be too much for Tom. I suppose the success he had had in hiding the real yield of Ulle from Sir Giles and the long months I was gone had lit a spark of greed in him.

I had hoped to spare myself the pain—and the danger to him—of meeting Sir Gerald, but I realized I could not avoid it. Old Beric, who had been as near a steward as my father had, would have to bring the records he had hidden to Sir Gerald, who would then manage Ulle and the other manors until Bruno regained the estate. It was unfortunate that most of the records were written, since Sir Gerald could not read—well, neither could papa; I had teased the skill out of Andrew because tally sticks for many small accounts are a nuisance. But I was sure Beric knew most of the amounts by heart, and if a question should arise, a clerk who would keep a still mouth could be found.

To Tom I said that I wished to speak to Sir Gerald to learn what he knew of my father and brother, and that I would tell him how it should be arranged when I next met him. He seemed to accept that and to be more resigned to the loss of his hope of being lord of Ulle in all but name, but my faith in him had been shaken. Somehow I would have to contrive a way for Sir Gerald to let me know what was happening and for me to get messages back to him.

My mind was so preoccupied with my disappointment in Tom Bailiff and the difficulty of relaying messages from a place as distant as Cumbria to a court that moved every few days or weeks that I did not bother to consider why Bruno was more than usually silent that afternoon and evening. Certainly, I did not associate it with my meeting with Tom. But that night Bruno made love like a man expecting to be starved of that joy forever after. He woke me four times, and would have had me a fifth, I think, except that I was so exhausted that I could not respond to his touch although I was dimly aware of it. I was annoyed also, although I cannot deny that I enjoyed our couplings, because it seemed to me that it was seeing Ulle that made me more precious in Bruno's eyes. Of course I was glad that Bruno liked Ulle, but I preferred to be caressed in response to my own charms, not my property's.

It was also very stupid not to suspect Bruno's convenient absence most of the next morning, but he so often rose before I did—and I had slept very late—that I simply thanked God for it and went out to meet Tom. I was pleased that he had come and had brought me the tally sticks as I ordered, because I do not know what I could have done if he had decided to avoid me instead. The habit of obedience is wonderful. I decided to take the sticks with me to examine, partly because I did not want to spend too much time away from the manor and partly because I wanted to show them to Sir Gerald. I told Tom only the first part of my excuse, but assured him I would put my mark on them to show I approved his accounting after I had read them.

Then I asked him to bring Sir Gerald to Ulle and bid him hide in one of the cottar's huts. I was not happy with the arrangement, but though I had racked my brains all day, I could see no other way to arrange a meeting. It would not be difficult to get Bruno to take me to Wyth, but I was sure it would be impossible to free myself of him for as long as I would need to talk to Sir Gerald. In Ulle, I felt I could contrive somehow to get free within a week. Since Sir Giles did not seem to know one man from another, I hoped Sir Gerald would be unsuspected for that long. When he saw me alone, I told Tom, he was to lead Sir Gerald to this place.

It was no problem to conceal the bundle of sticks under my furred cloak. I nodded to Edna, who was sitting on a stool in the sun by the doorway slowly and carefully stitching a seam, and bade her finish her task. Inside the little house I still thought of as Winifred's, I drew the traveling basket that held my clothes close to the hearth, pulled a shift halfway out, as if I were examining it, and began to read the tally sticks. To my relief, the amounts of grain garnered, lambs and calves born, and all else seemed much the same as other years—a bit more here, a bit less there, but I felt that the accounting was honest. I smiled as I heard Bruno's voice in the bailey, flipped the shift over the sticks, and thrust them down into the basket.

"And where have you been?" I asked, as Bruno came in.

"I have been along one of the trails that leads into the hills," he said, gazing steadily at me. "There are blocked-off side tracks on it."

I smiled at him, thinking he was hinting that he had not gone down those tracks deliberately to avoid discovering evidence of the true productivity of Ulle. "If you wish to see what is there, I will ride over with you."

"I would rather ride out to the smaller manors beholden to Ulle," he replied.

"Very well," I agreed. "There is Wyth, Irthing, Rydal, and Thirl." My voice quivered over the last, for I thought that house would probably be just as Mildred left it; I did not think that any part of the king's army had struggled over the snow-filled passes to Thirl. "Which would you like to see? If we go to Rydal early, we can also visit Wyth and then come back over the mountain to Ulle. It is a beautiful ride—if the weather is fine."

"Why do you not wish to visit Thirl?" he asked.

I told him, and he came to my side, put his hand on my shoulder, and said he was sorry. I thought his voice sounded flat, and glanced up at him but he was looking over my head, out the door. I suppose I should have been warned by that, but I was hurt because I assumed Bruno was growing tired of being sympathetic to sad memories. I resolved to do my best not to mention my family to him again—easy enough to do because, aside from shying away from what might wake pain in me, I was not sad.

That shows what a fool I was; it did not occur to me that it was Bruno's presence, not only his physical presence but the knowledge that I belonged to him and he to me, that sheltered me from grief. I had not yet quite absorbed the fact that Bruno did understand women far better than any man in my own family. I underestimated him at that moment and went on being very pleased with myself and quite blind to everything beyond my own satisfaction.

He had been silent, still looking out the door, his hand sliding up from my shoulder to my neck. I thought he could see something I could not and craned my neck upward, but there was nothing there, and Bruno's grip was growing uncomfortably tight. I did not want to complain that he was choking me; men are so easily hurt when one points out that their affectionate gestures are actually unpleasant—so I rubbed my cheek against his arm, then turned my head farther and kissed it. As I expected, he let go at once.

"Would it not be wiser to go to Wyth first if the morning is fine?" he asked hurriedly, more as if he needed something to say than cared exactly what he said, and then went on more purposefully, "Is not the road to Rydal easier than that from Ulle to Wyth? Should we not do the most difficult part first and not chance a change in the weather that will keep us from taking the trail over the mountain in the afternoon?"

"If you like we can go to Wyth first," I replied without

a hesitation. I was certain that Sir Gerald would be warned and have time enough to make himself scarce before we actually entered the place; besides, he might have already left for Ulle. "It is just that Rydal is a richer manor. There was a small income from it and there is more to see there, which was why I suggested we go there first. Wyth was to be my dower property, you see, and since papa was in no hurry for me to marry, he did not spend much effort on it. Papa planned for Magnus to have Rydal and made it as rich as he could because Donald would have had Ulle in the end."

I stopped speaking abruptly, annoyed with myself for forgetting so soon that Bruno was bored with my "might have beens" about my father and brothers. Absently, I closed the traveling basket, trying to think of something cheerful to say, but all that came into my mind was the sad thought that if Magnus had married Mary, he would probably have preferred Thirl, which was closer to her estate and that Donald would have been willing to make the exchange.

"Perhaps we should not visit Wyth at all," Bruno said suddenly.

I stood up and put my arm around his waist. "We will go where you please when you please, my lord. There is not a stick or stone in Ulle or any place beholden to it that is not beautiful in my eyes and I hope to make it all beautiful in yours, for you will get little out of it except the beauty."

"Beauty? In bare rock?"

Sir Giles's voice did not startle me, for I had seen a shadow fall across the open doorway and seen another bob up and then disappear. The second, I assumed, was Edna, jumping up and bowing, so the first must be Sir Giles. I was *very* glad that my words had been so ambiguous, and I laughed and said, "I am a simple soul and find great joy in the little flowers that grow among the scree."

Sir Giles sighed. "I sent your husband to bring you to dinner, but he seems to have forgotten."

"I beg your pardon," Bruno said. "We were talking about other places to visit and I did not realize how the time was passing. Would you like to accompany us? I am sure Melusine will make a reliable guide."

"In this season there will not even be the wildflowers you praise, Lady Melusine," Sir Giles remarked, lips twisted in contempt, "and I have seen enough bare stone. I thank you, but in weather like this, I prefer the fireside— such as it is. I will allow you to enjoy the beauty of Cumbria alone."

We did enjoy it; the stark beauty of this country is not, at least to my mind, diminished by a cloudy sky. There were no flowers, of course, but some red and gold leaves clung to the trees on the lower slopes, bright against the grey-green hills, and the lake glowed like a burnished helm. I took Bruno around the head of the lake. Bird calls preceded us, some from birds that I knew had flown away for the winter, and the stubble fields showed only a few cows. A few sheep were scattered on the low knolls that stretched south and west.

Bruno must have known that the land would carry more sheep than what he saw, but he did not ask where they were and I leaned from my horse to kiss him as he turned north to ride the east shore of the lake then inland past Silver Hill and around Lough Crag to climb The Dod. We did that on foot, leaving the horses at a shepherd's hut below. It was no great height, but the land ran away in folds, and Scalehow Beck lay like a silver ribbon below us.

The next day the wind was all from the lake and the high clouds moved slowly with large breaks that sent lances of sunlight down upon the hills. I was sure there would be neither rain nor much wind inland, and I told Bruno that it would be a good day for riding. To my horror, while we broke our fast, Bruno repeated his invitation to Sir Giles to ride with us, telling him that we intended to visit the other manors. Sir Giles only laughed scornfully and refused again, saying he had been at each several times during the summer, had ridden through the hills, and had seen nothing of enough interest to take him out on them on a cold November day. If we discovered anything, we were welcome to it. I had raised a foot to step on Bruno's toe, good and hard, if he tried to say any more but it was not necessary.

Later, on the road, he told me he had asked Sir Giles to

come because he felt the man deserved another chance. "If he had questioned you and watched you as we rode and examined the manors, he could have learned a great deal that you did not mean to tell him."

"That was just what I feared," I exclaimed. "Do you or do you not want to recover Ulle?"

For some reason the angry question seemed to please Bruno, who smiled at me. "I want to recover it honestly," he said, then laughed at my snort of contempt. "I am sorry, but I do not have a woman's single-minded way of looking at problems. I suffer from a man's tender conscience, and must assuage it."

"And daring a disaster has patted and oiled your tender conscience into smoothness? I am surprised that you did not force Sir Giles to come at sword point, rub his nose in every bramble closing off a cart track, and help him to count each stubble stalk so he could know how many grains of corn were lacking."

He laughed again. "It was the knowledge that I would have to do so if he came along that convinced me to let the stupid dog lie. But his repeated refusal to accompany us can, I think, be used to imply to the king that he is not an assiduous steward."

I drew breath to point out that his entrapment of Sir Giles, who he must have already known was lazy and stupid, was no less unscrupulous than my concealment of Ulle's worth, but that would have been idiotic. Bruno was, in fact, far too honest for his good or mine. He *would* have pointed out the oddities in Ulle's management if Sir Giles had shown any interest; why should he not use that lack of interest if he could? Bruno was also far too honest to tell me outright that he would conspire with me to keep Sir Giles in his present state of ignorance and then betray my confidences. This gave me the freedom to talk seriously with him about the value of the land and the fresh-water fish that could be caught in abundance in our lakes and tarns.

"For now," I summed up, "there is little above what we would need to live in comfort, but over the years as the other manors begin to yield profits instead of needing support, Ulle could be rich."

"Not if there is war," Bruno said.

"God forbid!" I exclaimed. "King Henry came once and never again. King Stephen has been here already. I pray God that once will suffice him also."

Bruno had been watching me so closely that I began to feel uneasy, but he burst out laughing at my last remark. "I hope so too, from the heart. I do not want ever again to creep with an army over your roads."

Then he put out his hand and touched mine as we came out on the crest of a hill. The thin soil had been washed away to bare rock and the wind was like an icy steel blade against the skin, but the sun made every stream into a jeweled ribbon and gilded the crags beyond us to the west. He stopped and I reined in Vinaigre.

"You need not fear that I will try to obtain some richer land," Bruno said firmly. "I do not desire riches. I am accustomed to a hard land called barren by others." His lips twisted wryly as he let his eyes sweep from the glint of Ullswater away in the distance to the mountains we still had to climb. "Not so hard as Ulle, perhaps, but not so beautiful either."

We rode on then and I was happy. To say the truth, I had forgotten all about Sir Gerald being at Wyth. I did not even think of him when we came out of the wood at the top of a rise and were able to look down into Wyth's bailey for a few moments. I could see movement and faintly hear voices, but they struck no fear into my heart, and when Bruno looked at me, I smiled and said, "There are few visitors to Wyth. Perhaps they think it is Sir Giles. But if they are running about hiding kegs of fish at this late hour, I will have their skins."

I was a little annoyed when Bruno did not answer; I felt that to pretend now, after I had confessed all and he agreed with me, that it was wrong to conceal most of the catch from Sir Giles was pompous and silly. It was not until we had passed the narrow fields and saw a few men and women standing by the gate of the palisade that I felt a prick of anxiety. Would Bruno realize that they already knew I was at Ulle? They cried out on seeing me, and one woman clung to my skirt, weeping and thanking God that I had come back. She was the chief weaving woman and used to a small house and servant of her own and the comforts of life in an established manor. I think she liked me, but her fervor was for regaining her old life.

As I explained that I had only come for a visit but that my husband, Sir Bruno, would listen if they had any complaints of ill-usage and do what he could, I dismissed the anxious qualm. So what if the people of Wyth knew I had come? There need be no reason besides natural interest to send the news from Ulle to all the other manors. And since I had told Bruno the truth, I asked openly for the tally sticks. The headman—Wyth was not large enough to dignify the man with the title of bailiff—was out fishing, but his wife knew where the sticks were, and I sat down in a patch of sunlight in what might some day be the manor garden to read them, leaving Bruno to look about as he pleased.

He came directly from the hall, waiting while I cut the M with a U under its arches that was my mark into the stick that summed the whole year ending the last day of February. I was slow about it, not noticing that Bruno was looming over me because I was thinking that it would not be long now until the sticks marked the end of 1138—and I could remember none of it, except the last two months.

"The hearth is warm," Bruno said.

"Warm?" I repeated blankly. "What of that? I think the servants who fled from Ulle are living here. I suppose they settled into the hall—they are used to living in a hall. Besides, there are few houses here and no one would be fool enough to build more and give away that there were new folk here. And they have no right to build more."

"Only the old servants live in the hall?"

I almost burst out and told Bruno the truth, hoping that if I pleaded with him not to betray my father's old friend that he would keep secret Sir Gerald's escape from the battle where my father died. But how could I dare take such a chance with a friend's life? I knew Bruno's devotion to what he believed his duty. Neither pity nor mercy would stop him from dragging Sir Gerald to the king to suffer whatever punishment Stephen decided was proper for a man who had done no more than obey his overlord.

"I do not know who *lives* in the hall," I replied,

lowering my eyes to the tally stick in my hand and cleaning a splinter out of one leg of the M.

I was not lying. I had seen several open, half-filled barrels of salt fish standing in one of the outbuildings that I thought had been a house rather than a storage shed. In fact, it seemed more likely that Sir Gerald would live in one of the common folk's houses because it would be much easier to conceal his identity if he should be surprised by a search party or a visit. Most people would not realize that one barrel had been set where it would conceal the firepit and all had been left open so the smell of fish would be stronger than any lingering trace of smoke.

There was a brief silence after I spoke and I felt Bruno staring down at me, but I hurriedly began to carve my mark on a second tally stick so I would not have to lift my head. If that one was incorrect, I would have to accept the loss. I was growing frightened wondering whether Bruno could somehow have heard about Sir Gerald, when he remarked that he saw no sign of stores except salt fish. That made me look up at him with a frown.

"That would be right since Sir Giles must have taken lord's share of what little came from the fields already. Wyth does not harvest enough grain to feed even these few folk. They trade fish for produce. The pigs are still in the woods. Slaughtering has not yet begun, except for a single animal now and again for food. What would you expect to find here?"

I felt another stab of fear; Bruno was not looking at me, and his face was set like stone. But in another minute he said, "You are right. There is nothing here. Let us go on to Rydal."

"Let us eat first so I can finish with these tally sticks," I protested.

"Very well," Bruno said flatly. "I will go down to the mere and look about for a few minutes."

That reply seemed very peculiar, for we had brought our food and could sit down and eat in a sheltered sunny corner any time. Nonetheless, my fear diminished. There had been no threat in Bruno's voice or manner. Instead he seemed very disappointed. I could not imagine why; I had told him that Wyth was the poorest and least developed of the small manors my father had founded. And disappointed or not, I still had to make sense out of Bruno's deciding to take a walk by the lake when all we had to do was open a pair of saddlebags and eat. All I could think was that perhaps Bruno wanted to sit in greater comfort at a table or felt it to be below the dignity of the lord of the manor to perch on a log or sit in the dry grass.

In a few minutes a table and two stools were brought out and I sent a man after Bruno. I laid out the small cloth I had expected to set on the ground, and one of the women who had been a maidservant came running with wooden bowls and spoons and a large pot of hot fish stew. It was delicious, the perfect addition to the cold roast venison, cheese, bread, and wine we carried. Perhaps the food made Bruno more cheerful, but he seemed happier after we were on the road to Rydal, and he certainly approved in every way of that manor.

The bailiff there had wanted to take me aside, but I explained that Bruno was my husband and would not betray him. He did not seem entirely comfortable—and for an instant I was terrified over giving so broad a command, fearing that some other rebel folk might be sheltering at Rydal—but the fear was baseless. The bailiff was only worried because he had been less successful than Tom in hiding the arable land from Sir Giles, and that greedy sloth had taken nearly half their crop. If they gave full lord's share to me, they would starve.

I acknowledged that it was more difficult to conceal the arable land around Rydal. The hills here were all low and much of the forest had been cleared. He addressed most of these remarks to Bruno, but it did him no good because Bruno shrugged, said he knew nothing of the crops in this area, and wandered away to inspect the hall and outbuildings, leaving me to ask for the tally sticks. I assumed Bruno's actions implied that I should settle the matter and I did. The bailiff did not get what he wanted, but the folk of Rydal would not be more than lightly hunger pinched—and with my father and brothers absent they could hunt more freely and fill any empty corners in their bellies with game.

It was just as well we had visited both manors that day

because it poured rain and blew a gale on the next. I barely
ran from Winifred's house to the hall without being blown
away. On the second day there was only a light drizzle and
the wind seemed less, but it came off the mountains out
onto the lake. Bruno said, as we broke our fast, that he
would ride to Thirl with any guide who knew the way,
since I did not want to visit that manor. He did not
understand that the wind would be worse in the hills, and
it would sweep through the passes in a roaring fury that
could easily lift a horse and rider and toss them over the
side of a trail—but I dared not tell him that. There might
come a day when I would have to send him out in such
weather to rid myself of him. A great hand seemed to
clutch at my chest and squeeze the breath out of me at the
thought so that I gasped for air.

All I could do was to plead with him not to go. I saw his
eyes go to Sir Giles—I think he had had enough of that
one's company—and he argued a little, but he yielded to
my pleading much more readily than I expected and he
was much easier to amuse than papa or Magnus when they
had been thwarted. I ran back to Winifred's house to fetch
another item the maids had packed in my chest because it
was clearly meant for traveling—a small chess set wrapped
in a cloth that served as a board. I had taken it along when
Bruno and I left Winchester, and we had used it a few
times. I knew Bruno took pleasure in the game, though
neither he nor I had much skill. We played for an hour or
two, and then began to gamble for silly stakes with marked
bones, which I unearthed from beneath a slab of stone
bordering the hearth. Sir Giles stared at me, but I only
laughed when he tried the other hearth stones, and the
bones, although painted with symbols and very old, were
worthless. I had often wondered where papa had found
them and why he kept them buried by the hearth, for they
were the bones of a man, but I had never asked, and it was
too late now. We hardly noticed when the wind died.

The next day dawned clear, with hardly a breath of
breeze from either lake or mountain. It was almost warm,
and when Bruno asked if I would change my mind and
ride to Thirl with him, I nearly said yes. Then I thought of
the unchanged state of Thirl—of Donald's chair by the

hearth with the cushion Mildred had embroidered and the stool by it on which she sat. Perhaps Thirl had been stripped by some raiding party—but what if it had not? Would I see Donald lying back in the chair, laughing at me? Mildred with her hand outstretched to draw me to her? I swallowed hard and shook my head, my voice beyond control.

Bruno's face hardened, and I looked quickly away. Rage struggled with grief and fear in me until I remembered that for him nearly a year had passed while for me it was only a few months. I looked up, but he had already turned away, saying over his shoulder that he would see to Barbe's saddling as well as horses for his men and a guide and asked whom he should ask to lead him.

"Tom Bailiff would be best, if he has not left the manor," I replied. "I will walk down and tell him."

It took me a few minutes to find the man; he was outside the gates talking to the swineherd about bringing in an animal to slaughter to honor my arrival, and I told him sharply not to be a fool, since Sir Giles would want to know from where an extra plump, healthy pig had come if he had not ordered it to be slaughtered. We must eat from Sir Giles's table, not from my hidden stock, I reminded him. Then I told him I would like him to guide Bruno to Thirl. He looked startled, then said that Peter Huntsman would be a better guide for the party and shouted to a passing boy to fetch him to us.

I was not pleased by Tom's resistance to my order, but by the time the shepherd had been sent off, the huntsman was in sight and it was too late to insist on my own way. Besides, I was not sure how to make Tom obey if he would not. Everyone had always obeyed me because papa and my brothers would have enforced my orders, right or wrong. I was not at all certain Bruno would do so—and in any case, he did not have the right; Sir Giles was legally master here. So I swallowed my pride, nodded a greeting to Peter, and explained that he was to guide my husband and his party to Thirl and home again.

"There can be no danger in riding in the hills on so still a day," I said to Peter finally, "but remember the men are riding English horses, not mountain goats, so go through the pass of the Stick, not over White Side. I wish to ride White Side with Sir Bruno myself.''

"I will look forward to that,'' Bruno said from behind me, but he did not look at me, gesturing Peter toward a horse one of his men was holding.

His face was blank and there had been a peculiar note in his voice, almost like longing, that made me wonder whether he had been disappointed rather than angry when I refused to go with him to Thirl. I had noticed that Bruno was much more desirous of my company since we lay together as man and wife. But we had not coupled last night because my flux had begun. Surely the man could not be so silly as to add my refusal last night to my refusal to go to Thirl and believe I was angry about something? I almost started after them, and just barely choked down a cry for Bruno to return when Tom said, "I will bring Sir Gerald to the hollow as soon as the party is out of sight.''

Well, if Bruno were silly, I was far worse. I had almost forgotten that his visit to Thirl was a perfect opportunity to meet with Sir Gerald. Still, I could not help glancing back over my shoulder at the riders. Again I called myself a fool. I could explain everything just as well after Bruno came home. Foolish once, foolish twice; without thinking I went back inside the gates intending to go to Winifred's house to change to stouter boots and get my cloak, and of course I fell into Sir Giles's clutches.

At first I could not understand his arch looks and self-satisfied smiles as he made unnecessary and foolish flattering remarks about how lovely I looked that morning. So indifferent was I to the cloddish creature that I did not even suspect his intention when he asked if I would play chess with him. I was surprised by the request—it was largely his impatience with the game and his remarks on it, which even such poor players as Bruno and myself recognized as totally inept, that had driven us to abandon it. I looked down at my toes, trying wildly to think of some excuse, and Sir Giles, totally misunderstanding, took me by the arm and murmured into my ear that there was no need to feel shy; he would be happy to serve so lovely a lady. While I gaped, wide-eyed with disbelief, that wet cow-flop dared stroke my arm and say he would accompany me to my bedchamber to get the chess set and then, no doubt, I could find an errand on which to send my maid. *Then* it burst on me like a thunderclap that the stupid clod thought I had sent my husband away so that I could be alone with him!

I should have boxed his ears, of course, or better yet, spit in his face, but the whole idea that *any* woman, including a feeble-minded crone of sixty, could desire him enough to cheat on a husband, no matter how bad, was too ludicrous to take seriously. Besides, I was not yet ready to leave Ulle, so I decided I had better decline civilly.

"I am afraid I do not feel like playing today," I said. "I do not feel very well. And I cannot allow you to accompany me to Winifred's house because I must change my bleeding rags. It is kind of you to wish to amuse me, but I am better off alone on such days."

The truth was that I was never much aware of bleeding and sometimes messed my garments from forgetting my condition. It was Mildred who had trouble, sometimes flying into rages or weeping for nothing just before her bleeding began and sometimes being so racked with cramping in her belly while she bled that she could do nothing except lie in her bed and grit her teeth against moans. Sir Giles stared at me open-mouthed, and then turned from me with a foul curse and a look of disgust. I had much ado not to laugh for a moment, but then tears rose to my eyes as I silently blessed my lost sister for spreading the mantle of her torment over me to protect me.

After that I got my boots and cloak, but I had to send Edna out to discover where Sir Giles was before I could sneak out of the manor to meet Sir Gerald. As I left, I also bade her sit outside the closed door and tell him I was abed if he should happen to ask for me and she nodded, grinning. I doubted he had the brains to suspect me of plans of my own, aside from being convinced that I would engage in the lecherous deceptions attributed to every woman, but I did not want him to learn that I had gone out. Edna's ready understanding pleased me; in fact, I was very well pleased in every way with Bruno's choice of a maid. Edna's ability to sew had progressed rapidly; she had made herself a new gown, refitted the old one to her figure, and begun a tunic for me in a fine, rose-colored wool that Audris had given me. So far I had had no complaints about her behavior with men, and she was certainly circumspect when I was present.

Thinking hard as I could about Edna could not mask completely the growing pain in my throat and chest. I had always been fond of Sir Gerald, but that he should live and papa die was hard, very hard. Yet I was also glad he had survived; he was someone, one lone thread stretching back into the part of my life that was over. My steps slowed, then quickened, then slowed again. I swallowed and bit my lips and recalled the many, many times I had been in Sir Gerald's company, and yet, when I saw him waiting for me, his eyes alight with eagerness, I burst into tears. He rushed to me and took me in his arms and also wept as he patted me and tried to comfort me.

At last he put me away a little and said, "Come, Melly, they are dead almost a year. This is too much . . . or . . ." His arms tightened around me again. "Melly, is the man cruel to you? Tom said you spoke well of him, this Sir Bruno."

"It is nothing to do with Bruno," I sobbed. "To me it is as if they died less than two months ago. All the while the king held me, I was mad. Oh, Sir Gerald, I do not remember half the winter, the whole spring, and part of the autumn."

"Too much grief," Sir Gerald said softly. "Too much grief for any woman to bear. Hush, child, it is over now. They are at peace, and with God's help you will find some peace too. Now, what of this man? He must have been forced on you. What do you wish me to do?"

My tears did indeed dry up as I realized that Sir Gerald thought I had called him to free me of a hated husband. I had to bite my lips to keep from laughing, and then blink back more tears. Poor Sir Gerald; my Bruno would have killed him in . . . "my" Bruno?

"Forced on me, yes," I said quickly, hiding from my own thoughts as well as seeking an answer that would satisfy Sir Gerald if it should ever become possible for him and Bruno to meet. "For I would not have willingly married a man who must have been papa's enemy, but he is a good man and has been kind to me.'' I hesitated, thinking that if Bruno did get back my lands, they would come from the king, and Sir Gerald had better know that Bruno was Stephen's man heart and soul. If Sir Gerald could learn to accept the king, perhaps Bruno could win him a pardon also, so I added, "I think also that the king and queen meant well when they chose Bruno for my husband. Although he—he is not so well born—''

"A bastard, eh?'' Sir Gerald remarked.

I wondered how he guessed that, and then realized that Tom must have said Bruno was a lord, and the common folk are very quick to detect their fellows dressed up in rich clothes to deceive.

"Yes,'' I admitted, quickly deciding that there was no need for Sir Gerald to know the whole truth, "but he is recognized and dearly loved by his half sister and her husband—the lord and lady of Jernaeve. Sir Hugh offered to take him as vassal for a good property.''

"A strong man, then, and a good leader?''

"Yes, and a great favorite with King Stephen, and—and he refused vassalage because he believes that in time he can convince the king to enfeoff him with Ulle.'' I said that in a rush, fearful that Sir Gerald would be angry, but he only patted my shoulder.

"You want me to leave here then,'' he said slowly.

"No!'' I cried. "Oh, no! This is your home. Where would you go?''

"You must not think of that, child,'' he replied. "I will find a place, never fear for me.''

But he was old. I had never noticed that before, but now I saw the lines on his face and the grey in his hair. He would not find a place, not really. Someone might take him in for charity, but that would destroy his pride.

"No!'' I exclaimed. "I need you.''

I could see that he was about to go on arguing, so I shook my head vehemently and opened my mouth to explain my lack of confidence in Tom's continued honesty under the strain of lacking a master. Just in time I remembered to ask softly if Sir Gerald was sure the bailiff was gone, and he assured me he had sent Tom away with the excuse that his absence might be coupled with mine if he stayed. Then I explained how Tom Bailiff was hiding most of the produce of my estate but that someone must oversee Tom.

"Sir Gerald, if you will not stay and be my deputy," I ended, "there may be little left to build on by the time Bruno gets the lands."

To my surprise, he looked shocked. "Melly," he protested, "that is not honest. Forgive me, my dear, but your father did an unwise thing. Little as I like it, Stephen had the *right* to do as he did. It is the law. And the yield of the land is his by right."

"Perhaps," I snapped, "but *I* did no wrong. I tried to stop papa from going to King David. I am of Ulle, and England and Scotland both can be sunk in the sea for all I care. Why should *I* lose my lands?" I saw that he was about to tell me what others had in the past, that a woman had not sense enough to consider such matters, and that was why she must be bound to the will of her menfolk. But I was not in a temper to listen to pious mouthings—which were clearly false, since if papa had listened to my "lack of sense" he would still be alive and the lands ours—and I hurried on to explain that Sir Giles would swallow all, and whatever was yielded, none would come to the king. "Moreover," I ended, "I have shown all to Bruno, and he agrees with me."

"So he does!"

I flung myself before Sir Gerald, trying to hide him or protect him, I do not know which, with my body. How Bruno had crept up on us, I have no idea, but there he was, smiling down at us from the little rise that sheltered the hollow.

CHAPTER 17

Bruno

THE DISCOVERY that the purpose of Melusine's secret meeting with Sir Gerald was a conspiracy about nothing worse than making sure her bailiff did not cheat her filled me with such joy that I would have committed a far greater crime to please her than concealing Sir Gerald's escape from the battle at Wark. I was very sorry to have caused her the terror I saw in her face when she cast herself between Sir Gerald and me, and I would have told her so directly—which would have been a grave mistake. Fortunately Sir Gerald put her gently aside, telling her not to be a fool.

"Am I your prisoner, Sir Bruno?" he asked steadily.

"I know of no ill you have done sir," I replied. "Nor do I remember seeing or hearing your name on any list of proscribed men." That was the truth; I had been searching my memory for Sir Gerald's name since I heard it when Melusine bade Tom Bailiff bring the man here, and he had not been proscribed with Sir Malcolm and Sir Donald. I nodded at him. "I have come to Ulle on a visit with my wife and have no official standing. Unless you have recently taken up a career of rape, murder, and arson, I have no reason to take you prisoner."

"Then why have you been searching for me?" he asked.

"Do not flatter yourself, Sir Gerald," I answered. "My purpose was of deeper and more abiding interest to me. I have been examining what I hope will be my property if I can earn it by service to the king. That cannot be very soon, unfortunately, and," I could hear my voice grow harsh, "I want to know what to take out of Sir Giles's hide when I can rid the place of him. As to you, if I had found you, I would have told you what I have just said."

Sir Gerald passed a hand over his face. "Have I been hiding for nothing then?"

"I do not know," I told him honestly. "Certainly you are not being *sought*, yet if some enemy should bring you before the sheriff and swear that you had fought for King David, you might be imprisoned in hope of ransom."

Sir Gerald laughed loud and heartily. "I would be in prison a long time in that expectation. I have nothing, not horse nor arms nor armor. I was left for dead before Wark and stripped like the other corpses. I have no idea how long I lay there, but it must have been two days at least from the growth of my beard. Why I did not freeze I do not know, nor do I know when I crawled away from the battlefield, only that I woke up the second time in a wood." He turned away from me and drew Melusine to him. "I never saw your papa and Donald struck down, Melly. I went first, so I have nothing to tell you. I am sorry I was so careless. Mayhap . . ."

Melusine pulled away from him and ran wildly away toward the manor. I looked after her but did not follow. She was best alone in the first moments of her grief; God forbid that grief should suddenly wake her memory of me as the invader of her hall. Besides, I needed a few more words with Sir Gerald.

"Does she still hope?" he asked, also looking after Melusine.

"I do not think so, but she still hurts," I said grimly. It seemed that the queen was wrong about Melusine. Poor girl, she had no reason to lie to her father's old friend, and she had told him that she had been mazed in her wits by grief. Then I saw how tensely he was watching me, and I shook my head. "They are dead beyond doubt. The king was not at Wark, nor I, but Sir Malcolm and Sir Donald must have been marked by one who knew them. I know they were listed as buried because I examined the scroll myself soon after Melusine and I were married.''

He nodded quietly, but I thought his shoulders slumped somewhat and his face became a little greyer. He had been hoping that Melusine's father or brother had survived I guessed, even though he knew it unlikely. I was sorry for the old man and I hesitated because I found it hard to ask the question I must ask. To hurt Melusine again, if the answer was wrong . . . but my life was sworn to Stephen.

"I said I knew of no ill you had done, and that is true, Sir Gerald, but as Melusine told you, I am a king's man. I *must* ask—if there is war again between my lord and King David or the party that supports Empress Matilda, what will you do?''

"Nothing,'' he said, looking steadily into my face. "I am of no party, and I have no overlord to order my loyalty now. I am landless, masterless, penniless. What could I do? And if you are asking whether I am willing to sell my sword . . .'' He laughed bitterly. "I do not have one, and who would buy the sword of an old man anyway?''

"That is not good enough. A man of your experience, who knows the ways of this dangerous land, *would* be of value and could be dangerous to my lord,'' I pointed out—and I was glad to see his eyes brighten and his shoulders go back with renewed pride. "I cannot ask you to swear to me,'' I went on, "because I am little richer than you, and can offer you nothing. A useless master is a bad master.''

I paused and was delighted that he did not rush to protest that he was eager to be my man without benefit. That would have marked a man who lied easily to save his skin. Then I went on, "But I must ask you to give your word not to aid the king's enemies. In turn, I will gladly give mine to return Irthing to you—or one of the other manors, depending on what the king will give me, if he gives me anything.''

He thought that over for another moment, then said slowly, "I will promise not to take service with any man who is bound to King David or Empress Matilda for the purpose of overthrowing King Stephen, but I cannot swear any general oath not to oppose you. I must reserve the right to protect Melly. She said you were kind to her, but I do not know you, Sir Bruno, and she must be my first concern.''

"Then we are easily agreed," I said, smiling. "I will tell you truly that I was no more willing to marry than Melusine in the beginning, but she has become very dear to me. I will do my uttermost to protect her. But there is one thing I must tell you. When Ulle was taken, I was the first man in, the first man she saw. She—she does not seem to remember that, but if she should do so and take me in distaste for that reason—''

"I certainly will not encourage such silliness in her." He answered my unspoken question immediately and without hostility, then frowned. "Unless . . . You did not harm her, did you?''

"I did not touch her, not even come close or speak to her. No one harmed her. King Stephen took her under his protection immediately," I assured Sir Gerald, glad I could tell him something favorable of my lord that the servants of Ulle would confirm.

"Then Melly has no right to be angry with you, and remembering that you obeyed your master is no reason for her to turn on you. You obeyed your overlord as I obeyed mine, and she must learn to accept that. I know women do not understand such matters, but I will not break my promise to you for that reason. I will explain it to her and tell her that Sir Malcolm would honor you for doing your duty.''

I breathed a sigh of relief. I was sure that Melusine trusted this man, and I knew that she had been devoted to her father. If she should remember, perhaps Sir Gerald could convince her that I had not deprived her of Ulle of my own will. He nodded, acknowledging my relief, but said only that he would stay until first light tomorrow in case Melusine wished to speak to him again. He hesitated and I was sure he would ask me to arrange another meeting—she was his last link with his lost past—but he only grimaced, I thought in recognition of his own foolishness, and told me to assure Melusine that he would demand accounts from Tom Bailiff and the headmen of the other manors, to remind them that Ulle still had a master.

I thanked him and as he turned away, called him back and told him, if he should be betrayed by an enemy—more likely now that he intended to take an active role in the management of Ulle—to send a message to me at court and another to Jernaeve, one of which would surely reach me. I was not certain I could help him, I explained, but I did have the king's ear, and there was a chance Stephen would spare a friend of mine and of Melusine's.

We did not remain in Ulle much longer, only a few days, during which Melusine, as she had promised, took me up White Side and any number of other mountains. I admit I hope never to see the top of some of those again despite my wife's enthusiasm for perching on the edge of windy crags to admire a fine stretch of wilderness. However, at those few moments when my attention was not wholly fixed on not toppling off a trail a mouse would have found narrow, I noted that the area was thick with hawks.

I had thought then that Ulle could have a mews that would rival the one at Jernaeve, and I thought it again as we rode across the mouth of Grisdale and on south toward Brothers Water, where I saw the graceful birds circling. That was a resource Melusine's father had not used, it seemed. Perhaps he had had no taste for hawking and I knew he had no friends in high places, but I was different. I recalled how Sir Oliver had used the beautiful and well-trained birds with which Audris filled Jernaeve's mews. Often a fine hawk brought great benefit to Jernaeve or bought peace and well-being. I could do the same for Ulle, and service with the king had taught me just which people to gift.

Not that I was about to allow Melusine to climb cliffs and trees as Audris did, but I knew Audris would gladly teach her skills to our . . . My thoughts checked. I had been about to call the folk of Ulle "our people." I must stop dreaming, at least stop fixing my hope on so real a thing as Ulle. Vague dreams may be renewed when disappointed; but dreams fixed in reality shatter, and shards pierce the heart. Anyway the hawks would be gone south soon, for the weather had changed and Ullswater lay grey and still under a cold steel sky.

Melusine had taken one look that morning and said we must go, that snow would come that night or on the morrow and we would be trapped with the passes closed if the snow was heavy. I did not argue, having learned that she was right too often about Cumbrian weather but went to tell Sir Giles and to apologize for our abrupt departure. He had shrugged and grunted that we were indeed fortunate to be able to flee the horror of a Cumbrian winter. I commiserated with him, but did not suggest that he could easily leave and no one know or care. If he left the place and were removed from his office as steward too soon, another more efficient man, or worse yet, someone who knew Cumbria and could manage the people, might be appointed. It would be much harder to obtain estates that were flourishing and paying taxes into the king's coffers.

Aside from that, I really had little sympathy with his distaste for the winter months; I was used to long, snow-heaped winters at Jernaeve, and sitting by the roaring fires of winter with Audris and Sir Oliver was among my sweetest memories. My heart stirred to think that I would spend such winters at Ulle with Melusine.

Again I told myself not to fix my hope on so uncertain an objective, but I could not resist trying to smooth my way to it, and Melusine and I often discussed how to convince the queen that Melusine in Ulle would be no more dangerous to King Stephen than Melusine at court. We never found an answer—how could we "prove" something that depended on what was inside Melusine's heart and head?—but even our fruitless talk gave me joy. Just to be with Melusine gave me joy.

We had more than enough time to discuss that and to sit by the fire or lie warm together because Melusine had been right about the snow. We were not actually trapped, but what should have been two days' ride took five days. Even after we came out of the mountains the roads were seas of freezing mud. Until then I had not minded the delay, but I had sent Cormi to Jernaeve for our chests, and after we met him in York, I often had cause to regret the need for court clothes. With the cart we dared not try to shorten the distance on side roads. Even on such great ways as Watling Street, which we took south of Leicester, we came close to being mired more than once. We did not reach London until the third day of January, and came into the city so late that we found lodging not far from Aldersgate rather than struggle through the dark to Westminster, where we would not be expected and likely find no place to sleep.

Not that I was aware of the date when we arrived, although I knew it was past Christmas—we had celebrated that in some small town. I lost count of the days again on the road, and did not bother to ask since we could move no faster than we were already going. My temper would only grow worse with each day I knew I was overstaying my leave, so it was useless to count them. I was relieved to find out the evening we arrived that the twelve days were not yet over, and that we were not as late as I feared. So instead of rushing off to the king, I rose early, left Melusine sleeping, and hurried to the West Cheap, where I purchased a pretty pair of long earrings, a necklet of gold wire so cleverly twisted that it looked like lace set with very small pearls, and a tiny bejeweled knife for paring nails—I could not resist that as a reminder of her reaction to our marriage.

I had not realized how long I had taken choosing and chaffering for the gifts. They cost more than I planned too, yet I could not buy false, bright dross for Melusine. However thin the gold wire, it was real gold; and each pearl and jewel, though minute, were true in color and form. I expected to find sharp words waiting for me, but Melusine hardly listened to my excuse, pointing to my court clothes laid out and bidding me change quickly while she packed away what I was wearing. She too was in court dress, all else packed and ready so we could go at once.

I was surprised and said so because Melusine had often told me she thought of her service to the queen as a kind of captivity, but she did not respond to my remarks and uttered vague assurances when I asked direct questions. I wondered whether she was angry about my unexplained absence—I had said only that I had business to do. If so, the cure was in my purse, and I would enjoy applying it.

Considering how and when to offer my gifts kept me

pleasantly busy during the short ride. The king's palace at Westminster was only about half a league from our lodging, and even after battling the men, women, horses, dogs, mules, carts, wains, and all else that flowed through the streets, it did not take long to get there. Still, by the time I found a place to leave my men and my cart and shepherded Melusine and Edna through the crowded courtyard, we arrived barely in time to present ourselves before dinner, I to the king's chamberlain and Melusine to the queen's.

I do not know what greeting Melusine had, but Geoffrey of Glympton, the king's chamberlain, was not well pleased to see me, growling that he did not know if another herring could be packed into the barrel. All he could offer was a pallet in the king's chamber. There was no room for my men. Westminster was filled to bursting; every lord in the land seemed to have come to this Christmas court. Although this spelled discomfort for me, I was glad of it. The great attendance must mean that rebellion was at an end and all acknowledged the king's power.

Stephen himself was more welcoming, and he only grinned at his chamberlain's complaints. In high good humor, he embraced me in a huge bear hug and smiled at me when I said I had a confession to make. He told me he had no time then to let me ease my conscience, but bade me with a laugh to attend him after the evening meal and then dismissed me to find lodging for my men. I ate no dinner that day. It took me all the forenoon to accomplish what should not have taken an hour's time. Each page I sent with a message to let Melusine know I must lodge with the king never returned, and I had to assume the boys had been captured by a more important person and sent on a different errand. I had to accompany my men to see that my chest was placed in the king's apartment, and Melusine's was three times sent to the wrong place by officious, ignorant servants before Edna recognized my men and directed them.

I almost fell on her neck and kissed her when I saw her coming back with the men. Although I had had the forethought to tell them to bring her with them, I had almost given up hope that they would find her and had begun to fear that I would have to ask admittance to the queen's chamber to explain matters to Melusine and get her good clothing to her. I did not want to take the chance of drawing the queen's attention to me though; I was sure if I did, Maud would seize on me and ask questions I did not wish to answer until after I had spoken to the king. Now Edna could tell Melusine to seek lodging with the queen; there was another problem Edna could solve for me also. She understood the ways of the city, and if I sent her out with Fechin to find lodging and stabling, she would not permit him to be cheated.

Edna listened and nodded, asked a question or two about where I would prefer the men to be placed and what I was willing to pay and whether area or cost was most important, then said she would find something. I thanked her and gave her a silver penny, and to my surprise she laughed and said she would keep it because she had been bred up to take money from men but that she had been paid and overpaid already for any service she could do for me or for Lady Melusine. And I really looked at her and saw that she spoke the truth, for she was a different woman, carrying herself with pride and without fear. I was glad I had not asked Edna to spy on Melusine in Ulle. The girl had a place in the world now; it would have been a shame to stain her loyalty.

A glance at the sky told me it was both too late and too early to ask for food, dinner being long over and the evening meal not yet started. The nearest cookshop was too far, so I turned toward the kitchen sheds, where I hoped to be able to wheedle some bread and cold meat to fill my hollow belly, when my arm was seized in a powerful grip.

"Bruno! Where the devil have you been these two weeks?"

I bowed, masking my surprise as well as I could when my eyes met the pale blue gaze of Ranulf de Gernon, earl of Chester. "I was lately married, my lord," I said, "to Lady Melusine of Ulle, and the king gave me leave to make my wife known to my half sister, Lady Audris of Jernaeve."

This was the first time in my life that I had openly named my relationship to Audris, and my statement of

Melusine's full name was also deliberate. Ranulf of Chester had a claim to Cumbria, which his father had held and surrendered to King Henry for the right to inherit the earldom of Chester. If Lord Ranulf ever won his claim, he might be overlord of Cumbria, and I wanted to remind him that I had a deep interest in the north.

A moment after I spoke, I regretted it. Chester had opened his mouth to say something, but he closed it abruptly, a gleam of interest making his eyes even paler. His brow creased in thought, then he nodded and said, "Ulle? I know that name, I am sure. That is a place not far from Carlisle. So your new wife is from Cumbria?"

"Yes, my lord, but she was disseisined because her father was a rebel, and—and we have no further interest in Cumbria."

Chester smiled broadly and I had all I could do to keep my rage at my own stupidity from showing. In trying to recoup one blunder, I had made one much worse; I had betrayed by denying it my desire for Ulle. And Chester was a man who understood such desires—all too well.

Pretending I did not understand his broad smile, I asked, "Is there some way I can serve you, my lord?"

My heart sank as the words echoed in my ears. It was only a formal question, one I had asked many lords many times during my service to King Stephen, but in conjunction with exposing my desire for Melusine's lands, it rang with implications I had not intended. Chester would doubtless interpret that question as a hint, for he was just the man to dangle Ulle as a bait, asking for a trifling service, a trifling favor, and implying that when he had regained his father's lost power over Cumbria, he would remember those services and favors.

"Yes, you can," he replied, smiling again. "You can tell the king that I am leaving tomorrow, but I would be glad of a word with him in private if he can spare the time tonight."

"I am not summoned to service until after the evening meal," I said, keeping my voice flat and my face blank. "If you need someone to speak earlier, you will have to seek another messenger, my lord."

"No, no. If I desired to see the king in the middle of a

rush of other business, I could have presented myself now.
I said tonight. I wish to find Stephen at leisure.''

"Very well, my lord," I said.

He clapped me familiarly on the shoulder, as a man
might do in thanking his own upper servant, and nodded
and turned away, leaving me much shaken. There was no
other answer I could have made to his request because I
knew that the king wished to conciliate the earl of Chester.
He was too powerful to offend, and for my master's sake, I
must do as he asked—which gave the impression that I
did wish to serve him. Yet Chester was the last man I
would wish to see as overlord in Cumbria. I did not trust
him; I could not decide whether he was greedy and power-
hungry or whether he was simply obsessed with reestab-
lishing his right to Cumbria. But whichever was true, I
was certain that no oath of fealty would override that
desire, and his loyalty would go with the prize he sought.
For me—if I should be enfeoffed with Ulle—an overload
who changed sides from Stephen to Matilda would be a
disaster.

Three months away from court and I seemed to have
forgotten all I had learned in two years! I was disgusted
with myself; I had not spoken with such thoughtlessness
and naivety even in the beginning of my service. Between
lack of food and anxiety, my stomach was flapping against
my backbone, which reminded me that I would be an
unknown, nameless face in the cookshop and all too well
known almost anywhere in Westminster. Without another
thought about the long walk, I went out through the nearest gate and set out along the river.

It was almost dark when I returned, my stomach very
full of tasty food and my heart much calmer than when I
set out. It was true that I should have been more careful
about what I said, but doing what I knew the king would
want me to do did not commit me to Chester's service, no
matter what the earl thought. So it was in good spirits that
I came to stand behind the king's chair, placing myself so
that he would see me as soon as he rose and turned away
from the table. His eyes lit when they fell on me and his
smile warmed me. I spoke only the truth when I bowed
and said, "I am very glad to return to your service, sire."

"And I to have you back." He shook his finger at me. "I thought you might have forgotten me, you were away so long."

"Only because I spent near six weeks lifting a cart out of one mudhole after another," I said ruefully. "Our journey took much longer than I expected." I felt rather than saw someone approaching to get Stephen's attention and I added quickly, "You have not forgotten that I have a confession to make, my lord. I meant no ill and no ill came of what I did, but I would not wish you to hear of it from another man."

Stephen looked surprised, not as if he had forgotten what I had said earlier but as if he had thought it was a jest. But when he glanced at the gentleman sidling around to block his way to the door of his closet, he shook his head and said, "I am sorry Pembroke, but I have promised to play confessor to Bruno—and hear his news also." And he made his way firmly to the door and through it, drawing me, and me alone, in with him.

Inside, he laughed. "Did you say that to save me from Pembroke?" he asked. "Or have you really committed some crime against me?"

I grinned back. "You are very kind to make a mousehole out of Pembroke's greediness for me to escape into, but I dare not accept that escape. Twice I have nerved myself to confess. I will never manage a third time." I was speaking lightly, but I saw a flicker of doubt in the king's eyes, and I hurried to put that doubt to rest. "I have not committed a crime, my lord, only yielded to my wife's desire to see her old home and took her to spend a week in Ulle."

"And?" Stephen urged, seeming to expect some unpleasant news.

"There is no 'and,' my lord. That is all I had to confess. I wanted you to know we went there. Melusine has a great love of the country, and it is very beautiful despite being poor. I saw no signs of disaffection in the people, but we did not visit any of the local gentlemen. I would say the common folk care for nothing but their small farms and fishing boats."

The king raised his brows. "You needed total privacy to tell me this?"

I laughed. "No, my lord, although I was eager that you should know. What I wished you to hear in private was that the earl of Chester stopped me in the courtyard and bade me tell you that he wished to leave tomorrow but would be grateful if you would spare him a few minutes alone tonight." The anger I saw in the tightening of the king's lips made me add, "If you do not wish to see him, I can go to him in the morning and say I found no time to give you his message."

"He has not asked me for leave to go," Stephen said.

I remembered that Chester had said he *was* leaving. I had assumed that he already had the king's permission, but apparently he did not feel he needed it. Heat rose in my face as I flushed with anger at the way Chester had used me to deliver a subtle insult to my master.

"Let me bring him a message forbidding his leaving," I snarled, "and challenge him to meet me man to man if he will not obey."

Stephen met my eyes, his own bright with anger and his jaw set, but after a moment, he shook his head. "It is too dangerous. I doubt if he would accept challenge, and anyway, I would have to forbid the meeting. No one would believe I did not know of it, and it is the king's business to keep the peace when he holds court. Another thing, Bruno, I do not know why Chester came to court at all. He has not joined the council of barons to do any business; he has not asked me for any favors—aside from his usual complaint of how Cumbria was reft from his father unjustly. So why did he come?"

"To see if the court was thin after the troubles in the summer to decide whether a new and greater rebellion was brewing?" I suggested furiously.

But my sneering remark had an odd effect on Stephen. The anger faded from his face, and then I realized I must have called to his mind the crowded court, the many nobles who now fawned on him seeking favor and recognition. "If he hoped to see me weak, he has had a round answer," the king said with smug satisfaction. "No, I will not deny him. Go bring him to me, Bruno. Let us see what he desires."

I was still angry, but I realized that by accident—and

partly against my will—I had done the right thing in calming the king. The trouble was that Stephen was virtually helpless against so great and powerful a noble. He could not seize him and imprison him here in Westminster even for open defiance. During a holding of court, strict custom decreed that all who came had safe conduct to depart after the king did so or earlier by permission. It was a good custom; without it, few men would have found the courage to bring a complaint to the king or answer a summons to decide even a just cause. And for minor knights or barons the custom of safe conduct was a protection without any license for defiance or contumely. A minor gentleman could be caught and punished any time after the holding of court was over, but once a great lord like Chester was back on his own lands, he was too strong to be attacked by the king's mercenaries. It would be necessary to summon a baronial army to fight the earl of Chester, which would most likely revive the rebellion that Stephen had just seemingly put down.

It soothed me somewhat to find Chester near at hand and watching the door of Stephen's private closet out of the corner of his eye. I had almost suspected that his only purpose in stopping me was to have me pass on the insult of his leaving without permission. I was wrong about that it seemed. Chester did have some request to make of Stephen. Yet he did not seem pleased when I nodded at him and said, "The king will see you now, my lord." But that might have been because I used the same phrasing to him that I would have used to any minor nobleman, or perhaps my tone was not all it should have been.

I felt even better when, as Chester entered, Stephen, who had seated himself beside the fire while I went out to fetch the earl, looked up and said, "You desire permission to leave our court? You have it."

I had not expected so perfect a response, for the king was not particularly apt at quick responses, and I had to swallow hard to hold back a little crow of laughter. The blow went home too; I could not see Chester's face, but I saw the way his back stiffened and the slight check in his stride. By the time I closed the door and came to stand beside the king's chair, however, Chester had bowed slightly

and come erect again, wearing a faint smile. He shook his
head—to indicate he had not come to ask permission to
leave? If so, he was not ready for open challenge of the
king's authority because he said nothing about that.

"I have a small problem with my bishop about the
selection of a priest for the manor of Ridley," Chester
said, "and I thought since you have just approved
the election of Theobald as archbishop of Canterbury,
that . . ."

The earl continued to speak, but I heard no more. I was
shocked deaf, dumb, and blind. *Theobald* had "just" been
elected archbishop of Canterbury and that election had
been approved by Stephen? Who the devil was Theobald?
How was it possible that anyone except Henry of Winchester could have been approved by the king to be archbishop? Henry was Stephen's own brother and had done
more than any other man to win the throne for him.

When the old archbishop had died not long after Stephen was crowned, it was common gossip that Winchester
would be the next archbishop. When he was not elected
immediately, some said the canons of Canterbury, who
were responsible for the election of the archbishop, were
resisting the king's will because Henry's interests were too
secular. Others said the king himself was delaying the
election to obtain the rich revenues of the see, which
flowed into his hands while there was no archbishop. I
thought it was a bit of both, having heard the king claim
he was waiting for the pope to send a legate. This was an
excellent excuse for delay while Stephen filled his purse at
Canterbury's deep well and could not be blamed on the
king. It was, after all, the pope who bade legates come and
go. In addition, the legate could more easily influence the
canons so that Stephen could be sure his brother would be
elected. But whatever the cause of the delay, I do not think
it occurred to anyone that Henry of Winchester would not
be elevated to the archbishopric.

As my shock receded a little, sadness came. Surely
Stephen could not be so petty as to deny his brother the
crown of his ambition over a quarrel a year in the past?
Yet I could see no other reason for the king to permit the
election of another man, not even, as far as I had ever

heard, a notable churchman. I was no expert on episcopal virtue and I knew that Winchester was no saint, but he was certainly no worse than others who had held the office. He was not lazy or stupid; he was cautious and careful and a good negotiator, which was necessary for the management of the suffragan bishops; he might not be a great scholar, but he loved the Church and would have striven for a smooth working between the Church and the king, which would benefit both and the realm also.

I never discovered what Chester asked of the king so I never found out whether the request was his real purpose or an excuse for testing some unstated idea. I blame myself for that. Perhaps if I had been more alert I would have seen some sign—but I doubt it. I am not even sure that Chester was a practiced deceiver. I think the angry remark I had made—that he had come to examine the king's strength—was more true than an angry burst usually is, and little to Chester's taste as it was, he had decided that he must moderate his demands and live at peace with Stephen or be locked in a struggle he could not be sure of winning.

It is wonderful how years of service teach a man to keep some small part of him alert to a demand by his master no matter where his thoughts may wander. Thus I responded smoothly when the king asked me to pour wine, but all I saw was that Chester was not dissatisfied with the meeting and the king was openly pleased. They drank a cup of wine together and bid each other a cordial farewell before I was told to open the door and invite others into the king's chamber.

I was not surprised when Waleran de Meulan was the first named, but his name brought a new idea into my mind of why Henry of Winchester had been passed over for archbishop of Canterbury. Waleran hated the king's brother, not for any injury Winchester had done him but for his influence over the king, and of course as archbishop of Canterbury that influence would be greatly increased because Winchester would be speaking for the Church in England rather than for himself. Suddenly it occurred to me that Theobald had one all-important virtue in Waleran's opinion—he was *not* Henry of Winchester.

As I went about among the men talking in the great hall, seeking out those the king wished to see in his chamber and deciding whether to invite those with them or wait until I could discreetly separate them from their companions, the subtle struggle between Waleran and Henry of Winchester replayed itself in my mind. It seemed to me that Dame Fortune had been lifting Waleran up on her wheel for a long time. Part of the king's love for Waleran was natural—they were much alike in their tastes and humors—but it seemed pure good fortune that Waleran was absent when Henry blamed the king for yielding terms to Redvers and when William of Ypres's attempt to ambush Robert of Gloucester caused the failure of the campaign in Normandy.

Not that Waleran left matters in Lady Fortune's hands completely. I had always suspected that the reason the wound Henry had dealt Stephen in that year-old quarrel had never healed was that Waleran had continued to pour salt into it. And it seemed that I might have been mistaken about why Waleran had been so eager to be rid of me. I had thought it was to collect news about who opposed the elevation of his relatives to one earldom after another; now it seemed more likely that he wanted me out of the way so I could not impede his efforts to worsen the relationship between the king and his brother.

I liked Henry of Winchester and I did my best to smooth his way, showing him particular courtesy, and making sure the younger squires did too, so that he would feel he was welcome to the king. And those times Stephen refused to see him, I gave the message—or related it to the messenger—with soothing apologies and regrets. If those courtesies were discontinued, Winchester might grow suspicious and angry; his anger and suspicion would irritate the king, who might speak thoughtlessly and harshly; and that could only make Winchester even more suspicious and angry, and round and round. Oh, yes, considerable damage could be done in three months, particularly if Waleran subtly encouraged the discourtesy of the younger squires, who admired him.

With Winchester's defeat and probable withdrawal (I had not seen him among the men in the hall) and with

William of Ypres still in partial disgrace (I had seen him and spoken a few words, but his company was his own mercenary captains and a few minor courtiers), Waleran was now preeminent with the king. I did not like that at all. Waleran was a fine soldier and in his way shrewd, but I had never seen in him a wider view than the increase in his own wealth and power. Of course Fortune was fickle; Waleran might fall. I would not mind that at all—except that tied so close to him, the king might be dragged down too.

Altogether, I was in a black humor by the time I went to my pallet that night. What I had learned from listening to the talk in the king's chamber sickened me. Not only had Winchester been deprived of an elevation I knew he wanted, but Stephen had not had the courage to tell him and explain to him. The king had secretly summoned the canons of Canterbury to Westminster on the twenty-fourth of December, the day Henry had to perform an ordination of deacons in St. Paul's in London, and the election of Theobald, abbot of Bec, had been carried out in Stephen's presence and that of the pope's legate, Alberic of Ostia.

I was long past weeping over the weaknesses of the king, who was always kind to me so that I could not stop loving him, but I bitterly craved the comfort of Melusine's body. I needed to talk to her too. The skewed view she had of all events, which had meaning to her only as they affected her personally or might affect Ulle, sometimes made me laugh. But just as often, her view lifted me out of a rut in which my thoughts went round and round and helped me see and accept a fresh truth. I had done a great deal of talking as well as coupling with Melusine in the past three months, and now I desired her as some men desire drink.

Next morning I had reason to wonder if that desire had been so strong that some thread of it had disturbed the queen's dreams as well as my own. Before I had gone in to the king, a page from the queen was bidding me come to break my fast with her. I begged admittance to the king's closet, where he was in the middle of dressing, and asked his permission. It came so promptly and with so little remark, as well as with eyes that would not meet

mine, that I realized he had been with his lady that night
and she had already spoken to him about me. His uneasiness was also a warning that the queen was angry; I had
expected that and was rather glad to face it so soon. I do
not mean that I did not respect the queen and fear her
anger, but I felt that the results of the chance I had taken
were all good and I hoped to be able to bring her to see it
that way.

Her expression was not encouraging as she gestured me
to the end of a bench that was drawn beside her chair.
Melusine stood on the other side, her black eyes wide
open. I thought she was holding back mingled alarm and
indignation, but she went quietly when the queen bade her
bring us wine, bread, and cheese.

"You have failed me!" Maud said bitterly as soon as
Melusine was out of hearing.

"No, madam," I answered steadily. "I have proven to
my satisfaction, and I hope to yours, that my wife is no
danger to you, to the king, or to anyone."

"You have proven nothing but that you are completely
ensorcelled by her. I thought I could trust you."

I smiled at her; I could not help it. "I will admit freely
that I am happier in my marriage than I expected to be. If
you wish to say Melusine has bewitched me, I will even
agree to that. But I have nonetheless fulfilled your trust as
well as I could, not betrayed it."

"Do you think I do not know you took Melusine to
Ulle?" she asked.

"Madam, I am not a fool," I protested quietly. "I
never intended our visit to be a secret either from you or
from the king. I told my master as soon as I could. From
what you say, I must assume Melusine did not tell you. I
cannot imagine why, unless she was afraid, but—"

Melusine's low, musical laugh interrupted me. "I was
afraid, madam," she said, laying a loaf of bread, a large
piece of cheese, a flagon of wine, and three cups beside
me on the bench. "But that was not why I did not speak.
You know I had no chance. In the press of great ladies
attending you, I could not come near until you summoned
me this morning. And then you called me a witch, a

corrupting witch, and then Bruno came before I could even ask why you missaid me.''

Maud's eyes flicked from me to Melusine. "Why did you go to Ulle?"

"For three reasons," I replied. "First because I wished to look at the lands when I was not part of an attacking army—I will, if you will permit, explain why I wished to see them in a moment.''

"You need not." Maud's voice cut at me like cold steel. "It is clear enough why you wished to see Ulle. You hope to get those lands.''

CHAPTER 18

~

Melusine

THE QUEEN'S voice was cold and hard as she accused Bruno of desiring to obtain my lands, and my heart froze within me. Why I had not expected her to guess so obvious an intention, I do not know. I had been annoyed with Bruno yesterday morning for disappearing as he did because I had been eager to get to court early. I had thought I could explain to the queen that once we had ridden into Northumbria I had become terribly sick for a sight of my old home and had wheedled Bruno into taking me there, but I had no conception of the number of great ladies who had come to court with their husbands. I had not even been able to beg for a private word. Now I was sure all was lost, and I did not know whether to admire Bruno's unshaken demeanor or be contemptuous of him for his stupidity.

"Yes, madam," he replied with perfect calm, "every man desires land of his own, and I would be a great fool if I did not see the suitability of Ulle as a reward for good and honest service on my part. But there is no need for you to think me presumptuous enough to expect that reward soon. I have done nothing to deserve it. All the favors have flowed the other way. I do not forget what I owe King Stephen, who raised me from nothing to a knight of the royal household." Suddenly he grinned mischievously and glanced at me. "And much against my will you have done me a greater favor and given me my heart's desire."

"I am glad you are happy," Maud snapped bitterly, "but I did not expect you, of all men, to lose your head. How could Stephen dare trust a vassal in thrall to a disloyal wife?"

"Melusine is *not* disloyal," Bruno said, staring back at her, but he was still grinning. "Of course, she is not loyal either. I would never try to tell you that—"

I thought him mad. "Will you give me leave to retire so that you can discuss me more freely," I cried, barely holding back my tears as I saw all my hopes in ruin.

"No! Sit down and listen!" Maud ordered. "It will do you good."

I stood still for a moment, startled. To my surprise I had detected just a hint of amusement, the faintest thawing, in those last words. Before I started to move toward the bench on which Bruno was sitting, Maud pointed to the wine. Bruno took the flagon and poured a cup for her. I was beside him by then and he looked up and smiled as he gave the cup to me, touching my fingers before he let go. Maud took the cup, darting a swift glance at me, then fixed her eyes on Bruno again, nodding for him to go on. He was still smiling faintly.

"My second reason for going to Ulle," Bruno said, "was that I thought if I promised to take Melusine there, she would not try to escape me on the road, which would save me infinite trouble."

"I said I would not try to run away," I protested, but neither of them looked at me.

I was angry, but under that was a thread of relief; it was infuriating to be ignored by people who were discussing me—one of them my own husband—but I also felt I would be ground to a powder between those two implacable wills if I should interpose myself. And all mingled in with the rage and fear and relief was admiration for Bruno. I had always thought of him as an obsequious servant in the court, but he was not bowing now.

"My third reason," he hesitated and then went on in a rush, "was that I could think of no better time or place to

determine whether your suspicions that Melusine was an
inveterate rebel were true. I brought her to Ulle; I gave her
what seemed to be freedom to do what she wished; I set
my men to watch what she did.''

"You spied on me!" I cried.

He turned to look at me that time. "Yes," he admitted.
"Merwyn followed you that first day when you met Tom
Bailiff in the hollow. You are very innocent, Melusine. I
do not think you ever looked behind."

"Why should I suspect such a thing?" I gasped. "You
only pretended to want to go to Thirl. It was a trap."

"Yes." He was half laughing, half shamefaced. "But
the innocent do not need to fear traps. Madam," he turned
again to the queen, "I swear that all Melusine cares for is
the well-doing of Ulle. I cannot tell you that she will ever
support King Stephen, but neither will she lift one finger
to help King David. I heard her say—and she did not
know I heard—that for all she cared both England and
Scotland could sink into the sea, so long as Ulle was safe
and quiet."

"That is not much advantage to the king," the queen
remarked, but I thought I saw the smallest quiver at the
corner of her mouth.

Bruno shrugged. "Nor is it any great disadvantage.
Come, madam, you know that it is a common condition
that women do not care much for kings and great causes.
They care for their children, for the land that supports and
shelters them, and sometimes—" Bruno cast a glance at
me that brought color to my cheeks before he looked back
at the queen and added slowly, "sometimes they care for
their husbands."

I was not as brave as Bruno. I was too much afraid of
the queen to scream aloud that I was no more slave to my
lust than he was, that I would not follow blindly any path
he laid down for me just because I did care—no, no, I
must not allow myself, not yet—and certainly, I thought,
biting my lip with rage, certainly not when he had just
implied I would give up everything papa wanted for him.
While I was choking back my anger, I missed a few brief
exchanges between Bruno and the queen. She looked more
amused than enraged when he rose and nodded, implying

permission for a request that may have entered my ears but had not penetrated my thoughts. When he took my arm, I almost pulled away but I dared not, not knowing what had been said.

"The queen has given permission for us to lodge outside the palace—if we can find a lodging," he said, as he drew me toward the door of the hall. "When you do not need her, Edna can go with one of the men to look for a place. She knows the town and knows people who are familiar with London. We can ride in, if you are willing to rise early."

"I am not so eager as you think to share a bed with you," I muttered, choking on rage and shame. "If you think you can use my lust to tame me, you are mistaken."

We had come to the doorway, and Bruno stopped. "What are you talking about?"

"How dare you say 'women care for their husbands' after looking at me as if I were some man-sick—"

Still holding my arm, Bruno put his free hand on my back and pulled me close. I did not resist because I knew it would be useless and make me look ridiculous, but if I had had a knife, I think I would have plunged it into him.

"Fool!" he murmured into my ear while seeming to embrace me. "To believe you will be loyal for my sake will wake the queen's sympathy for you as nothing else could. *She* adores Stephen." He let me go then and touched my nose with his lips. "Send Edna soon."

Then he was gone, leaving me so confused that I stood staring after him—until I realized I was confirming what he had said to Maud by my behavior. Then, I turned about and hurried back to her and dropped a short curtsey.

"I think you should know, madam, that despite what Bruno says, I am not a bitch in heat unable to free myself from my dog's cock."

She burst out laughing, and cocked her head to look up at me. "Touched your pride, did he?" But the laughter seemed good-natured, and when she gestured toward the bench and said, "Come, break bread for me and give me a slice of cheese, and then you may go and break your own fast," she seemed somehow satisfied.

My outburst had calmed me a little. I had told the truth,

whatever the queen wished to believe. I served her without saying any more and when she had smiled graciously at the earl of Warwick's wife and beckoned that lady to come to her, I retreated gladly, eventually finding a quiet corner with a stool in it where I could sit and eat. It was cold there, too far from the fire, but my gown was warm and it was worth numb fingers and toes to be overlooked by the younger and lesser ladies attending the queen. I had been right about my absence from court curing my problems with the queen's ladies. Most of those who had served her before I went away had been already granted leave to go home or would go in a few days. The group now in attendance did not know me at all or remembered me only dimly. If any recalled my slowness and silence, they doubtless put it down to my fear and uncertainty in the past.

I had found being part of a group of chattering, gossiping women interesting and amusing—it had been a long time since papa had taken me to a council in Carlisle or on a visit to Richmond where a large group of ladies was gathered—and it had distracted me yesterday from my concern about being unable to speak to the queen. This morning, however, I did not wish to be distracted. Bruno's remark had given me a severe shock, wakening my fear of abandoning my lost loved ones for a false, new toy. Yet what had he done wrong? He had promised me he would try to win back Ulle, and every move he had made certainly aimed toward that purpose. Had not his whole conversation with the queen been designed to soothe her? And was it not worth a small slight or two to gain her forgiveness *and* fix in her mind that he desired Ulle as his reward? Even his spying on me—perhaps it had not convinced the queen, but certainly it had shaken her conviction that all I desired was the success of King David and Empress Matilda.

It seemed I had been fortunate that circumstances had prevented me from telling the queen a lie. She would never have believed me, and my lie would have made the truth Bruno had told seem false. He had known just how to manage the queen. I kept forgetting that Bruno was not like papa, who often spoke before he thought and said what was in his heart. Bruno was cleverer—was it disloyal to think that, even if it was true? So long as Ulle came back to papa's blood, did it matter how?

Should I send Edna out to seek lodgings? Mary help me, was all this musing on how clever Bruno was and how wrong I was to be angry only an excuse to lie with him again? But the queen *had* been appeased. Suddenly I felt warm with blushing despite the chill in the part of the hall where I sat as I realized my denial had probably only convinced Maud of my desire for my husband. Well, let her think he could rule me. If Edna found lodgings for us, I could refuse him—that would show him how I felt and not betray me to the queen.

All my worrying was useless though. Edna did not think she could find us anything decent within a reasonable distance of the palace. The men had been no problem; she burst into giggles telling me. She had lodged them in the stable of the whorehouse in which she had served. They were welcome for their ability to keep other men-at-arms out, for the women of that place preferred to reserve their favors for the gently born, and they had had some trouble and threats when they would not open their doors to common soldiers. As to our men, the situation had been made clear to them, and if they had a fancy to slake their own thirsts, the older women in less favor or already degraded to servants would doubtless satisfy them. Lodging for Bruno and me was a different matter. Edna agreed to go out and ask, but she thought finding a place before those who had come to court were gone would be impossible.

I agreed with what indifference I could summon up, but I was ashamed that I *felt* disappointed. And before I could decide whether to send her anyway or tell her to forget the matter, the queen's servant came to me and plucked my sleeve, bidding me come to her mistress. I assumed Maud wished to question me again, and my heart sank, for I was equally afraid to lie or to tell the truth. I was bitterly disappointed, for I had thought my trial was over—but I had guessed wrong.

"I have heard that you can read and write," Maud said abruptly as I came up from my curtsey. "Is that true?"

"Yes, madam." I stared at her, uncomprehending. Surely

the queen had clerks enough and my ability to scribe was unimportant. She was staring back, her brow wrinkled with doubt, and I thought I might add to my answer so I would not appear stubborn or sullen. "I learned from my brother Andrew, who was a priest, more for mischief than any real reason, but I found the skill useful for I acted as my father's steward in the accounting of the estate. I am no practiced scholar though. I know only the common tongue, no Latin."

"I do not need a practiced scholar," Maud snapped. "I need someone who can keep accounts and who will not get my maidens with child while counting linens in my own bedchamber, as did that little priestling who served as scribe to my chamberlain and almoner."

"I promise not to get your maidens with child," I gasped between chuckles. "My ability to keep your accounts must be tested. I am afraid, madam, that keeping track of bushels of wheat and casks of fish at a poor manor like Ulle is far different from dealing with a queen's estate."

"Not so different as you think," Maud answered, and called to two men I had not noticed, addressing one as almoner and the other as chamberlain. They were standing near the wall, well away from her chair, and came forward, both looking very cross and protesting as soon as they could be heard when speaking low that it was unheard of to have an inexperienced lady keeping accounts. They would find an older scribe, one less likely to fall into temptation.

"One in his dotage, you mean? What man not nearing his deathbed and eager to serve in a court does not have an eye to a pretty, young woman?" The queen's anger and scorn, though soft-voiced, made the men blench, and I had to bite my lip. In fact, I had yesterday heard some talk about the almoner, himself a priest, that I had not then understood. Now I did.

When there was no answer to her accusation, the queen continued, "I need a strong scribe, one who can ride as far as I must go and who can be near me. Here is one young and clever who can be trained to the work—and who will cost me nothing. I will take no more chances that the daughters of noblemen entrusted to me to be held safe and taught virtue will be befouled by those supposed to guide them. Who will compensate a father who has lost a marriage prize? The blame will be mine, the cost mine. Lady Melusine is my chosen scribe. If you cannot work with her, you are free to leave my service."

The chamberlain only raised his brows disdainfully, but the almoner looked furious. I was not happy about working under the direction of two men who did not want me, but I had not been asked what I wanted any more than they had. Thus I became the queen's scribe for her closet, and the rest of that morning I spent poring over the accounts the dismissed priest had left with one or another of the queen's officers sneering at me.

At first I was frightened and thought I would have to tell the queen I was unfit for the post. The priest's hand was unfamiliar and he used many short forms that I did not recognize; however, I was afraid the queen would think me unwilling rather than unable, so I struggled on. Then the chamberlain left, saying he had business that could wait no longer on an idiot woman who could read no better than a pig. Nonetheless, his leaving meant I could put aside the accounts of purchases made for the queen's household, which were far more varied and thus more difficult to decipher than the almoner's record of charities.

The almoner was even less accommodating. He hardly gave me time to glance at a sheet before he snatched it away, and when I held tight, he pointed to one item after another, asking, "What is this? this? this? Stupid! No woman can read or keep accounts. All you are good for is between your legs."

The more the almoner sniped at me, the angrier I grew, until I answered him roundly that I was no stupider and far less interested in what was between my legs than a priest who meddled with one of the queen's maidens. Moreover, I told him, holding fast to a sheet he seemed very eager to snatch away, I was not set to a guessing game but to learning, so he had better teach or I would go to my mistress and complain that he was trying to drive me to refuse her orders.

We went better after that in one way, worse in another;

the almoner grudgingly explained what he could—at least I
thought he was explaining what he could. At that time I
believed he was almost as ignorant as I and resigned
myself to discovering bit by bit what the forms meant, for
I was determined to spite both men and please the queen.
Still, I knew I had made a bitter enemy of the almoner.
One would think that when after dinner the king called for
dancing and Bruno came to lead me out, this matter,
which might be of grave importance, would burst from my
lips. Far from it, as soon as I laid eyes on him everything
but the fact that I would sleep alone again that night flew
from my mind. What I said at once was that there was no
hope for lodging until court was over.

Bruno's grip on my hand tightened. "I must talk to you
alone," he said, "and I cannot find a moment's freedom
until the king is abed. Also, I do not think we can wait
until the court disperses. I am afraid the king will leave the
same day he dismisses his vassals."

"Leave?" I repeated, my shame over my desire for him
driven out by surprise and alarm. "But will not the queen
accompany the king?"

"No." He stared at me in warning as we joined the row
of dancers, and I realized he would not tell me more where
others could hear.

"Perhaps we could meet—" I began, but I could not
really think of a private place, and then we were separated
by the figure of the dance.

By the time the set ended, I was furious with Bruno
again. He had asked permission to lodge away from court
not because he wanted me but because he needed a private
place to give me instructions. But I am not a complete
idiot, and angry as I was I understood that there must be
matters of real importance he needed to tell me. Moreover,
I had to tell him about the queen's peculiar behavior to
me. In my anxiety over the actual records and the disgust
of the chamberlain and almoner, I had not considered what
she had done carefully—but I knew it was peculiar.

I had no chance either to express my hurt feelings or to
mention my problem. Richard de Camville was waiting to
take my hand from Bruno's for the next dance at the last
note of music. I was about to refuse him, but Bruno shook

his head, bowed to me, and said he must go, glancing toward the entrance to the king's closet. So I danced with Camville and then with other gentlemen. I am sure they found me pleasant company; I had experience enough answering my brothers while my mind was on other matters. And since I would not think about Bruno's indifference to me compared with my weakness for him, I thought instead about the almoner's uneasiness.

When the word came into my mind, it rang like a bell. There had been a real difference in the chamberlain's attitude toward me and the almoner's. The chamberlain had only been annoyed and contemptuous; he had not cared how long I studied any record except that I wasted his time. The almoner had not wanted me to look at anything slowly and carefully. Uneasy, that was the right word.

As soon as I could manage it, I pleaded exhaustion and made my way back to the queen's hall, where I found the chest that held the records and drew out those for the last month and began to look at them item by item. After a time, although I could not determine what each item was, I began to find a repetition of certain forms that I took to be specific religious institutions. Each amount was not great, but added together they came to a fair sum and it seemed strange to me that Queen Maud should give several small sums to the same places over a short time instead of one larger sum. Still, I could not believe this to be what made the almoner uneasy. A "fair sum" to me must be near nothing to him.

Some time during the night I woke with a start with the realization that there was another use for what I had discovered the previous day. Surely the unusual pattern of giving had a purpose that the queen would remember. If so, I would have several names to match the forms on the record, and I might be able to use those to help me make out the meaning of others. Thus I came to the queen's bedchamber and begged admittance before she was dressed and surrounded by the great dames of the court.

Queen Maud was sitting up in bed propped by bolsters and attended only by two of her oldest and most trusted servants. She seemed surprised when I mentioned my

trouble in understanding what the previous scribe had written and how I hoped to decipher some of it. All she said
was that I was not responsible for the records before I
began to keep them and I should write them as best suited
me without regard to what had been done in the past, and
waved me away. I was a little disappointed, for I was
curious, but then I thought that there might be some
private significance in those regularly given small sums
and bowed my acceptance. I was hardly out the door,
however, before I was called back, told to fetch the chest
in which the records were kept, and asked to find and
display the sheets and point out the entries.

There was a silence while the queen considered, then
shook her head. "Not by my order," she muttered. "I will
discover what these are, but by my guess the sums went
into his own pocket."

"The almoner?" I gasped. I could not believe it.

"No," Maud said, "the priestling."

"But then why should the almoner be uneasy? I felt it,
and I was angry because he insulted me. That was why I
looked so carefully."

"Because the priestling was his choice—probably his
son—and he knew of it and did not stop it. And there is
little I can do, for the Church reserves the right to try its
own criminals."

"But surely you can dismiss the almoner from his office? Why should you endure—"

"Hush!" The order was peremptory, and the queen
looked startled, as if she had just realized that she had said
more to me than she intended. She sat still for a time, her
hands lying quietly on the parchments, her eyes on my
face, but not seeing me, I thought. Then she said slowly,
"A queen is not as free as a simple baron. The almoner is
cousin to the bishop of Salisbury, the king's chancellor,
and was recommended to me by him. To offend the bishop
of Salisbury over so small a matter as his cousin's dishonesty would be very foolish." There was a significant pause
and then she added, "Therefore, you will say nothing of
this matter to anyone."

"No, madam," I breathed, appalled that my pique at

being thought incapable of keeping accounts should have led me to knowledge that I did not wish to have.

"I am not angry, Melusine," she assured me, the tight line of her lips growing softer. "You were clever to see the oddity, and wise to come to me in private. If you should come across any other oddity—something you do not understand in what you are told to write down—do not fail to come to me again. Now you may go."

I reached for the sheets, to put them away, but the queen shook her head. She smiled at me as I curtsied and may have intended to reassure me, but to my mind I was caught between drowning and hanging. I liked neither cheaters nor tale bearers, but I must be the one or excuse the other. Worse, what I thought a small matter, like the few shillings the priest had taken, might have roots and branches reaching far away that touched great people. And to turn a bad day worse, just after I had broken my fast without much appetite, Edna brought me a message from Bruno that he would be away from Westminster. He had left Fechin in case I wanted an escort, and he hoped to be back by twelfth night but could not be sure. As a cap to my misery, hard on Edna's heels a page came to summon me to the chamberlain, who threw a handful of tally sticks onto a table in the queen's chamber and bade me record them.

I had a small revenge—and in this case did not make an enemy by it—because while I was still cutting a quill (I had broken the old one after ruling off the old records from the new ones, which I headed with my name) one of his young assistants came in with a few more tally sticks. He seemed stunned to see me, but more amused than offended at a female scribe, and willing to explain the markings on the tally sticks for the pleasure of seeing me write—as if I were a dog walking on its hind legs. Thus when the chamberlain returned later to prove I was incompetent, he found a neat, clean record and was honest enough to praise my work although as he left me he still shook his head over what he considered an unnatural act.

The small victory raised my spirits enough to make me notice that a number of the great ladies, as well as the queen herself, were not in the best of tempers. Usually, the queen was a good mistress, too clever or perhaps, for I still did not know her very well, too truly good-natured to be unkind to her servants. However, I heard more than one whispered complaint that day about unreasonable demands and sharp words, and Edna told me while I was dressing for another feast and entertainment that one of the younger maids, who had carried in washing water last night after the king left, had hinted the queen had been crying and had been slapped by an older woman. That was when I began to wonder if at least part of my fear and anxiety was not owing to the work I had undertaken so unwillingly but was infecting me from the company around me.

I had my answer to that the next night. The queen had retired to her chamber and I was sadly allowing Edna to pack away the rich, red bedrobe I had made for Bruno. Audris had given me the cloth and silver and gold thread, and most of the work had been done at Jernaeve, but I had still needed to sew and embroider in every private minute I could snatch both at Ulle and on the road. Now twelfth night was over and I had given up hope that Bruno would come back when there was a knocking at the hall door and a minute later a grumpy door warden came and told me my husband wanted me and said I had leave to go with him.

I do not remember if I thanked him. I know I forgot all about the robe Edna was still holding in her arms. So eager was I that it was a miracle that I remembered to snatch my cloak from the top of my chest before I ran. Nor did I pause at the door to ask Bruno if he wished to come in but threw myself right into his arms before I realized how unseemly was my behavior. He kissed me warmly but then lifted his head and laughed.

"I feel that I hardly need to make the apology I had all ready," he said, seeming unaware that I had begun to pull away and squeezing me tight against him.

"What apology? What have you done?" I hardly knew my voice, it was so thin with the jealousy that had seized me by the throat and choked me, but Bruno did not seem to notice that either and laughed again.

"I have found a room for us for the night—but it is in the whorehouse where our men are lodged." One of our men was holding a torch nearby. I could see Bruno's face—full of merriment, it was—and I know he could see mine, which I suspect was not so merry. I am not sure he realized I was angry; perhaps he thought I was shocked, for he went on, still merrily, "Now, now, Melusine, no one could suspect you of wishing to use the women and I am not likely to complain about your coupling with the man who took you there."

"You think that a fit place for me?" I cried, wrenching myself away from him.

There was an instant's pause, and then he said, "It is not a fit place for any woman but some have little choice." He was no longer laughing. "I will make sure the way is cleared so that you need not see or speak to any of them."

I had forgotten that his mother was a whore, and when the flatness of his voice reminded me, I was so filled with horror and remorse that I could not speak or move.

"I am sorry to have offended you," he went on in that expressionless voice, "but I thought . . . no, it does not matter. It is not necessary to take you there. I can say briefly what must be said. I have been to Nottingham to tell the captains of the king's mercenaries to make ready to march north the day after tomorrow. The king will—"

"You are going to war?" I breathed. "Tomorrow?"

"Yes." A hint of a wry smile curled up one corner of his mouth. "If you still desire to be rid of me, Melusine, you can pray for it." He hesitated, but I could force no sound out and the little smile disappeared. "I will knock and get the doorwarden to let you in."

Still unable to speak, I flung myself on him and held him away from the door. I could feel his head bend over me, but my face was buried and he could not see it. After a moment he said uncertainly, "We cannot stay out here in the cold much longer Melusine, and there is no place to go. Every hut and cot is filled. There are men sleeping between the horses' feet in the stables. I—"

"Let us go to—to where you have a chamber," I said, shivering, but he did not move at once, and I forced myself away from him, and took his hand and started off.

"You are going the wrong way," he said gently, and drew me close, pulling up my hood and opening his cloak so he could put it around me atop mine.

I was shaking with fear, not cold, but I dared say no more lest I begin to weep. A guard opened a small postern in the palace wall at Bruno's order, and our way lighted by Cormi with the torch, we walked the few streets to the place in silence. Bruno stopped at the door of a house that looked to me exactly the same as any other and began to tell Cormi to go in and order any woman there out to the kitchen, but I cried, "No, no. I do not care about the women. You did not understand me." So we went in, but I saw nothing—only a large chamber dimly lit by a lively fire in a hearth on the short wall near the far end. Perhaps there were shadows on the floor not far from the hearth, but I was still too wrapped in my misery to find the curiosity to look carefully. However, my first agony of terror was beginning to abate as I realized that Bruno might be leaving tomorrow but it was not possible for the fighting to begin the same day.

Had we lingered a few minutes, I would have looked about more carefully, but Bruno pushed me gently toward a stair—a real wooden stair, not a ladder—going up to a loft. I was much surprised to see that this was not the open space I expected but was divided into small chambers. I think some were in use, but Bruno guided me quickly ahead down the narrow aisle to one at the far end. Here I was surprised again for it was brightly lit by four scented wax tapers in holders fixed to the walls, and it was warmed by a large brazier of charcoal standing in the far corner well away from the low bed that filled the space from the outer wall to the planks closing off the central aisle.

"You will be warm soon," Bruno said. "Come sit down on the bed. Do not fear; it is clean. I came here before I came for you and made them change it."

"It is not the place or the cold," I whispered, letting him draw me down beside him. "I am afraid."

"Of what?"

I turned and stared at him, but he looked surprised and honestly puzzled. "That I will be a widow, you fool!" I exclaimed, quite exasperated. "Did you not tell me that tomorrow you leave to fight in a war?"

He burst out laughing, then pushed back the hood of my cloak, lifted my face, and kissed me hard, laughing again when I pushed him away. "But Melusine," he folded my hands in his, "I have fought in many wars. There is nothing to fear for me. I am sorry I teased you about wanting to be rid of me. Truly, there is as little chance of it as of your doing me a hurt with this little toy I have for you." Letting go of my hands, he threw off his cloak and fumbled in his purse, putting into my lax hand a tiny jeweled knife. "There, that is a keepsake to remember how ill was our beginning together, and these—" he put a small cloth-wrapped packet in my lap, "—are a very small mark of my gratitude for the joy you have given me."

I opened the packet and touched the earrings and the necklet, delicate and beautiful. "Oh, I forgot your gift," I cried. "And now I cannot give it to you—and you will have no use for it if you must go to war."

"It is enough to know you remembered me," Bruno said, stroking my hair.

"But I should have brought it." I began to weep; somehow I felt it was no disloyalty in me to weep for my thoughtlessness in forgetting to bring Bruno's gift, whereas to weep for Bruno's danger when I no longer wept for my dead—was that not very wrong? "It is a bedrobe," I sobbed. "I saw you had none. That very first day when we were wed, when I should have been thinking of where to find a knife, I saw you had no bedrobe and wondered if I should make one for you."

"Melusine, do not weep. I cannot bear it."

He kissed my lips and then delicately licked the tears, first from one cheek and then the other. I began to tremble again, but not with cold or fear. Indeed, I sought his mouth again, and mine clung to it as he pulled out the pin that held my cloak and pushed it off my shoulders. I do not know how he rid me of the rest of my clothes or managed to take off his own for I gave him no help and must have hindered him by my unwillingness to let him go. I was ashamed, but I could not restrain myself. I needed to feel his body on mine, to hold him within me. As long as I could feel him, warm and strong, I did not need to fear being alone.

Does fear make lust stronger? Not fear of being hurt or forced—that kills all desire—but fear of losing the joy coupling brings? For me, that night, it did. I tried to suppress the waves of pleasure that rose higher with each thrust, but I could not. That final convulsion, which is akin to pain in its intensity, took me against my will. Bruno's too, I think, because he stopped moving and tried to hold me still, groaning when I thrust against him in my frantic need.

We were both still afterward, until I sighed and said, "I think you chose our lodging very well."

"I did not choose it. It was all I could get. I thought it more important that we be together than what particular place we were together in."

I felt Bruno stiffen as he spoke, and he began to lift himself off me but I held him tight. "I think so too," I whispered in his ear. "I only meant that I do not think myself so much better than the other women here. I am as lustful—"

Bruno squeezed me tight, then raised himself on his elbows so he could see my face and laughed aloud. "Silly girl! A whore is not lustful. Mostly they hate men and what they do. A few are indifferent. A few manage to keep alive some feeling for a special man or two, but even in those it is hard to wake any real response." He bent his head down and kissed my forehead, my nose, and my lips, then laid his cheek against mine. "Melusine, there is very little pleasure for me in coupling with a whore, not much more than pissing in a pot. Lying with you—that is different. You have given me joy in many ways, but now I am talking about joy of my body that no whore with all her practiced tricks could give me. A trick is a trick, but you give me your own pleasure which doubles and redoubles mine."

And his pleasure doubled and redoubled mine too. We were both fast in a trap. I remembered how the queen had accused him of being ensorcelled. She had thought that his experience with women who sold themselves would armor him against me—but seemingly it was just the opposite. So I had a real weapon, as I had guessed in Ulle, but what did it matter? Tomorrow Bruno would ride away—

"Teach me some tricks," I cried. "Let us see if what I do to you makes me feel more strongly too."

My purpose was to wipe from my mind my terrible fear of loss. And for the hours of that short night—short to us although it was one of the longest nights of the year—I washed away that fear in a warm sea of pleasure, finding to my surprise that the tricks were not—except for touching with fingers and lips—what I did to Bruno, but what I tempted him to do to me. I slipped the loops of my earrings around my nipples and tangled my necklet in the hair between my thighs and danced and bade him undress me with his mouth.

Less than half an hour before that he had sighed, "Enough, I must ride at dawn," but my little game gave him such renewed life that he hurt me a little in his eagerness to take me. I was tired myself by then. I would not have wakened him and tempted him if he had not reminded me that this was all I would have—perhaps forever.

Of course, I only remembered to tell Bruno that the queen had made me her scribe on our way back. He thought it as odd as I, but we were both half dead by then and not much interested in Maud's notions. At the door of the queen's hall I clung to him, and he kissed me a last time as passionately as if we had not been kissing until our lips were sore. Then the cold grey sky flushed red, and Bruno put me aside, closing the hands I stretched out to him on each other and telling me not to be a goose and that he would write to me so that I did not need to worry. That promise and my exhaustion saved me from the most acute agony when the men rode out. I was so sated and dazed with tiredness that even grief and fear were dulled.

The only thing that really pierced the haze in my head was the fact that the queen was as sick with fear and grief as I would have been if I had not been numb. It was a strange, painful comfort, and in the months that followed while King Stephen took the keep at Leeds and went on to ravage Scotland until King David yielded up his son Henry of Huntingdon—this time as hostage, not guest—and then rode south to besiege Ludlow, it forged a bond between us because we were the only two who craved their missing menfolk in the same way.

I do not mean there were not other ladies attending the

queen who were worried about their male kin. Almost
every lady had some relative in the king's army, and I am
sure the pain of a mother for her son is every bit as sharp
as that of a woman for a husband she craves. It is as sharp,
but it is *different*. Queen Maud and I were the only two
who shed most of our tears in a bed in which one lay
where there should be two.

However, I did not shed nearly as many tears as I
expected, nor did the terror long continue, which in the
beginning came over me in waves so that I burst into a
cold sweat and could not move. Maud noticed one of the
worst of these; she stared at me, for I had dropped my
bread and wine—we were breaking our fast the morning
after Bruno had gone—and sunk down on the floor whimpering. I should have been ashamed to show such weakness, but I was too far gone to care who saw my misery,
my whole world having narrowed to the knowledge that
every person I loved and who loved me soon died. Then
the queen had come and stooped above me, putting her
hand hard on my shoulder so she hurt me and saying
harshly, "You will be better soon. It is impossible to be so
afraid for very long—and I have work for you."

I did not believe her, but she was right. I was soon so
busy that I had little time to indulge my fears. Later I
thought she might have spoken from her own experience,
but I never dared ask. I discovered the real work of the
scribe of the closet during the three days after the king
rode north when the queen's Household went to Dover. It
was my duty to keep track of the queen's possessions each
time her Household moved. And we moved constantly—
from Winchester to Dover; from Dover to Hastings; from
Hastings back to Winchester; from Winchester to Windsor—
staying only about three weeks in each place. Fortunately
only necessary items were unpacked when we stopped and
guested at keeps along the road and at each new place or I
would not have had time to eat or sleep.

The work was a poultice over my terror—fixing my
mind on sheets and pillows, ewers and basins, chests and
stools suppressed it—but in the night and other times too it
could burst forth. It was Bruno's first letter from Leeds,
which reached me at Dover in a packet sent by Stephen to

the queen, that cured the worst fear, leaving only my natural longing for him—for the pleasure he gave me, for the way he could make me laugh, for the way he talked to me. Maud had summoned me from the hall and handed me the folded parchment. Perhaps I should have gone away, but in my eagerness I only walked a few steps to the side before I began to read.

Aside from some light words about taking care to keep the earrings and necklet he had given me packed away until he could try putting them on as he had taken them off—which made me blush despite knowing that no one but I could understand his meaning—Bruno's letter was mostly full of small complaints about mislaid baggage and bad food and the fact that the king's advisors kept Stephen back from the fighting, which also kept his fighting companions, the Knights of the Body, from engaging the enemy.

That matter was not set apart in any way, not coupled with soothing phrases about not worrying. Because it was mingled in with all the other complaints I did not suspect it was only a lie to comfort me, as indeed it was, for Stephen and Bruno with him were in the thick of every fight—although it was true enough that the king's advisors did not like it and tried to hold him back. But I did not discover the truth for more than two years because I did not suspect Bruno of such deviousness. At the time, as I felt a lifting of the heavy weight that had lain on my heart no matter how busy I was, I suddenly remembered how the queen had tried to hearten me, and I cried out to her, "Oh, madam, listen," and read her those lines.

Maud looked up from the writing she was studying and blinked, and I was appalled at my stupidity in intruding so unimportant a subject into her news, which must be about affairs of state. I began to stammer an apology and withdraw, but she rose from her chair and came to me and bade me show her the letter. She was so eager to see the words that promised safety for her husband she made a mistake and let me guess by the way her eyes went at once to the right place that she was not reading my letter for the first time, only reading more carefully what she had let her eyes pass over too quickly before. For a minute I was angry, but then she looked up and smiled at me like dawn breaking.

That was the first time I truly understood what Bruno had told me many times—that everything the queen did was for Stephen's sake. I wondered then if she herself would rather have lived quietly on her own lands in Boulogne but yielded to Stephen's need to have his own, greater estate. I could forgive her for prying if it was to increase the safety of one she loved. Would I not have done that for my own? I would, and gladly.

Even though I understood, it troubled me and came back to my mind again and again over the next few days, each time I reread my letter for the comfort it gave me. I knew that Bruno had taken Cormi and Merwyn with him to act as messengers and had no need to send his letter in the king's packet. At last I realized that Bruno had sent the letter in the king's packet just so the queen *should* read it. That was a hint, I thought; he had left Fechin with me, but it would be most unwise to allow Maud to suspect I sent secrets with a private messenger—specially when I had no secrets any longer and it was my purpose to convince the queen that I would not be a traitor if my lands were restored. So the next time I had a chance to speak to her, I asked her if I could send a letter to Bruno when she wrote to the king.

Permission was given immediately, and Maud suggested I write as soon as I could because she intended to send a messenger off within the next two days. Naturally I did as I was bidden, but knowing that another would read my letter made any intimacy in what I wrote impossible. I would not have written anything that could shame me in any case, but I could not even add little jests or reminders of pleasant moments. I felt that I was writing to a stranger, and the best I could produce was a tone of courtesy. I also wrote every bit of news I had—where we were; how we had traveled to get there; the gossip I had heard in the keeps where we stayed along the way; everything I saw, each rumor I heard, and what I guessed about Dover and Maud's purpose for coming here. I was curious to know whether the queen would admit she was reading my letter by reprimanding me, scratch out what she preferred Bruno not to know, or let the letter go intact, knowing that all I wrote was harmless and desiring to let me believe, if I could, that my letter was sent unexamined.

I received no reprimand, so either the queen had no objection to the gossip and guesses I related or she had decided to let me twist a rope long enough to hang myself. I waited eagerly to learn what Bruno thought of my letter, but I was disappointed. It was the end of February before I heard from him, and what came was only a note—again part of the king's packet—thanking me for writing and saying he was too busy to answer as I deserved. He did ask me to write again though, which I took to mean he approved of my gossip. Later in the day I discovered he was also trying to tell me that I would soon have more important matters to relate because Maud bade me order her maids to begin packing for a long journey. And then I heard we were to meet King David in Durham to negotiate a treaty of peace with the Scots.

Waleran de Meulan's twin brother, Robert of Leicester, met us at his keep five days later. He carried another long letter and further instructions to Maud and was to accompany us to Durham and remain with us. I had learned enough of matters of state from what Bruno had told me during our journeys that I wondered why the earl of Leicester was coming. Was he to be the queen's advisor rather than the bishop of Salisbury, who had for many years been the chief negotiator for King Henry? Considering what Bruno had told me about Waleran's opposition to Henry of Winchester, I did not dare ask about Salisbury, but I wondered whether Waleran was fomenting a dislike and distrust in the king for his own chief ministers.

That was no business of mine, but peace with the Scots *was* important to me. Perhaps when King David and King Stephen were no longer at war, the queen would have less reason to oppose the return of Ulle. So I was much troubled by the substitution of Leicester for Salisbury, who Bruno considered astute and who must be experienced after so many years of service to King Henry. I remembered King David very well, having been presented to him in Carlisle and even danced with him several times. His manners were gentle and very polished, much more what I

thought of as French than like a barbarian Scot, but despite
the outward gentleness papa had respected him and said he
was a strong man. I was certain that Waleran's overbearing ways would only arouse David's animosity.

Thus, I was afraid that no treaty would be made and my
case would become more hopeless, but Leicester was a
very different man from his brother, not so much in looks
as in his manner and, I think, character. Waleran was
quick and loud; arrogant even with his equals and utterly
contemptuous of anyone less powerful; prone to suspicion
and envy; and distrustful of, if he did not actually hate, the
Church. Robert was slow and thoughtful, courteous in
speech to all, unless he had reason to be angry, and he was
religious. He also seemed fond of his wife, Emma, and I
could not help but like him despite his twin.

That was just as well because I soon learned that we
were to be much in Lord Robert's company as we traveled
to Durham, and I am sure I would have betrayed my
hatred if I had been forced into such close companionship
with Waleran. After the evening meal, the queen gathered
her ladies and explained that she could not take most of
them because of the distance, the uncertain weather, and
the dreadful condition of the roads as the frozen mud
thawed at the end of March. She chose from among us
only strong riders who were not likely to fall ill or complain about wet and cold, which cut our number to four. I
did fit the conditions, but I am still not sure whether Maud
included me because she was well satisfied with my work
as her clerk and did not want to take an inexperienced one
on a long journey or because she distrusted me and hoped
to catch me in some indiscretion when I was among the
Scots.

The next day, while the queen was conferring with
Leicester and I was sewing with the other ladies in the
hall, a page came to tell me that my man-at-arms needed a
word with me about the horses. I sprang up at once and
fetched my cloak, much alarmed because I did not want to
leave Fechin and Edna, who rode pillion behind him, but I
had not enough money to buy a new horse. That fear was
put to rest as I reached the stable and followed Fechin to a

far corner. There I found Merwyn, who handed me a letter from Bruno.

"How is he?" I gasped as I caught at the folded parchment, fortunately too surprised to cry aloud.

Fechin made a gesture of caution and looked nervously over his shoulder, and I clapped a hand to my mouth. No doubt Bruno had ordered his men to be secret, and he was quite right. If Maud learned that a private messenger had come from Bruno, her doubts and suspicions would be redoubled, worse because of the care we had taken to calm them.

"Is my husband well?" I asked in a carefully lowered voice, hoping it would not tremble as I trembled within, suddenly torn by a mixture of longing and jealousy.

"He be very well, m'lady," Merwyn mumbled, looking down at his boots, "but m'lord bade me go soon as the letter be in your hand and not to stay for any answer."

I was a little surprised at Merwyn's awkward manner. None of the men ever intruded on me, but if I spoke to them, they had always answered easily. However, I tried to accept his unease as owing to his wish to obey his master and leave, violently suppressing the suspicion that Merwyn was embarrassed because he knew I had been supplanted. It was a ridiculous suspicion—with whom could Bruno supplant me in siege or war? What did it matter if he relieved his body with some serf in the fields or the kind of whore who followed an army? I would not *let* it matter. If I did, I was lost. Besides, it was useless for me to keep Merwyn and, in a way, torture him. I knew he *would* not answer the question I could not allow myself to ask, and he surely could not answer questions about the king's doings. Nonetheless I was bitterly reluctant to let him go, and only fear that the queen still had eyes that followed my doings forced me to nod permission.

When he had slipped away, I opened the letter and read it while pretending to look at the horses. From the first lines it was clear why Bruno had sent this privately. He was furious with the king, criticizing him for the first time and actually calling him a fool over the terms of the treaty that was to be offered to King David. For nothing, he wrote, simply for the promise of good behavior, David

was to have all of Northumbria and Cumbria, and all the
blood shed in driving the Scots out was wasted.

For me, of course, the news was not unwelcome, no
matter how bitter Bruno was over the hurt Audris and
Hugh and other northern friends had suffered. However,
my satisfaction did not last long. The real reason Bruno
had written was not to express his anger and disappointment but to warn me not to approach King David with a
plea for the restoration of Ulle. The peace could not last,
he warned; most of the Northumbrian barons would not
accept it and would make trouble enough to provide David
with an excuse to violate the treaty at any time. When that
happened, Stephen would be twice and thrice as bitter
against any who had been favored by the Scot.

I read that more than once and thought of my doubts
about the queen's reasons for selecting me to go with her
to Durham. Perhaps there was no hope of convincing her;
perhaps I should ignore Bruno's warning and appeal to
King David—had not my father and brother died in his
cause? And if Bruno was not loyal to me, why should I be
loyal to him? I began to fold the letter and saw there was
more to it, a few lines that had been hidden by the fold on
which the seal was set.

"Beloved," Bruno wrote, "take care for your health
and that you do not tire yourself with too much labor, I
beg you. I grow so weary of this life. I desire only to sit in
quiet with you by my own fireside though we eat no more
than black bread and salt fish."

Hot with shame, I returned to the hall and my sewing. A
thousand pretty verses could not have carried the caring
and longing in those few lines. At that moment I would
gladly have painted my face blue to do as Bruno asked,
but as we traveled north my anxiety about being noticed by
the king faded. It was many years since David had met me
and kings see many, many people. It did not seem possible
he would remember me, and during the time the treaty was
being negotiated he did not seem to do so, although we
dined in the same hall several times. However, on the day
of the feast to celebrate the signing of the treaty, as I
finished a dance with some man whose name I do not
remember, the king came up to me and took my hand.

"Do I not know you?" he asked. "Are you not Lady Melusine, daughter of Sir Malcolm of Ulle? Why did you not come and speak to me?"

I curtsied to the ground. "Your memory is far more keen than I could dare hope," I murmured. "I would not presume so far."

King David laughed. "I do not forget beautiful women who dance as gracefully as you do. Will you allow me to renew my memory of the pleasure you gave me in the past?"

The music was beginning again and I could scarcely refuse, but though I could not see the queen, I could feel her eyes on me. Mostly the steps of the dance separated us, but as we walked down the center of the set together, the king said softly, "I think my surprise in seeing you with the queen made me slow to recognize you. Are you a hostage for your father's good behavior? If so—"

He did not know! Did he think papa and Donald had fled, deserting his service when the tide turned against him? "My father and brother are dead. They died at the siege of Wark. Ulle belongs to the Crown."

He looked shocked and grieved but could not answer because we came to the head of the row and were forced to stand apart. When we came together, he said, "I grieve for you, but I can do nothing about Ulle—not now."

I nodded. The terms of the treaty were not quite as favorable to Scotland as Bruno had described. Northumbria and Cumbria were not being ceded to King David himself. Instead his son Henry would do homage for those shires as vassal to the English king, so Stephen would still control them, at one remove. Even I could see that Henry, who must swear to be a faithful vassal, would not dare—at least for the present—to restore anyone disseised as a rebel against Stephen.

We had been performing the last of the turns and bows of the dance while those thoughts ran through my head, and King David took my hand for the final bow and curtsey. "I can offer you a place as my wife's lady," he began, but I shook my head.

"I am married, sire, to Sir Bruno of Jernaeve, Knight of the Body to King Stephen."

He stared at me and then nodded slowly. "If it is well with you, I am glad," he said. "But I will not forget you, Lady Melusine, and I will do what is in my power to do for you if you need my help."

He raised and kissed my hand, and I curtsied low a last time. That time I saw the queen and caught the glance of her black eyes. There was nothing to be read in her face and it was too late for regrets, but I had time to think about what I would say when she summoned me. She was in bed, having kept me waiting as long as she could—to allow time for my fear to grow?—and asked me why King David had chosen to dance with me.

"He said it was because he never forgot a beautiful woman who danced gracefully," I replied. "I had danced with him some years ago in Carlisle. I told him of my father's and brother's deaths at Wark," I went on, "and that I had been disseisined."

"You are very bold," Maud said quietly.

"Not so bold, madam," I sighed. "But I could not bear that he should think papa and Donald deserted him when he was losing." I wiped tears from my eyes and met hers. "And we said nothing to each other worth lying about. He offered me a place as his queen's lady, but that is not what I want."

CHAPTER 19

Bruno

I DO NOT know why, when all was going well, I felt the cold hand of disaster on my shoulder. Leeds fell to us with little loss. Our foray into Scotland did not weaken the king's forces, although I could not see that we accomplished anything either. Ludlow yielded also, and Stephen himself saved Prince Henry from death or capture by rescuing him when he was pulled from his horse with an iron hook by one of the defenders. Even before that the prince seemed fond of King Stephen, and that attachment boded well for keeping the treaty, despite my distaste for it. And if it were kept and there was peace in the north, Stephen's control of the south would be firmer.

Nor had the king grown cold to me when I spoke my mind over the terms he had offered to make peace with King David. He had been kind as ever, saying he understood my fear that those I loved in Jernaeve might suffer, since they had always withstood the Scots. But it was not fear for Audris and Hugh that chilled my blood. Prince Henry, who would be their overlord, was not a vindictive person nor the kind of man to blame Hugh for loyalty, and King David would not urge unjust behavior on his son—far from it; King David was a good man. Besides, Henry's investiture with the shires of Northumbria and Cumbria

was hedged about with restrictions forbidding any changes
in the tenure of those who held lands from Stephen and in
the laws and customs that were current in those shires.

I felt some uneasiness about the reaction of the earl of
Chester. He had long claimed Cumbria had been reft
unjustly from his father by King Henry and that his loyal
support of Stephen deserved the restoration of those lands.
He had been pressing that restoration at the Christmas
court, and I remembered Stephen soothing him with bland
words. But if Chester had taken those words as a half
promise, he would be more bitterly angry than before.

I do not think Chester's disappointment would have
troubled me as much if it had not been for the secret talk
about the treachery of the bishop of Salisbury. That made
me feel as if the earth were unsteady beneath my feet.
Salisbury had been the mainstay of the kingdom for all of
my life, and I did not trust Waleran, who was the chief
spokesman against him. Only I knew myself that the facts
Waleran stated were true. He did not exaggerate the secular power that had accumulated in the hands of Salisbury
and his kin—among them, the bishops of Salisbury, Lincoln, and Ely controlled the gathering of the wealth of the
entire kingdom and held six great keeps. There was no
doubt that if they turned on the king and the earl of
Chester joined them, the realm would be lost.

If it had been only Waleran who claimed that the bishops were just waiting for Matilda to step ashore to repudiate their faith to Stephen and raise her to the throne, I
think I would have contrived to warn the bishop of Winchester that the king's mind was being poisoned. But it
was not only Waleran. Before he left for Durham, Robert
of Leicester, who had as deep a love of the Church as his
brother Waleran's distrust of it, admitted that he felt the
king's hold on his realm might be in danger. And William
of Ypres, who was not a man that liked to contend with
the Church either, no matter what he felt about it privately,
warned Stephen that the castles the bishops held were too
strong for easy capture and could make whole districts
rebel strongholds.

Others faithful to the king and not of Waleran's party,

although they did not come forward with warnings, said when questioned by Stephen that they were made uneasy by how much power lay in Salisbury's hands. Among them were men I respected—Geoffrey de Mandeville, who was sheriff of Essex, Aubery and Robert de Vere, Robert de Ferrars, earl of Derby. All agreed that although the bishops had seemed to serve the king loyally, it would be wise to convince Salisbury and his kin to give up their offices and castles . . . if possible.

That "if possible" worked on my soul like a shower of sleet despite the mild weather and sunny skies of June as we moved toward Oxford, where the king was to hold his summer court. If Stephen dismissed Salisbury, Lincoln, and Ely from their offices and demanded that they yield up their keeps, would they obey him? Most of Stephen's barons clearly felt the bishops were more likely to flee to those keeps, where a great part of the money they had collected was stored, and fight the king, crying out that they had been unjustly deprived. Their defiance might convince Matilda that the time was ripe to come and demand her throne. If she came with her half brother Robert of Gloucester to lead her army, surely the rebellions that Stephen had quelled this year would burst out anew.

It seemed a hopeless tangle, but there was one thought that warmed me despite all other evil: Melusine would meet me in Oxford. The queen had finished her work with King David and was coming to join her husband. This time I made sure there would be no chance of being deprived of Melusine's company. I spoke to the king as soon as the place and time of holding court were settled, and though he laughed at me and teased me for my uxoriousness, recalling how I had resisted the marriage, he gave me leave to go ahead and find lodgings—and gave into my hands a good deal of the business Geoffrey of Glympton would ordinarily have done with the castellan of Oxford.

My pleasure in my foresight and in the fine, cool chamber—with a bed—I obtained raised my spirits. Being so early into the town, I had my choice of places, but I was not fool enough to consider any of the large, rich houses along the street that led to the castle or even those north and south of Carfax, where the market would be held. I chose a place less convenient—not far from the North Gate and Saint Michael's church—and a house too small to hold a nobleman and his retinue. Even so, I paid more than I could afford, but for the price had the guarantee that the widow who gave up her solar to my needs would house my men and horses—the horses in the yard, the men in the workroom—during the time the king was in Oxford.

Later Melusine told me I had been cheated, that if I had presented Cormi and Merwyn first, the price would have been lower. I said she had a lecherous mind, but to tell the truth, I am sure she was right; the widow and the woman who worked for her doing embroideries, which were sold by her son, who carried on his father's business as a mercer, also lodged below and from the sounds that drifted up to me did not lodge in the shop but chose the workroom too. I never would have thought it; the widow and her helpers were not young—but my men-at-arms were scarcely in the first flush of youth either.

Perhaps the fortunate, if lamentable, weakness in the moral fiber of the women was partly my fault. It was not possible for me to spend much time in my lodging until the king came because of my role as deputy to the king's chamberlain, and I did not trust my hostess—after all, it would be natural to wish to make as much profit as possible from an event that took place only once in a few years. So I bade my men stay at the house to make sure she did not rent it to several other people, despite our arrangement, and insist that we share the place. I bade Merwyn and Cormi make themselves agreeable and useful so that she would not suspect their true purpose, so perhaps I led to her downfall—but why should I regret something she enjoyed so much?

My work was not so pleasurable. Glympton had given me a list of the men who were to be lodged in the castle, their names written in the order of importance they had to the king. Did this mean the most important should be lodged closest to the king or in the grandest state, I had asked, whereupon Glympton had shown his teeth at me—it was not a smile. Part of our trouble was that in Oxford nearly all the great nobles had to be lodged in the keep or the town, unlike Westminster, where many of the barons had their own houses.

A further complication was that we had several foreign visitors, among them Alan, count of Brittany, and a man called Hervey de Lyons—that one was so haughty that he never deigned to see me, and his lips curled and nostrils flared every time Stephen put a hand on my shoulder or asked for a service from me with a "please." I am not certain why Stephen was so eager to please Lord Hervey; he was not a man the king would ordinarily have welcomed as a companion. Looking back and considering the fact that King Louis of France betrothed his sister Constance to Stephen's eldest son, Eustace, the following year, I have come to think that this Hervey might have been a secret envoy sent to determine whether the English court was a fit place for Constance. Whether he was or not, he was so dainty in his ways that Robert de Vere and I decided he must have his own house, not lie in the common hall, no matter that he be closest to the door of the king's chamber.

Forty-two of the houses in Oxford were Crown property, and four on the south side of the road that led to the drawbridge were very fine. Sir Robert and I bade those living there to remove and set their servants to cleaning and furbishing. Just opposite Saint Peter's church I found one house that seemed perfect for Lord Hervey and Lord Alan. It had a luxurious solar for Lord Hervey, whose small escort could occupy the lower floor, a large hall attached, and a yard with plenty of stabling for horses. I asked Sir Robert if he would approve having men screen off a chamber to the rear for Lord Alan, so his men—God knew why, but he had brought thirty men-at-arms as well as servants—could be housed in comfort in the hall. Sir Robert pointed out that the hall was really too large for the purpose and could serve the escorts of four or five noblemen, but after looking at each other—and bursting into laughter at one another's expressions—he approved my plan.

Day by day as my mind moved the queen's cortege and
with it my Melusine closer and closer to Oxford, I thought
less and less of the troubles that might befall us. I was
busy and a little concerned lest I make a mistake and cause
offense among the king's great vassals, but that did not
worry me deeply. I was not an official, only a deputy
pressed into service. I was sure Glympton could find an
excellent reason for the need to use a deputy, at least a
better reason than that one of the king's knights wished to
be sure of sleeping with his wife. And as an ignorant
deputy I could be used as a convenient scapegoat and yet
escape punishment. From time to time a chill would pass
over me as I remembered that there might be a confrontation between Salisbury and Stephen, but it was easy to
divert myself here in Oxford. I only had to look in the
market and see a small, pretty, hammered brass bowl to
hold flowers for Melusine, or any other toy I thought
would please her, and I was warm and happy at once
buying it.

I never had a doubt about how Melusine would feel or
whether she might have met some charmer among King
David's men who would have been more to her father's
taste—and thus perfect in her eyes—until the very last.
When I rode out with the king's retinue to meet the queen
and her people, an honor I suspect few kings paid their
wives and a mark of Stephen's eagerness to see Maud, I
suddenly recalled how cool and indifferent my letters must
have seemed to her. Would she know that I could not write
what was in my heart because I knew the queen would also
read the letters? Would she believe me when I told her
that? Now I remembered that I had wasted no words on
my desire for her in the one private letter I had sent either.
I had been too worried and angry. Nor would that letter
have pleased her in any other way. Had she obeyed me?
She had not answered, neither in the queen's packet nor in
any private message.

Barbe danced and fretted as the foreriders came into
view, responding to my unsteady hand on the rein, and
someone cursed me; however at that moment Stephen
started forward along the road, which was only wide enough

for three horses abreast and was lined with thick hedges.
Because of that it seemed years to me before I was able to
work my way around the more important folk who were
greeting each other and reach the mounted ladies. Then,
like a fool, I reached for Melusine before I turned Barbe
and that accursed Vinaigre nipped me on the thigh. In
jerking my left leg away, I pressed against Barbe, who
obediently danced aside, ramming another horse to my
right, which surged ahead into the hindquarters of the
preceding animal; that beast, turned left somewhat by the
impact, also started ahead, bumping into the mount of a
gentleman riding beside the lady one down the line from
Melusine.

I am not a coward. I have faced death and injury and the
rage of my superiors without flinching—at least outwardly—
but there are some things for which my courage is not
sufficient. One of those was admitting responsibility for
the growing chaos ahead of me, full of plunging horses,
shrieking women, and the shouts and curses of infuriated
men. Perhaps if I thought my confession that it was all my
fault would have done some good, I would have confessed. I say perhaps; I am not at all certain.

The lady immediately behind Melusine had pulled up
her mare in surprise and alarm and turned to look at the
confusion. There was now a clear space ahead of me wide
enough to turn Barbe. I did so at once and brought my
stallion beside Vinaigre, who was standing like a rock, so
completely unaffected by the noise and excitement behind
her that she could butt her head affectionately against
Barbe's neck. How I resisted drawing my sword and cutting off that mare's head I will never know.

There was a choked sound beside me, and Melusine's
voice, low and shaking, followed. "I am very sorry."

"It is time for me to buy you another horse," I said.

I heard Melusine gasp and I tore my eyes from Vinaigre's
head, where I was imagining a large, large hole. There
were tears on Melusine's cheeks and she was shaking,
getting out between gasps, "She likes you. She bites much
harder when she does not like someone."

"Why are you weeping?" I snarled at her. "You know
I will not harm your accursed mare."

Melusine sniffed and hiccupped, then bit her lip. "I was not weeping." Her voice was very small and meek. "I was laughing. I am very sorry but—but that"—she gestured behind us, where the chaos near us was quieting while farther down the road it was growing—"that is a very large result for one little affectionate nip."

I drew a deep breath, now considering whether Melusine's head would not look better decorated with holes. I do not know what showed on my face, but she lowered her head and looked at me sidelong. I could see her swallow and then swallow again and I knew she was fighting an impulse to giggle. I was balanced on a sword edge between rage and laughter when the lady behind urged her horse forward and said, "What in the world is going on?" and then continued ahead without waiting for an answer.

That was fortunate because Melusine's face turned puce in her effort to restrain her laughter and I gave up and burst into guffaws, leaned from the saddle, and bussed my wife soundly on the cheek.

"God knows this was not how I intended to greet you," I gasped. "I cannot tell you how much I have missed your company and how glad I am to have you back, but I did not mean my celebration to take the form of a public riot."

Melusine started to laugh with me and then stopped and asked, "Will we be together? Queen Maud said this court will be as well attended as the one at Christmas, and Oxford is smaller than Westminster if one counts the lodgings in London, so there will be less accommodation."

Her voice sounded eager to me, but she did not meet my eyes, and I thought her smile was strained when I told her of the chamber I had rented for us—it was later that she teased me about our hostess's weakness for my men. Then she reminded me that she could not come until her work for the queen was finished, and that would be late, she feared, because Maud and Stephen would be living in state—which meant that all the queen's richest gowns and every hanging, rug, and ornament would have to be unpacked and recorded separately. I pressed her hand and assured her that no matter how late, I would be waiting by the stairs that went to the women's quarters—or, if the king had some duty for me, which I did not expect because I was sure he would be with the queen, Merwyn would be waiting.

It was fortunate I had made that arrangement. After idling away hours after the evening meal, I was sent for into the king's private closet. Maud was, as I expected, with Stephen, but I was surprised to see that even the squires of the body had been dismissed. As soon as I came to the two chairs in which they sat side by side and bowed, Maud said to me, "Did you know Melusine was a favorite with King David?"

My heart sank at the words. I had hoped to hear no more of Melusine's feelings and connections with the Scots, and was disappointed. The particular question made my dismay worse. From it, I could only suppose that Melusine had ignored my instructions and approached King David with an appeal for the restoration of Ulle.

"I knew she had been presented to him," I replied warily. "I cannot see how she could be a *favorite*. King David could not have known her well enough for that. I do not believe her father ever served David—her brother did, but she would not have been sent to court then, she was too young."

"You are very hot in her defense," Maud snapped.

There was a weary pettishness in the remark that made me feel much better. If Maud had a real complaint against Melusine, she would have stated it. This attack seemed to owe more to Maud's being tired and worried in general than to any real anger at me or at Melusine, and the king smiled at me behind Maud's back and made a little gesture of apology. Then I realized he must have told Maud—possibly as a small, cheerful item of amusing gossip to relate among many troublesome matters—about my desire to come ahead and reserve a chamber, and that must have reminded her that I was no longer indifferent to my wife and, to her mind at least, not capable of controlling her.

"I beg pardon, madam," I protested, smiling, "that was not a defense but the facts as I know them. Will you tell me what Melusine has done wrong?"

"She told David she had been disseisined."

"She just walked up to King David and told him that?" I asked incredulously. "Right before your face? Or did she seek him out privately?"

Maud looked a little ashamed and Stephen began to laugh and patted her on the shoulder. "I think my dear wife is annoyed because for once I have seen deeper into a person than she." He leaned forward and kissed her cheek, then spoke to me again. "Melusine did not approach David at all. He approached her and asked her to dance. The rest followed from that. I *said* she was a sweet, gentle girl."

"I am not so sure of that still," Maud insisted. "Even Bruno admits she wants Ulle back. Now that she has established that David owes her a debt . . . Just you be sure, Bruno, that she does not ask Prince Henry for those lands. Treaty or no treaty, they are not his to give."

"Why do we not give Ulle to Bruno?" Stephen suggested, laughing again, but I thought only half jesting. "The lands are worthless. Not a penny over the livelihood of the steward can be wrung out of them. Then you could stop worrying about it."

"Not now!"

Maud spoke so sharply that the smile I had given the king, part gratitude and part acknowledgement that he was only teasing his wife, froze on my face as I turned to look at her.

She laughed then and said lightly, "Melusine is too useful to me now. I cannot spare her—and you cannot spare Bruno, my lord."

I could have promised that Melusine and I would serve as willingly after we had Ulle as before, but I knew Maud would not believe that, and I was not sure I believed it myself. Instead, I bowed and said, equally lightly, "I am not yet very hungry. The promise of the carrot on the stick will serve very well."

"A hope you may have, not a promise," Maud replied before Stephen could speak. Then she looked down at her hand enclosed in her husband's and added softly, "I will not promise what may be impossible to perform." She turned her hand in Stephen's and gave his a squeeze. "It is late, my lord, and I am weary."

The king put his arm around her shoulders and nodded dismissal at me as he murmured some apology to her for not taking her to her chamber earlier. I was out the door before they rose, but had only to look across the nearly empty hall to see that Merwyn was gone from the foot of the stairs. That meant that Melusine must have come down from the queen's apartments and gone ahead with Merwyn to our lodgings. I hurried down the stair in the forebuilding, but they were not in the courtyard or the outer bailey, so I moderated my pace, guessing that Melusine must have come down only a minute or two after I was summoned and I would not be able to catch up.

When I came softly into the solar, I caught Melusine in the act of undressing, wearing only her shift. The way she cried out and clutched to her the tunic she had just removed enchanted me completely. "I adore you," I muttered, striding across the narrow room and embracing her. Her arms were caught between us, and for an instant I thought she was pushing me away, but then she dropped the tunic to the floor and laid her head on my shoulder.

"Beloved, I am sorry my letters were so indifferent, but the queen—"

"I understood," she murmured huskily.

I hesitated, but she did not say in turn that she had written like a gossiping friend for the same reason. It occurred to me just then that Melusine had never said she cared for me. I was tempted to press her for a few sweet words, which I had never had from any woman except my sister Audris—for I was not so foolish as to ask a whore to call me beloved—but I did not. If she refused, even out of shyness, the sweetness of this moment would be lost, and the moment *was* sweet, for her arms had crept around me, one stroking my back and the other clinging to my waist. I tilted her face up and kissed the full red lips; her eyes closed.

"Are you cold, dear heart?" I asked softly after a moment. "Do you want to get into bed?" I should not have kissed her, for I was aching with need already and the feel of her mouth made it worse.

"No, I will help you undress," she whispered.

I was glad of it. She could have called Edna to help me, but her willingness to serve me herself was precious to me. My grip on her had relaxed while we spoke, and she let herself slide down my body. The way she went down, her arms still around me, her whole body pressed against mine, nearly brought me to a premature spilling of my seed. Yet, I was not sure she had intended to raise desire in me. If she wished to hide her face or her body, she might have done the same thing. A small uneasiness drifted about inside of me and shadowed Melusine's actions. Ever since she had yielded her body to me there seemed to be two Melusines, one warm and eager and the other reluctant and doubting—but at that moment it would have taken a far stronger chill to divert me than the moth-wing brush of doubt I felt. Sword and belt, tunic and shirt, were off and cast away anywhere before Melusine had both my cross garters untied. As the second loosened, I had the tie of my chausses undone and could rid myself in one sweeping push of all my nether garments.

Then I bent to lift Melusine from the floor, to strip off her tunic, to sup the sweetness of her body with my mouth and take in the strong woman-smell of her. And when my mouth was not busy with kissing I praised her. I do not remember everything I said—all of it was silly beyond measure, like calling her my sun and my moon—but it was true. I was spilling out all the need to love that had been buried in me all the years I had been parted from Audris. But this was a far fiercer caring, far stronger, a need so great that though it was all joy it was like torture. Caring for Audris was a glow of warmth and a sweet tenderness. The tenderness was there for Melusine also, but it was like a honey that bound together a burning ginger concoction of passion in the body and the soul.

Later, after we had loved—and that was better than ever with Melusine's strong legs urging me deeper and her body rising to meet mine; there was no reluctance there nor did I fail to bring her, crying out, high and sweet, like a bird's song, to a rich joy—but later, when the soft words and small tired kisses of repletion had been exchanged and she lay quiet against me, I thought she looked sad. And I wondered then whether there had been just a moment of resistance when I first lifted her up to caress her before we joined bodies. If there had been, I know it melted with my first touches and sweet words.

Again it was a moth-wing brush of doubt and I flicked it away as one brushes at a moth. But it was there, and perhaps to avoid the far greater pain of doubting Melusine's affection for me, I turned to a faint renewed irritation about her leaning toward King David and mentioned the queen's remark that she was a favorite with him. She pushed herself up on the pillows, away from me, and frowned, but I saw at once that she was more anxious than angry.

"I do not think I could have avoided the meeting," she said. "Maud would have been even more suspicious if I refused to come to the hall to eat with the others. And I did not believe he would recognize me after—it must be four or five years." She hesitated and then went on slowly, "Maud is a very strange woman. I could have sworn that she had thought the matter through and accepted what I told her—which was the truth—as the truth. She was so easy with me on the journey here, even sometimes jesting with me, I thought I had eased her mind . . . yet she has carried that suspicion—"

"I am not sure of that," I interrupted. I certainly did not want Melusine to feel the queen had been deceiving her. "I do not think the queen is really suspicious of your talk with King David in Durham. I think Maud was angry and frightened about something else and to divert her the king told her how I had asked to come to Oxford before him to secure a place so we could be together—Stephen thought it very funny and teased me for days about how I resisted our marriage and how much I have changed. Then because of her fear, Maud recalled that she had urged our marriage because she thought me impervious to women and found I was not. She was only lashing out at you and me because she is afraid. And I am almost sure now that we will have Ulle in the end, although . . . No, let me finish one thing at a time. The king said, 'Let us give it to Bruno'—only half in jest—and Maud did not say 'No,' she said, 'Not now.' "

"Not now?" Melusine echoed, and then, quick of wit as she was, also repeated, "The queen is afraid?" And putting the two together asked, "What has happened?"

"Nothing as yet," I told her, "but the king fears treachery from the bishop of Salisbury, and I believe the bishop and his nephews will be asked to give up their offices and the keeps they hold."

"So that was why Maud once said she did not dare anger Salisbury over the dishonesty of one of his cousins and why Leicester rather than Salisbury came to Durham with us." Melusine nodded briskly as if things that had puzzled her had now become clear. Then she frowned again. "But why should the queen be afraid? If Salisbury plans some treachery, is it not best that he be stopped before he can accomplish it?"

I explained then about the power of the bishop and his party, how they might resist and cry that they were unjustly used, since it was true enough that there was no proof of disloyalty against them, and how that might reawaken the rebellion and even make it more dangerous by bringing Gloucester and Empress Matilda to England.

Melusine listened although I could see her eyes were closing. When I was done, she slid down beside me again, with a shrug of her shoulders. "A cause to deprive them of offices and keeps will be found."

"But I think they are too experienced and too clever for the king to catch them out in any real crime," I said, pulling her close and laughing silently at myself because I was so happy now and only two weeks ago the same thought could make a bright summer day turn grey.

"I did not say any crime would be discovered," Melusine murmured sleepily. "Do not be silly. I said a cause would be found—or mayhap made. Hmmm. Could be that was why the queen is afraid, because she does not think the cause the king will create is sufficient. She is very clever, very . . ."

There is a woman for you. Melusine's voice faded and faded and she fell asleep right in the middle of a crucial remark. What she had said horrified me, and I wanted to argue with her because it all rang too true. I remembered the plot to assassinate Gloucester in Normandy and grew cold despite the warmth of Melusine's body nestled against me. No, that was not possible. Maud would have had a fit not been only worried if there had been a plan to attack the bishop. I could not and would not believe it. Yet it stuck in the back of my mind all the next week while more and more noblemen arrived in Oxford.

By the date the king had set in his summons, I could have sworn that the dog kennels and pigsties had been rented out despite the fact that it was summer and perfectly possible to put up a tent in a field near the town. Some of the lesser folk did so, poor knights and barons who had come to court to plead a case or beg some small favor from the king. I suppose the great men thought their dignity would be lessened, and it was a wet summer. The fair days of June gave way to hot weather, alternating with terrible thunderstorms. These were so frequent that Melusine moved most of her fine gowns to the queen's apartment and changed there from coarser clothes, which she did not mind getting wet and muddy. But no matter what the weather, we both made our way back to the widow's house every night.

On the night before the king was to greet his court officially, the bishop of Salisbury still had not arrived. I could not help wondering whether he had discovered that some plot had been devised against him. Later I learned that he knew nothing for sure, but he had sensed the king's coldness toward him—well, I had seen examples of that myself and Salisbury was no fool. I think myself that the one bred the other, that is, when Stephen was first crowned Salisbury truly intended to be a loyal servant and it was Stephen's suspicion that caused the bishop to begin to lean toward Matilda.

In any case, Salisbury did come, just in time for the king's greeting. I was standing below the dais near the king, ready to perform any necessary service, when the bishop entered the hall, and my heart clenched hard when I saw how all made way for him and how many bowed

deeply, unlike Waleran and his party who gave only stiff
and shallow acknowledgement. This was no time for an
accusation, I knew, but I was not prepared for, and, I must
admit, I was sickened by Stephen's overcordial greeting.
Whether it deceived Salisbury, I do not know. He thanked
the king for his kindness, said a few words about a meeting of the inner council, and then withdrew from the king
to greet others in the hall.

I did not sigh with relief—a good servant to a king does
not give way to such expressions of feeling, good or
bad—and besides, I was not sure that I was relieved. The
trouble had to come. Even if Stephen had begun to doubt
that Salisbury was as black as he was painted or if Maud
had urged him to wait until the bishop showed a sign of his
intended treachery, I was sure Waleran would prick him
into action with new accusations. So if the break had to
come, I wished it to come soon so that I need not see my
master shaming himself with falseness.

There was no more that day, at least. Salisbury was an
old man and could claim he was tired by traveling and
must rest in private. Unlike other latecomers, lodging was
no problem for him or for Lincoln and Ely and Roger le
Poer, who was the king's chancellor. However, for their
guards and clerks and servants—of whom there were a
great number; perhaps because of their fears they had
come with a force large enough, they thought, to protect
them—it was not so easy. Only a few were allowed space
in the castle. Most were left to fend for themselves, and
since nothing better was to be had, a good number had
settled in the sheds and outbuildings in the churchyard of
Saint Peter's.

Saint Peter's church was closest to Oxford castle—aside
from Saint George's, which was within the grounds—and
made it easiest for the men to get to their master. That
need and the bad weather and the great pride of Hervey de
Lyons, which had rubbed off on his retainers, caused the
trouble—I am sure of it, although it is widely said that it
was by Stephen's order that Alan of Brittany's men invited
attack with insult.

I am sure, but I can offer no proof although I myself

was embroiled in the attack by accident. There had been two days of quiet, at least as far as Salisbury was concerned, while the king disposed of most of the business of the minor knights and barons. This was the sort of kindness and considerateness that always made me put aside Stephen's other faults. He knew it was difficult and expensive for a poor man to come to court, and he never made his lesser petitioners wait and wait to see him. Their business was done first, and each was given permission to depart "when it pleased him thereafter"; they were welcome to stay and enjoy the feasts and entertainments and hunts if they so desired, but they were not required to do so. He even made sure that there was a great feast and merrymaking the very day the minor pleas were finished so that those who did intend to leave early would not miss all the amusements.

I had been on duty from dawn on both days—another mark of Stephen's kindness, not to me but to those lesser subjects. The king thought my manner and dress, which were simpler than those of many of his high-born servants, would put the petitioners more at ease. Perhaps the king felt I had been too much engaged in serious business and that was why he bade me stay after the feast and continue merrymaking with some other young men, all of whom I knew well. I was not at all loathe to do it. I adored Melusine and enjoyed every moment spent in her company, but there is a different kind of pleasure in a hard drinking, loud talking group of men, and I suddenly realized I had not been in such a party since my marriage.

The night was everything I expected, but I stayed longer than I originally intended. I was only a little merry with wine when I got up to leave because I did not want to frighten Melusine by coming to her roaring drunk. On reaching the outer door, however, I discovered there was so violent a thunderstorm in progress that I would have been swept away and drowned if I had set a foot outside. I returned to my companions only to wait out the worst of the weather, but somehow by the time I reeled back to the widow's house the stars were paling in the cleared sky.

Naturally after my initial attempt to leave, I had been

well roasted for being henpecked and had received much advice on how to school my wife if she objected to my condition, but I had no need of it. Although I wakened her from a sound sleep, by stumbling over something, probably my own feet, and falling on her, Melusine received me with good humor. Indeed, I must have afforded her considerable amusement, for I recall how much she laughed when my nose nearly touched my knees and she had to catch me to save me from falling over as I tried to undo my cross garters.

Actually, I do not remember much after that—Melusine must have undressed me and got me into bed—until she shook me an hour or so later and told me it was dawn. She began to laugh again when I groaned piteously, and if I had had the strength, I would have used one of the suggestions I had been given for curbing a wife and beaten her soundly. However, I knew that would hurt me more than her at the moment, so I only told her I was excused from duty to the king for this day and to leave me in peace. She was still laughing when she departed, and I cursed her under my breath and vowed to make her rue it, but I forgave her when I woke some hours later. I found the chamber pot set ready for me on a small bench beside the bed so I did not have to bend and seek for it, and next to it, a goblet of wine redolent of strong spices.

That worked so well on me that I, who woke hoping I would never have to eat again, was able to enjoy a hot pie I bought in the market and then have another with a jack of ale so I could escape sitting down to a court dinner. Markets are always noisy, and at first as I walked down the road toward the castle I thought I was still hearing echoes of the hawkers' calls. However, the sound grew louder, not softer, and I realized it was men shouting in rage and the clang of weapons somewhere ahead of me. I started to run, then hesitated; the noise was coming from the hall in which Count Alan was lodged. I had my sword half drawn, but if there was a quarrel between the men of Count Alan and Lord Hervey, I wanted no part of that.

Suddenly a man with blood pouring from a wound on his head appeared in the doorway of the hall and began to shout, "À Salisbury, *à l'aide! Au secours!*" and a mass of men came boiling out of Saint Peter's churchyard. I leapt between, drawing my sword and shouting for them to keep the peace in the king's name, but I hesitated to strike any of the bishop's men, and I was thrust aside so violently that I was knocked backward into the front wall of the house. By then Count Alan's men were pouring out of their hall, and the battle was joined in earnest—not with fists and feet, which is common enough when men are crowded together with strangers, but with knives and even swords.

Plainly no one man on foot would be able to stem what was rapidly growing into a riot, and it would take far too long for me to try to go around the fight, so I charged forward, laying about me with the flat of my blade until I forced a way through, and ran for the castle. There were men enough in the guard who knew me and responded when I called for a mounted force to stop a riot, but the horses had to be fetched and saddled, and by the time we rode back the damage had been done.

Several of the men-at-arms were down and bleeding, but far more important was that Count Alan's nephew had been badly hurt. I recognized him at once and drove Barbe at two men fighting directly over him. Angry as they were, they knew too much of destriers to dare Barbe's teeth and hooves and they broke and ran. The other guards did even better, since they were experienced in quelling market troubles, and in minutes I was able to dismount and take the young man into my arms and carry him into the hall.

I laid him on the table, pushing away trenchers of half-eaten food and cups of wine, some overturned by the violence with which men had left their meal. I slashed his clothes into strips with my knife (I could see no reason to ruin my own; I was angry enough at having my tunic stained with blood) and bound his head and his arm, shouting to the servant boy who was cowering in a corner to run for a chirurgeon, or if one could not be found, for a barber to sew up his wounds.

A guard came in then, and I ordered him to watch by the young man while I rode to the keep and informed the

king. Had the count's nephew not been hurt, I would not
have thought the matter important enough to trouble the
king, but I found that I was not the first to report the fight.
Lord Hervey himself was already recounting the insult and
hurt the bishop's men had done to his servants. Stephen
soothed him, promising that the insult and damage would
not be overlooked, even though it was the men of the
highest official in the land who had committed the of-
fenses. The king looked angry, but something about his
voice shocked me; there was a kind of satisfaction under
the anger that told me Stephen had found a cause for
stripping Salisbury of his power.

I suppose I made some movement, or possibly Stephen
was growing a little restive under Lord Hervey's unending
complaints and let his eyes wander, and the king started up
out of his chair, crying, "Bruno! You are all over blood!
Are *you* hurt?"

"No, my lord," I assured him, "not at all, but I saw
the fight and brought men to quell it. All is quiet now, but
I am afraid Count Alan's nephew was injured. It is his
blood you see, my lord."

"I will send my chirurgeon to him at once." Stephen
gestured to a page and told him to bring the chirurgeon,
then turned back to me. "Will you wait and guide him,
Bruno? You will need to go back to your lodging to
change your clothes anyway."

"Yes, my lord." I could say nothing else, but I knew
the purpose for keeping me there was for my bloodstained
clothing to start questions going among those who had not
heard Hervey's protests—or who would be overjoyed at
his men getting a drubbing, only regretting it was not he
himself who had received it.

That thought was amusing, but what followed was not.
Salisbury was summoned, the complaint was lodged, and
restitution demanded. The bishop first said his servants
were not wholly at fault; they had been swamped and
terrorized during the terrible storm the previous night and
had gone peaceably to seek lodging in Count Alan's hall,
where they knew there was space aplenty. The three men
who had gone with the request were not only refused but
beaten and had naturally called for help. The captain of

Count Alan's troop protested vigorously, admitting that the lodging had been denied but claiming that it was Salisbury's men who, in fury, struck first, crying that Salisbury was a far greater man than Count Alan and that they would drive all Alan's men out and Alan himself too and take the lodging for themselves.

Salisbury refused to accept this version, but said it was the duty of the Church and its servants to keep the peace even under provocation. For this reason, he was willing to give satisfaction for the ill behavior of his men, whereupon the king demanded the surrender of all his keeps and his offices, and those of his nephew also. I do not think the bishop was really surprised, but he pretended hurt and deep shock and cried out that the punishment was too severe for so small an offense and one not even given by himself. Still he did not refuse; he asked for a day or two to consider, but only a few hours later he was arrested in his chamber in the castle and his nephew Alexander of Lincoln was seized in his lodging in the town.

The arrests were dreadful to me because they violated right and custom, which decreed that any man who came to court must be allowed to depart in peace. Yet I could see the necessity. King Henry had been strong enough to let go a man who had defied him and punish him later; Stephen's rule was still too uncertain to allow men of such power to escape. I did not like the cruelty with which the king forced the bishops to yield their keeps either, starving them and threatening to hang the bishop of Lincoln, but their sufferings were brief and many would have suffered worse and died too if the king had let the bishops go and fought to take the places. Perhaps it was a sin to lay hands on the anointed of God, but it saved much bloodshed both for the bishops' men and ours.

At first the king was jubilant, his optimistic nature leading him to believe that his troubles had been solved, but Melusine told me, when the army returned from taking the six keeps that had been held by the bishops, that the queen was sick with worry. A number of the great ladies who served Maud had expressed their horror of the king's action, among them King Henry's widow, Lady Adelicia, who was now married to William d'Aubigny. Worse yet,

Henry of Winchester had come to her and begged her with
tears to convince Stephen to restore the keeps and the large
sums of money in them to the bishops. He would be
forced, he told her, to call Stephen to account if he did
not, and it would break his heart to need to admonish his
brother. The queen had responded that the bishop of Winchester had no right to admonish the king of the realm, and
Winchester had riposted that a legate of the pope had the
right to admonish anyone who offended the Church.

I was at first stunned to hear that Winchester had pro-
cured legatine power. There might have been time if he
sent to the pope after Theobald had been made archbishop,
but considering the snail's pace at which the curia worked—
and their habit of delaying to see if larger bribes could be
extorted—I doubted it. And then I recalled how Winchester had thanked Melusine for her "warning" just before
we had started north, and I realized that he must have
begun his negotiations to be made legate at that time. If
the plea had been presented then and the details worked
out, the legate who had confirmed Theobald as archbishop
could have carried back Winchester's request.

I could see why Maud was worried. Kings had defied
the Church before over questions of secular power, and
Stephen had not demanded any change in administration or
tax from the bishops' sees. Nonetheless, it was always bad
to be at odds with the Church. There was something that
worried me far more, however, and that was the rage
generated in the sheriffs, most of whom had been appointed by King Henry and had long ruled the shires under
Salisbury's administration. I had a taste of it once or twice
as the army moved about the country and I was sent with
messages. If they would no longer serve the king faithfully, the whole government of the realm would be shaken.
I warned Stephen, but he only smiled and said he knew
how to manage that problem; he would appoint earls from
among his own supporters to oversee the sheriffs.

In August the first overt reaction to the treatment of the
bishops burst out. The king was summoned by Henry of
Winchester, acting as papal legate, to a council of bishops
that was to judge his actions. Stephen did not attend

himself but sent Aubery de Vere as his spokesman—Aubery de Vere and a crowd of bull-throated, newly created earls. When they returned they were all very pleased with themselves because the council had broken up in confusion with no decision.

I heard Lord Gilbert Fitz Gilbert praising Vere's defense, which I myself found convincing, I must admit. Vere claimed that the king had *not* interfered in any way with the property or privilege of the Church; he had not deprived the bishops of their power over their sees nor had he demanded that anything belonging to the Church be delivered into his hands. Stephen's quarrel with the bishops had been reserved to their activities as ministers of the Crown and their control of secular property, both of which were rightfully the business of the king. What I liked much less was Hugh de Beaumont's laughing comment that Vere's defense might have been masterly, but what sent the bishops home with their tails between their legs were a few suggestions as to what would happen to them and their precious churches if they voted against the king or took their case to Rome without Stephen's permission.

I think that was the final blow to any hope of peace in England. I am sure that many appeals had been made to Empress Matilda and Robert of Gloucester to come to England over the three years of Stephen's reign, particularly during the sporadic rebellions of 1138, but they had not come to help their adherents. I am also sure that there were many reasons for their lack of response, some of which had nothing to do with England, but I think that one cause of their reluctance to commit themselves was the nearly universal support for Stephen from the Church.

King Henry had controlled the Church diplomatically, but also with an iron hand. When Stephen came to the throne, English churchmen had held high expectations of a gentler relationship with the Crown, with more freedom and opportunity to expand their wealth and power. The fierce double blow the king had dealt them—taking two of their most powerful number prisoner and sending his earls to threaten the whole council—had changed that attitude.

A second good reason, to my mind, for Matilda and Robert to delay their coming was that they were waiting

for Salisbury to tell them the time was ripe and he was
ready to support them. It seems to me that Salisbury's fall,
taking from them all hope of a quick and easy victory,
rather than discouraging them, made them desperate. They
must have seen that Stephen would gain complete control
of the country if they did not act at once. While the fury of
the bishops was still hot and Salisbury's subordinates had
not yet been replaced or fully controlled by Stephen's new
earls, there was still hope for them.

The council that destroyed the bishops' hopes for a
compromise ended on the kalends of September; on the
day before the kalends of October—in a month less a
day—Robert of Gloucester and King Henry's daughter
Matilda arrived in England, landing at Arundel by the
invitation of William d'Aubigny and his wife Adelicia,
who by her earlier marriage to King Henry was Matilda's
mother-by-law.

CHAPTER 20

Melusine

QUEEN MAUD'S MOOD had been so bad since the court in Oxford that when Bruno told me Robert of Gloucester and Matilda had escaped the patrol ships and come safely to port in Arundel, I nearly wept with despair. It was not so much that the queen was unpleasant or unkind but that a gloom so dark hung over her that it seemed an abomination to be happy oneself. So I felt split in two, because I was happy. From the end of August, after the king had taken possession of the bishops' castles, the queen had joined him and Bruno and I were together.

The only small cloud in my personal sky was that I thought I might once have got with child and lost the babe. I was not certain; I had only missed my flux by a few days when we started a progress from Northhampton to Windsor, and it started on the second day. I said nothing to Bruno—I am not sure why. He certainly never reproached me for not conceiving, although he worked very, very hard at the activity necessary to making a baby; on the other hand, I do not think that was his major purpose. To be honest, it was not my major purpose. I had not been completely overjoyed when my bleeding was late, and I felt more guilt than grief when it began because I knew Bruno would have insisted on taking me to Jernaeve once he knew I was with child. But the flux was not heavier than usual when it came, so perhaps I had not conceived after all.

It was a little shadow in my mind though, which made me more sensitive to the queen's heavy heart—thus my despair when I heard news that I thought would make her more sorrowful. To my amazement, the effect was quite different from what I imagined. At first I did not notice much change in her, even when the king reacted with his usual swiftness, gathering an army and marching south. Perhaps that was because I felt so terrible myself; all the light seemed to have gone out of my life when Bruno rode away. At least when the king and queen were together, we sometimes met during the day, and Bruno was always so steady and practical that he lifted my spirits. And we had our evenings and nights together to talk over the news and gossip of our different portions of the court and to laugh and jest . . . and love.

Then we had the news that Gloucester had escaped from Arundel, taking with him the hundred and forty knights he had brought from Normandy and leaving his half sister Matilda at Arundel, which the king promptly besieged. I wept—not because Gloucester had escaped; I did not care a blown egg about Gloucester, but a siege meant that Bruno might be away from me for months and months.

It was then that the queen's mood changed. Not that Maud was happy, but it was as if a blow she had been dreading had fallen, and the worst had *not* occurred. She shook herself out of the heavy cloud that seemed to have deadened her feelings and dulled her mind. Now her tears flowed. She wept over the danger her husband might encounter if he decided to assault Arundel, but she did not let the tears interfere with a spate of activity in which she made ready to summon more men to the king's aid and to ascertain that supplies flowed in a steady stream toward the king's army. I knew something of that because I wrote some of the orders. She never would have trusted me to do that in the past, but Maud had softened toward me, especially after she had found me weeping over the news of the siege. I had not told her my real reason—she did not ask.

I could have saved my tears though. Before a week had

passed, Bruno arrived with a request that I return to Arundel with him to perform a service for the king.

"What service?" Maud asked unbelievingly, and I fear I was standing with my mouth open, so shocked that I could not even force out the same question.

"Melusine knows Empress Matilda," Bruno replied.

"Knows her?" Maud repeated, turning to look at me.

"I was presented to her twice, but that was eight years ago. I was only fifteen."

That was all I said, but I recalled that during the second of those meetings Matilda had singled me out several times. Once she even sent a page for me, summoning me by name to my intense disgust; there was no way to avoid the summons if she knew my name. She had infuriated me thoroughly because by her august attention she had deprived me of the opportunity of dancing and talking with friends whom I saw only a few times a year. And there was not a thing in her conversation worth losing that pleasure. She had nothing of interest to say; she did nothing but complain about the crudity of English ways and the lack of manners and respect shown her in contrast to the refined practices of the court of the Holy Roman Emperor— from which she had been gone over five years.

My fury made me dumb in her presence; in fact, I did not even dare raise my head and look at her for fear she would see the contempt in my face, and I knew better than to offend King Henry's daughter no matter what I thought of her. I can only suppose that she took the silence and the bent head for awe and favored my company for that reason. Some of the other ladies were not so careful as I, but most of them were daughters or wives of men much more powerful than my papa. Also, I knew that King Henry did not much trust papa, so it was more important for me not to add insult to injury.

My face must have shown that there was more than a simple presentation to remember and Maud said, rather dryly, "For the daughter of a simple knight, and a poor one too, you seem to have many friends in high places, Melusine."

"I would not say I was Empress Matilda's friend," I answered equally dryly. "There are few people in my part of the realm, madam, so there is never a great crowd attending even the most important persons. Thus, each of those summoned may be noticed more particularly. The empress thought me meek and talked at me.''

Maud laughed. It was not a sound heard frequently these days, and I found, to my surprise, that I was glad I had amused her.

"Talked *at* you," she said. "Very good. That is a good description of Matilda's conversation." Her eyes went back to Bruno. "But I do not see what service Melusine could perform despite her acquaintance with Matilda.''

"I suppose she is to serve as a—a kind of hostage," Bruno replied.

We both stared at him. "Ridiculous!" Maud exclaimed, and I agreed, my sense of the inappropriateness of the idea temporarily overwhelming the hurt I felt that Bruno would agree to use me in such a way. Hostages came from families of power who could exert influence on the king to prevent him from violating whatever pledge the hostages were surety for. There was no sense in taking a poor, powerless hostage. But then Maud frowned and repeated, "Hostage? Is Arundel not besieged? Has there been a battle? How could Matilda demand—"

"I beg pardon, madam," Bruno interrupted, looking contrite. "I did not mean to cause you any anxiety. The king is safe; the siege has not been broken; there has been no battle. It is my fault for beginning the tale at the wrong end."

The queen, who had started to rise from her chair, sank back and gestured to Bruno to continue.

"From the beginning then," he said, smiling faintly. "The advantage of strength is all ours, so much so that she who was Queen Adelicia and her husband sorely repent inviting Matilda to come to them."

"I will make her very welcome here," Maud remarked with a grim smile.

"Unfortunately their honor is too much engaged to give her up to imprisonment," Bruno said.

"Did I speak of imprisonment?" Maud retorted. "She will be my guest, and I will swear on whatever she desires to maintain her in greater luxury than my own until the day she wishes to return to her husband and swears she will never set foot in England again.''

Bruno smiled but shook his head. ''You know that offer will not be accepted, madam. The choice was only to assault Arundel keep at great cost with much loss of blood—they cannot be starved out; it is impossible to surround the keep completely because of the river—or to make an offer Aubigny and Adelicia could accept with honor. The king himself wished to try assault and to encourage his barons offered to lead the assault in person, but his advisors felt that would be too costly and too dangerous.''

''Assault *is* too dangerous,'' Maud agreed quickly and emphatically, paling as she spoke.

Clever devil Bruno, I thought. I knew he had put in that little bit about the king leading the assault just to frighten the queen. He had succeeded. Maud valued her husband above ten kingdoms. She would agree to any proposal that would prevent assault. But it troubled me that Bruno should use his cleverness against the queen, and it reminded me how far he set his duty above my well-being that he would send me as a hostage into enemy hands. Only just then his eyes flickered toward me, with a glance that warned me he had more to say to me alone and enjoined me to silence. Perhaps I should have been more hurt and angered by that silent command, but that fleeting glance had been more like a sharing of trouble than an order, and I held my tongue.

''So it was decided,'' Bruno continued, acknowledging the queen's remark with a nod, ''although there was some difficulty in convincing the king, who was torn between his desire to be merciful to his cousin and his wish not to appear weak before his barons. However, by the consent of all, it was decided to send Empress Matilda to her brother in Bristol.''

''But surely it is wrong to free her now that she is trapped in our grasp,'' Maud cried, common sense conquering the fear she felt about Stephen engaging in war.

''Perhaps, but to capture her would mean bloodshed, much bloodshed,'' Bruno reminded her.

The queen made a furious gesture. ''Well, since you

have promised her freedom," she said angrily, "what more does she want?"

"A token of faith, madam," Bruno said, and before she could burst out into a tirade of rage and frustration, he hurried on. "She desires a woman companion in whom she believes she can trust, and after many ladies were considered, the bishop of Winchester suggested Melusine; the king felt she would make a perfect envoy, and the empress recalled her and found her acceptable."

"And you agreed to this?" Maud asked. "You will let your wife be dragged to Bristol in a crowd of enemies with Matilda as her sole female companion. Well, you do not know Matilda, but she—"

"Forgive me for interrupting you again, madam, but I fear you do not understand the whole conditions. Naturally the king, having the upper hand, would not permit Aubigny to escort the empress. That is why a lady companion was deemed necessary. It was decided that Lord Waleran and the bishop of Winchester will escort the empress."

"Waleran and Henry—" the queen began with a quick intake of breath, but then she added, very quickly, as if she hoped to overlay her first words in our memories, "I still think it not safe for Melusine. I am afraid that—"

"I will escort my wife, madam," Bruno said, his mouth grim. "I would agree on no other terms. If Melusine could have joined the bishop of Winchester's people . . . but that was impossible. I am aware of Empress Matilda's reputation although I do not know her in person, and I would not endure that Melusine be Matilda's plaything or the butt of her jests."

The queen asked some further questions to which I paid little attention. A great joy had burst over me when Bruno said he would go with me, and I no longer cared much who else would be in our company. I already knew Matilda to be an arrogant fool, and an arrogant fool stripped of her power, so I did not fear her at all. If all she desired of me was silent attention with a meek little "Yes, my lady," at each pause, I would provide that gladly to keep her happy; but if she thought she could take any liberties with my person, she would soon learn her judgement of me as a meek pet bitch was mistaken.

At a pause in the conversation, I came forward and bowed and asked, "My accounts, madam, to whom should I give them? And should they be proved before I leave?"

"Do you not expect to return?" Maud asked.

"Of course I do, madam," I replied, smiling. "Otherwise, why should I care that the accounts be proved? If I take them up again after some mistake or dishonesty is recorded, how could I prove that mistake or dishonesty was not mine?"

"I assure you, Melusine," the queen said, chuckling, "that I would never think any dishonesty or mistake yours. A dishonesty in goods or money would be impossible, and any mistake you made would have my seal or my name writ beside it. Still, you may do as you did in the beginning. Rule a line below your last entry, sign it, and bring it to me and I will set my seal there so anything writ after the rule will be another's work."

I do not really remember the rest of that day. Although he had concealed it in the queen's presence, Bruno was nearly crazy with impatience to leave. He made me leave my chest and bundle all my court gowns and toilet necessities into a blanket, which was strapped behind Cormi's horse; Edna was to ride pillion behind Merwyn and Fechin in turn; and we set off in the late afternoon at a pace which soon became unsafe in the gathering dusk. We rode until we could not see, then rested until the moon rose and rode on. I am a strong rider, but I found myself swaying in my saddle more than once, and after a time I heard one of the men telling Bruno that he thought the girl must be allowed to rest.

"She must endure until we come to Steyning," Bruno said. "Tie her to the horse if you must." He turned to look at me. "Do you want to ride before me so you can sleep, Melusine?"

I made myself laugh, although I was ready to weep with weariness. "Do not be a fool. I am no feather like Edna. Barbe will founder if you add my weight to yours. Besides, it is not so much my eyes that are tired as a certain other part, and exchanging your saddle for mine will not mend that."

"You are a treasure, Melusine," Bruno muttered, leaning from Barbe to kiss me. "I will explain when we get to Steyning. There is a chamber awaiting us there."

"At this time of night?"

"Yes. I told them I would be late."

He must have paid them thrice or more too, because the house was all alight, though it was near to midnight. A man came hurrying to take the horses with a boy behind him to help him curry and feed them. Another man urged the men within the lower floor, and a woman showed us the way to the solar, where a warm pie and mulled wine were set on a table in the chamber as we entered the door. The woman curtsied deeply and withdrew and the girl followed her.

"Royal service, Bruno?" I asked, smiling. "Is this to accustom me to life with Matilda?"

"I wish it were, but I think it more likely you will play the girl who curtsies and goes out."

"So much the better." I laughed. "I will prefer your company to hers—and that is no great flattery, so do not begin to preen yourself." He stretched and yawned, and I could see a greyness under the dark tone of his skin. "You look very tired. Come, sit and eat, if you will, or go to bed at once. Shall I help you undress?"

He touched my face. "You are my life and my joy, Melusine. I did not know that there were two such women in the world as you and Audris, never complaining and always kind. I must eat. I have had nothing since dawn, when I set out, but even my jaws are tired."

I turned away and made myself busy at the table, pouring the wine into cups and setting pieces of the meat pie on trenchers of bread. "I hope your tongue is not as tired as your jaws because you will hear complaints very soon if you do not tell me why we need to hurry so fast."

"I did not lie to the queen." He sighed, lowered himself to the bench by the table, and drank off the wine. I filled the cup again and sat beside him. "But I did not tell her all the truth either."

"I guessed that much," I told him, breaking off a piece of the pie and beginning to chew.

"There really was no question of assault," he said. His eyes were on the food, but I do not think he recognized it for what it was. I broke off another piece of the pie and put it in his mouth. He chewed slowly, not as if he were tired but as if he had little appetite. "The king is very angry. He wishes to fight, not to do Matilda harm; he would only send her back to Anjou if he took her prisoner. But he is bitter against Aubigny, and he thinks Winchester proposed freeing Matilda because of spite. It is true that Winchester was deeply hurt by being passed over for archbishop of Canterbury and also felt Stephen was wrong in his harsh treatment of Salisbury and his kin—in that there may be some private concern, for Winchester has built and fortified more keeps than Salisbury—"

"Never mind all the past causes," I broke in. "I can guess that Winchester is the one who proposed that Matilda should be sent to Bristol rather than being taken prisoner, and I can guess also that there have been some voices whispering treachery. What I want to know is now the matter is decided, what difference could a day or two make? Why have we nearly killed our horses to get here a day sooner?"

"Not by order," Bruno said, staring ahead at the small fire. "The king—Stephen always sees the sun shining, but I see the black clouds all around. There is an ugly feeling in the camp, Melusine. Half the men, or more, who answered the king's summons were connected in some way with Salisbury or owed him favors. I think they are wondering when Stephen will turn on them. I think many are beginning to ask themselves whether they were forsworn when they did homage to Stephen. I wonder, if Stephen had been a little slower in coming here in force, whether some or many of those now in his army would have risen in revolt to follow Matilda. I do not know whether Winchester's reasons for proposing this solution to being rid of Matilda are the same as mine, but I feel that an assault would more likely begin a war among the men supposedly supporting the king than take Arundel. I want Matilda away from these people."

I put my hand on his and with my other put another piece of pie into his mouth. "I cannot see why," I said, opening my eyes wide to achieve a look of innocence. "I think you should better encourage them to go to her, not try to prevent it." And when he turned outraged eyes on me, his mouth being too full to allow speech, I laughed. "They would be back behind Stephen in a week, and they would never waver again. One taste of Matilda is usually enough. I know you have great and important reasons for the different things Robert of Gloucester has done—why, for example, he did not cry defiance at once after he was nearly ambushed by—oh, I do not remember his name—"

"William of Ypres."

I waved a hand to dismiss the name, which was not important, and presented another piece of pie, which Bruno accepted, grinning, because he had already guessed what I was about to say.

"Yes, well the reason was, simply, that Robert could not stand Matilda either. It is a good reason for him to go ahead and leave her here too."

Bruno contemplated that while he chewed, not seriously —I had not offered the notions seriously, only as an amusing fantasy in which there was just enough of a shred of truth to lighten the moment. We both knew that Matilda had stayed behind because she hoped to rouse the barons in the area to rebellion. Whether that would have happened, we would never know because Stephen had arrived too quickly with a show of force that pushed waverers to his side.

"Yes, well." He drank most of the second cup of wine and sighed, the smile I had brought to his eyes disappearing. "That is the cause of my haste. I agree with the bishop of Winchester that Matilda can do little harm—" briefly his smile returned, "—and if you are right about her effect on people, perhaps she can even do our cause some good, once she is confined to Bristol. That city and the whole shire have been steadily rebel from the beginning. To my mind, the quicker she is gone, the more it will seem she fled from the king's strength."

Others had come to the same conclusion, it seemed, because we wasted no time after arriving at the king's camp outside Arundel. Even Stephen seemed caught up in the need to remove Matilda from her present place as quickly as possible, for he spent no more time than to ask if I were willing and to hear me say I was, so long as Bruno accompanied me, before he sent us off to Arundel.

Despite my calm words and manner, I was not easy as Bruno and I rode alone to the keep. All that protected us was our insignificance; Aubigny knew that our fate could not influence the king in any way so it was useless to hurt or kill us—at least I hoped he knew. That could be why I had been chosen rather than a lady of more consequence.

When we approached the keep, the drawbridge came down and a large party of men thundered across. I gasped with alarm, but Bruno seized my rein and said, "Do not be frightened, Melusine. They will do us no harm. They are only taking precautions that our coming cannot be used as a cover for an attack. See, they have stopped. Now they will part to let us through."

Everything happened as he said, but I did not like it when we were followed closely across the bridge, and I felt stifled—which was ridiculous, since we were in the open space of the outer bailey—when the bridge rose again, sealing us inside. We were, however, civilly greeted and asked with courtesy to follow the captain of the troop to the inner bailey and the keep itself.

"The empress is much concerned that this offer is only a trap," the captain said.

I looked at him in some surprise, since troop captains did not usually discuss the affairs of important guests. He was a large man with a broad, fair face—what I could see of it around the nasal of his helmet—and worried blue eyes.

"It is no trap, my lord," Bruno replied.

I realized then that this must be William d'Aubigny himself, and I thought, from his expression, that he was just as eager to be rid of Matilda as the king. That made me feel somewhat more confident.

"King Stephen," Bruno went on, "desires no harm to come to his cousin. Even should worse come to worst and it be necessary to assault Arundel, Matilda has nothing to fear—you may assure her. In that case she would still have her choice, to go in honor and safety to Bristol or to be taken to France or Anjou, whichever she wishes."

I nearly squeaked with surprise, thinking that if the empress were taken as a prize of war Stephen could not be so foolish as to release her, and if Aubigny had not been staring fixedly at Bruno, I might have ruined the impact of Bruno's remark. In the next moment I realized my husband was being clever again. He had deliberately omitted any assurance of pardon for Aubigny, who was looking more grim by the moment. Clever Bruno; Aubigny would now do all in his power to be rid of a guest who was about to bring destruction on him and escape scot-free.

"I do not think it would be wise to tell her that," Aubigny said, "not if the king wants her to go. Here she could be a cause of unrest among his vassals."

"It might be so," Bruno answered indifferently, "but it would be of little account. The queen has already dispatched orders for her ships to bring more mercenaries, and then to lie at anchor to prevent reinforcements from reaching you by sea."

I did not know whether this was the truth; likely it was what Bruno and the queen had been talking about while I was thinking only of how glad I was that Bruno would come with me. I saw, however, that the pleasant, calm manner in which Bruno made these statements added greatly to Aubigny's discomfort. He said no more while we crossed the inner drawbridge and dismounted in the courtyard. I looked up at the keep with a distaste that was growing stronger and stronger. I did not wish to be shut up in there with Empress Matilda, and I carefully ran over in my mind what I had heard and what of it I could use to convince her to go. She would not care about the harm that could come to her hosts, of that I was sure, but perhaps I could use Stephen's promise not to harm her in a different way.

It was just as well that I had given my thoughts to my new duty on our way in because as soon as I was brought to Matilda and had curtsied to the ground, she rose from the chair on which she was sitting and said, "You may rise, Lady Melusine, and come with me. I wish to speak to you in private."

"But madam," Aubigny cried, "it is almost time for dinner."

And Lady Adelicia, who had also got up from a stool to the left of the chair, cried, "Matilda, let us allow Lady Melusine to take off her cloak and brush away the dust before we begin to question her."

Matilda did not even glance at Adelicia. She raised her brows and uttered a thin, high laugh. "To give you time to tell her what to say, my dear William?" I had to swallow hard not to laugh myself at Aubigny's expression. He was remembering, I suppose, what I must have heard while he talked to Bruno, ignoring me as if I had no existence—as, indeed, women ordinarily did not in any talk of war and politics.

"Oh, no," Matilda continued, her voice as sharp as her features, "I intend to hear what she has to say before she has been made to repeat it ten times over so it comes easily from the tongue. She may have been instructed in the king's camp—that I expect—"

The dislike I had cherished for years was renewed with new force as the empress called me "she," as if I had no name, no being except to fulfill her purposes. "I beg your pardon, madam," I interrupted in a faint, frightened—at least I hoped I sounded frightened—whisper. "I swear the king said no more to me than to ask if I were willing to come to you and to hear me reply that I was willing."

"And no one else instructed you what to say?"

I let my eyes slip to Bruno, then pulled them back to her. "No, madam. There was no time for—for instruction. We came from Rochester yesterday forenoon."

"Not one word about this situation or what you were being brought for?"

I shook my head. She did not believe me, I could see that. Again I glanced swiftly at Bruno and away. I hoped she would think I was afraid of him. "Oh, yes, Sir Bruno—my husband, you know—told me that I had been asked to be your lady on a journey if I were willing, and of course, I was."

She smiled at that, a little softened by believing I was eager to renew the joys with which she had filled me the last time we met. I think the troubled look Bruno gave me, the mingled fury and anxiety on Aubigny's face, and the fear in Lady Adelicia's all helped confirm the idea that I was guileless and could be squeezed free of all information I had once I was alone, away from dumb-show signs to threaten and curb me.

I followed where she led, which was up the stairs and

into what I was sure was her host's bedchamber. There she
signed for the maids to leave and then at me to close the
door behind them. She sat in a chair—I guessed it was
Lady Adelicia's chair carried up from below, for there I
had seen only one high seat. Since the lands were Adelicia's,
willed to her on King Henry's death, there should have
been two. Yes, I was right. I remembered there was a
stool to the right of her chair as well as from the one which
Adelicia had risen. So Matilda insisted her mother-by-law
sit on a stool even though she had been a queen, and
Adelicia got her revenge by addressing her as "Matilda,"
without any title, as if she were a child. Not a happy
household. I grinned at the door before I turned around,
thinking of the rage Aubigny and Adelicia must feel at her
ingratitude.

She treated me no better, seating herself and at once
demanding that I tell her everything I had heard and seen
from the time I was fetched. She must have known it
would be a long history, but she did not ask if I wished to
take off my cloak or whether I had ridden far to come to
her, nor did she offer me a cup of wine or invite me to sit
on the stool near her chair to tell the story as Queen Maud
would have done. Since I had decided to play the role
Matilda seemed to have envisioned for me—the poor
knight's daughter who had cherished for years the glow lit
in her heart by the empress's condescension—I did not
plop down on the seat without her permission, as I would
have liked. Instead, I began my tale, only emphasizing
Maud's protest at letting a netted fish escape.

Matilda told me angrily that she was not a netted fish
and that if she remained the whole shire would soon rise to
support her. I did not deny this, although I heard fear in
the strident tone of her voice and knew I could play on it.
But the fear woke a thread of sympathy in me, and I hoped
for a moment that I could bring her to see that it would be
best for her as well as best for the king if she accepted his
offer to be taken to Bristol. So I told her more gently than
I had intended what I had heard Bruno say about the
mercenaries and Queen Maud's ships.

"Then let them bring down Arundel," she cried, her
voice even more strident with what I now recognized was

fury, not fear, because her face blazed red with rage and fear is a pale, cold thing.

Later I learned that Matilda's one great virtue was her courage; whether or not she felt fear I do not know, but she never showed it, and if she saw any chance to win what she desired, I believe she would face down the devil—or God—without blenching. At the time I had no way of knowing this. All I knew was that she would be safe no matter what happened to everyone else in Arundel— that she did *not* know it and did not believe Stephen's promises did not occur to me. Thus, all I could recognize in her cry of defiance was a gross selfishness that destroyed what little sympathy had touched me, and I determined to use any weapon I had to get her to leave. The first was to paint her humiliation when Arundel fell.

"Oh, madam," I whispered, covering my face with my hands, "what a shame that would be, to see you dragged out of the rubble and driven away like a stray dog. I could not bear it."

That touched her. She jumped to her feet and turned on me so enraged that I thought she would strike me. I stepped back and that seemed to remind her I was an envoy, not a servant girl.

"What choice have I?" she spat. "I know they are all lying. I have been sold like a slave. If I go now, my dear cousin Stephen will cast me into prison."

"No, madam!" I exclaimed. "I am sure it is not so because the queen—"

"I am the queen!" Matilda shrieked.

"Yes, madam." I curtsied and bent my head, chagrined to have made so stupid a mistake. "Forgive me," I begged, most sincerely because I could not manage her if I offended her. "I meant Stephen's wife. But I am sure you are to be taken safely to Bristol. Why else should Maud be so furious? At first she would not listen to the plan and called the bishop of Winchester a traitor for offering it. She could not stop my husband from bringing me, but I fear she will write to Stephen opposing your release. Perhaps the king, who is the kindest of men as you know, madam, wishes you gone to Bristol so that you will be saved the humiliation of bowing to Maud and calling her madam."

That bit hard too. Matilda was a very handsome woman, with a proud stance and a good figure. To see herself bowing to homely, dumpy Maud must have cut like a sword slash. "Why should I believe you?" she snarled at me, again raising a hand as if to strike. "You are one of Maud's ladies now and fawn on her just as you do on me, no doubt."

"No, I do not!" I had to bite my lip to keep from laughing after that indignant remark burst out. It was not only true but implied I feared and respected Matilda more than I did Maud without needing to say so and lie. In addition it led naturally to an explanation of why I was Maud's lady if, as I hoped Matilda believed, my heart was Matilda's. "I have been as much Maud's prisoner as her lady," I said—and it was perfectly true in the past as I put it. "My father and brother died fighting against Stephen, and my lands were taken from me."

"Oh." She thought that over without a word of sympathy for my losses, staring at me with an eye that only weighed and measured me to see what my adherence to her would be worth, and then nodded. "You have a good reason to want me to go free and I will give you another. I tell you now, sooner or later I will take the throne—or my son will. Stephen is a fool. He does not know how to rule. If you have told me the truth, I will give back to you some part of the lands Stephen has reft from you. If you warn me now that this is a trap, I will give them all back."

"You tempt me to lie to you, madam," I said very low, "but you would find me out. There is no trap. You will reach Bristol soon and safely."

CHAPTER 21

Bruno

I CAN ONLY THANK God that the weather that October was no exception to the general rule. The dry, bright days were a benefit and permitted us to advance swiftly toward Bristol. I must say also that despite her arrogant manners the empress did not slow us down. She rode as hard and fast as any man, and the only thing she did not complain about was the distance we covered. Perhaps she was afraid Stephen would change his mind. It was no secret that his army was following our track west.

Aside from that, Empress Matilda was all empress, at least to me. Waleran had appointed me to be in charge of lodging and victualling—I think out of spite, although the reason he gave me seemed logical. He said he would not trust the task to any of Winchester's men, who might deliberately place us where we might be betrayed to Matilda's supporters, and on the other hand, Winchester would undoubtedly protest if he appointed any of his own people. There was just enough truth in that, added to the fact that I had no other duties, to keep me from refusing; however, I knew the "honor" would expose me to Matilda's wrath.

There was some justification for her complaints about the lodgings. I did not dare arrange for her reception in places that would have been usual for a queen, like the great abbey hospices, where I feared she might flee into the church, claim sanctuary, and wait for her brother to bring an army to rescue her. Nor did I dare stop in the keep of any great independent vassal; I had no idea any longer which of them might cast us into the lowest floor of the donjon—or cut our throats—to please Matilda, and the loyalty of any man grew more suspect the farther west we rode. Thus we were confined to those few keeps held for the king by men of unimpeachable loyalty or to those small places that would not dare challenge the might of the army that moved west a few days behind us.

I never replied to her tirades on that subject; if she had the brain of a pea she would have understood why I chose the places I did, and Melusine agreed with me that Matilda was stupid. Not that there was anything wrong with her ability to learn; she could read and write, which was a feat far beyond any ordinary woman. It was more as if she *would* not understand anything that did not fit into life as she planned it, as if she *could* not look ahead and see any outcome to a plan that she had not arranged—until disaster struck.

Matilda was a very strange woman. She never said please or thank you; she *ordered* Melusine to tell me nothing of what she said to the bishop of Winchester or Waleran—and she never seemed to realize that an order delivered in her overbearing manner was sure to inspire just the opposite of what she desired in any normal gentleman or gentlewoman. Had she forgotten that Melusine was not her servant and there was no way she could hurt her? Or did she believe the greatness of her station awed all into instant obedience? I suspect there were some things Melusine did not tell me; I am sure, for example, that Matilda had said she would return Melusine's lands to her when she was queen, but by then I do not think Melusine would have wanted Matilda as queen, even to get back her lands.

The empress gave me orders too, most often to beat servants who had not responded quickly enough to her wishes or had not anticipated them. Usually I simply drove the servant out of the chamber, which seemed to satisfy her without doing the servant any harm. If poor Edna had been whipped each time Matilda ordered it, the girl would not have had a sound place on her body.

Once, however, the empress went too far and ordered me to burn a shop where a merchant had refused her a bolt of cloth without payment. Naturally the man then offered the cloth, but I would not take it nor burn the shop, and I told Matilda that King Stephen did not permit his subjects to be defrauded. She simply raised her voice to overpower mine, not seeming to hear me when I said I was not her servant and would do what I believed was my duty to my master, King Stephen.

That time I thought I would come into conflict with Waleran, who arrived in response to Matilda's high-pitched commands. I think he would have agreed to burn out the merchant, but he saw my hand on my sword hilt and instead threw a handful of coin at the man and gestured one of his men to take the cloth. Waleran de Meulan was not afraid of me, although I think I could have won a man to man battle, but there were too many witnesses. Waleran would not have wanted the king to hear of his acquiescence to Matilda's demands, which would have disgusted Stephen or, worse, perhaps made the king suspicious.

I do not think Waleran was tempted by the empress's offers—not then, although it was those veiled temptations to treachery that Matilda forbade Melusine to mention to me, as if I would not have guessed without telling that Matilda was wooing both Waleran and the bishop of Winchester. I never gave the matter much thought because I could not conceive that any man in his right mind who had spent a week in Matilda's company could believe for a minute that she could rule. I do not blame myself for not reporting her long conversations with her escorts to Stephen; he would, as I did, have assumed such talk could bear no fruit. Moreover, Matilda must have given Waleran one order too many, for he turned back to join Stephen's army when we reached Calne, leaving Winchester and myself to finish the journey with her.

In one way that made matters easier, removing any chance of another open confrontation, but I did not want Matilda to complain too bitterly to Winchester about my behavior. Thus, most of my attention was given to getting around the empress's unreasonable demands without angering her more than necessary. I do not think I could have succeeded without Melusine, who most often interposed herself between us by carrying Matilda's orders to me. I fear I would have lost my temper and taken that idiot woman over my knee, which she surely deserved, but Stephen could not have overlooked such an offense against his cousin's high birth. And Melusine and I had our nights together, for another order Matilda gave Melusine that she would not obey was to forsake my bed and sleep in her chamber to serve her during the night. Abed Melusine turned all Matilda's tantrums into subjects of laughter.

That made it possible for me to face each new day, but I have never been more relieved than when, about midway between Bath and Bristol, we met Robert of Gloucester by arrangement and handed Matilda over to him. As soon as his force was in sight, she ordered Melusine to come with her. I do not know why I seized Vinaigre's rein and held her back. Melusine looked at me most strangely, but she made no protest, and Matilda rode ahead with the bishop of Winchester without a backward glance. I do not think she realized Melusine had not obeyed her until the groups were separating. Then I heard her voice raised although, shrill as it was, I could not make out the words. I saw Gloucester look toward us, and laid my hand on my sword. He sent a man after the bishop of Winchester, who also looked toward us as he answered, but the man rode back to Gloucester. I saw Earl Robert shake his head at his sister and then turn his horse back toward Bristol though Matilda had not moved and I could still hear her voice.

The men Gloucester had brought moved out into the road to fall in around her, casting long shadows that reached toward us. I almost backed Barbe to avoid the touch of those dark fingers. That was foolish; shadows could do no harm, as Matilda herself was no threat. But Matilda's claim to the throne with Robert of Gloucester to control her was another matter entirely. I saw the shadows touch the bishop of Winchester, who was watching the group move away—Matilda was now either silent or speaking quietly and was riding beside her brother—and I wondered how many more slights Winchester would endure from Stephen, brothers though they were. For a moment I thought the bishop was about to ride after Gloucester, but he turned back and came toward us.

"Lady Melusine, did you tell Empress Matilda that you wished to be her lady?" he asked when he reached us. "She seemed convinced that you wished to leave Sir Bruno."

"I do not know how she can have thought that, my lord," Melusine replied calmly, although her voice sounded strange to me. "She knew I would not take night service because I wished to be with my husband. I may have said I was glad to be able to serve her. I could not with civility say other than that."

"Yes, yes, of course," the bishop said, but rather absently, as if his mind was elsewhere. "Well, then, let us return to Bath," he added more briskly after a moment, "and decide whether we will continue on together."

There was no question in my mind but that my duty was to join the king at once, since he was in action in the field, and of course I could not take Melusine with me. I told Winchester that if I had to, I would send her east with my three men and Edna, but I was relieved and grateful when Winchester said he would take her to the queen. I thought Melusine would also be pleased; however, when we were alone in our quarters, she unleashed a blast of fury that made no sense to me. For the first time in our marriage, she would not listen, although I explained until I was hoarse that when the king was fighting, my place was at his side, not escorting my wife about the country. At last, unable to think what else to say, I assured her that she would be perfectly safe with Winchester—at which point she slapped my face and I stormed out and slept in the stable loft.

We parted only a shade more civilly. When I lifted her to her saddle, I said one more time, "I am sorry not to be able to take you myself, Melusine," and she replied, "Do not trouble yourself, I understand very well," and turned Vinaigre toward the bishop of Winchester's mount. I cursed Empress Matilda all the way from Bath to Wallingford, where I joined the king. Perhaps it was unjust to blame the empress for my quarrel with Melusine, but I had never known my wife to be unreasonable before. It was as if a poison flowed out of Matilda and fouled everyone who came near her.

I was in the mood to kill when I rode into the king's camp, but there was no action at Wallingford. Stephen had tried some feints, but the keep was plainly too strong to take by assault without great loss. When I arrived the army was engaged in building two small wooden keeps at no great distance from Wallingford from which Stephen's men could prevent Gloucester's vassal from dominating the area. That did not improve my mood. Had I known, I could have escorted Melusine to the queen. I did not endear myself to anyone over the week it took to make the little keeps defensible, but the work went faster when anyone saw me.

Fortunately, as we marched west toward Bristol, which only meant another siege that would give me no relief, a keen-witted captain of a troop of foragers brought word that the enemy-held keep at Cerney was ill guarded. We were upon the place that very night, and the next day took it by storm. I had killing enough that day, for I was first up a scaling ladder, and I had three—one through the throat, one through the belly, and a third over the wall after I lopped off a hand—before I got onto the walkway. I did not count the full total, but Stephen awarded me an extra share in the loot so I must have made a mark during the assault. After that day's work, I felt somewhat better, and two days later I felt even more cheerful, seeing the prospect of more fighting when a deputation from the town of Malmesbury came and begged Stephen to rid them of the tyrant who had taken Malmesbury keep by a mean trick.

Stephen had heard the keep had fallen into the hands of Robert Fitz Hubert, but he had done nothing because the man was kin to William of Ypres. However, on hearing of the abominations Fitz Hubert had inflicted on the town and the surrounding countryside, even Ypres was disgusted and had not a word to say in the defense of his kinsman. He did not protest when the king garrisoned Cerney and changed the direction of his march from southwest to northwest, but that did me no good. I was foiled of the chance to relieve the fury that tore at me because, the town having opened its gates to the king, Fitz Hubert cravenly yielded the keep without a blow being struck.

In deference to Ypres, Fitz Hubert was allowed to go free and all—except me, and I knew I was in the wrong—rejoiced that so strong a place and one so near rebel strongholds had fallen into the king's hands undamaged. There was a bright feeling of confidence in the councils called to determine where next to strike. I stayed apart as much as I could and held my tongue, for I felt like a black crow ready to caw disaster.

I know that one man's black mood cannot call down ill upon others. Often enough bad news came when I was in the best of spirits, but I could not shake off a feeling of guilt when trouble struck. The king, having taken the advice of the other leaders of the army, had determined to take Trowbridge. This, with Malmesbury and Cerney, would give us a half circle of strongholds from which powerful attacks could be launched at Bristol. Moreover, taking Trowbridge would be a sharp stroke against Miles of Gloucester—an ungrateful devil who had declared for the empress as soon as she landed despite the favors Stephen had done him—because it was held by Humphery de Bohun, Miles's son-by-marriage. We were camped within a few miles of the place considering when and how to attack when a few ragged and bloody men arrived with the news that Miles had marched a large force, almost as strong as Stephen's army, around our rear, had attacked and demolished the keeps the king had built to control Wallingford, and threatened to attack London.

I was on duty in the king's tent, and I saw the sudden bleakness in the faces of every man there. William of Ypres's lips thinned to nothing; Waleran snarled an obscenity; Geoffrey de Mandeville looked down at the ground with a face turned to stone. Although I was no great leader, I had been in the king's service long enough to understand that it was not the setback of the destroyed strongholds or the loss of men that troubled Stephen's vassals. Had it been the men of Wallingford and local supporters who inflicted the defeat, the king's men would have been angered and annoyed but not deeply disturbed.

What struck them so hard was that Miles had been able to
march an army halfway across England without a word of
warning from the shires through which he had passed.

That could not have happened in King Henry's time.
Any knight through whose territory so large a force passed—
even if it did no harm—would have sent messengers to the
sheriff, who would have sent the news to the king at once.
Indeed, the reason that Stephen had been able to quash the
rebellions of 1138 and move so quickly that one rebel
could bring no help to another was because he had just
such warnings from the sheriffs and often from the bishops
who held sees in those places and had news from a local
priest that a baron was arming and buying men. But that
was before Stephen had struck at Salisbury; now both
Church and sheriffs were silent.

Only Stephen was not downhearted. He ordered the
army to march east immediately, for London must be
protected at all costs. He was sorry to miss the opportunity
to take Trowbridge and then strike directly at the source of
Goucester's strength; however, he pointed out to his glum
council, the situation was not all bad. If Miles was marching toward London, he had no stronghold east of Wallingford. He could be caught in the open, forced into battle,
and utterly destroyed.

There was no answering light in the vassals' eyes nor
did my heart lift. The same lack of support that had
permitted Miles to march east in secret could easily prevent the king's army from coming close enough to force a
battle. Stephen was not unaware of this. He sent riders out
both to the sheriffs and to spy out the country—only Miles
was not marching on London. That news had been false.
While we searched to the east, riding all the way to
London, Miles of Gloucester had circled around us again
well to the north and sacked Worcester.

Waleran was beside himself, for he had been made earl
of Worcester and had no warning from his own sheriff. I
was as angry as he, but for a far different reason. The king
had sent a messenger to bring the queen to London, but
she had not yet come when we had the news of the attack
on Worcester, so I missed seeing Melusine and any chance
of making peace with her before we went west again—to

no purpose; Miles was gone, safe behind the high walls of Gloucester. Stephen took some small revenge by assaulting and capturing the little keep at Sudeley, but I think he might have followed Miles and attacked Gloucester, despite the danger of ourselves being struck from the rear by forces from Bristol, had not news come of the death of the bishop of Salisbury on 11 December.

Leaving a strong garrison at Sudeley and a substantial force at Worcester with Waleran, the king moved swiftly to Salisbury to secure the see. To my great joy, Stephen sent messengers ahead to the queen and she arrived in good time to keep Christmas with us. For others it may have been a sad time; few came to Stephen's court that season. But for me, light returned to my life. It was not the same light; there were shadows it did not reach and a flickering that made it unsteady, but I did not see that at first. It was light, and there was warmth in it. After more than a month of total darkness, it was so bright to me that I was blinded.

I am not certain to what I owed Melusine's forgiveness—not that I felt she had anything to forgive; as I had told her twenty times over when I left her in the care of the bishop of Winchester, I was only doing my duty to the king. However, I was not such an idiot as to mention our parting, and neither did she. Perhaps she had reconsidered her unreasonable anger and realized that I was right, but long acquaintance with Audris's humors told me that was unlikely. Probably the fact that I was limping had more to do with the softness of her greeting than any acceptance of the concept that my service to the king must precede my attention to her as long as she was in no danger.

The king did not ride out to meet the queen because he, and all of us who had come to his court, was attending the funeral services of the bishop of Salisbury. We had already been standing in the church for an hour when a messenger sidled discreetly up to Stephen and whispered that Queen Maud's cortege was in sight. The king's face lit with eagerness, and he looked toward the door. To my shame, I found I was praying he would leave instead of that he would stay, although I knew word of such an outrage would spread like wildfire and do him harm. Geoffrey de

Mandeville laid a hand on his arm, and Stephen turned back to the altar.

Perhaps we should have walked out for in the end the seeming respect did no good. Those priests kept us for three hours more—I am sure apurpose—and for all I know would have gone on all day had not the king signalled Camville, who spoke softly to the most elaborately robed priest, one whose paunch was visible under his robes. He was not intoning prayers at the moment and I saw his face redden and his eyes flick toward the king, but he brought the service to an end within the next quarter of an hour.

We found the queen and her ladies at the back of the church. Maud moved forward to speak to the priests even before she greeted the king, and my heart nearly stopped when I did not at first see Melusine. I thought she had not come just to avoid me, or that she had even left the queen's service, which shows the state I was in; the only place Melusine could have gone was to King David, and Maud would never have permitted that. But that was only the depth of my fear making me stupid; she was there, very near the door of the church so that when she offered her hand in greeting, I was able to step outside and pull her into my arms to kiss. She did not pull away, and I asked for no reasons.

"You are hurt," she said softly, her voice shaking, when our lips parted.

"Only by stupidity," I said, grinning like an idiot to see her anxious frown. "I tripped when we entered Sudeley and hurt my foot."

I did not bother to say that I had tripped over the king, who had lost his balance climbing over the splintered logs of the palisade, and if not for the happy chance that I had fallen backward, shield and sword uppermost, we would both have been dead. Stephen managed to spit the man in front of him by thrusting up and catching him between the legs, but I would never have been able to turn over in time to get the two coming from the side. As it was I had only to sit up, and I hit the first in the groin with my shield and caught the other with a blow that tore the sword from his hand and cut his thigh to the bone. Actually my foot was not hurt by tripping. The second man-at-arms I had wounded fell on my leg and must have broken one of the small bones in my foot, but the action was so heated just then that I jumped up and walked on the foot until the keep was secured. It was only then that I fell, and my boot had to be cut off because my whole leg was swollen.

Having already gained Melusine's sympathy, there was no need to describe any of this. I had learned my lesson with Audris. What I thought amusing had turned Audris pale and sick with terror. Let Melusine think I was just clumsy. She would tend my foot and some other bruises I collected at the same time just as tenderly, and not be set imagining all sorts of horrors that had not happened but might happen in the future. I remembered, too, that her father and brother had died in battle and did not wish to remind her of that.

"If you hurt your foot," Melusine said sharply, but without releasing my hand, "why have you been standing on it for hours? Do you think that will do it any good?"

"No," I answered meekly, "but I did not think of it at first, and once in the church you know I could not leave while the service was going on. That would be looked on as another deliberate offense I am sure. But it hurts, and I can ask to be excused from duty for the rest of the day. Stephen will be with Maud and will not want me. Will you ask leave from the queen to tend to me?"

"Do we have lodging?" she asked.

I could feel my face twist. "So few have come that you can pick whatever you like, inside the bishop's palace or without, if you do not care for the chamber I have chosen. I took what must have been one of Salisbury's clerk's rooms. They all fled, you know, but we came too quickly for much to have been stolen. I could have looked for a lodging outside—we would have been more comfortable I suppose—but . . . but the palace was so empty . . . it echoed."

Melusine stared up at me without speaking for a moment and then said softly, "I did not realize things had come to so bad a state." I do not know what she read in my face, but she looked down, away from me, then took my arm over her shoulder and went on, quite briskly, "It is just as well, with your bad foot, that the chamber is

close by. Let us go there; then I will ask the queen if I may
stay with you, and if she gives permission, I will ask her
to tell the king where you are. Then I will bring us dinner
to eat in our chamber.''

I opened my mouth to protest, but I saw that dark from
which I had just emerged closing in on me and I shut my
mouth again. Every minute of the light was precious, so I
let Melusine help me to the room, which was in a wing of
the palace given over to cells for priests or clerks or I
knew not what. It was a small room, but I had collected
two braziers and a good store of charcoal, so it was warm.
There was no bed—there had been a cot, but I had taken
that out and replaced it with two fresh, newly stuffed
pallets. The blanket I used on the march was underneath to
take up most of the cold from the floor; a fresh blanket I
only used when I was with Melusine lay atop, and I knew
she would have her own to add. I had collected two stools
also, and she pushed one of those close to the pallets so I
would have a place to rest my foot and bade me sit.

I saw Melusine look about with pleasure, but when she
turned to me, I would not meet her eyes. She said nothing,
so I do not know whether that meant anything to her; she
only dropped her cloak, unpinned mine, and helped me to
sit down; then she unbound the strips that held my boot
together and slid it off. Finally she ''tchkd'' and drew her
cloak over my foot to keep it warm—and she touched my
cheek as she rose and went out.

That touch was full of tenderness, but it only brought
the dark closer. I was sure that Melusine had hurried me
into the privacy of our chamber to try to induce me to
leave the king—not to join the empress, Melusine was not
a fool, but to seek the neutral sanctuary of Jernaeve.

That we would be safe there and not openly connected
to either party was true. Stephen had sent no summons for
men to the northern shires. Although Prince Henry was
nominally his vassal and had given oath to send support if
Stephen ever needed it, the king was too wise to test that
oath, specially since he did not need men. His army was
already larger than any that could be gathered by the
rebels. Thus, all that would be necessary to send us into
safety—without loss of my position as Knight of the Body

and protected from any chance of open conflict with King David or the empress—was an excuse to take Melusine north, and I could think of several, the easiest being that she had discovered she was with child.

Without loyalty to any person, except perhaps to me, Melusine would never understand my refusal. She would feel that I was deliberately exposing her to danger, and it would be useless for me to offer to send her to Jernaeve alone. If I fell with the king, she could not hope to win back Ulle, for she had offended Empress Matilda by not going with her. Worst of all, she would feel I did not return her loyalty, and her rage would be far worse than when I would not take her to the queen myself.

By the time Melusine returned, laden with two large baskets, I had reduced myself to the condition of a child ridden by nightmare. And, of course, I had totally under-estimated her. It must, indeed, have been the strain of dealing with Matilda that drove her into open fury when I crossed her in Bath. I should have remembered that Melusine was used to managing eight headstrong men (not all at one time, of course, but she had told me a great deal about her father and her brothers) and knew perfectly well that con-frontation was not the path to getting her own way.

What she did was to kneel down beside me and say, "Are we so close to disaster, Bruno? You look as if you had seen Armageddon."

"Not for the realm," I answered, "but for me."

"What do you mean?" she asked, looking astonished. "I know the king is not angry with you, for by chance—I do not know this place and took a wrong turn and came out right at the door of the king's chamber just as Stephen and Maud were going in. So I told him your foot was all swollen and he was most concerned for you."

There was something in the way she spoke of the king and queen that sparked a hope I had been a fool, and I laughed and took her face in my hands and said, "Oh, I do not fear the king. He cannot bring my Armageddon. Only you can do that, woman."

I cannot swear she knew what I meant. I think her eyes widened with realization, but perhaps she thought I was remembering our quarrel in Bath. Whatever she knew she kept to herself, for she also laughed and said, "Well, I did not bring it in my baskets. Shall I bind up your foot first, or shall we eat what I snatched from the kitchen?"

"I have a stronger appetite," I murmured, leaning forward and kissing her. "It is too early for dinner, at least by half an hour, and it eases my foot to lie down."

"And having nothing else to do in an idle half hour you choose to toy with me? Lecher! The time will be as well spent tending your foot." She spoke sharply, but her eyes laughed, and when she twisted free of my hold, it was to move the baskets safely out of the way.

"I do not believe in wasted motion," I said, snatching at her and catching her around the buttocks without much effort; she did not try to escape. "Since you must take off my chausses to see my foot, you might just as well attend to the other swelling too."

"Disgusting," she said haughtily, but her fingers were busy untying my shirt as mine were undoing her laces. "You have had a bath," she murmured when we were lying on the pallet.

She had good reason to know, for she had been playing with me, kissing my belly and thighs and Sir Jehan's red head too. And she laughed when I answered only with groans, but there seemed to be red flecks in her dark eyes, like the red glints the shaft of sunlight from the small window brought alight in her dark hair. And when I seized her and pulled her atop me, her mouth was hot against mine and she was ready.

Later, when I could speak again, I said, "You do not need a bath. I love the woman smell of you."

She laughed and answered that I would not love it long if she did not bathe at all, but I saw the way she was looking at my shoulder, where the rings of my mail had cut through my arming tunic and into my skin under the pressure of a blow I did not even remember. There were a number of other bruises on my body, and despite the sweet sated feeling that filled me, I began to wish I had left our loving until the dim light of a night candle would have concealed the marks.

"That was a bad fall," Melusine said, frowning. "Were you drunk?"

"No, it was on the palisade," I said, recalling what I had told her and delighted that she seemed to accept it. "I fell against a broken part, and rolled down—well, it may be that we had been celebrating our victory with a bit of wine. If you will let me up," I added quickly, "I will show you something prettier than scrapes and scratches." The less she thought about my story the better I would like it.

"Beast," she remarked. "You think I am too big and heavy."

"God, no!" I exclaimed. Then I laughed uneasily, remembering that I had thought that at first. Had she felt it and said nothing until now? I hoped not, but the rack would not make me admit it. I said what I knew would please—and it was true too, "But if you do not let me up, I will have more swellings."

"A threat or a promise?" she asked, but she slid off me and sat up, pulling the blanket around her.

I did not answer that, only reached under the top of my pallet and drew out a roll of cloth, which I opened and set in her lap to show a headband of gold set with pearls. To my surprise, she did not touch it, and her eyes went all black and dull.

"You have been fighting," she said.

"It is not loot," I assured her. "I bought it here. I will take you to the goldsmith—"

She threw her arms around my neck then and hugged me. "Forgive me," she cried. "I cannot bear to wear what was torn from some poor woman's grief."

"No, dear heart," I soothed, "but I am glad you told me. You may be sure that I will bring you no gifts that will burden your spirit."

I did not say that the money I had used to buy the headband had been an exchange for my share of the cattle in Sudeley, which I could not use because I had no land. I had thought at the time of sending them to Jernaeve to be kept until Ulle was ours, but in the black cloud in which I had been living then I had lost hope of Ulle and did not think it worth the trouble to have the cattle driven all those miles north. I did not regret that now, seeing the pleasure with which Melusine set the band on her head and preened herself as I admired aloud how fine it looked against her dark hair. But she was not truly vain, and in a moment she had taken it off, dropped the blanket on me, and pulled on her clothing.

After I sat up and laced her gown, she bound up my foot and helped me dress. Then she laid out our dinner. At first we both ate with too much appetite to talk, but when the first edge of hunger was dulled, she said, "Tell me how bad our state is in the west."

"Actually we have gained more than we have lost," I replied. "Stephen is a great battle leader." I saw her hand hesitate in bringing a piece of bread to her mouth, and I added hastily, "Even when he does not fight. Our trouble is not taking keeps nor defeating our enemies, it is meeting them." And then I explained about the holding back of information, if not open treachery, of the sheriffs and the bishops and that because of that, even the yeomen and minor knights were afraid to support the king. Before I had even finished Melusine was nodding her head.

"You will not have that trouble in the south and east," she said. "The queen has been busy." Then she sighed. "We have traveled and traveled and traveled. I think we have been in every shire—and in every chartered town— from Durham to Dover."

"Every town?" I echoed. "But—"

"Men!" she exclaimed. "You say burghers will not fight—"

"I say nothing of the kind," I protested. "They will fight, but only to protect their own town."

"But you do not need men, you need news—and where does news come quicker than to a town?"

I sat staring at her, remembering that it was the townsfolk of Malmesbury who came to the king for help, and it was again the townsfolk of Worcester who had brought the news of the attack—too late, but they had not been told to watch and warn the king; he had expected that service from the officers of the Crown. And Bath held steady for the king despite the nearness of Bristol and the rebels; the townsfolk had helped Stephen's garrison fight off many attacks.

"The burghers favor Stephen," Melusine continued,

"and they have reason to love the queen. I do not think any army will move east of Oxford without the king knowing. And I think the barons will be more faithful too. Some did not greet us very warmly—oh, did you know the queen has a small army of Flemings?—but I saw how they were eased and their loyalty confirmed after she spoke to them."

I doubted much could be done with the barons of the west unless the king had a great victory there, but the towns were another matter. Surely it could do no harm to use the queen's idea, and I was certain Maud would convince Stephen to do so without difficulty. The king had little pride of birth, perhaps because he was sure of his nobility, and he had always valued and treated well and fairly the burghers of the realm. The trouble was that the west was less populous than the east; there were fewer towns, and many of those were already in rebel hands.

Still, there were free towns, and they did favor Stephen. I will not say that hope leapt free and full in my breast. To speak the truth, I still saw nothing ahead but years of battle, but with the southeast at peace and solidly for the king, the situation looked much different. I felt less concerned at the idea of a long confrontation with the rebels, and Melusine brought snippets of news that, always good, supported hope.

For more than a week, I kept to that single chamber so my foot could heal. I did not once ask to leave. I did not want to know how the court progressed. While I was with Melusine I was at peace. We played games—chess, and when we felt silly, riddles, or fox and geese, or nine man morris—we played other games too, in which no pieces or boards were needed, only soft words and soft touches. And we talked of many things, of her family and of mine, such as it was, which, of course, brought us to Audris and Hugh and Eric and Jernaeve . . . and Ulle.

It was strange that it should be I who remembered most vividly the beauty of the land, of purple hills against the sky and deep tarns with glints of silver streams falling into them from cliffs. Melusine saw Ulle as it must be now—so quiet it must be in the hills now with all the passes filled with snow and the lakes frozen over. I even told Melusine about the cattle, not saying they had been my share of the loot, but speaking of another man with land in the north and his doubts about having the beasts driven home. She smiled and said it was fortunate I had no part of that herd for such cattle were useless for Ulle. They needed a hardier breed, like the little wide-horned red cattle of Scotland—a good reason, she added, why Cumbrian men seldom raided south or east and had so little interest in the wars of England.

At the time I was aware of only the faintest twinge of discontent at my prospects of sweat and blood and pain compared with the long pleasures of holding Ulle and *not* caring a whit about wars. It was only a twinge, but it left a little sore place in my breast, and over the dreadful year that followed that twinge grew to an ache that gave me no rest. It was then that I realized what Melusine had done. She was much too clever to place hands on hips and scream at me like a shrew that all loyalty to Stephen could bring me was death; she had not that quicksilver lightness with which Audris could bedazzle and get her way. Melusine, dark and warm and sweet, held out peace and joy and pleasure to wean a man from a hard duty turned bitter with shame.

Mary the Merciful knows how that memory of Ulle ached within me, but the pain did not come at once for the king and queen did not separate immediately after Epiphany and I still had Melusine. Then, too, despite the poor attendance at the court, at first the situation looked hopeful. A huge treasure had been uncovered in Salisbury's strongroom, and Stephen had determined that so much could not belong to the Church but must have come from state revenues. I thought that likely, not that I would have cared much if it was Church coin, for the son of a whore does not get a very good view of priests and the Church. Moreover, neither my father nor Sir Oliver paid more than lip service and the smallest tithe they could manage to the Church. The one priest I knew as a child who was all good, Father Anselm, did not know what money was, I think. He had never taken more than the food he ate and the pallet he lay upon. He never asked even for a new robe, though his own was in such rags that Audris took it away and replaced it.

Everyone benefitted—although one of the benefits made me anxious because it meant that Melusine would have to go to France with the queen. There had been some talk about betrothing Eustace, the king's eldest son, now fourteen years of age, to the sister of the king of France. I knew Stephen desired it, hoping that Louis would help him recover Normandy from Matilda's husband, Geoffrey of Anjou, if he made Eustace duke of Normandy. But promises for the future, particularly when they can only be made good by large expenditures for armies, are a poor inducement to forming a relationship. Now with a huge bribe (called a bride price) available, Maud and Stephen were able to plan for the queen to go to France as soon as a safe passage seemed possible.

I was not pleased at the thought of losing even the chance of seeing Melusine for months, but I knew we would be fighting most of the time and comforted myself that she would be less likely to discover my lies and be worried if she were in France. Also, the benefits from Salisbury's hoard even trickled down to me, and when the king offered me the two payments of my pension that he was in arrears and a third for the coming quarter, I took it gladly and did not worry about where the coin came from. It was very welcome, because I found I spent far more than was sensible when I was with Melusine. She scolded, but I could not resist buying her little things that caught my eye—beads and thread for embroidery and rich cloth, red and gold; I loved to see her dark beauty glow in those colors.

After the queen left for France in February, the well of joy that had bubbled through my blood as long as I had Melusine died down. The spring was darker than the winter. It seemed as if a contagion of greed and madness tainted the whole land. All bonds of loyalty and reason burst asunder. Every little man who could raise an army turned on any other weaker than himself. And the king could not prevent it because great lords, some of whom he had favored and had no reason to rebel and indeed did not declare for the empress, suddenly seized royal property.

The summer was worse than the spring. There is no use in trying to recall exactly where we fought or how many marches we made—many to no purpose because before we arrived at our objective, we had to turn back to some more urgent fight. I had always enjoyed a good fight, at least after my blooding, in which I came to terms with the fact that use of my sword and lance would bring pain or death to other men whom I did not know and wished no harm. Now, for the first time in many years, I needed to find that place inside myself very far away from the blood and the stink of loosened bowels and the screaming. But worse even than the battles were the constant signs we stumbled upon as we crossed and recrossed the realm of that madness of greed, that loss of all honor, all mercy, all humanity. Again and again we found whole villages and manors where every person had been ripped and disemboweled and burnt for what could not be more than a few coins, a few ells of cloth, or for nothing at all.

Yet in the blackest moments of that summer and into the autumn there had been some hope of peace. The queen and the bishop of Winchester were attempting to negotiate a truce with Robert of Gloucester. But it came to nothing. Waleran de Meulan played on the king's too optimistic nature, reminding Stephen of our many successes and saying that all would think him faint of heart to give up half a royal crown—and to a woman too. Perhaps the queen could have changed the king's mind, but she was not with us and within the week news came from the townsfolk of Lincoln that the earl of Chester and his half brother, William de Roumare had taken Lincoln keep by a strange stratagem. They had sent their wives to visit the wife of the constable. After some hours, the earl of Chester had arrived, saying he had come to fetch the ladies. He was unarmed, except for the sword by his side, and he was accompanied by only three knights, so he was welcomed without any uneasiness—whereupon he and his knights turned on the guard, seized every weapon they could find, and held gate and drawbridge until his brother came galloping in with a strong troop, with which he ejected the royal garrison.

Stephen rushed north, but Chester and Roumare had not been idle. They had brought in more men, many more, enough to hold not only the keep but to cow the burghers and hold the walls of the town. Now Waleran spoke for peace. He pointed out that Chester and Roumare had not declared for the empress and that it would truly be a disaster if so powerful a baron changed sides. Then he reminded Stephen how bitter Chester was about the treaty with King David that had given Cumbria, which Chester felt was his, to Prince Henry. If Chester and Roumare would swear loyalty and swear to defend Lincolnshire against Matilda and Gloucester, it would be better to let them hold the keep and town.

It was sensible advice. I remembered how troubled I had been about that treaty with King David and how I had even mentioned Chester's claim to the king when I spoke against the treaty. Yet now I had to bite my tongue to keep from crying out against Waleran's ideas. I had begun to feel that Waleran was the king's evil genius, a clever, perverted creature that brought ill even when what it suggested seemed fair. But in this case all agreed with Waleran. I do not think there was one dissenting voice, except for the displaced constable, and his prejudice because of his shameful expulsion from his keep made his objection ridiculous.

A peace was patched up, although this time I do not think the king was pleased with Waleran. I thought his acceptance of the vows of Chester and Roumare was sullen; however, they swore on the holiest of relics, on their own souls, and the souls of parents and children that they would be faithful vassals and support the king in all ways without fail. I think they were sincere. I think the great keep at Lincoln and the governance of the shire—even though it was placed in Roumare's hands, not Chester's own—was a salve that eased Chester's sense of ill treatment over the loss of Cumbria, which was a poorer land. In addition, Chester knew well that peace with Scotland might be of short duration while the empress was in England because King David might be induced to break the peace to support her. In that case, Chester might still obtain the restoration of Cumbria.

Perhaps with that in mind, Chester set himself to be

agreeable, and I believed the king had been reconciled to the arrangement by the time we left Lincoln. However, I thought very little about Stephen because we were going to London and I knew Melusine was waiting for me there.

The next few weeks I performed my duty in a kind of dream, not wishing to hear the plans for more war and still more war in the future. I had Melusine, and we danced together at the feasts and we laughed and played and made love, but I could not talk of Ulle. I know that made Melusine uneasy; I was sorry for it, but I could not bear even a shadow of pain in the little circle of false peace I had made for myself.

I was not even to have a full measure of the peace my wife brought me. On the last day of December, a new messenger came from the townsfolk of Lincoln, crying to the king of Roumare's cruelty. Lord William and his brother, he complained, were hanging and fining the people of the town for having warned the king that the keep had been taken. I was hardly listening, only alert for my name in my master's voice, but I sprang to attention at the king's roar of rage and the heated words in which he promised he would not permit such practices. I had a fleeting thought of the burnt-out villages that he had ignored in seeking a greater enemy, but I thrust myself between the king and the messenger when the man suddenly stepped forward.

"Let him come," Stephen said.

I did so, but stood close for I thought it foolish to take a chance, even though I felt myself that this man meant no harm. He came right to Stephen's feet and knelt down, taking hold of the king's gown in his anxiety.

"If you wish to punish them, sire—" His voice was harsh, but hardly more than a whisper and his eyes burned with eagerness. "Chester and Roumare and both their wives are at ease in Lincoln keep—and they have sent away nearly all the men they had summoned to hold the keep and the town. If you come quickly, we will open the town to you. You could surround the keep and take them with great ease. We will even fight with you."

"I—"

I thought the king was about to say, "I cannot do that. I

have just taken their oaths of homage and sworn to protect them from their enemies as they protect me from mine.'' I could understand why he hesitated, having only just promised, too hastily as usual, to help the folk of Lincoln. Instead, he said, ''I must take counsel with my barons. Go now, but come back after the evening meal. Bruno,'' he gestured toward me, ''will bring you to my private closet.''

Years past, I had come to terms with the fact that the king's honor was not mine, that my duty was to serve him not to be his conscience, but until now Stephen's lapses, at least those of which I knew, had been omissions. He had chosen not to know certain things. This was different. This time when he told his chief men to order their troops to make ready to march and told them where to go, even Waleran and Ypres, whose own souls were not spotless, looked taken aback, and Geoffrey de Mandeville looked disgusted.

They all protested, but Waleran and Ypres were soon won over, and Mandeville, although he still looked like a man who had bit on something very sour, became silent when Stephen pointed out that once Chester and Roumare were safely imprisoned, there would be no chance at all that they would turn rebel and no need to give them more and more to keep them loyal. Moreover, Stephen reminded his men, Chester's wife was Robert of Gloucester's daughter, which would give them a strong pawn for bargaining with Gloucester. In addition, the king swore that when Gloucester was defeated and Matilda driven out of England, he would make restitution to Chester and Roumare. This was only a necessary expedient in a time of great crisis.

To be more swift and more secret, every man-at-arms who could sit a horse was mounted, and we rode in small groups by different ways. We were in Lincoln by the sixth of January, but Chester and his brother were not quite as off guard as the king had been told. Although we came to the town by night and the gates were opened as promised, somehow warning was given. The earl of Chester escaped, and Roumare had drawn his men into the keep and sealed it tight.

We had not men enough to take the keep by assault.

Although the townsfolk were willing to fight, they were
not trained for such work and would be useless. However,
Lincoln had not been stocked for siege, the king was told,
and it would not take long to starve them out. Stephen was
not so sure; he sent summons to war to the local barons,
and many came so we had a decent army. Still, Lincoln
was very strong and it seemed reasonable to wait and try to
induce Roumare to yield. We set up the siege machines to
pound the walls and we made feints of attack to tease the
garrison into wasting arrows and wear them down with
lack of sleep and constant alarms.

But there was a side to mewing up the earl of Gloucester's daughter that had not been properly considered. We
soon discovered that Chester did not flee to his own lands
but to Gloucester himself, and although Gloucester had
had reason for ill-feeling against Chester in the past, he did
not hesitate. From the army that came against us, it was
apparent that Gloucester had sent Chester back to his lands
to call upon his men and hire Welsh archers while Gloucester summoned his own supporters. Together, they marched
west—and again the evil sown by the destruction of Salisbury bore bitter fruit. We only learned of Gloucester's
advance when he was less than a day's march distant, and
it was far too late for the king to collect a greater army.

As too often happened these days, the king's council
was divided. The more cautious of the king's vassals,
Ypres and Mandeville, advised him to ride south before
Chester and Gloucester arrived, leaving one or more of
them in Lincoln with their troops to hold the town and
continue the siege of the keep. The king could then return
with a greater army and attack Gloucester from the rear
while those within could come out and assault his front.
Caught between the two armies, Gloucester would surely
be defeated and probably captured. Simon de Senlis, William d'Aumale, and others agreed, offering to ride south
with the king and raise more men. I had my doubts about
their reasons, and I did not agree with them.

Now I know it would have been better, far better, for
the king to have taken that advice. At the time, I found
myself, unwillingly, in agreement with Waleran, Alan of
Brittany, and most of the younger barons, who all cried

that it would be a shame to flee Gloucester. I was less concerned with the shame—to my mind there is no shame in retreating from a certain loss so that one may triumph later—than with the loss of opportunity to end the war. If we failed to meet him now, who could tell when we would again find Gloucester so exposed, and we seemed to have at least a small advantage. The reports we had made the rebel force out to be smaller than ours, if we included the townsmen who would fight afoot, and Gloucester's men had had a long, hard march while ours were well rested.

Aside from reason, I knew the king would not go. This was too close to his father's betrayal of his men in Antioch. Stephen might refuse battle in the open if he saw no chance of victory, but I was not sure that he would retreat, even from certain disaster, once he was committed to the protection of a city. I do not think he considered fleeing south for a moment. He barely waited for the voices to cease before he committed us to battle.

I slept well that night, possibly a special gift from Mary the Merciful, for I lit a candle to her and prayed, not for myself but for Melusine. My death might grieve but could not really harm her, but if Stephen fell to Gloucester, the queen would likely flee England. Perhaps she would take Melusine with her, but to what uncertain and dreadful future? And if Maud left Melusine in England, could she travel the whole length of the war-torn kingdom to reach Jernaeve? And once there, what? She would be cherished, but what purpose could her life have? There was King David and a second marriage and Ulle—but I put that from my mind. Perhaps I should have loved her enough to wish for it, but I was not that good a man. No, that was a thought to keep for the battlefield, where I could draw it out and it would give me a berserker's strength.

The following dawn there was a misfortune at Mass. The flame on the thick white candle, which was the usual royal offering, went out, and the candle broke as the king placed it in the hands of the bishop of Lincoln. The church was full to bursting, mostly with the men of the town who were joining us to defend their city, and a cry went up from them as they saw what happened. Then the pyx holding the body of Christ fell out of the bishop's hand,

and a silence more profound than should be induced by the Mass followed. If it would not have caused even more terror, I would have broken Alexander of Lincoln's neck, twisting it between my hands like a chicken's. I do not know how the bishop of Lincoln caused the candle to break, but I am sure he did as I am sure he broke the hasp of the pyx. It was Alexander whom the king had threatened to hang before Devizes keep in front of the bishop of Salisbury's eyes—could either event have been an accident?

The king knew too, but he could do no more than I. If we prevailed, Stephen would have his revenge. But because he no longer trusted them to stand firm, he chose to fight afoot with the burghers of Lincoln, a detachment of his mercenary men-at-arms, and such knights and barons as wished to join him. While Stephen was telling his battle leaders of his decision and giving orders that they form in two lines to defend the flanks of the foot battle, we heard the messengers crying that Gloucester's army had somehow made its way through the swamp created around the Fosse Dyke by the flooded Witham. The king hastened his instructions, and we all made for the gate and marched out on the plain, which was mostly level except for one small rise, upon which the king stationed himself.

I held my usual place to Stephen's left and half a step behind, and a leather-lunged baron called Baldwin Fitz-Gilbert, who would exhort the men, Stephen's voice being too soft, stood to the right. Camville, who had given way to Fitz-Gilbert, was behind him, and in their usual places, although on foot instead of mounted, were the others who shared my duties. I was glad to see that our own group was well fortified by a number of the local knights. I did not know all their names, only Richard de Courcy on my left and Ilbert de Lacy behind him, near me; but they were all in good spirits.

Marsh or no marsh, Gloucester's army came on to the field in good order and advanced on us until I could make out the arms and blazons of the leaders. Chester lead the center, and he was already reviling the king and his supporters. I could hear a few words and had to bite my tongue to suppress a cheer when I heard him call Waleran crafty and perfidious, but like most exhortations much of it was lies. He called Waleran a coward and pusillanimous in deeds, and neither was true—even though he certainly acted the part that day.

I heard nothing more from our enemies because Fitz-Gilbert was paying them back insult for insult and lie for lie in a voice like a brass gong. Certainly what he said about Miles of Gloucester, Chester, and Earl Robert was untrue, and he had not quite finished his exhortation when roars from the enemy line and shouts from our own men cut him off. In fact, Chester was in the act of proving he was no coward by charging at the footmen's line well ahead of his troop. He and the men who followed hoped to shake the footmen and force them to break their close formation. Men on horseback are at a huge advantage over individual men on foot, but they cannot penetrate a solid line of pikemen without sacrificing many horses.

Our line held, and Chester sheared aside just before his horse was spitted, leaning far out from his saddle to try to strike with his lance. And then I could make out little more for there was a confusion of shouting, screaming men and screaming, plunging horses. I turned my eyes away; I could never bear to see horses hurt, and I looked at the king who was staring eagerly to the right where Ypres was leading his troop at nearly a full gallop against a motley crowd of Welsh. They were deadly as archers, but not disciplined to stand and receive a charge, and Ypres, rightly, wished to scatter them before they could begin to shoot or make their way around the flank of our footmen to use their long knives.

They scattered, and the king laughed and brandished the huge, gilded war axe he had been given by the people of Lincoln. I heard Chester bellow orders and the mounted troop began to gather itself and ride across our front to the aid of the Welsh. A few arrows followed them, but not many of the burghers had crossbows and our men-at-arms had no time to reload for behind the horsemen, as they cleared our front, came the footmen. I drew my sword, and almost struck Sir Ilbert de Lacy who was next to me as I heard Stephen cry out in anguish. I looked wildly about to find the cause, but it was no physical blow that hurt him. It was Waleran riding headlong, his men fleeing in

disorder without having struck a single blow, as Robert of
Gloucester charged.

I knew then. Even as the first wave of footmen reached
us and the king charged forward, swinging that axe, I
knew the battle was over. We fought a long time. I do not
know how many men died for no purpose at all. The king
killed until the ground before him was carpeted with bodies, until the great axe broke in his hand, and I leapt before
him and took the arm off a man who had shouted aloud in
glee, thinking he had found easy, unarmed prey. He fell
away and two more advanced. I took one blow on my
shield and slashed at the other man, catching him in the
hip. I do not think my weapon cut through his gambeson,
but he backed and stumbled on a body and Fitz-Gilbert
killed him.

I should not have looked, for my shield dropped and I
was hit on the shoulder, but the blow was given by a dead
hand and only bruised me. Stephen had drawn his sword
and hacked the man's head half off. He killed another,
pushing past me so I could catch my breath, and in that
moment I heard cheers and looked west hoping against
hope that I would see Ypres coming back. But it was
Chester, not Ypres, and his men charged our line again. It
was already raveling away, not because the men had
panicked—I will never think ill of burghers' courage again—
but because they were so engaged against the enemy footmen that it was impossible to hold a solid line.

So we were driven back and back again, up the little hill
where we had first stood with high hopes, and every foot
of the ground around our group was covered with dead and
dying. Still the king fought, and while he stood and fought
so would every man until we were all dead. Camville and
Lacy had been driven away from us. Gilbert de Gant was
beside me now, poor boy, he was only a squire and too
young to be caught in such a hopeless struggle. He could
hardly stand, but his courage had not broken and he thrust
away a man with his shield, turning him so I could cut at
his neck. He fell and Gilbert stumbled over him. I stepped
back to give him room to rise and was struck a heavy blow
on the back that pushed me forward. My feet caught on
Gilbert, I half turned even as I fell and saw that what had

hit me was the king, his helm gone, his face all blood. I thrust blindly at a form reaching out toward Stephen and opened my shield from my body so that we fell together. He crushed the breath from me and the world darkened as my head slammed into the earth, but I was able to lift my shield across his body.

"Here!" It was a thin voice, far away in the swirling darkness. "Here! I have taken the king."

CHAPTER 22

Melusine

I SAW BRUNO before he saw me in the church in Salisbury, and I had time enough during that interminable funeral to consider how I would greet him. Not that I had not been considering it since we had parted, but now with his strong back and his dark, curly hair just within my sight if I leaned my head to the side, I did not feel quite the same. I had told myself that if he did not care enough for me to hold back his lust for fighting the few days it would take to escort me to the queen, it was time for me to break my shackles. If I could not bend him in so small a thing, how could I bend him in greater ones?

When I saw him, however, I suddenly realized that I had not tried to bend him. I had attacked him in a rage, scolding like an alewife. That was good enough for dealing with a servant, but mama had beaten me when I raged and told me she did so to save me a worse beating from papa if I offended him in such a way. But Bruno had not hit me. And then I had another revelation. Bruno had not left me in contempt but because his own temper had been roused and he would have beaten me if he stayed. Still, he had been wrong and selfish, and I would *not* say I was sorry and beg forgiveness.

There was no need. Bruno's face as he sought me in the

group of women advancing with the queen toward the king wiped out all the hurt and rage that had eaten at me. The anguish I saw told me my fears had been silly; if I asked for the moon when he found me, he would try to get it. I asked for nothing, just held out my hand when he saw me at last and I was repaid manyfold for that gesture of submission by the joy that made him look ten years younger, like a boy who has been given his heart's desire.

We never mentioned the quarrel again, but I had a chance to scold him and breathe out a few flickers of heat remaining in my head. The fool was walking on a broken foot without even a stick to take some of his weight. No doubt part of the anguish I had seen in his face was pain, not anxiety, but it was too late to take back what I had offered. Besides, the broken foot was not all bad. I got leave for him from the king and for me from the queen to tend him, so we had eight sweet, quiet days, and Bruno needed them.

Something more than our quarrel was troubling him. He tried to put a good face on it for my sake and I tried to draw out the trouble to soothe it, but that made it much worse so I pretended I did not see. I was sorry he would not share the burden, but at least Bruno did not act as if I were a fool and pat me on the head as papa did. I was deeply worried at first because he told me freely of the shattering of trust in the realm caused by Salisbury's overthrow, which I knew to be the queen's greatest fear, and if Bruno's trouble was worse it might be dangerous indeed. However, as the week he kept only to our chamber passed, he grew so much more cheerful that I began to wonder whether the trouble he had been hiding had to do with our quarrel rather than the king's problems.

That made me wonder what meaning he had read into the quarrel that I did not see. Later I learned—at least I learned words that expressed his trouble, but I never understood Bruno's crazy notion of duty any more than I understood papa's crazy attachment to a country he had left when he was hardly a man. At the time all that concerned me was whether he had bad news about Ulle he was afraid to tell me lest we quarrel again, that it had been seisined on another man, for example, or that he had changed his mind about accepting so poor an estate when a richer one was offered. But it was not Ulle; I was surprised by Bruno's passion when he spoke of it and a little amused that it was he who described again and again the beauty of the land. Usually it is a woman who sees that kind of beauty; men see what is good for defense or for grazing or plowing or hunting. I could not doubt his determination to have the place, so that was not his trouble.

As Bruno grew more cheerful, I would have forgotten his original misery had I not caught him looking at me more than once in a strange way. And he was so good to me, so eager to please me both with his body and his sweet words that first I wondered whether he might be jealous, fearing I had looked elsewhere while we were parted. That was not an unpleasant notion. I would not lie and hint I had seen a man I liked better; it was not true. There were fair men I thought handsomer than Bruno simply because they were fair, but I had only to think of them touching me with lips and tongue as Bruno did and I felt cold and sick, my skin rising in bumps and my stomach turning over.

Then another idea slid into my head that was not so pleasant. What if Bruno had been unfaithful because I had angered him? That made better sense of his unhappiness; no doubt my welcome to him had made him feel guilty and the strange, sidelong looks were because he wondered whether I had guessed. When I first thought of it, I was ready to scratch out his eyes and show him that my scolding in Salisbury had been a bare sample of what I could do, but we were back on duty by then and I had regained my common sense before we were both free. Acting the shrew was no way to hold a man, so I was sweeter than honey. I could not tell whether that made Bruno feel more guilty, but he was barely polite to any other woman though more than one of the queen's ladies gave broad hints of favors if he would respond.

I suppose it was really my jealousy that made me so discontent with being chosen as one of the ladies who would accompany Queen Maud to France. At the time I convinced myself that I was angry because Maud still did not trust me and would not let me go to Jernaeve with

Bruno because that would bring me too near the Scots. However, I did not ask to be left behind. I was not sure enough of my power to wrest Bruno from his hateful duty. Likely all I would accomplish would be to separate him from Cormi and Merwyn, whom he would send to join Fechin and escort me to Jernaeve. If I went with the queen, Bruno would have a third man-at-arms, for Fechin would be useless in a country where he did not speak the language.

I was becoming truly expert in lying to myself and thus hiding from fears that might have pushed me back into the madness to which I had lost eight months of life. Thus I did not permit myself to think *why* a third man-at-arms should be useful to Bruno. I did not question the cause of the bruises I tended and clung to the lie he had told me about the king and his Knights of the Body taking no part in the fighting. It was better to suffer some slight pangs of jealousy than to ask Bruno to take me to Jernaeve and be told the truth.

Aside from those pangs of jealousy, which were greatly assuaged by the amount of attention I received from the gentlemen of King Louis's court, I enjoyed myself. I only learned after we arrived that the queen's purpose was to make a marriage contract with King Louis's sister. I suppose it was kept secret so that the king's enemies would have no chance to interfere, and if Louis refused, no one in England would know. I was not privy to the negotiations, but there was enough to interest me without that. Woman as I was, I was fascinated by Louis's young queen, Eleanor of Aquitaine.

She was not beautiful, at least not to me, but I was very glad Bruno was not with us. When she turned her eyes, darkly bright and burning with the brilliance of her mind on me, I could understand why any man would adore her. Bruno would not have spoken of duty to *her;* like others he would have fallen to his knees before her and offered his life in her service, even if it meant being false to his precious master. She had only to look, to smile, and to speak and all else was forgotten. I saw Maud, who was a woman too, stare at Eleanor and, when she left the young

queen's presence, shake her head as if to free herself of
some clinging enchantment.

I said every man was her victim, but some of the priests
were not. They were already muttering ''witch'' and recounting the tale of her grandmother, who had so ensorcelled
her grandfather that he put aside his own wife, stole ''the
witch'' from her husband, and defied man and God to
keep her with him all the days of their lives. It was said of
Eleanor's grandmother that she did not die a natural death,
but having been tricked into church, she changed to a
monster and flew out the window when the Host was
elevated. Devout as he was, King Louis was not listening
to the priests; nor were his political advisors. They were
encouraging Louis to pamper his wife since her lands were
wider and her wealth greater than those of the French
monarchs.

I never thought Queen Eleanor was a witch. I had seen
that kind of charm before in my sister-by-marriage Mildred. Nor did I believe that Eleanor intended to bewitch
and enslave any more than Mildred did. Just to be near her
woke excitement—not of the body, that would not have
affected me, although I think she could have roused that
too in a man—of the spirit. She was so full of life, of the
desire to give and receive ideas, that she filled those
around her with a kind of joy in everything. It was as if a
great and brilliant light was cast into places one had never
troubled to look before, and old, dull thoughts took on a
new luster and appeared new and curious in that light. One
could see the reflection of that light in her husband's eyes
and one could see that the priests that clung around Louis
were not pleased with what the light of Queen Eleanor's
eyes showed him.

I liked her better for that; I remembered how the priest
in Ulle had hated Mildred for her oneness with the earth
and the nonhuman creatures of the earth. I only wished I
could catch from Queen Eleanor that ability to enchant
men. Not that I lacked for attention; I never missed a
dance or a man to sit beside me at the great feasts and
offer me the tenderest cut of meat, the best of the winter
roots, the most delectable piece of subtlety. But that was
only for the beauty of my face and the rich curves of my

body—and those would fade with time. I knew that Mildred, had she lived, and Queen Eleanor would be as desired, as sought, when they were worn and wrinkled with age.

I watched and I listened, hoping to find the key to Queen Eleanor's powers. If I could catch just one strand of the rope with which she tied men to her, it would be enough. After all, I had only one man to bind, not a whole troop of courtiers. Then I thought of the long winter days in Ulle; to me such days, spent sitting by a roaring fire, had been full of rich contentment, but I wondered whether a man used to court life might grow dull and restless, and I expended the purse Bruno had filled before we parted. I did not buy the fine fabrics or ornaments he had urged me to get for myself—what would I do with silk brocades or jeweled earrings in Ulle? I bought leaves of parchment on which sweet songs and tales of love were written. I bought a few lengths of cloth too, silk thin enough to float on air. One length was white, another rose. Even in a dim light a man could see through shifts made of that cloth.

News came from England, not all of it through Queen Maud, and when someone who knew the country put together this and that, the news was not good. King Stephen suffered no defeats; indeed, he put down several rebels and struck some shrewd blows very close to the rebellion's heart. But one man cannot be in many places at once, nor can he long rush from one end of a kingdom to another without failing. I could not think about that, not without seeing Bruno's face grey and haggard. I worried instead about whether King Louis would think as I thought and refuse to allow the betrothal of Constance and Eustace.

Queen Maud had her own form of power, however; she could not fascinate as could Queen Eleanor, but she could bind men to her will also. Although Maud's manners were gentle, she had great strength and authority and she was every bit as clever, though much less learned, as Eleanor of Aquitaine. I know she had a great sum of money to use as bribes, and perhaps that was the greatest of her powers— but that would not have worked on King Louis, who was fond of his sister and too high-minded to take a bribe if he believed the arrangement would place Constance in danger

or bring her unhappiness. Possibly Maud was also skilled
in lying with great conviction and managed to convince
King Louis that, despite reports, Stephen was in control of
his country.

Whatever power Maud used, she brought the negotiation
to a successful conclusion. By April we were on our way
home, taking Constance with us, only to learn that the
situation was even worse than we had heard and that the
whole country had burst into little private wars as a leper's
skin bursts out in weeping sores all over his body. It was
fortunate that the queen had traveled with a strong troop
from her own land of Boulogne to make a show for the
French and had brought them back with us because the
king could not come to meet us. His army was engaged in
the west. The Boulognese escorted us to London, where
Maud found the bishop of Winchester waiting for her.

Many evil things have been said of Henry, bishop of
Winchester—that he was mad for power and had built and
otherwise gained more castles than Salisbury had, that he
had counseled the release of the empress out of spite
because Stephen had denied him the archbishopric, that the
request he now made to the queen to allow him to propose
terms of peace to the empress and her brother was also out
of hatred for Stephen. I never believed it. I always liked
Winchester. I am not saying that he was not vain and
ambitious or that he was not hurt and bitter about the way
his own brother had turned on him after he had won a
kingdom for him. From what I saw, and I happened to be
caught up in both the release of the empress and the
dealings Maud had with Winchester over the proposed
peace, I think he was doing his best to reduce the agony of
a country he saw being torn and burnt and ruined.

Maud had heard enough both in letters from the king
and from petitioners for her help that she agreed at once to
Winchester's request. I was never so glad of anything in
my life for I had a letter too, and it frightened me half to
death it was so strange. There was not a word about
fighting, nor one word of news of any other kind either,
only a long lament of Bruno's need for me. It is true that
the pretense that Bruno did not care for me had long since
been abandoned, but Bruno's letters never held serious

complaints. They were always designed to soothe me or to make me laugh; this, although it did not ask openly, was a cry for help. I would have gone to him, despite the fact that it meant coming onto a battlefield and even though Edna and I would have to ride without Fechin to protect us—but I did not know where to go. By the time we reached London, the action we knew of had been broken off and the king was hurrying east to quell Hugh Bigod, who had broken into revolt.

That was the story of the whole spring, summer, and autumn. Each time I thought the king and queen must meet to discuss the terms of the peace Winchester was trying to bring about, a new attack or new need to attack drew the king away. There was no other letter like that first one, but then it might be said that there was no other letter—except a few lines now and then that mentioned the king's favorable reactions to Winchester's peace treaty. Oh, I received words written on parchment, but Bruno was not there. They were letters from some stranger who discoursed on the weather and the state of the roads. One time I raged, the next I wept, telling myself that he had taken another woman because I would rather believe that than that Bruno was now as mad as I had been before we married.

I should have saved my tears. After the bishop of Winchester had spent all the months from May to November crossing and recrossing the country to bring one set of terms after another to Maud and to Robert of Gloucester, after he had even gone to France and Blois to consult with King Louis and Stephen's brother Theobald of Blois, after the empress had been brought to accept the terms, Stephen put them aside "to consider at a more propitious time." I thought Maud would faint when she had the news, although at the moment I had not yet heard the king's phrase and did not know why her face grew so grim and so grey. I had come near when the packet was brought to her, hoping—or should I say fearing—there would be a letter from Bruno in it, and I cried aloud, "Oh, madam, what is it?"

"The earl of Chester has taken Lincoln Castle, and Stephen is too busy trying to get it back to consider the peace treaty at this time. He will think about it at a more propitious time," she said, but I am sure she did not know to whom she was speaking or what she was saying.

"The king is not going to assault the castle, is he?" I whispered, for the moment the real meaning of what she said being lost on me because of my fear for Bruno.

"No, it is too strong," she replied still dully, as if she were speaking by rote, without thinking. Then her voice changed, growing shrill and angry. "You are as blind as he, you fool! Cannot you see that if Stephen had agreed to the peace, Chester would have *had* to yield the keep? There would be none to help him. Why, Stephen could have called on Gloucester to help drive Chester out. All rebellion would have been at an end."

It was the first time I had ever heard Maud say a word of criticism of her husband, and I knew it was only her fear for him that made her do it, but I was nearly stunned by what I finally understood. "The king does not like the peace terms?" I asked in amazement. "But he has known every proposal and approved it—Bruno wrote that. What—"

"Waleran de Meulan"—Maud nearly spit the name— "explained that it was better to fight on for a whole crown than live in peace with only half."

"May he rot outside as he is rotten inside!"

Maud seemed to shiver and focussed her eyes on me, first realizing now to whom she was speaking. "What reason can *you* have to hate Waleran?" she asked.

"If it had not been for his pride and arrogance, my father and brother would be sitting alive at the table in Ulle talking about whether we had supplies enough for the winter. My father answered no summons from King David; he went to fight in Scotland because he had been insulted by Waleran de Meulan."

"I did not know that," Maud said softly, but she looked away from me and I could not tell whether she was thinking of what I said or had simply gone back to her own problems, but then she looked back at me and said, "There is no letter for you, but Stephen has assured me that he will meet me in London to celebrate Christmas."

They came before Christmas, at the end of the second week in December. I suppose being close to the city, the king decided to leave the army to make camp outside of

London and rode on, though it was already dark, desiring warmth and the comfort of a real bed. Certainly we did not expect to see them that day and had only a few minutes warning when a page came running, crying to the queen that the king had come. I was sitting and sewing, and I remember that I got to my feet, dropping my work, but I did not move from my place.

I think by then that I was more afraid than eager to see Bruno; I thought he might greet me as a stranger, but that was silly. It was only when our eyes met across the great width of the room that I understood how that first letter of longing fit with the other "polite" missives. I cannot see how I could have missed so simple an answer. Bruno had said what he felt the first time; thereafter, he dared not even think it or think about me lest he lose control of himself and violate his precious duty.

How can I explain how he looked? I have lived all my life in a land that has water in great abundance, much rain, many streams and rivers, many lakes; but there are tales of other places where men went on crusade, where the sun blazes without a cloud to give relief, without a tree to give shade, and where there is no water, no water at all. The storytellers who recite these tales speak of the great agonies of thirst endured by the crusaders, a thirst so great that the lips crack and the tongue dries to leather. I can only say that the thirst in Bruno's eyes when he looked at me was the same as a man in that state who looked on water. And he walked away from the king, without a look, without asking leave, and came to me and asked, "Where is our chamber?"

Thank God I had had sense enough to send Edna out to seek a place as close to the Tower as she could find and had still a few silver pennies to pay for it. I had not slept there alone, but I had gone twice to see the bed made and that all was clean and ready. Unfortunately, having no notion when Bruno would arrive and not expecting he would come so late, I had not ordered a fire to be set. I shuddered, thinking of the icy room, of cold, damp sheets, expecting that Bruno would all but leap on me to satisfy the needs of his body starved for nearly a year. But, seeing how he looked, I did not try to explain nor even go to find my cloak nor tell Edna I was leaving. I took his hand in mine, with as little thought for the duty I was abandoning as Bruno had given to his, and I led him down the stairs to the forebuilding, out of the Tower, and out through the postern gate.

It was very dark, even to eyes accustomed, and I hesitated, feeling for good footing on the rutted road. Bruno gave a little shiver and said, "Wait." Then he went back to the postern and shouted for the guard to give him a torch. When he came back, he looked at me in surprise.

"Where is your cloak?" he asked.

"I did not stop to take it," I answered as steadily as I could, for it was frightening to be reminded that once I had also looked straight at things and had not seen them as Bruno had looked at me. "Shall I go back for it?"

"No!"

The exclamation was so sharp, I jumped, and he caught me to him, holding the torch well away and murmuring that he was sorry he had startled me. Then he bade me hold the torch while he took off his cloak, but I laughed and said, "No, take me under it with you. I will be warmer so."

Bruno opened the cloak for me, and I caught my breath for he was all in mail and there were dark splotches on the rings. Then I was enfolded and saw no more; perhaps I had been deceived by shadows from the flickering torch-light, but my voice froze in my throat and I could not warn him about the cold, unwelcoming chamber. We walked down the mound on which the Tower stood and into the street that led to the East Cheap. The house Edna had found was less than a quarter of a mile from where the houses began. The merchant from whom I had rented the chamber had moved in with his son-by-marriage, but when Bruno pounded on the door with his mailed fist, the journeyman, who slept at the back of the shop with the two young apprentices, came and asked what was wanted. I answered, giving my name, and we could hear the bar of the door being lifted.

"Take the torch in," I said to Bruno, as I saw him lower it to roll in a puddle on the ground. "The room is not ready. I did not expect you. I can use it to light the fire quickly.''

He kissed me swiftly as the door opened, then pushed me into the house and said to the journeyman, ''I am sorry to disturb your sleep, but I will need the back door opened so I can get water from the butt and wood.'' Then he threw his cloak over my shoulders, put the torch into my hand—there was a night candle burning in the shop and a dim glow from the back showed there was another there—and said to me, ''Go up and hand down an ewer,'' but his voice was light and he was smiling.

That confused me so much that I do not remember doing as I was bid or lighting the fire and the tapers. I must have done so because the room was bright and the wood laid ready by Edna was blazing when Bruno came up the stair—little more than a ladder with broad treads set at a steep angle along the wall of the shop—carrying an ewer filled with water. He handed it to me, cocked an eye at the heap of wood near the hearth, and said he would fetch more. I got the flat stones for warming the bed, thrust them under the fire, and sat down to wait for what would happen next. I did not think the kind of need Bruno had showed when he saw me in the hall of the Tower could be shed by walking a few streets and entering a house.

Yet it seemed that was just what he had done. He came up with his arms full of wood and atop that load a big wedge of cheese and half a loaf of bread held down by his chin and the strap of a leather jack round his arm. I ran to take the bread and cheese before they fell, and held the jack, which I discovered was about half full of ale, so it would not spill when he put down the wood.

''There,'' he said, grinning at me, ''this is not as elegant an evening meal as you would have had in the Tower, but at least you will not go hungry.''

''Where did you get it?'' I asked as Bruno slid his arm out of the strap and bent to put more wood on the fire.

I knew he must have bought the apprentices' breakfast from the journeyman, but I could not think of anything else to say. I was hurt and angry, and at the same time I knew I had no right to be offended. It was not Bruno's fault that I had misread his expression when he first saw

me and thought he felt an overwhelming hunger for me. I
should be grateful that he had not overlooked the need of
his belly, and my own, and that he did not really wish to
tear my clothes off and throw me into an ice-cold damp
bed because he could not wait until the sheets could be
warmed. Still, my eyes were full of unreasonable tears,
and I had to turn away sharply and pretend I wished to put
the food on a small table by the far wall, which was a
stupid thing to do since the table would have to be moved
to the fire or we would freeze while we ate.

I never got there. I had no sooner turned my back than
Bruno seized me around the waist, thrust my veil aside,
and began to kiss the back of my neck. "Let go, you
fool," I cried angrily. "Do you want me to spill the ale?
Go and get the table so we can eat in the warmth." And
then I burst into laughter at my own silliness. I was angry
because Bruno's passion was not as hot as I first believed,
so I shrieked at him when he showed that it was.

We nearly did spill the ale, but not in the grapplings of
passion. We fell into each other's arms, crushing the bread
and cheese and ale between us, both laughing like idiots. I
have no idea about what we were laughing, but it made me
light and happy so that I did not flinch when I helped
Bruno take off his armor and saw again those dark stains
on it.

"Rust," he said, when he saw where my eyes were
fixed. "It has been devilish wet and not safe to go
unarmed."

Did I believe him? I do not think so, but he was
grinning at me like a mischievous boy, as Fergus grinned
when he had done something dangerous, for which papa
would have beaten him black and blue if I told. I never did
tell, and now I laughed, as I had laughed with Fergus, and
gave Bruno the food while I ran to get the bedrobe I had
made for him from his chest. He had left that in my care,
fearing to lose everything in the quick marches and
countermarches in which the baggage train was often left
behind. The bedrobe covered his arming tunic, marked
with the same dark stains, and when they were hidden I
shut them from my mind.

There was nothing else to remind me of those marks.

Bruno's movement was easy even when he carried the table to the fire; he was not favoring any half-healed wound, except that he still limped a little and that, I knew, was because the cold and damp made the old break in his foot ache. We laughed again when we discovered that my eating knife was too small to cut the hard cheese; Bruno was not wearing his and drew his sword to cut it, which was ridiculous, but we had no other tool. While he was massacring the cheese, I pulled the warming stones from the fire, wrapped them in the warming cloths, and put them in the bed. Then we both sat down to eat. We had to drink from the jack of ale, for I had not thought to bring cups. And then we had more cause to laugh when I remembered the brass bowl Bruno had bought for me, which we could have used.

I know we talked, but only of the lightest things. He said he was glad they came too late for the queen to ride out to meet Stephen because Vinaigre would surely have bitten him again, and he reminded me of the disaster we had caused when we met at Winchester. And I told him about Queen Eleanor and about the writings I had bought, at which he groaned—not that he did not like to hear the poems and tales, he assured me, but that my purchases had reminded him of Audris's passion for such things and the agonies he had suffered when she made him learn to read and write.

Sometimes our hands met when we reached at the same time for the bread or a piece of cheese. Then we did not laugh, and our fingers clung together, but only for a moment, and we both looked aside and took the food. There came an end to eating, a time when our hands met and Bruno lifted mine and held it to his lips. I touched his face with my other hand, and he looked at me. Then he rose from his stool and lifted me from mine.

I have never known a loving like that. If it were not blasphemous, I would have said that Bruno worshipped each separate inch of me. He took off my clothing as if it were holy, a piece at a time, folding each garment and laying it aside. And when I was naked, he laid me in the bed, drawing back the coverlets—it was warm enough in the room by then, and the sheets were warm too—and began to kiss me, first my hair, then my forehead, then my cheeks and lips, my throat, my breast. He was not hurrying, not grasping greedily at me like a hungry man, nor was he teasing me, playing with me to excite me.

He said nothing, so I do not know what was in his mind, but to me the touch of his lips seemed as if he needed to reassure himself that I was real and, perhaps, to thank me—just for being. Whatever Bruno's purpose, that light touch, touch, touch of his mouth on my body brought excitement nonetheless, but it came slowly. I was ready and willing but not half mad as he sometimes made me. He drew the coverlet over me at last and turned away, pulling off his bedrobe. I lay quietly when he went to take off his clothes and waited patiently, watching the fire leap in the hearth. The pleasure in my body was like that of a fire in winter, a beautiful thing, glittering and glowing and giving warmth and contentment.

Bruno caressed me again when he came to bed and said such extravagant things that I would have laughed, knowing how imperfect I was compared to his words, but I dared not. His face and voice were so intent; for that time I was his whole world. I responded with caresses; I stroked his hair and face, his shoulders and arms, and I kissed him gently, but I could not echo his words of love. I *would* not lie to this man who was offering me his soul, and I dared not love him.

I do not know how long we lay entwined, taking and giving comfort. My desire for his body grew slowly more intense, and I could feel Sir Jehan pressing harder against me. The kisses, which had been light and tender, became longer and more passionate. I pulled gently at Bruno's body, and slowly he lifted himself atop and entered. We hardly moved at first. I only closed my eyes, relishing my easy, warm delight when I was filled, and I think it was the same for Bruno, who seemed in no hurry to spill his seed. So it continued, each slow thrust giving a tiny bit more pleasure until a new joy broke over me in slow rolling waves that made me sigh and sigh again but not cry out.

Bruno's release was very like mine, or so I judged from how he acted, and he raised his head and smiled at me then slid to the side and slept. Usually he was very careful to say a few words of thanks and love after we coupled, but tonight there was no need. We had said everything already with touches and kisses purely gentle. I lay awake for some time—I had done nothing all day but sew—and I thought I would never be jealous of him again. Perhaps he had coupled with a woman now and again in animal need. There was nothing in that, although I would never come to like the idea. What was important was that he would never give another woman a night like this.

Perhaps because I felt less strongly, I teased Bruno in the morning about how he had contented himself over the long time we had been parted. I almost expected him to be angry and tell me his sins of the body were between him and God. Instead he looked as if I had given him a chest full of gold and jewels. He seized me and kissed me and laughed long and loud. Then he frowned and tried to look stern, only his eyes were still bright with laughter, and said a good wife did not ask such questions. But he burst out into chuckles again before he finished and asked if I wished to see the dingy drabs that followed the army. I would not need to ask again once I saw them; such women, he assured me, were more likely to inspire chastity than lechery.

"There are better women than that as spoils of war," I remarked, still teasing and remembering what Donald had told me.

But Bruno's laughter stopped abruptly, and he seized me by the shoulders. "Never! Never in my life have I taken any woman as a prize of war. I could not, Melusine. I would see you and Audris. Can you think I would use threats or force—" He stopped and the pain in his face was terrible. "Do you still hate me for our wedding night, Melusine?"

"No, no!" I cried, throwing my arms around him and clinging to him. "I did not mean to hurt you, Bruno. I had forgotten that, truly forgotten it, or I would not have been able to tease you. I was only jesting. I—I am a little jealous."

Truly repentant, I admitted openly what I would have denied to my last breath, despite having exposed myself by my questions. But my purpose was accomplished. Although Bruno undid my arms from his neck and held me away from him so he could see my face, the tension in his body had eased, and when he saw I was blushing, he began to smile again.

"You need not be," he said. "Having the mother I did, I was never much of one for women—"

"Not much of one for women!" I echoed indignantly. "What am I, a frog? You do not give *me* much rest."

"Do you desire it?" he asked, pulling me close again. "You never say no."

I pushed him away with all my strength. "What I desire," I snapped, "is the last word, just once!"

He took my hands in his, smiling again. "I beg your pardon. That was neither a polite nor a clever remark—I spoke before I thought because your gentle compliance makes me so happy." Since my compliance was more often violently enthusiastic than gentle, I felt a strong urge to pull his hair and my hands jerked in his grasp, but he did not release me and went on blandly, "But on this subject you shall have the last word. I can do without women, and if you want my word on it, I will give it."

I could feel myself blush again, and Bruno laughed aloud, let go of me, and cast up his hands in a signal I had seen men use to call a halt in fighting exercise.

"Forgive me!" he exclaimed. "I do not know how I came to make two such stupid remarks in succession. Of course you need not ask. Even if you do *not* desire that I be faithful, I swear I will take no other woman while you live, Melusine—not whore nor serf nor fine lady."

Although Donald had taught me what men's oaths are worth on such a subject, I felt a definite satisfaction. Bruno was my husband, not a man promising the moon to win a mistress, and he had no need to pacify me except for his own desire to please me. However, all I said was, "With such a beginning, I know what that oath is worth."

He caught my chin in his hand and held my eyes. "I do not give any oath lightly, Melusine, even if I smile when speaking it. I smiled because you had the deed without need of oath. You should know I have not touched any woman since I first lay with you."

He embraced me again, but I laughed and pushed him away. "We must go. I did not tell the queen or Edna that I was leaving, and I wonder where Fechin, Cormi, and Merwyn slept last night.

"They will have found a place easily enough in the stables or even in the hall." Bruno's lips twisted. "This court is not likely to be overattended. But you are right, we must go. I am very late."

There was a note of indifference in Bruno's voice that both pleased me and made me uneasy. I thought perhaps his duty was not so precious or pleasing to him as it had been, and that would make me more important to him. Yet the happiness that idea brought was not unalloyed. I found the notion that Bruno would be lax in keeping his oath to the king disturbing. What had been a character of solid rock was no longer a place to rest with utter trust.

I found over the next weeks that I was right in half and wrong in half about Bruno's duty. His character had lost none of its solidity. The pleasure was indeed gone from his duty, but it was as precious as ever. He had given his oath to the king, and that oath was adamant. Until Stephen released him, he would serve. But he *was* different. In the past he had attended eagerly to the king's plans and hopes and as eagerly discussed them with me, most particularly as they applied to our hopes of obtaining Ulle. Now he would not talk of anything more serious than my beauty, the latest gossip—and Bruno had never cared for gossip—and what was to be found in the shops in London.

I was hurt, at first, thinking he was keeping secrets from me, but I soon realized that Bruno was not listening to the king and his advisors as he used to do. He said bitterly that all they did was plan for war, and none of the plans was new to him. I saw that Bruno was tired, not in his body but within himself, the way papa had been tired after mama died. I did not understand over what Bruno grieved. He would not talk about it, and I wondered if he was as bitter as the queen about Stephen's rejection of the peace treaty. If that was what had made him withdraw his affection from the king, he was more loyal than Maud, for he said no word against his master.

What I did understand, even if the cause was unclear,

was that Bruno had to have a time of peace in which he did not need to strive for anything, not even for so dearly desired a goal as Ulle. Besides, from other men's talk I learned that the war might go on for a very long time; if so, our hope of settling in Ulle would be far in the future, and tired as Bruno was, that thought must be painful to him. It was reasonable for him to avoid any talk of Ulle.

I did not press the subject, since the queen had told me we would remain in London through January. I was the center of Bruno's world; I was very happy, and I wanted him to be happy. I felt there would be chances toward the end of our time together to show Bruno the letter I had had from Sir Gerald with the accounts of the harvest and quarterly income from the fisheries. The accounting was some months out of date, but I did not blame Sir Gerald for that. He had first had to find a priest who could write and would not betray him, and then the poor messenger had twice arrived in towns the queen had just left.

I was eager to give Bruno Sir Gerald's news because the accounts were cheering; the harvest had been good and the fish were bringing higher prices than ever because of the war. The hidden strongbox was filling with silver, and when we came to Ulle, there would be money to buy sheep and pigs, even cattle, to replace any depredations Sir Giles made. And the war had not touched Ulle; it might be tearing apart most of the realm, but the deep valleys of Cumbria were quiet. I should have made him listen; it would have been something good to think about, something to cling to during the nightmare that followed.

One would think that, at twenty-four years of age and bearing on my heart the scars I bear, I would not have the simple expectation of a child that the war everyone talked of could not touch me. I had been "promised" that Bruno would be with me until the end of January, and I expected that "promise" to be kept—as if the queen's remark could order fate. I had no suspicion that our time of peace and play was over when Bruno sent a message that his duty would keep him late and I should go to our lodging with our men's escort. Even when he came and flung himself on me with such violence that our coupling would have been rape, except that his urgency roused me quickly to desire, I only laughed, glad of his need of me. But when he began to shake after his release and I felt his tears wetting my shoulder, my pretty bubble burst.

At first, I was more shocked than frightened, and I held him and soothed him. I remember saying that though the whole world burned, we had each other and would find a corner in which to live in peace. I could not well make out his answer because his voice was thick and he would not raise his head; it was as if he were ashamed. He said something about pitch spreading from the guilty to smear those who stood watching. I supposed he was speaking of something the king had done, but I did not care and only told him that there was no way one man could change the world—unless he thought he was Christ in his second coming. He was too sick, with disgust I think, to smile, but the reminder that he should not be so proud and think the fate of the world rested on his doings finally calmed him. He sighed and let me see his face and told me he was sorry he had been so rough. A little later he loved me again with his usual tenderness, and then he slept. I did too, not knowing what was to come.

Before dawn Bruno woke me. He held me and kissed me tenderly and said he must go and he did not know when he would come back, so perhaps I had better give up the lodging. That was when I realized he was all in mail. I was so stunned that I could not even weep—thank God for that. My poor Bruno had enough to bear; he did not need the memory of a weeping wife. And I thank God too that out of some inner urge, I called out, "Take all three men, Bruno. I do not need a private messenger, and I think Fechin is lonely without his friends."

It was Fechin who came back to me, riding Barbe, though he could scarcely sit the horse, and leading Merwyn's mount with Merwyn tied to the saddle. Cormi was dead.

In times of utter and complete disaster, one thanks God for small mercies. When I heard that Bruno was alive and not sorely hurt, I thought it a wonderful thing that he was a prisoner rather than dead. Thus it was I who brought to the queen the news that instead of taking Lincoln, the king had been surrounded by Gloucester's army and defeated. It was not until Fechin stood before her that I thought she might not believe him and call him a liar or even punish me, but Fechin began the tale at the right end by saying that the king was alive and not much hurt before he said that Stephen had been taken prisoner.

I had not waited to hear the whole story. Once I had been assured of Bruno's safety, I stayed only to call a servant to see that Merwyn was put in the hands of a healer before I brought Fechin to the queen. Her shock was less than mine—when I saw Barbe with Fechin, I thought Bruno was dead. Once Maud learned that Fechin had actually seen Stephen safe after the battle, riding a horse beside Robert of Gloucester though hemmed in on all sides by rebels, she had every detail out of him even though I had to translate most of what he said; Maud did not understand soldiers' patois. Some events Fechin had seen himself and others Merwyn had told him, for Fechin's right arm had been broken early in the battle, and he had withdrawn to have it set and then stayed with the horses. When he saw the king could not win, he had stolen Gloucester's colors from dead men for Merwyn and himself, and thus escaped.

"I didn' go before I saw I couldn' get Sir Bruno free, m'lady," he said, turning to me in the midst of his explanation to the queen. "He be ridin' right behind the king. I made like I was Gloucester's man and followed, right in the city, but they be goin' on to the keep."

The queen was not unkind. She called for wine for Fechin and a stool for him to sit on, but she did not let him go until she had heard everything he knew at least twice, and it took several tellings interrupted by many questions before she was sure she had drained him dry. She gave him gold coin and told me to see to his comfort. She never thanked me—one does not thank the bearer of such tidings. I went to see Fechin settled near Merwyn, who was not so near death as I had thought, only exhausted, and made sure that Barbe was stabled beside Vinaigre and being cared for. But when I returned to her, Maud took my hand and held it. Then, with a face like stone and in a voice so soft that I do not think anyone save me heard, she cursed every earl that Stephen had belted and made rich.

Most especially did she curse Waleran de Meulan, who

had most influenced the king to reject the peace treaty, and then had fled the field. I said, "Amen" and "amen" again, but I do not remember feeling anything but relief that day. The shock of thinking Bruno dead followed by the joy of learning he was alive numbed me to all else. In the days that followed my mood swung from hope to terror and back again. As a prisoner, Bruno would fight no more, so I had hope that he was out of danger; but other times I had visions of him being tortured and starved, chained in a black dungeon.

And then we waited. Two days after Fechin came, William of Ypres rode into London. The early news Fechin had brought was of value to Queen Maud. It gave her time to absorb the shock and control her rage, to think what she must do to save her husband—and what was first and foremost was to keep the good will of any who were still faithful to the king. She was specially gracious to Ypres, who had at least not fled without striking a blow and whose power was in Kent, which gave her access to ports close to Boulogne, from where she could get money and mercenaries.

A month dragged by. In the beginning of March the queen sent for me to tell me that a messenger had come from Henry of Winchester with news of the king and Bruno. The bishop had assured the queen that Stephen was well and being treated with honor and that he had with him his own servant Sir Bruno of Jernaeve. She did not then tell me the real purpose of the message, which was to announce that Winchester had repudiated his oath to his brother and accepted Matilda as queen and that he had called a council of bishops to convene on 7 April. At that council, the bishop intended to use his authority as legate of the pope to announce that Stephen had been cast down by God and deprived of his crown for his trespasses against the Church and call for an election of Empress Matilda as Lady. When I heard, I wondered why the title of Lady rather than Queen had been selected. I never discovered the answer, but I think perhaps it was because Stephen had been anointed as king and the bishop feared that even his legatine authority could not wipe away God's chrism.

Although Winchester did not obtain the enthusiastic ap-

proval he expected, even from many of the other bishops
of England, most of the country withdrew into a kind of
fearful neutrality. Even London, where Stephen was loved,
in the end dared not resist openly and agreed to allow the
empress to enter the city when Geoffrey de Mandeville,
keeper of the Tower of London and thus master of the
troops that guarded the city, was bought by Matilda's
promise of rich new lands. When Mandeville broke faith,
Maud was deeply shaken. She wept bitterly and then wrote
to the empress offering to yield if Matilda would only
release Stephen under bond never to seek to regain the
throne of England.

The empress refused—well, I expected that; I knew
Matilda well by now and pity and mercy were not in her
nature—but I did not expect her answer to be so coarse
and cruel. And Matilda's messenger not only insulted
Queen Maud but told her Stephen was now chained like a
slave and it was the empress's intention that he should die
in those chains. That was a great mistake on Matilda's
part. It made Maud desperate. The queen would fight now,
with every device and resource she could muster, and
Ypres began to gather an army for her.

As Matilda approached London, we retreated, but only
to Rochester, less than ten leagues from the city and in
easy reach of Ypres's strongholds in Kent. We did not lack
news from London, for the burghers sent news nearly
every day; and it seemed to me that the empress was
fighting on our side, so ill did she manage friend and foe
alike. We heard how she would not rise to greet even King
David, a fellow monarch, and how when her own half
brother, who had fought for her, knelt to request mercy for
an offender, she bawled a refusal at him almost as coarse
as that sent to Maud.

Most foolish of all, within days of entering London,
Matilda demanded a huge tallage of the city, which I
understand she had no right to do, being not yet crowned.
Then the burghers, who still desired peace even with so
harsh a mistress, sent a delegation who knelt and begged
her to reduce the sum. The city was drained of its usual
resources by the damage to trade owing to the war. Matilda would not listen and roared at them in a rage that she

would not abate her demand a penny and threatened to punish them for having in the past supported King Stephen.

Had Matilda agreed to Maud's pathetic terms, London would have had no one to turn to, no help in rising and driving out the empress and her supporters. Now men came and whispered in Maud's ears and Maud whispered back. In the second week of July, Maud's army marched west and we with it, but for us it was just another journey; there did not seem to be any connection with the large number of men talked about by Maud and Ypres. Even when the army began to ravage the district south of London, I saw nothing of it. The queen and all her women had taken refuge behind the high, thick walls of Southwark priory, with a strong troop of Boulognese to protect both her and the priory.

The most I saw was the red light of fires reflected on the low clouds and sometimes I heard a low, dull noise. But the ravaging of Southwark was the signal, given on the very eve before Matilda was to be crowned, while a feast was being readied to celebrate the event. I did hear when all the bells of London suddenly began to toll, and my eyes met the queen's. I almost laughed, for she looked as I felt—eager, and hungry. We knew that those bells were calling the men of the city to rush out to attack Westminster, where the empress was making ready for her coronation.

The burghers were as good as their word. As Ypres and Maud's army marched toward the bridge and began to seek boats in which to cross the river, London rose. Unfortunately there were those among the empress's party who were not befooled into believing that the bells were ringing in celebration of the coming coronation. The surprise was not complete and Matilda had time to flee with her supporters, but they went with what they had on their backs. In her haste to escape, the empress even left behind the royal crown, which she had been carrying with her since Winchester had opened the treasury to her. Ypres arrived before the Londoners who were looting the palace had broken open the strongboxes that held the royal regalia and plate, but I am sure Maud would have preferred to lose the crown than Matilda. Yet she could not blame Ypres; he did not know until he entered the palace that the empress was not there. He set out after her as soon as he was sure she had escaped, but no one of importance was captured. We learned later that they had broken up into small parties and fled in different directions so that there was no clear trail to follow.

I have told the events, many of which I only heard about days after they happened, and in the telling I have not mentioned how they affected me. I can hardly bear to do so now. After Matilda had refused Queen Maud's proposal of peace, my days were too busy to give me time to think, and much of my employment concerned the attack on the empress in London. That sustained me because I hoped that the empress would be captured and we would have her to exchange for Stephen and Bruno. But the nights were terrible. Awake or asleep, as soon as it grew dark—as it might be in a dungeon—I saw visions of Bruno, chained so he could neither sit nor stand and was in continual torment, all wasted and covered with running sores as I had seen prisoners in Carlisle and Richmond. And when I came into Westminster with the queen and learned that Ypres had returned without a single prisoner of note, I slipped back into the emptiness that held me for so many months after I learned my father was dead. I must have lost a few hours or a day, for I came to myself in a start of pain in an empty room in the palace when the queen slapped my face.

"You coward!" she shrieked at me, slapping me again. "You spoiled, self-indulgent monster! What right have you to sit staring at the wall? Selfish beast! Will you let your husband die in chains rather than make the effort to save him?"

CHAPTER 23

Bruno

I HAVE BEEN so often praised for sacrificing myself for the
king, that I must confess my shame. I did my duty to the
utmost of my ability in the battle of Lincoln, though I was
appalled at the dishonor of the attack, but my refusal to be
parted from Stephen after we were captured was purely
selfish. Did no one save me realize that to be one with the
king was my best hope of freedom? Where could I find a
ransom? Melusine had nothing except the few coins I had
left with her when I departed; Audris and Hugh would
pay, I was sure, but why should I drain their slender store
and take on a debt I might never be able to repay? Moreover, I was assured of far better treatment in captivity as
Stephen's servant than as a poor knight with no estate.

It was fortunate that Robert of Gloucester, to whom our
captor delivered us, recognized me as one of the men who
had brought his sister to him from Arundel. I was supporting the king, who was still partly dazed from the blow to
his head, when we were brought before Gloucester, and he
stared at me a moment and then said, "You are Bruno of
Jernaeve. My sister had a good deal to say about you when
I was escorting her back to Bristol."

I thought I was a dead man in that moment, but I could
not change the habit of a lifetime, and I stared back at him

and said, "I am sorry to have displeased Lady Matilda, but I am not sorry for the cause. Free or captive, I can see no reason to beat servants for not being able to guess in advance what was wanted of them nor to give up my wife to a service she loathed."

"A round answer, and what I might have expected from a man who puts his hand on his sword hilt in reply to a look," Gloucester said.

His voice was sober, but to my amazement there was a slight crinkling of the skin near his eyes and a twitching at the corner of his mouth that looked like a desire to laugh. It gave me hope, and I shrugged. "I am sorry for that too, but I could not bawl across the distance between us a denial to a question that had not been asked."

Then Gloucester smiled. "Just so, but we are far from the business at hand. Kahains here informs me that he and his men had some difficulty in making you lift your shield away from Lord Stephen when they captured him. You are a loyal servant. Do you wish to remain with your master?"

Before I could answer, I felt Stephen turn his head. "Stay with me, Bruno," he muttered. "Stay and show me one candle worth of loyalty in the black night of treachery that surrounds me."

Despite my anger at the king and my feeling that he had shown his nobles the way to their treachery with his own, I think I would not have denied him even if I had not already seen the advantages in being Stephen's fellow captive. "You need not ask," I said to Stephen. "I have given you my oath, my lord king, and that oath will hold me until you release me." And then I looked at Gloucester. "Thank you, my lord. I beg you to let me go with my lord king and serve him."

I had given Stephen his full title because Gloucester had called him Lord Stephen—and whatever Stephen had lost in attacking Lincoln, nothing could take from him his anointment as king. Gloucester looked at me, and for a moment I thought he would take back his offer of allowing Stephen to have his own servant, who might, as I had just done, attempt to keep up the king's spirits and thus interfere with attempts to make Stephen renounce his crown. But he said no more to us, only ordering that horses be found for us so we might be taken into Lincoln keep. Gloucester was a fine man, and I thought it a great misfortune that he should be a bastard and—by his own honor and his love and respect for his father as much as by any other cause—be deprived of the right to the throne. Better, far better for our unhappy realm had Gloucester the bastard sat on the throne than either Stephen or Matilda.

That is true, even though I may have overestimated Gloucester's kindness in allowing me to remain with the king. Gloucester knew Stephen of old, and may have known him better than I in certain ways. I had never seen the king truly cast down, except for very short times until something diverted him from whatever had disappointed him. Gloucester may have realized that nothing I could do could lighten the king's mood once he realized the finality of his condition as captive. That he did not realize it in the beginning soon became clear.

By the time we were mounted, Stephen was fully recovered from the blow on his head. We were both wounded, as was Gloucester, but not seriously, and none of us had lost enough blood to induce weakness. Still, I could hardly believe my ears when I heard Stephen talking quite cheerfully to the earl about a ransom. I wondered if the king believed what he was saying, or if he was simply putting off the time when he must face the truth—that there could be no ransom on earth that would free him except the yielding of his crown.

For over a week Stephen resisted this truth. It was not until we came to Gloucester and Stephen was forced to do reverence to the empress that he realized his situation was nigh hopeless. I was not there. I was sent on ahead to Bristol, and I thank God I do not know what actually happened at that meeting for it broke the king. For a few days after he arrived in Bristol, he still seemed stunned. Then, instead of recovering his usual optimism, he sank into alternating periods of grief and rage in which he first wept and lamented his misdeeds and cried he had been justly chastised by God and then cursed those who had fled the battle without even trying to save him.

The poor king was thrust even deeper into a pit of despair when in March he was summoned to the hall to

hear, before a crowd of his enemies, a special messenger
from Matilda. With sneering satisfaction, that messenger
announced that Stephen's brother had betrayed him and
had offered—of his own free will and without conditions—to
proclaim that Stephen had been cast down by the judgement of God and that Empress Matilda was the true ruler
and Lady of England. The king wept for a day and a night,
moaning of his brother's ingratitude. I do not know how
often I bit my tongue to keep from reminding him of the
many times he had affronted and slighted Winchester,
beguiled by the smooth flattery of Waleran de Meulan.

To tell the truth, I was nearly as despairing as the king.
The news was a bitter blow to me too. I had not thought
Matilda could be crowned until the king had agreed to
yield the throne. If Matilda were crowned without Stephen's abdication, it might profit her more to keep him a
perpetual prisoner—or be rid of him entirely. I felt myself
fittingly punished for my selfish decision to cling to Stephen, not for honor or loyalty or his many kindnesses to
me but because I thought service a cheap way to win
comfort and freedom. My solace was that I had done my
master no harm despite my selfishness and I began in good
earnest to try to cheer him.

I told Stephen—and it was true—that Matilda was proud,
cruel, and thoroughly venomous and that he must not
believe all that her messengers were bidden to tell him. I
pointed out that Winchester's change of heart might not
last long. As soon as Matilda showed him her true character, he would regret bitterly what he had done. But the
king would not listen to me and sank deeper and deeper
into apathy, wandering listlessly about the hall or sitting
silently in his chamber. He no longer even walked on the
walls, which was allowed. We were not confined harshly.
Mostly we were treated as guests and given much freedom—
only certain places in the keep, like the armory, and
leaving the inner bailey were forbidden to us.

I could not rouse Stephen, even when toward the end of
March, Theobald the archbishop was allowed to visit him
to ask his permission to transfer his allegiance to the
empress. I stood as usual beside Stephen's chair, but I

could not tell whether Stephen even heard the archbishop. The man spoke low; I suppose he was ashamed, as he might well be, for his election was probably the major cause of Winchester's defection. Stephen stared at him, and I pressed the king's shoulder hard enough that he winced and looked at me in protest.

"Say you will consider," I murmured, bending over him. "Then we can go back to your chamber."

Stephen repeated my words obediently, and went with me like a sleepwalker, but he had indeed heard Theobald. "Why do you want me to delay?" he asked, standing and staring into the fire. "Does it matter whether I say yes today or tomorrow?"

"You should not say yes at all, my lord," I urged. "Are you not angry with that creature? You gave him the power he now has. How dare he come and ask permission to change faith! Do not give him that ease of soul! If the highest member of the Church is so weak that he will forswear himself and betray the man who lifted him up from nothing, let him be forsworn before all men's eyes. If that less-than-man has a soul, let it be wrenched and blackened. Do not give away your crown."

He smiled wearily at me and rested a hand on my shoulder. "Did I not choose him because Waleran said he was weak and I hoped to rule the Church in England as I ruled the realm? Is it not just therefore that this weakling be unable to help me? And why should I complain of one more traitor or try to make his change hard when others change even faster without asking my permission?"

"My lord, listen to me—"

But he shook his head and soon after that he absolved Theobald of his oath to serve him and "graciously" permitted him to swear to the empress instead. Next, I knew, would come the formal abdication, and I was torn between my hope that it would lead to freedom and my fear that it would lead to death. I felt helpless to bring the king to resist, and no longer was sure I should try. Why should I cause him pain when his case was hopeless? And then I wondered if I was so ready to believe the case hopeless because I hoped for freedom once the king yielded his

crown. It was no merry treadmill my thoughts went round
on, but I never did need to decide what to say or do. The
date of the council, which Theobald had told the king,
passed, but no triumphant message came from Matilda nor
any word of a coronation.

Then one day near the end of April when I was pacing
the wall, looking north toward the hills of Wales, beyond
which though many miles away lay Ulle, a middle-aged
man came and stood in my path. I did not know him, and I
did not much like his looks. He had the face of one who
has suffered too many disappointments, hard eyes and a
thin mouth that turned down at the corners. I almost turned
and went the other way, but then I thought it wrong to be
so churlish—some of the men in Bristol keep had sought
out of kindness to lighten my captivity with talk and
invitations to gamble or drink with them—so I nodded at
him but without speaking, hoping he would let me pass
by.

Instead, he put out his hand to detain me and said,
"You are the king's man, are you not?"

"I am," I said, instantly alert because he had used the
word king. The other men in the keep either avoided
referring to the king, called him "your master" out of
politeness, or named him Lord Stephen.

"I have a word of news for him. Tell him, from Sir
Grolier d'Estaple, that the council did not go as the Great
Lady desired. Few bishops came and the delegation from
London did *not* invite her to come to their city or to be
crowned at Westminster. Instead they begged the council
to free the king. Moreover, Winchester could not prevent
Queen Maud's clerk from reading aloud a letter from her
begging the bishops to remember their oaths to King Stephen. It is said that some were much shaken."

There was no one near enough to hear, and he smiled as
he spoke, as if he talked of some light matter. "Thank
you," I said, shaking my head as if denying an invitation.
"I will tell him."

He shrugged to show he had accepted my "refusal,"
and we parted, he going on past and I continuing ahead.
To tell the truth, the news confused me more than it made

me happy. Until now we had heard nothing except what
Matilda or Gloucester wanted us to hear. We had been
given news of each defection from Stephen's cause to that
of Matilda and heard that Hervey Brito had lost Devizes
keep to a crowd of common folk and had fled back to
Brittany as had Count Alan, who had lost control of
Cornwall. I knew, of course, that we would be told only
what could lower the king's spirit; nonetheless, over the
two months we had been imprisoned, without realizing it,
I had begun to believe that the whole country, like so
many of his earls, had deserted Stephen without a struggle.

It took me a long time to absorb what I had heard, and
part of that time I kept telling myself Sir Grolier was
lying, that I did not like his looks, that it was not reasonable that one of Gloucester's men should carry good news
to Stephen. I was pacing fast along the wall; when I
realized I had gone all the way around, no short distance,
and was back where Grolier had spoken to me, I stopped.
Then I had to ask myself why I was denying the truth of
the news Grolier had brought? The answer was not flattering to me. I resisted because I was, at heart, as bad as the
king. I had given up hope, and I did not wish to hear good
news because it woke hope in me—and hope hurt.

Then I asked myself whether it was the king's fault or
mine that my efforts could not cheer him? The answer was
that I had doubtless done the king more harm than good.
Now I realized I had always spoken like a beaten man,
urging Stephen to stand firm in defeat but never holding
out hope that those loyal to him could bring about his
restoration. Full of guilt, I now went quickly to the chamber where I had left Stephen lying on his bed and staring
into nothing. He was still there, and I shook his arm.

"Thank God you had not gone out into the hall," I said
when he looked at me. "I have good news, my lord."

"*Good* news?" Stephen echoed.

"One came to me on the wall where none could hear,
by name Sir Grolier d'Estaple—"

"Estaple?" Stephen interrupted. "That is near by
Boulogne."

"Can he be the queen's servant?" I breathed and then

told the king what Sir Grolier had said about Winchester's council.

"So London has refused her," Stephen said slowly.

"But is it true, my lord?" I asked uneasily. "Of course, if Sir Grolier is Queen Maud's man . . . I have never seen him here before that I can remember."

"I do not know the name," Stephen admitted. "What does the man look like?"

I described him, but the king shook his head. "I do not know him, not by word anyway. If I saw him, perhaps—"

"I do not know where he went," I said. "He acted as if he did not want to draw notice, and if that is true it would be a mistake for me to seem to be seeking someone."

"He found you once," the king said, "he will find you again if necessary." He seemed to have lost interest in Sir Grolier, and looked away from me, but he murmured to himself again, "So London refused her."

The king was quite correct that there was no need to seek Sir Grolier. A few days later, he found me again while I was pacing the wall. He had more words of hope. William of Ypres had never wavered in his loyalty to Stephen. Ypres now had Kent under firm control and mercenaries were coming from Flanders.

"Can you not come to the king?" I asked. "I left him in his chamber, and I am sure he would wish to thank you himself for your kindness in bringing this news."

His mouth twitched. "You are generous," he said. "Most servants prefer to carry good news themselves and only invite the bearers of ill tidings to speak directly to their masters."

I do not know why that struck a sour note with me. It was, I suppose, true for some, and as I have said, Sir Grolier had the look of a disappointed man, but I told him, "There is no need to call me generous. The king said he would like to see you himself."

"Then I will gladly go, but I do not think it would be wise for us both to walk in together. If you will give me your cloak, I doubt any will look carefully enough to see that it is not you."

That made me uneasy, but why should I doubt the man?

What purpose could he have other than seeking favor with the king? And if he sought favor, was that not a hopeful sign? Surely the king could do him no favor until he came into power again. Then Grolier certainly must hope and possibly even expect that Stephen would be restored. We went into the shadow of a tower and exchanged cloaks, and I stayed there, leaning against the wall so I would be out of sight. Sir Grolier was not long away, and when he had given me back my cloak I went down to the bailey before I returned to Stephen's chamber, as if I had carried a message to the kitchen so that none should wonder why I went out twice.

Because I was uneasy, I asked as soon as I came into the king's chamber whether Sir Grolier was Maud's man.

"No," Stephen replied, smiling broadly but speaking in the same hushed tone I had used. "He is sworn to Gloucester and left Estaple many years ago, but for old deeds done by Maud's father, he says, he feels obliged to do for me what he can. Is it not excellent to find a friend amongst our enemies?"

This answer made me no easier. Could we trust a man who, in a way, was betraying his master? Yet did he think of the news he brought Stephen as a betrayal of Gloucester? Likely he thought it could do his own master no harm, or did not think at all. Probably I was again drawing too fine a line, and I could not bring myself to mention my doubts to the king. This second dose of hope had affected him more than the first. Why should I be a black crow and spoil the brightness for him by mouthing suspicions for which I had no real cause? Stephen's eyes were bright, but he was sensible enough to keep his voice low as we discussed the chances Ypres and Maud had of protecting London and thus preventing Matilda's coronation.

I must admit the talk did not lighten *my* heart much. If Queen Maud was successful in her resistance and the war continued, Stephen, and of course I too, had no hope of being freed until the rebels were desperate—and from the way the war had gone until the battle of Lincoln, that might be many years. Stephen was not thinking about that problem yet. I do not believe he was really thinking about

the military situation he was talking about. At this time
what was most important was that he had *not* been abandoned by all.

Over the next few days, Sir Grolier came twice more,
each time speaking to the king alone by coming to him
while I was out. That did not trouble me, although now I
think I should have wondered why a man in Gloucester's
service should be so eager to speak alone with the king.
Then I did not think of it; I was accustomed to the fact that
men who wished to curry favor with the king preferred to
present their cases in private. Each time Sir Grolier brought
the king a few tidbits of fresh hope, as if he spent his time
fishing for news and brought in his catch every few days.
One time he had discovered that the earl of Surrey and the
earl of Northampton had gone to the queen and pledged
their support; another time he reported that William Martel
had refused to yield Sherborne Castle even in the face of
excommunication.

After that visit the king had begun to think in terms of
waging war rather than in terms of being still loved by
those he had uplifted and enriched, and he soon came to
the unpleasant conclusion I had reached immediately. "I
am glad I still have friends, Bruno," he said, frowning,
"but unless some great victory is achieved very soon, you
and I are likely to grow old here."

Since it was highly preferable to me to have a lively and
hopeful companion than one who lay and looked at the
walls or wept and raged, I temporized rather than agreeing. "That may be true, my lord," I admitted, "but it is
also possible that some other medium of exchange—"

Stephen cut me off with a sharp negative. "There is too
great advantage in keeping me. They have a leader; my
force has none. Even the faithful grow weary when there is
no symbol around which to rally. Time will favor them.
There is only one answer. We must escape."

Every particle of my being leapt up in response to those
words. I am sure the king saw my eagerness because he
gripped my arm so hard his fingers left marks. God knows
for me it sounded like salvation. I had never been asked to

give my parole—I do not know whether Gloucester had simply forgotten me or considered me unimportant or believed I would be bound by the king's vow; whatever the reason, he had not asked me to swear to accept captivity in lieu of physical chains. But the king had so sworn.

"My lord," I whispered, "you know I am willing, but you will have violated your assurance to Gloucester that you would not seek to gain your freedom. If we are not successful, I think you will be made to pay."

"Pay what?" Stephen asked, his voice hushed but his eyes alight. "My life? That will not be so high a price. Can what we live here be truly called a life? And even if I die, there will be gains. Matilda will then hold no pawn that can be used to blunt an attack on her. Eustace is nigh old enough to rule, and betrothed to Constance as he is, he can call in the full power of the king of France. No, Bruno, I am not afraid to die. Are you?"

When he spoke like that, gaily and proudly in the face of danger, a finger of the old magic that had bound me to him touched me—but it was only a finger, not a hand that could grasp me and hold me. I loved him, for he had great courage and it was true he did not fear death—but that was only because, like a child, he did not really believe it could happen to him.

"Yes," I said bluntly, "I am afraid to die, but I am not much worried about dying. Remember that Gloucester never threatened death. You said yourself, my lord, that you are worth too much alive. He said chains. If you are caught, they will make you suffer, not kill you."

"Well, that will have a benefit too." He grinned at me. "If Maud hears that I am ill-treated, she will move heaven and earth to free me at once. She is cautious by nature and might delay long waiting for the best time if she believes I am safe and comfortable."

Later that remark added to my anxieties, for I knew what the king said was true, and if the queen was made desperate, she might attack and fail. But at the moment Stephen named his wife, all I could think of was my own. I had not thought about Melusine by day for a long time—I was not quite so successful at keeping my fears and my desires out of my dreams at night and woke quite often sobbing, my pallet all wet with tears. At first I had spent a great part of my many idle hours recalling our times together. However, as my captivity lengthened, I found it necessary to stop myself from thinking of Melusine. It was not only my desire for her that tormented me—I would have welcomed that torment gladly—but I was afraid.

I knew that it was only Maud's fear of Stephen's displeasure that had protected Melusine and forced the queen to keep her among her ladies before we were married. Perhaps Maud had come to suspect Melusine less, but would she welcome my wife as a companion in this dreadful time? Was it not more likely that the queen would use her as a scapegoat for the real enemies she could not reach?

I told myself again and again that Maud was a kind and sensible woman and that she must have come to like and value Melusine, but with each piece of bad news I grew less hopeful. I had visions of Melusine abandoned without money, without a single man to protect her—for I thought then that Fechin, Cormi, and Merwyn had been killed or taken prisoner in the battle. What would Melusine do? How could she make her way across a war-torn country to the safety of Jernaeve? When I imagined what might happen to a woman traveling alone through a country infested by outlaws and marauding war bands, I beat my fists bloody against the wall.

After that, I knew I would have to give up the joy of thinking of Melusine or go mad. But when Stephen spoke of Maud, I was off guard. Maud's name instantly brought into my mind what I had seen so often in the past: the queen in her chair by the fire and Melusine close by, sitting on a stool with her embroidery on her lap, looking up and holding out a hand to me. I was seized by so violent a pang of longing that my eyes filled with tears and I turned away. Stephen seized my arm.

"Have you changed your mind at the thought of chains? Do you fear them worse than death?" he asked with a sneer.

Rage leapt up to burn Melusine out of my mind. How dare Stephen sneer at me? It was not I who wept like a

babe with hopelessness and blamed everyone but myself
for my ills. "Yes, I fear them worse," I told him coldly,
"since they are more likely to be my fate than death, but I
fear nothing so much I will not perform my duty and obey
you."

As soon as he saw he would get his way, Stephen was
all smiles again. He had not even noticed that he had hurt
me and that I was angry. He thought his sneer had erased
my doubts. "You worry too much," he said. "We will
not be caught. When shall we go?"

Did he expect me to say, "Now" and lead him out of
the keep and through the city of Bristol? If so, he was
sadly disappointed. I pointed out the difficulties and the
need of making plans. "The guards may have grown less
watchful than they were at first, but even blind guards
would notice if we just walked out."

He laughed and struck me lightly with his fist. "Then
let us make plans if we must, but they must not delay our
freedom too long lest the rising hope of which Grolier
speaks be crushed."

Stephen's idea of making plans was suggesting that we
enter the forbidden armory, seize weapons and armor if we
could find it, and fight our way out. When I remembered
the dead around him at Lincoln, the idea did not seem
quite as ridiculous as it would have been for another man;
however, as I reminded him, numbers would pull down
any man at last, no matter how strong.

"They did not pull me down," he said pettishly. "No
man could come so close. My helm was lost, and I was
stunned by a stone. There are no stones here."

"No," I snapped, "but there are clubs and knives and
spears. And even if we could fight free of the keep, there
is the whole city to traverse. How can we do that if a hue
and cry were raised?"

"How can we escape without a hue and cry being
raised? I did not mean that we should start a fight here in
the keep. I thought we could go quietly, kill the guards at
the gate, and run. You said yourself that we cannot simply
walk out."

"We cannot walk out as ourselves, but if we were

disguised as serfs who have come in to do a day's labor, we could walk out. It is possible that none would notice we were missing for some hours, and by then we could be out in the countryside. Who would notice two poor hinds trudging from one task to another?"

Stephen looked at me as if I had grown two heads, but after some discussion he began to see the merits of the idea—or to think that it would be an amusing adventure. Anyway, he entered into my attempts to obtain disguises for us with an enthusiasm that grew greater with each of Grolier's continued tidbits of hopeful news. The first step was to get my hands on money—that did not have to be done secretly; I could pretend I wanted it for the games of chance I had often been invited to join.

It was easier than I expected. I was able to sell, as a keepsake, one of Stephen's shirts embroidered by Maud with the arms of England. I think the man who bought it believed I had stolen it from my master, but it was Stephen who had suggested that I sell everything I could. He pointed out, we could not take anything with us so we might as well get what we could from the garments we would have to abandon. Unfortunately I could not sell much because I was afraid that would arouse suspicion.

The next step was to steal from the serfs. I hoped my depredations would arouse no outcry because I left a silver coin for each ragged garment I took, and that hope was fulfilled. In less than a week, I had collected two ragged cloaks and two dirty tunics. Such garments were often laid aside for mornings were cool in May, whereas hard work warmed a man in the afternoon when the sun shone. The tunics gave me the most trouble because there were few serfs who were as large as Stephen and me. I could not get braies or shoes and stockings at all. Men do not take those off, and I could not get into the outer bailey where the huts of the demesne serfs were. Finally I realized I could make those from our own garments by tearing and befouling them with water and soil.

I had to be careful in gathering and bringing in the soil, but there was still some awe of the king and I think Gloucester had ordered that he be treated with respect.

None came into his chamber without invitation, so I could hide both what I did and the besmirched garments without danger. It was just as well for another reason too. Once Stephen had got over the shock of the idea of wearing torn and soiled garments, he seemed to find it a novelty. Twice I came in to find him trying them out to see which filthy tunic and ragged cloak better befit him. I warned him of the danger to us if anyone at all saw him, and I thought he looked guilty and that there was an uneasy note in his laugh when he assured me that no one knew of the disguise. I suppressed my doubts. I could not believe he would lie on so important a subject.

We were ready by the middle of May. It was a poor time for such an escape because dusk lasted a long time, unlike winter when dark came swiftly on the setting of the sun. However, to delay would only make that problem worse, and we were presented with a temptation we could not resist only one day after I had assembled everything I could for our escape. Because the king was confined in Bristol keep, many more men than usual were quartered in the place. That meant that more supplies came in, that more garbage was created and needed to be removed. It was the coming and going of serfs and villiens who were not well known to the guards upon which I had counted to allow us to leave without question.

I had intended to make the king watch the behavior of these people and try to imitate it for a few days. He laughed at me at first, but when I insisted he come down to the bailey with me and pointed out the differences, he admitted grudgingly that the demeanor of the knights, who walked proudly erect with heads high and eyes either fixed ahead or staring haughtily at some person or object, was not like that of a serf. A serf, even the young whose bodies were still straight, always went with bowed head and with eyes that flicked here and there, watching for a summons or an order or a blow.

When we were alone again, Stephen praised me for my ability to notice such a thing and asked how I had come to look so carefully at the serfs. I reminded him flatly that so had my mother walked and looked and so would I had not

Audris loved me and Sir Oliver been a good and honorable man. The king then looked a little embarrassed and agreed to practice that evening after we were supposed to be asleep, but he seemed to scorn his role. To my fury he laughed and appeared almost proud at his lack of success. After I pointed out that failure and a life in chains would be the price of his pride, he worked a little more earnestly at being humble and frightened. I think I would have given up then if I had not known that nothing could turn Stephen from this attempt.

Then, before my resentment faded there came the temptation that seemed so good a stroke of fortune that we would deserve to fail if we ignored it. Not only were more supplies needed owing to the large garrison in the keep, but the garderobe filled more quickly so it was necessary to remove the waste often. Usually this was only done when the lords had left and the keep was near empty, but Gloucester was taking no chance of transporting the king around England. For one thing, there was no equally safe and strong place to keep Stephen; for another, taking him into the open was just asking for an attempt to rescue him by a strong attack. Thus, the very day after Stephen had taken so lightly the need to imitate a serf, a large group of them was admitted to clear out the garderobe in addition to the group delivering supplies and carting garbage out to be rotted and used on the fields.

Stephen saw them from the window of his antechamber and rushed out to find me on the walls. I had seen them also and cursed them for coming a few days too soon, but when the king gripped my arm and said, "Today I will go," I did not protest. I knew protest would be useless; he was so set now on this escape that he would go without me if I refused, and that my duty would not permit. Besides, in such a crowd we might truly go unnoticed, and the need to clear the garderobe would not come again for several months.

"Very well, my lord, today," I agreed. "Do not eat your dinner—I will give you mine if you are sharp-set— and go down several times to the privy wearing your cloak. If someone asks, say you are chilled. I will ask for a physician later in the day, saying you are purging. Do not let him bleed you. I will replace the medicine he compounds with wine or water. One of the times you go to the privy, I will come and we will choose a place for you to hide. Just before dusk, go again to the privy, hiding the serf's garments under your cloak. Change, and remain hidden. I will come in a few minutes, don your cloak, and return to your chamber.''

''Then how will you come out? I am not so sure of how to slip into a group of those people.''

''I will make your cloak and other garments into a body in your bed and just walk out, saying the physician's remedy has worked at last, that your belly gripes are finally stilled, and that you are asleep. I am so often in and out of your chamber that none will remember I have not returned, or they will think I am walking the walls, as I often do, even after dark.''

I was not very excited at first. Stephen's light attitude toward the details of our escape had lessened my hope of success, but as the day passed, my excitement grew. The king's acting of his illness was so fine that he not only fooled the physician into real anxiety but nearly convinced *me* his belly pained—enough so that when we were alone I asked if he were too sick to go. He laughed at me so hard, he nearly brought up what he had eaten of my dinner.

He was perfect too in groaning that this was an evil day for serfs to be working in the garderobe. He cursed the physician roundly for saying, sick as he was he should use the chamber pot, shouting that he was not a babe nor yet so weak—although he knew they all desired he grow weak and die—that he must perch on a pot. The physician swore a hundred times that the last thing any of them desired was that he die and that Gloucester would doubtless have his head if Lord Stephen did not recover. Then he bade him use the garderobe anyway, saying it would not matter to the creatures cleaning it if he shit on their heads, but the king said indignantly that he would not so treat a dog or a horse, nor even a pig, and would not so treat a human servant either.

Then he shouted at me that he needed no man to watch

him and drove me out of the chamber. Nor would he allow me to help him to the privy when I offered to lend him my arm because he seemed doubled over with pain. Thus, out of courtesy the men looked aside and did not stare at him when he struggled down the stairs to shit and crept up again as if spent.

I managed to dispose of whatever medicine the physician compounded, and Stephen cleverly pretended that the dose had helped, sending for the physician and thanking him for his new ease. But late in the afternoon, he staggered out of his chamber again and called for another dose of the drug. Then he pretended to sleep until the last time. After I had crept back in his cloak, I came out in my own and went for a third dose. Then I remained in the chamber for a little while before I came out with my own serf's garments under my cloak. My heart leapt into my mouth when the constable stopped me, but it was only to ask how my master fared and I said he slept but lightly and I thought I would leave him alone until he was deeply asleep, so that any small noise I might make would not disturb him. I hoped, I added, that none other would disturb him.

When I had changed, I found a broken fork and a dull wooden spade and we went and joined a group that was dumping soil into a nearly full cart. Stephen did far better at looking cowed and frightened than I expected. We had smeared our faces with dirt and to my joy it had started to rain, so we could pull our hoods over our heads. Still when the cart moved out, I could not believe we would escape. I was so sure we would be stopped that I had to force myself forward as we drew near the gate, and I did not dare look back at Stephen, who was a step behind me, but I was sure he had forgotten to slump his shoulders like a beaten man and hang his head. But the guards on the gate of the inner bailey seemed indifferent, and the cart went onto the inner drawbridge with us behind it.

That changed everything. It was the guards on the inner gate that I feared most; they would be the ones most watchful for an attempt at escape. So when we came off the drawbridge, I began to shake with eagerness, needing to think of holding my feet to a dull, exhausted trudge when every instinct bade me run ahead out of the outer gate to freedom. It was torture to keep to the slow pace of the oxen, but they did advance foot by foot, and after what seemed like a thousand years, I heard a kind of echo of the creak and groan of the cartwheels that told me we were near the wall. Then I risked a glance and caught my breath. We were right at the gates, which were open, and the attention of the guards was on a group of men who seemed to have just entered.

Just as I lowered my head to better hide my face, I heard a cry of pain from one of the serfs ahead. I reached out for Stephen to remind him he must not resist—but it was too late. I saw a staff rise and strike him, heard his roar of rage, saw him leap on the man who had struck him and bear him down. I leapt too, knowing we were lost but throwing myself over the king to save him, I thought, from being beaten to death. But it was a knife not a cudgel that came down and struck me.

CHAPTER 24

Melusine

SELFISH! Self-indulgent monster! The voice was the queen's, but the words were those my mother had said to me after my brothers died of the plague that had taken so many lives in Ulle on my thirteenth birthday. I felt dazed and confused, most aware of the stinging of my cheeks where Maud's slaps had struck.

"But that was because of papa," I said. "Because I was making papa sick with worry."

"Your father is dead!" the queen shrieked, slapping me once more. "Long dead!"

I lifted my head and focussed my eyes on her face. She was bent above me, and to my surprise it was concern not rage that I saw, but I could not answer her.

"It is your *husband* to whom you owe your support," she said fiercely, although she was no longer shouting. "He has supported you and protected you, even against my will. Do you owe him nothing? And he is in prison, chained like a beast by the order of that monster Matilda. Melusine, do you hear me?"

"I hear you, madam."

"Then listen well. I will not stay long in Westminster. I will go first to Essex and root out any man who has ever been favored by Geoffrey de Mandeville and at the same time draw a heavy war levy, leaving some Boulognese troops to protect the province. As soon as I have news of where Matilda lies, I will follow. I will raise every city she enters against her, for the towns love Stephen, and I will hound her from place to place until she disgorges my man. You may not care that Bruno will rot in captivity, but I am not willing to accept that fate for my husband. I will be glad of your help and your company, Melusine, but if you wish to sit and stare at walls as you did when the king first put you in my care, I will leave you. I have no strength to carry dead wood with me now."

She straightened up, turned, and left the room, and I suddenly realized that I was sitting on the floor in a chamber looted of everything. I put my hands to my cheeks, which burned anew, this time with shame. What kind of woman was I that my answer to a disappointment was to become mad? No more. Never again. If I could not face the horror and grief of my life, I would take my sister Mildred's path and walk into the water. I would *not* be dead wood, a burden to everyone, needing to be told to stand and sit, to eat and drink.

I tried to rise, but my whole body was stiff and my legs would not support me. How long had I been sitting thus? I tried again, but this time there were hands under my arms, helping me, and Edna's voice, trembling as she asked, "Are you well, my lady?"

"I am well now, Edna," I said.

"I did not know the queen would be so angry," she whispered. "I tried and tried to make you get up or tell me why you were sitting there, and then I grew frightened and . . . and I told the queen."

"Thank God you did," I said, leaning on her and walking about the chamber. Now I saw it was not totally empty. In the corner behind me there was a stool. I moved toward it, tempted to sit down again, but each step was easier, and in a few minutes I let go of Edna to walk on my own. When I was steady on my feet, I came to her and put my hand on her shoulder. "Thank you, Edna. That was a brave deed. Queen Maud is so busy, it could not have been easy to get leave to speak to her."

"It was not hard." She grinned up at me. "I did not ask

for leave. I just walked up to the guards and called out to her. Everyone was so shocked that I should walk past all the great ones and cry for help, that no one tried to stop me.'' Then she grew solemn, her eyes large with remembered amazement. ''And the queen was so good. She bade all those high-born men wait and came at once when I told her you were sick and I could not rouse you.''

I felt tears sting my eyes. Maud *had* been very good to leave such important matters to come to me. Her words and blows were sharp, but so had my mother's been, and only for my good. ''Yes,'' I said to Edna, ''she is a good woman. I am sorry I frightened you, but if it should happen again that I do not answer you for a long time, do as the queen did—I mean, cause me pain. That will wake me.''

''But my lady—''

''Never mind that now,'' I interrupted. ''I am famished. See if you can find me something to eat and drink. Anything will do.'' As I spoke we walked to the door. I hoped Edna did not notice how my breath caught and I said quickly, ''Bring the food here. I fear I will have no chance to eat if I go where the queen is.''

I was afraid to admit to Edna and to myself too, that I did not know where I was, so I turned my back on the huge empty chamber and gestured toward the small room. Edna ran off and I turned back to the great chamber. It was a hall, a hall in Westminster—surely the queen said we were in Westminster. I was not so mad as not to be able to remember what had been said to me only a few minutes before, was I? And the place was not completely empty. As in the smaller chamber, I had not noticed that there were broken bits of this and that—a leg of a stool, a strip of cloth that had been white and was now marked with smudges where someone had stepped on it, half a trestle for supporting tables. And then I suddenly knew where I was. I had not recognized the place because each time I had seen it before it had been crowded with tables and benches and people—people eating, laughing, talking, sometimes dancing. I was looking at the king's hall, and the chamber in which I had been sitting on the floor was the king's private closet.

My first sensation was shock, my second regret that my foolishness had forced the queen to come here; it must have hurt her to see the place empty and looted. Then I fetched the stool and sat down and asked myself what I was doing here. It was not a place that could have drawn me by familiarity; the place I knew best in Westminster was the queen's hall and her private chamber where I worked. Why should I come to the king's hall? Why should I, who had never entered it before in my whole life, sit down to wait—forever if need be—in the king's private chamber? What was I seeking here in my madness? I never came to the king's hall except . . . except in Bruno's company or to find Bruno.

Bruno. I had come seeking Bruno in my madness. I could not lie about that to myself any longer. And if I sought him when I was mad, then was he not the center of my life? The center of my life . . . yet he was the man who most likely killed my father and my brother. That was how it was done, to give the female to the victor. He had been the one to burst in the door of the hall at Ulle; he had taken the manor, that was certain. And I had been given to him, that was also certain. Was it not most likely that he had been allowed to take Ulle because in a sense he had already won it over my father's and brother's dead bodies?

I shuddered so hard the legs of the stool creaked, but I hardly heard that. I heard the queen. "Your father is dead. Long dead."

Did that wipe out my duty to him? He had cared for me and protected me . . . But the queen's voice overrode that thought too, angry, demanding. "It is your *husband* to whom you owe your support . . . he has protected you even against my will." It was true. But only because he wanted Ulle. No, that was a lie and I had come to the end of lying—that led only to a dark place where I sat on the floor and stared at the wall. Bruno wanted *me*—not Ulle, not even my body, although he took pleasure in both—he wanted my love. Papa had also wanted my love . . . Had he? Papa had wanted my devotion, which was a very different thing, not an equal sharing but a greater and a lesser—and papa was dead. Dead. Bruno was in chains and might soon be dead.

I found myself on my feet, my hand on my eating knife and ready to run . . . to Bruno, to keep him alive. Papa was dead and Bruno was still alive. Papa was dead. I could remember him; I could still love him, but I could not let his cold hand again draw me down the path that led to sitting on the floor in an empty chamber, deaf, mute, and blind because my duty forbade me to do what I desired with all my heart, all my mind, and all my soul. The queen was right. I could no longer pretend that I was loyal to papa as long as I did nothing myself to help Bruno.

My duty was a dead weight on me, crushing me; I must cast that aside. There were things, real things I could do to help Bruno. I could bring men from Ulle and there was silver in the strongbox. I could hire other men to fight with the queen. Sir Gerald could lead them. I could go to Audris. Jernaeve was rich; Audris would lend me or give me money to buy more men. Some might even come for the pure pleasure of fighting against Matilda, even though King David's son was now their overlord and King David was with the empress. But King Stephen was Henry's overlord, not his father, and I knew the men of Northumbria did not love the Scots.

Edna came with my food—cold meat and bread and ale, and I ate with an appetite that I had not felt since the news of Bruno's capture. When I was full, I went to the queen's private chamber and waited, thanking God that I had done my accounts before Ypres returned with the news that the empress had escaped him. The queen did not come in until very late, and she looked tired. Nonetheless, I came and knelt beside her chair and thanked her for her kindness to me.

"So," she said, "have you decided who you are?"

"Yes, madam," I replied. "I am the wife of Bruno of Jernaeve, and I love my husband as you love yours."

"Very good." She offered me a tired smile and leaned her head against the high back of her chair. Her eyes began to close, and her hand lifted to wave me away.

I caught the hand. "Madam, a moment more, I beg you."

She turned her head a fraction. "Yes?" There was a weary patience in her voice, the patience of one who has begun a task, now almost regrets it, but cannot leave it unfinished.

"I can bring men to swell your army."

Maud's eyes snapped open and she jerked upright. I almost chuckled with amusement although I had deliberately said that to catch her attention when I knew she expected me to trouble her with some silly personal doubts.

After staring at me for longer than I liked, she said, "Yes, I believe you have decided who you are. But have you told me the truth?"

I was not shocked. Little as I knew about armies and battles, even an idiot could understand that an open enemy is less dangerous than an ally who knows your plans and betrays you. I knew too that Maud had never fully trusted me although I felt she had come to be truly fond of me. I had had several hours to consider what to say, and now I smiled.

"I have told you the truth, but if you will give a moment's thought to the matter, you will see that it does not matter. The only thing I am sure papa would want me to do—" A little chill went down my back as I thought of the kind of revenge papa would really want on the man who killed him, but that had nothing to do with who was king or queen. "—is to regain Ulle. I have a good hope of getting Ulle, or of Bruno getting it, from King Stephen. I have no hope of that from Matilda, even if I could get King David to make his son enfeoff Bruno or me. She would see me dead first for refusing her command to accompany her into Bristol. And she hates Bruno worse than me because he flouted her will more than once on our journey. And even if that is a lie and she promised me Ulle to come and spy on you, do you think me such an idiot as to still believe she will keep a promise to me, who will not keep them to the bishop of Winchester or to Robert of Gloucester?"

Maud herself had to smile at my reasoning, but the smile faded as she went back over what I had said and saw that I had indeed covered every excuse for disloyalty. She frowned and looked uneasy and there was a pettish note in her voice as she asked, "How many men, and from where?"

"I can only be sure of about fifty from Ulle with a

knight to lead them, but it may be possible for me to bring many more, several hundred I believe. Bruno's sister, Audris of Jernaeve, is rich. I am sure she will lend me, or even give me, money to buy mercenaries. There are many in the north who do not love the king of Scotland and who will come to fight against him—and against Empress Matilda.''

Maud knew that was true; she had received bitter and angry delegations from northern baronial leaders about the peace treaty she had made with King David. She shifted uneasily in her seat and finally said, ''I will mention the matter to Ypres.''

''Thank you, madam,'' I said. ''That is all I desired. I would not have troubled you with this today when I knew you to be tired, only I was afraid I would have no chance to speak in the morning and that might cost me another full day. Jernaeve and Cumbria are far north and west.''

To my surprise, the queen suddenly looked very pleased, patted my hand, and promised that if Ypres thought my idea worthwhile and if I indeed did bring several hundred men who fought well in King Stephen's cause, I _should_ have Ulle. It took me a while, lying sleepless on my pallet, to come to the conclusion that Maud's suspicions had been increased by my approaching her privately in her chamber. She had probably believed that I chose to speak when she was weary in the hope she would seize on my offer while her mind was muddled with fatigue and sorrow and let me go at once.

That gave me hope that the queen had found my offer very attractive—she always mistrusted herself when she had an instant liking for something—which meant my idea was good. Indeed, it proved so, for I was summoned from the queen's chamber to repeat what I hoped to do to Ypres. He did not seem much interested in the men from Ulle, thank God; I had been afraid to speak about Sir Gerald lest his connection with my father make the queen and Ypres more suspicious. What Ypres was most interested in was who I expected to lead the Northumbrian troops.

''I do not know,'' I told him. ''I know nothing of war, but Sir Hugh of Jernaeve—he that was Hugh Licorne before he wed with Bruno's sister—will find a man for me who will be wise, strong, and trustworthy, I am sure.''

"Licorne." Ypres's voice became eager. "If you are wise, you will beg him to come himself, Lady Melusine.''

"No!" I exclaimed. "You think me a selfish monster indeed if you believe I would call my sister's husband to war in the rescue of mine. I will beg for money. I will beg for men. I will do everything a woman can do to raise as large a force as I can. But I will also do everything in my power to *prevent* Hugh from being involved in any fighting.''

I did. I swear I did everything I could to keep Hugh from leading my small army, but it was all in vain. Despite my need, I would never have gone to Jernaeve at all if I believed he would think of joining the fight to save Stephen unless I asked it of him. I am sure Bruno never told me that Hugh had once promised to take service with the king when his old master, Sir Walter Espec, no longer needed him. The king had freed Hugh from that promise when he did homage for Jernaeve in Audris's name, but Hugh was like papa and Bruno; he did not forget old promises.

Did Ypres know? Was that the reason that he advised me to ride straight north to Jernaeve rather than northwest to Ulle? He said it was safer, that the whole central part of the country was seething with unrest, with war bands marching to and fro and outlaws attacking travelers and merchants. He took the trouble to speak to Fechin and Merwyn and describe a route that should safely bypass the strongholds of Matilda's supporters. And we did come safely to Jernaeve, only once having hidden in a wood while a troop marched by and once having outrun a party that rushed out at us from a ruined village.

Hugh and Audris were at the lower gate to meet us, Audris's face whiter than bone and her eyes round with terror. She had been weaving and from her tower window had seen Fechin on Barbe before we crossed the ford. As I had, she feared Bruno was dead. I had forgot she might recognize Barbe, and though I had written to Audris almost every month ever since I had been with her in Jernaeve, I had not told her Bruno had been taken prisoner because I knew she was with child again and was afraid to cause her worry.

So my tale burst from my lips before I had even dismounted from Vinaigre—at least I cried out that Bruno was alive and with the king. Before I could say more, Audris flew from tears to joy. I did not think that unreasonable, for I had felt the same, and she began at once to talk of ransom.

"Hush, love," Hugh said. "Bruno will not leave the king. If he had desired to be ransomed, we would have heard the terms long ago. Remember that the king was taken prisoner in February, and this is July. Let us go back into the keep so Melusine can rest and eat. Ride up," Hugh urged me, but I shook my head and dismounted.

"I hope you do not blame me for lying to you," I said, taking Audris's hand. "I was afraid—"

She patted her belly, which was large, with her free hand and shook her head. Then, still holding me, she began to walk across the bailey. Her step was not as light as usual, but she was breathing easily and I was astonished when Hugh picked her up and began to carry her up the steep path to the keep. She said once, "Put me down," but when he did not, she only sighed and did not protest again.

I poured out the rest of my news on our way into the keep, and Hugh shouted with pleasure when he heard that the empress had been driven out of London and had fled with no more than the clothes on her back. However, they would not let me explain my business until I had bathed and eaten, and I was glad of it. I found it harder than I thought to ask for money, but Audris laughed at me and waved her hand, brushing away any thought of debt.

"I am alive only because of Bruno's care of me," she said. "Between my brother and me there can be no thought of debt. Money is lightly come by. A few tapestries and a few hawks will pay for all."

"Bruno will not agree," I said, smiling at her. "You know that."

"Bruno will have nothing to say about it," Audris replied. "If you do not tell him, he will not know."

Hugh laughed. "We will see. Men may cost less than

you think, Melusine. I will send out a summons and send
this news to Espec. You may not need to bear the burden
of the force we raise. Leave that to me.''

''But will not that make trouble for you with your
overlord?'' I asked fearfully. ''I know Henry is King
Stephen's vassal, but he is also King David's son. I thought
he could not blame you if I hired men in the queen's
name. He could not know you had given me the coin to
pay them.''

''I hold directly from Stephen,'' Hugh said. ''Henry has
no right over my service to the king.'' Then he smiled at
me. ''And even if he did, I am sure he would look the
other way. Henry does not love Matilda. He was here not
very long ago, bemoaning his father's need to uphold his
oath to her—and Henry never swore that oath.''

I sighed with relief and gladly relinquished the gathering
of men in Northumbria into Hugh's hands. Then I asked
whether he knew a good man to lead them. ''I do not think
my father's old friend Sir Gerald could do it,'' I said. ''He
is loyal and will be able to lead the men from Ulle, but he
always served under papa, and I am not sure how he
would manage men who do not know him. I wish there
were time for me to bring him here so you could talk to
him, but there is not, and Ypres said I must have a good
leader.''

Hugh was looking at me strangely. ''What are you
talking about? If I summon men, I will lead them.''

''No!'' I cried. ''No!''

He looked shocked and hurt. ''Do you not trust me?''

''Trust you? What has that to do with it? Must I sacrifice my sister's husband to regain my own? No! Not you! I
will do without the men from Northumbria. Curse me that
I ever came here. No! Is it not evil enough on my soul that
I will send an old friend to die?''

Audris put her hand on mine. ''Melusine, my love, is
there something you have not told us? Is this cause so
hopeless?''

''No! I swear it is not.'' Tears began to run down my
face and Audris drew me closer on the bench and put her
arms around me. I tried to think. How did I know Maud's
hope was not illusion? I knew because William of Ypres

did not suffer from illusions in matters of war. "It cannot be hopeless because Ypres is burning to begin."

"Oh?" Hugh drew out the word in a pleased way. "How do you know that?"

"I had to explain to him what I wished to do before the queen would give me leave. He told me—well, I did not understand everything so I wrote down all I could remember —but the way he spoke told of his eagerness."

"Good." Hugh's brilliant eyes shone with pleasure. "William of Ypres has his head fixed firmly on his shoulders. He does not indulge himself in dreams. I will want to see what you wrote."

"No!" I said, setting my teeth. "You are not going to war on my account. Audris, forbid him! Beg him!"

"I cannot forbid him," Audris said slowly, "and it would be wrong to beg for what would hurt him. But I will ask." She leaned forward, the better to see her husband, who was sitting in Sir Oliver's chair. "Why, Hugh? Is there no one else fit to lead?"

That was when I learned of Hugh's promise to the king. Audris seemed to know of it, and nodded her head as soon as he reminded her. She sat back then, apparently content to let him go to war, but I did not yield so easily. I wept and pleaded, and Hugh came and joined us on the bench, also embracing and soothing me—but not wavering a whit— until at last I brought out the deepest horror in my mind.

"You must not," I pleaded, and then I wiped the tears from my cheeks and eyes and stood up to face them. "Do you not know that I am death. I told Audris. No man or woman who has loved me has lived out a natural span of life. And it will all be in vain too. When we have captured the empress and bought the king's freedom, Bruno will be dead."

Hugh looked from me to Audris and back again and, to my utter amazement, burst out laughing as he got to his feet. "Now I know why you two loved each other at first sight. One is a witch and the other a prophet, and both are given to imagining horrors that do not come to pass."

Then he grew sober, drew me close, kissed my forehead, and stood back with a hand lightly on my shoulder. "Melusine, you are a very foolish woman. I am sorry there has been so much sadness in your life, but it is not uncommon. I inherited Ruthsson for just the same reason. My grandfather had four sons and three daughters and a pack of grandchildren, and his brother and I are the only two still alive. I forget just what killed each one, but I know that plague and war played their parts as in your family. It did not hurt me as it hurt you because I never knew any of them, did not even know they were my family until long after all were dead, but I do not go about calling myself death personified because I inherited. Now, I will leave you to Audris to sort out, and I will start my messengers on their way.''

"Hugh is quite right," Audris said, holding out her hand to me and drawing me down on the bench beside her again. "Plague and war strike everywhere. You know, my love, that it was only by Bruno's care of me that I survived a plague that killed my father and Bruno's mother and nearly all the people in Jernaeve keep and village. It is no person's fault when such dreadful things happen." She smiled at me. "In some ways you are very like Bruno. He also blames himself for not preventing from happening things that no man could prevent."

I remembered saying that to him myself just before King Stephen had gone to attack Lincoln keep, where he had been captured. I uttered a sob, but smiled at the same time. I was comforted in a sense, but my fear for Hugh still lay, a great weight on my heart. I took Audris's tiny hands in mine.

"Forget my foolishness. But even if I am not something evil that puts a death mark on those who care for me, war is dangerous. Do you not fear for Hugh?"

"Yes," Audris said, "but not beyond measure. I fear for Hugh when he goes out to drive raiders off the land, and even when he rides a new, half-trained horse." She freed one hand and touched my cheek. "But you see, Melusine, in my life mostly good things have happened to me. Thus, I fear in hope, in expectation, that no harm will come to my loved ones. You fear in despair, and that must be an unbelievable pain. I can heal many ills, but I do not know how to heal that."

"It cannot be healed, but you bring me comfort," I told

her, pressing the hand I held. "And I think at long last I am learning to bear it without lying to myself to avoid the pain—which only makes it worse until I find myself sitting on the floor in an empty chamber looking at the wall."

"Oh, Melusine," Audris cried, embracing me and holding me tight. "What happened?"

I told her and was comforted again because she did not scorn me for my weakness or withdraw in horror. "But if no harm comes to Hugh and if Bruno—" I had to swallow as panic closed off my voice, but I did go on. "And if Bruno is restored to me alive, perhaps I will find the bearing easier." I sighed. "Even if I do not, I must learn to bear it, or some day I will go into that dark place and not be able to find my way out again."

"I do not think so," Audris said. Her expression was thoughtful. "I do not think it is the pain of grief you cannot bear. Perhaps the first time it was, that and the fear of your father's disapproval because you had lost Ulle—a fear that would be greater when you knew he was dead because one cannot explain to the dead or get their forgiveness. But in Westminster I think what drove you to hide from yourself was that you could not abandon your need for either your father or your husband. That was the child fighting against the woman. No one wishes to leave childhood behind, and it is true is it not that your father was quick to lift from you any burden you felt was too heavy?"

I stared at her open-mouthed for a moment. True? Of course it was true, all of it, but especially the part about papa lifting burdens from me; in fact, often papa would not give me burdens I wished to carry. Yet I saw at once what Audris meant. Papa was safety. I could turn my back on anything I did not like while papa lived. Bruno was different. He needed my strength as much as I needed his. I nodded at Audris.

"Yes, I was always papa's dear little child."

"Well," Audris said, "you are a woman now." Then she smiled. "I did not like it when it happened to me either. And it is true that a grown-up woman cannot run for help like a child, but a grown-up person may share a heavy burden."

"I have certainly shared mine," I said wryly. "It seems

to me that I have dumped it on you rather than sharing it. And this is a bad time for you, Audris. You are very near your time, are you not? Surely you want Hugh here when you are brought to bed.''

''Want Hugh?'' Audris turned eyes full of horror on me. ''I would not have chosen to have him go to war, but I am almost glad even of that if it will save me from Hugh when I am brought to bed. Is it not bad enough to bear the pangs without needing to comfort someone else? He is not so bad this time. He only asks me *ten* times a day how I feel instead of fifty and only twice or three times instead of ten times carries food to me because I do not eat enough. These last months *are* hard for me because I am small, but I am healthy and strong. You saw him carry me when I could walk. I know it is because he loves me, but still I must bite my tongue not to scream at him.'' Suddenly she giggled. ''Wait, your turn will come. Bruno will be worse than Hugh. I would not be surprised if you *prayed* for a war to take him away.''

I laughed in response, but somewhat uneasily, fearing she was putting a good face over reluctance so that her need would not come before her brother's. ''But you will be alone,'' I said.

''Alone? Do not be silly. My Aunt Eadyth is here and Hugh's Aunt Marie. Both of them have born children and will be of much more help than Hugh. And if strength is needed for something, there is Fritha, my maid. She is as strong as an ox.''

How foolish I was, I thought. Most women looked to other women for help and comfort; naturally Audris would rather have her aunts than an ignorant and frightened man when she was brought to bed. I would prefer women too. It was only out of habit that I thought of a man as bringing comfort. Then I realized that Hugh must not have yet considered that problem and breathed a sigh of relief.

''Hugh will *not* go,'' I said. ''He has not stopped to think how near you are to your time. Whatever you desire, he will not want to leave you.''

''He does not know how near I am to my time,'' Audris said, her eyes dancing with mischief. ''I did not tell him when I first conceived. You remember I wrote you how ill he took it when I lost that babe last year. He wept more than I. This time I waited more than three months, until I was sure the child was well set in me, so he thinks I have yet two months to carry."

"How can he be deceived?" I asked, looking at her.

Audris laughed. "Because this babe is smaller than Eric was even though he was born a month early. Perhaps it is a daughter. And perhaps Hugh does not really want to know, and in his secret heart hopes he will be away when I am brought to bed. I am not sure whether he is truly deceived or only very frightened, but he will go."

She was right, of course, but I left Jernaeve in good spirits, very sure that in the end Hugh would stay with her. My faithful three rode with me, Fechin, Merwyn, and Edna. I was much surprised at Edna's steadfastness, for I did not think the life she came from would have taught that virtue. I could see no reason why the poor girl should need to face a war, however, and when I asked it Audris offered her a home in Jernaeve. But Edna flung herself at my feet and began to weep and ask how she had offended.

"You have not offended me at all," I assured her, lifting her to her feet. "You have always been faithful and uncomplaining, Edna, and of late in a life far harder and more unsettled than you ever expected, I am sure. And now, I am afraid, there will be more danger as well as great discomfort. I do not see why you should suffer. Stay here in Jernaeve. You will be safe, and when . . . when I can, I will send for you."

"I don't know what you can be thinking of, my lady," she said. "How can you do without me? How can you think of traveling with only those two clumsy loobies, Fechin and Merwyn? Who will bring you water in the morning? Merwyn? Not without emptying the pail on your head, most likely. Who will beat the dirt and pests from your clothes each night? Fechin? No doubt he will beat them with the edge of a sword or a stick pulled from a dung heap instead of using fresh twigs. Who will—"

Laughing, I held up my hand. "Edna, I know I would miss you terribly, but I could manage—"

"Not without me, my lady," she cried.

Audris put her hand on my arm and said very softly, "And she can cook and sew, which I cannot."

For a moment that seemed to have nothing at all to do with Edna and I was lost, but then I remembered how on my first visit Audris had said there were many things she had never learned just so that her aunt could keep her pride in managing Jernaeve. She was warning me not to hurt Edna's pride—a strange thought to have for a servant, but Audris never distinguished very well between common folk and those gently born. And as I thought of the change in Edna over the time she had served me, I realized Audris was right. Perhaps because of her past, Edna was fiercely proud of her position. Likely she would rather dare danger and discomfort than sink into someone without importance or recognition in Jernaeve.

"Then I will be very glad to take you with me," I said to Edna, taking her hand as I remembered that she had already dared the queen's wrath in her concern for me. "And thank you," I added.

At least I was not wrong in my judgement of Sir Gerald. He was delighted to see me when I rode into Wyth and made no objection at all to fighting for King Stephen, saying frankly that it would surely win him a pardon and he was tired of hiding and living almost like a prisoner. Nor did he desire leadership. He was relieved rather than offended when I told him of the men coming from Northumbria and that he would command only the Cumbrian troops.

To my surprise, we made up a troop one hundred strong, and it took less than a month to assemble them. The armorers in Keswick barely finished altering Magnus's armor to fit Sir Gerald before the troop was ready. But it was a good time for gathering men. Lambing was long over, the heavy work of plowing and planting was done, the first haying finished. Harvest would not be for two months, and the boys and women could care for the fields and do the second, sparser haying of August. Even for men with farms of their own, the coin to be gathered by fighting for pay would be pure profit, not needing to be offset by loss from neglected farm work. And, one of the younger men who had no responsibilities said, grinning at me, that if one had to go marching all over foreign countries, the summer was a far better time for it than winter.

We came into Ripon, where I had agreed to meet the troops Hugh would assemble, at the end of the second week of August and the Northumbrians were not far behind. They marched in on the second day of the third week, and when I saw Hugh's great red horse I did not know whether to smile or weep. I was terribly afraid for him, but Hugh was so strong and so wise that to have him near lifted my heart despite my fear. He greeted me with a grin and a bear hug and reported that Audris had surprised him again and borne a girl while he was out gathering men. She had named the child Melusine, and she was well and the child strong. The naming upset me a little and for years I feared for Audris's Melusine, but she lived through the fevers of childhood and is still well and strong.

Aside from my fears for Hugh's safety, I was also concerned because he was so much younger than Sir Gerald, but there was no question about who would lead. Despite the difference in their ages, by the time Sir Gerald had talked to Hugh for half an hour, he was calling him "my lord" with the same respect he had paid papa. Later Sir Gerald told me that Hugh was trained to be a great lord, not a simple knight, and understood the management of armies as well as small troops.

It was just as well he did, because we soon became an army. Hugh had brought a little more than five hundred men from Northumbria, I had one hundred, and two days later at Cawood, south of York, another five hundred sent by Sir Walter Espec joined them. I was not with the army when the new troops arrived. I had ridden separately to York to see whether there was a letter from the queen. Maud had decided to write to me in care of the Church in York because the new archbishop, William, had not attended the council that elected Matilda. It was a good choice for another reason too. Although Hugh's foster father, Archbishop Thurstan, had died—not at York but in the Cluniac priory at Pontrefact—in February the previous year, Hugh still had good friends among the churchmen in York. The new archbishop, who had been the treasurer of the see in Thurstan's time, was one who had known him for many years, and when Hugh wrote to him, Archbishop William agreed to receive messengers from the queen with news and instructions for us.

The news was all good. The townsfolk of Oxford had secretly sent word that Matilda had come to rest in Oxford keep and was gathering together her scattered supporters. But now life had been infused into those faithful to the king by the rout at London. Men who had seemed to bring only lip service to the queen had arrived with troops. Even Waleran had finally come—but he had come only to say that his lands in Normandy were in danger and he was departing to defend them. The queen did not write "Thank God," but I could read it between the words that *were* there—good news, indeed—that Robert of Leicester had come in Waleran's place and had brought an army with him.

Best of all, Geoffrey de Mandeville had returned from Oxford. He had not knelt, weeping with shame, at Maud's feet to beg her pardon for his defection, as I thought he should have done, but he made many excuses, most to the effect that he had hoped by his taking up Matilda's cause when it seemed that Stephen's was hopeless, to help and protect the king. To me, Maud made no pretense of belief but said Mandeville was too powerful to offend. Moreover, Maud said she had made sure, through her contacts with the merchants of Oxford, that Matilda would learn Mandeville had returned to his allegiance to the king. Knowing Matilda's temper, the queen reported her hope that Mandeville would be threatened or insulted or both. As for the troops I was bringing, we were to march for Oxford as soon as we could.

Hugh was astonished at the details of the letter. It sounded, he said, as if I were the queen's closest confidant. That made me laugh.

"No, it is all warnings. She is trying to tell me that it would do me no good to betray her because events are moving in her favor."

Hugh sputtered with anger, but I pointed out how many had betrayed her husband and that she had long regarded me as an enemy steeped in guile, which had made Hugh laugh. Naturally, once he had news of his objective, Hugh

wanted me to go back to Jernaeve, but I would have none
of it. I could scarcely be in any danger in the midst of the
army with Hugh to protect me. I had promised to return to
the queen, and return I would. After some argument, Hugh
claiming that it was not so safe as I thought because we
would pass strongholds held for the empress and might be
attacked, I said very simply that I would go with the army
or alone. Hugh cursed me for being as stubborn as Audris,
but he yielded.

It was the first week in September when we came near
Oxford, and Hugh sent men ahead to discover whether the
city was besieged. But the men came back saying there
was no army, neither that of the empress nor that of the
queen, and no sign of any battle either. Hugh, Sir Gerald,
I, and two knights who led troops of Espec's men took
counsel together, but none had any idea of where to go
until an idea occurred to me. The bishop of Oxford had
sworn to Matilda, and the queen could not commit any
message to his care. But Maud trusted the burghers of the
towns, and I remembered from the letter that a townsman
had warned Maud that the empress had come to Oxford
keep.

I had her letter in my purse, and in it I found the name
of that townsman and his business. I wondered then if I
had maligned Maud. Perhaps she had sent all the details
not as a subtle threat but because she knew my fears for
Bruno and wished to cheer me with the hopes to which she
clung. I said nothing of that, but I proposed that I should
ride into Oxford alone and seek out that man. Hugh objected, fearing for my safety, but we called one of the men
he had sent out, and he assured us that although there was
an extra strong garrison in Oxford keep, the town was
peaceful. Finally it was agreed that I should go.

Maud had left no written message, but the townsman
had been told my name—I had been right in my guess that
Maud wasted no words, and his direction had been placed
in the letter deliberately—and he had news for me, again
good. The king's brother, the bishop of Winchester, had
been suspected of having a hand in the revolt of the
Londoners. He had quarreled with the empress not only
because she would not grant the Honor of Boulogne to

Eustace but over Church matters, on which she had promised much and violated every promise. Thus when Maud
wrote to him again and begged him to have mercy on his
own brother and work to restore him to his throne, Winchester met Maud in Guildford and agreed to lift the ban of
excommunication from the king's followers. Winchester
did not then offer to withdraw his support from Matilda,
perhaps out of shame for showing himself so light of
purpose; however, the result was the same. The empress,
hearing of his meeting with Maud and that he had lifted
the ban of excommunication on the king's supporters, had
taken her army and marched on Winchester to seize him
and punish him. He had escaped and cried to the queen for
help, but Matilda's army was attacking the keep Winchester held in that city.

That was clue enough. We marched south toward Winchester with a fan of foreriders to warn us of any large
force we might encounter. East of Andover Hugh's men at
last came upon a troop sworn to the queen making camp
for the night. Again I rode forward with only my three
servants, taking lodging in Andover and sending Merwyn
with a letter to the leader of that troop. He must have
passed the letter on as Merwyn asked, for the next morning William of Ypres himself came to speak to me. I was
frightened when he first came in, for I hardly recognized
him all in armor, but as soon as he spoke I knew his voice.

Ypres seemed much surprised that I had come south
with the troops and laughed when I said I had promised to
return to the queen with the men I gathered, remarking that
he did not think she expected me to keep the promise so
literally. Then he asked if my troops would be willing to
join his force, and I replied that I was sure Hugh would be
glad to do whatever he thought best. When he heard
Hugh's name, his eyes lit; and when I told him he had a
thousand men, he took my hand and kissed it.

Had there been fewer men, I think Ypres would have
merely told us where to meet his troops. Because we were
a force to be reckoned with by ourselves, he rode with me
to the camp to speak to Hugh, who was waiting for me
impatiently, also armed and ready although his tent was
not yet folded away. That was fortunate because it gave

Ypres a private place to talk. He told Hugh that the queen's army had come from Guildford and had split, the queen going south with the main force to attack Matilda's army, which was besieging Winchester's keep of Wolvesey in the southeast corner of the city. Ypres had led a smaller contingent of men due west, however, because the queen had had word that Gloucester had sent a strong troop to Wherwell to hold the road open for supplies. It had been Ypres's intention to attack the troop that had fortified the little village and close that route for support to the rebels. However, he was more concerned about the routes west.

"If the queen's attack on Matilda's army is successful," Ypres pointed out, "the empress and her accursed brother will flee west, and if I have not blocked the roads by Michelmarsh and Stockbridge, they will escape me again."

"I can close Wherwell," Hugh said, "if that is what you think will best serve the queen's purpose"—he raised his head to look at the sun—"before dark. Shall I then march on Winchester or join you?"

"No, hold Wherwell, set guards along the fords of the river—I do not know the name—that runs to Whitchurch, and close the road into Whitchurch too. I do not believe that Matilda or any major supporter of hers will flee farther east than that."

"Very well, my lord," Hugh agreed, after a moment's thought. "A messenger will find me in Wherwell if you wish to change this plan."

Ypres gripped Hugh's upper arm. "I cannot tell you how glad I am to have you with us, Sir Hugh," he said. "I will not forget this. Neither will the queen, and she will not let Stephen forget."

"I desire no favors," Hugh responded with a smile. "I have all I can handle—sometimes more. Also, I made a promise to Stephen to enter his service once. The king was kind enough to free me from it when holding Jernaeve became more important, but in this time of need I feel that promise still binds me. God willing we will be successful enough to free the king."

"God willing," Ypres echoed.

"One more thing," Hugh said, seeing that Ypres was about to call for his horse. "Will it be safe for me to send

Lady Melusine to the queen? I do not like to leave her alone in Andover. Either of the two armies might take to looting after the battle, and Andover is too close on too good a road, but to take her to Wherwell—"

"Do not leave her in Andover," Ypres agreed. "But I am afraid it will be impossible to get her safely to the queen unless you wish to send about a hundred men with her. There are war bands, both rebel and ours, all over the area, and there have been clashes. Even with the men and luck in avoiding a fight, it might be hard to find Queen Maud, and with her Melusine might be even less safe." He sighed. "The queen is not always willing to stay a safe distance from action. She is not so silly as to don armor or think she is a battle leader, but she rides with the troops and is often close enough to turn back any who would flee. Take Melusine to Wherwell. She will be safe enough in so small a battle."

I almost opened my mouth to cry a protest, but I did not. I had forced myself on Hugh when he wanted to send me back to Jernaeve, now I must accept whatever place for me that he thought would cause him the least trouble. I did not want to see the battle, no matter how small, not because I feared for myself but because I was terrified that I would see Hugh hurt or Sir Gerald, or even Fechin or Merwyn. And after that first moment, I had no chance to change my mind. Hugh had followed Ypres out of the tent when he left. I heard him bidding Ypres fare well and then calling for his troop leaders and telling them to form marching order.

I do not know whether I could have kept my resolve steady over the hours it took us to come to Wherwell, but again I had no choice. Hugh rode with his captains, I suppose to make battle plans because when we came to the top of a rise below which lay the village, all seemed to know exactly what to do. Then Hugh came to where I was waiting with Edna, Fechin, and Merwyn a little way off the road and said, "You stay just here. No matter what you see or hear, Melusine, stay right here. I must know where to find you. Fechin and Merwyn will be with you, and I will come for you." I promised readily, and he smiled at me—but I saw his heart and mind were on the coming fight.

Despite that promise and despite my terror we were all drawn forward by the sounds of battle. I watched as men struck at each other, as some fell, and those who had struck them sometimes struck again to make sure, sometimes ran forward at once to strike at others, sometimes were struck in turn and fell. In no time at all I could not tell which were our men, which the enemy. I could not even pick out Hugh, and Sir Gerald had also disappeared into the malestrom.

I had never realized how much confusion there was in a battle. Men killed and wounded each other without ever knowing whom they had struck down or whether the blow was fatal. I understood now that I could not have been Bruno's prize for killing papa. Even if Bruno had fought my father or brother, how would he know? A battle was not like the taking of a keep or a manor. Then the victor could know whom he vanquished. Perhaps I had been given to Bruno because he was the man who took Ulle, but papa had died in a battle greater than the taking of Wherwell. I would never know by whose hand he died, and I was very glad of it.

I do not think the fighting lasted more than half an hour. The sun had moved very little when the noise of battle died away and weapons and shields were thrown down by the vanquished. It took longer to collect the wounded and secure the prisoners, but soon after that Hugh came for me and took me to the largest house in the village, which had been cleaned and furnished for the baron commanding the troop that had held it for the empress.

I discovered when we came into Wherwell that all the folk of the village had been driven away. There were no women, and only one leech had been sent with his troop by Sir Walter Espec. I am no great healer, but I had sewed enough cuts in my brothers' skins and poulticed enough bruises so that, having gathered what healing herbs I could from the village gardens, Edna and I were of use to the wounded. I was glad to be busy.

The next day there was more fighting. Twice there were shouts and sounds of battle outside the village. Each time a few more joined the wounded in the barn and more men, stripped of everything except their braies and shirts, were driven in to be penned with the prisoners we already had. Each time I rushed out to watch as the prisoners were examined, hoping I would recognize some man of importance who could be traded for the king, but only two minor knights were thrust into the hut with our petty baron.

Still, the news kept my heart beating hard with hope. That morning, 14 September, the Feast of the Exaltation of the Holy Cross, the queen's army had attacked the force with which Robert of Gloucester was besieging Wolvesey keep and broken it. There had been heavy fighting in the town, Gloucester trying to hold back Maud's army and keep them from reaching the royal keep in the center of Winchester where the empress had been staying. Both captured knights insisted they had been sent to reinforce Wherwell to keep an escape route free, but Hugh did not believe them; he said they were just running from a battle that was already lost.

Of course it was better that the queen had won the battle than lost it, but I had not heard the news I wanted to hear. If Matilda or Gloucester was not captured, we would merely have to begin all over, and it was growing late in the year. Very soon most of my Cumbrian troop would have to go home to get in the harvest; many of Hugh's men and Espec's would also demand release. As the day passed and only stragglers were taken and brought in, my hopes waned. I was sitting outside the house I was using, trying to fix my mind on what to provide for an evening meal instead of weeping with disappointment, when I heard Sir Gerald, who had been away since the end of the battle yesterday guarding the road at Whitchurch, hail me.

"I may have brought you what you desire, Melly," he shouted, but he did not sound or look very happy as he jumped off his horse and turned to unbind and assist down another man, so muddied and bruised that it took me a minute to recognize him.

"Sire," I gasped, jumping to my feet and sinking to a curtsey before King David of Scotland, but I felt horror rather than joy.

His eyes were cold as he looked at me. "You have a

very faithful servant in Sir Gerald, Lady Melusine. I offered him a rich estate of his own if he would come north with me, and he refused. Well, I was lucky twice. My first captor satisfied himself with my purse, my second with my armor and the jewels I had hidden—but they did not recognize me. What will *you* take for my freedom?''

I looked up, my eyes full of tears. "Oh, my lord," I said softly, "I would gladly, so gladly set you on your way freely, only for the love my father had for you—but it is a whole realm, and my husband's life, your capture will buy."

He looked down at me. "If you think Matilda will free Stephen in exchange for my freedom, you are sadly mistaken." His mouth was twisted with bitterness.

Could that be true? If it were, I surely had no reason to hold King David. I desired no rich estate, no chests of gold. All I wanted was Bruno and Ulle, and without Bruno, I did not even desire Ulle. Then if the empress would not trade Stephen for David, why should Sir Gerald not have his estate? But I was not such a fool as to trust the words of a man trying to buy freedom.

"There will be time enough to speak of that," I said. "For now, come within and rest." He followed me silently into the headman's house and sank down on a stool. I poured a cup of the captive baron's wine and offered it, saying, as he took the cup, "I will bring you water for washing and food and clean clothing."

Sir Gerald had been watching from the doorway, but I drew him with me and closed the door as I came out. Before Sir Gerald could protest, I said, "Let him be alone to regain his balance, but set a guard of the men of Yorkshire around the house—they have no love for David whereas our men might more easily be bought—and send a messenger to find Hugh."

"Be careful, Melly," Sir Gerald warned me. "Do not get so close to the man. If he seized you, he would have a strong bargaining piece."

I nodded. "I will not go in again before Hugh comes. Merwyn can serve him."

Hugh was no happier than I when he arrived and I told him who was inside the house. "God in heaven," he groaned, "I almost wish Sir Gerald had taken that offer and ridden north."

"He says Matilda will not exchange Stephen for him. Is that true?"

"Very likely," Hugh responded, "but it is Gloucester who holds Stephen, and Gloucester is an honorable man. What I do not know is whether Gloucester will feel that he owes David the exchange. David is a king, but his importance to this struggle in England is nothing compared to Stephen's. Still, there is a chance—"

"Then perhaps we should let him go?" It was more question than statement. Compared with my desire to free Bruno, my horror at using as a trading piece one who had been a beloved overlord to my father was nothing, but I suddenly realized there was another problem. "Hugh, will there be danger for you in giving him to the queen? Close as Jernaeve is to the Scots border, it would be an ill thing to have the enmity of the king of the Scots."

Hugh was silent for a time, then said, "We cannot let him go, Melusine. If he is the only captive of note taken, the queen must continue to pursue and try to capture the empress, or bring her to yield. For that Maud will need gold and gold and more gold. She has been draining Boulogne for months and cannot go on; there is little she can extract from England as long as Stephen is in prison. Even if David cannot be exchanged for the king, she can wring a large ransom from him."

"But if it endangers you, Hugh—"

"He need not see me or know I was involved. I think the best way is for me to find Ypres and report who we have taken. Then Ypres can take David, you, and Sir Gerald, who deserves credit and reward for the capture, into his care to be carried to the queen. I will win considerable favor with Ypres for surrendering my captive to him; he will be blessed by the queen, but you and Sir Gerald will not lose your part of her gratitude either—so we will all profit."

"Except poor King David," I said softly.

Hugh hugged me comfortingly, but he did not change his mind. He beckoned to Sir Gerald and asked him to make up a troop of mounted men and accompany him. I went into the shed at the back of the house to examine the supplies. The least I could do for the poor king was to see that he had a good meal before Ypres got him. I did not think David would be mistreated, but looking at Ypres's gloating face would surely make food less appetizing than my regretful expression.

When I entered the house with Merwyn and Edna, carrying a variety of cold, sliced meats, King David was clean and attired in the best of the baron's garments. He had regained his self-possession, and we managed to find a few subjects for conversation that did not touch on the war. Later, I found a board and pieces and we played chess, but before we had finished the game, Hugh flung open the door and entered with Sir Gerald behind him, and their smiles added a glow to the candlelight that lit the room.

"Sire," Hugh said, bowing low. "You are free! Ypres has captured Robert of Gloucester, and the empress will have to free King Stephen to have back her brother—will she nill she. No baron in England will serve her without Robert of Gloucester to follow."

CHAPTER 25

Bruno

THERE ARE TALES for children that Father Anselm used to
tell Audris when she was very young—to which I listened
eagerly also, although I tried to hide my pleasure under
scoffing—that end, "and so they lived happily ever after." I cannot say precisely that; thanks be to God Melusine
and I have not yet come to our ending, and it is not wise to
claim much happiness with certainty before then. Still,
there is much hope in me now for "living happily ever
after," and when the king and I were discovered by the
outer gate, I had no hope of living beyond the next few
minutes at all.

I felt twice the burning agony of being stabbed and
hands dragging at me, but I clung to the king until there
was a pain in my head, a great burst of light, and then
darkness. I must have been very near dying because I fell
under those blows in the middle of May and I do not really
remember anything until September. I have vague recol-
lections of pain and crying for water, but no memory at all
of the passage of time until the day I became aware that
something heavy clung to my ankle and made it hard to
move my foot. I recall saying crossly, "Melusine, that
foot is long healed. You must take off the bindings." And
then I opened my eyes to see Sir Grolier looking down at me.

"You stabbed me," I whispered, remembering now who held the knife. I have never seen such hatred in a man's face, yet when I put an elbow behind me to push myself to a sitting position and could not for weakness, he lifted me most gently and placed something behind me so I could lean in comfort on the wall. While he moved me, his body blocked my view, but when he moved back, I saw he and I were alone in the chamber. "Where is the king?" I cried, terror giving strength to my voice.

"Curse you, be still," he snarled. "He is in another chamber hale and well. Shut your mouth or I will be beaten again for your screaming."

That remark astonished me so much that I fell silent. Perhaps I also slipped away for a time to wherever I had been since May, but it was not for very long. I woke to find Grolier feeding me, digging each spoonful of stew out of the bowl as if he intended to break my teeth with it but touching my lips gently so that I opened my mouth instead.

"Do you get beaten for making my mouth bloody too?" I asked.

He did not answer, but the glare he turned on me was enough. I then said I would feed myself, but I found I did not have the strength to hold the spoon much less move it from the bowl to my mouth. Grolier laughed, enjoying my distress, but when I choked on tears of rage, the petty rage of the weak, he pulled me upright and patted my back until I could breathe easily again. No one could have heard me choking, so why did he not let me strangle to death and be free of tending me? It was a puzzle I thought about while eating, and continued to think about after Grolier held a cup to my mouth and went out. I heard the scrape and clank of metal on stone as he moved and realized his ankles were chained together—so he was a prisoner too.

Over the next two weeks, as less and less of my time was lost to sudden unconsciousness, I worked out how Stephen and I had been duped into escaping and almost killed from a few furious, unguarded comments Grolier made and the facts I already knew. First, it had been Grolier's news that set escape in the king's mind, and for all I knew he may have directly spoken of escape. Second, the queen's father had destroyed Grolier's family, not helped it as he had implied, so he had a personal hatred for the king and had intended to kill him. Third, I knew that could not have been by Gloucester's orders, but Grolier could not have got into Bristol keep without some important person's authority, and the only important person foolish enough to think Stephen's death would benefit her cause rather than harming it was—Matilda. I have no proof that the empress actually ordered the king's death and never will have. I could not make Grolier speak on that subject, and perhaps she only ordered that the king be induced to do something foolish so that Gloucester would imprison him more securely. I know she opposed Gloucester's gentle imprisonment and desired from the beginning that Stephen be chained in the depths of the keep.

The remainder of the story I wrested from Grolier himself by the simple expedient of threatening to scream as if he were hurting me. He told me that my clinging to the king instead of trying to defend myself had drawn the attention of the guards, who seized him and his two servants—one the king had borne down and the other who had struck me on the head. When I was pulled away from Stephen and rolled over, one of the guards had recognized me and then the king.

William of Gloucester, the earl's eldest son, happened to be in the keep at the time. Before ordering Grolier's two servants executed, Lord William had wrenched from them the information that they had been given a description of Stephen, told to provoke him, and when he reacted, to help Grolier kill him. But he did not order that Grolier himself be executed. I had heard that William of Gloucester was a strange man; he certainly had a weird sense of the comical, and instead of executing Grolier he devised a weird punishment. Lord William had ordered that Grolier nurse me and serve the king. If Stephen was dissatisfied with Grolier's service or if I died, William told Grolier, he would be killed by slow torture, but one hour of torture would be remitted for each week I lived.

To ensure Grolier's close attention to his duties, Lord William had given him a sample of the skill of his torturers. His little toes had been removed on both feet, not chopped off but cut away slowly, a little at a time. Moreover Lord William had arranged that I be examined twice daily but at different times each day, and if I had soiled myself and had not been cleaned or if I showed sores from lying too long in one position, Grolier was to be whipped. Of course, neither Lord William nor anyone else expected me to live. Grolier was quite sure that Lord William had remained in Bristol far longer than he intended just because he hoped for my death each day so he could enjoy Grolier's torture. I do not know the truth of that. I had seen William of Gloucester a few times, but I do not remember ever speaking to him, and I could not judge the truth through Grolier's hate and fear.

I was sorry for my cruelty to Grolier after I had forced him to tell the tale. It was not important to me to know why Grolier attended me with such care when his hatred was destroying him, but I had grown spiteful in my feebleness over those weeks. I expected to gain strength quickly, and I did not. Although I felt I was starving before each meal, I could eat very little, and forcing myself was useless because I only vomited the whole meal when I tried. Second, being chained made it much harder to move so I could not exercise unless Grolier helped me, and that he would not do. Perhaps he suspected what would happen to him as soon as I could feed myself and reach for the pot when I needed it. I had managed that by the third week in September, and one day Grolier disappeared. He was a treacherous dog, but I wept when a manservant brought my dinner and told me, his purpose being ended, Grolier had been hanged.

After he was gone, I slipped back instead of improving. I was dull with weakness and despair, for I was alone all the time now except when a servant brought me food or came to empty my pot. The food was worse too—I suppose Grolier had picked out the best pieces for me because I ate so little, but the servant dumped a bowl on the floor beside me, always cold and the dregs, the meat all gristle and the vegetables rotten. I think it was the leavings, what the men had thrown away. Often it was too much bother to lift the bowl and try to eat, and I did without. The servant only took the bowl away, empty or full. I wondered sometimes why I was left in that chamber rather than being cast down into the lower dungeon. Perhaps it was because the constable had forgotten about me now that Grolier was dead.

I must have been near death again; I can remember that my last thought was whether I had strength enough to lift the pot to piss. I cannot remember whether I did or not. The next thing I knew was that the constable of Bristol keep was kneeling by my bed and calling my name and pleading with me to wake up. Behind him I saw Stephen with tears on his cheeks and rage on his face. I slipped away again, but even in my unconsciousness the sight of the king free and unguarded must have worked in my mind and given me strength. I woke again to the feeling of being washed and the sound of a woman weeping; it was the constable's wife who was weeping as her maids bathed me, and I was in the constable's bed. But even that puzzle could not hold my attention.

It was only several days later that I learned why, when I was strong enough for the king to come and visit me. He told me with huge delight that Robert of Gloucester's youngest son, Philip, had come with orders that he be released at once from his chains and with a large packet of letters. These told of the battle won in Winchester, of Robert of Gloucester a prisoner in the queen's hands, even of the part my Melusine had played. One letter had been to the constable from the queen, informing him that one of the knights captured by Lady Melusine's small army was the only son of the constable and his ransom was my life. I did not wonder then that the lady of the keep put me in her own bed and cared for me. Joy gave me some strength, but my body was slow to respond, and I still slept away most of the days as well as the nights of the next three weeks.

The king came each day to talk to me, but he had little more news, only glowing plans for the future, which included a huge army that would rise to support him as soon as he showed himself. His presence, he assured me, would reanimate the whole nation, but he would never again be tricked by sweet words that led him away from his own good judgement—or Maud's, he added grinning. I smiled in return then and as often as I could because I knew his intention in coming to visit me was kind. He

wished to revive my spirit, but the truth was that the more
Stephen talked about the future, the heavier grew my
heart. I knew there could be no quick victory. The schism
was too deep, the hurts too bitter. The war would go on
and on—and I was so tired.

I looked at the fire sometimes—there was a small raised
hearth in the chamber—but it was a poor thing, captive,
like me, barely flickering over the charcoal that fed it.
What I wanted was the roaring fire of winter that the
hearth of Ulle would hold—and peace. All I had was a
faint blue flickering and talk of war. So when the king left
me, I slept. Then on the afternoon of the first day of
November, I was wakened by a kiss—and Melusine was
bending over me.

I do not remember what I first said. It was some fearful
question about how she had come to be in Bristol keep, for
her eyes were red with weeping. I asked her why she
wept, and she said for joy—but there was a darkness in her
behind her smile. I struggled upright with her help, and
she raised the pillows behind me, laughing and hugging
me and bidding me to be of good cheer because all was
well.

"I have come with the queen," she said, "who, with
Eustace, is to be hostage for Lord Robert's freedom. But
you and I are not bound to that condition, and as soon as
you are strong enough, we will go."

I was too dazed to take in everything she said, and
anyway it faded to nonsense in comparison with that last
word. *Go,* to go was to be freed. "Go where?" I asked,
and then with a sinking heart I remembered my duty.
"And what of the king?"

"Ah, as to those questions, I am forbidden to answer.
You must wait until tomorrow or the next day."

There was so much mischief in her smile that I knew
whatever I was told on the morrow would be pleasant, and
when I opened my mouth to ask another question, Melusine
popped in a spoon of delicious broth, thick with minced
chicken.

"I am not so weak," I protested. "I can feed myself,
and it is not time for eating."

"All day every day is time for eating for you," she

said. "I did not marry a bag of bones, and I have always favored well-fleshed men. As to feeding you—it amuses me. I like to see your eyes bulge when I get a spoon in unexpectedly. What else have I to amuse me?"

Fortunately I had swallowed or I would have choked as I laughed at her ridiculous remarks, and I nearly did choke several times as food arrived in my mouth at odd moments. But I will say that Melusine probably got three or four times as much as I usually ate into me. All day Edna brought up a variety of small dishes, some cold, some hot, all delicious. Melusine never offered more than one spoonful of anything, but by evening, I found myself asking for the pot or bowl and eating an additional portion.

Nor did I sleep much. Melusine kept me wide awake with the tale of what had happened to the queen and to her after news came of the king's capture. I had asked, of course, for the most recent news first, but she looked mischievous and mysterious and said she could not tell me that until she had leave. And when night came, she took off her clothes and climbed into bed with me. I must have looked surprised because she laughed and asked if I wanted her to sleep on a hard, cold floor when there was a feather bed available. I had not thought at all, except that I was sick and the sick lie alone—but Melusine did not act as if I were sick, so I laughed.

"I thought you might be afraid to be stabbed by the bag of bones," I teased.

She smiled at me as she slid under the covers and pressed herself against me. "I even love your bones," she whispered.

It was the first time, the very first time that Melusine had said a word of love to me. She had cared for me when I was hurt, she had coupled with me with open enjoyment; she had been a perfect wife in every way—but she had never said she loved me. I was afraid to ask whether the word was said knowingly, afraid she spoke the word only because I was sick. If it was the last word of love as well as the first, at least I had it. I would take no chance it would be withdrawn. So I took her in my arms and held her in silence until, being very tired from more activity than I had had in many months, I slept in joy.

I woke in joy also, to Melusine's merry voice. "Let me go, you monster," she whispered, kissing my ear. "If you do not let me rise to piss, you will soon be swimming."

My hand and arm were so stiff I had a little trouble letting go, and I realized I had been clutching Melusine all night. "I am sorry," I said. "You must have been uncomfortable with me holding you and not letting you move."

"Oh no." Her voice drifted up from below the bed on the other side where she sat on the pot, and somehow I knew she was smiling. "I managed to wriggle around." Then she stood up and leaned over me and spoke much more softly. "I do not think I have ever known the kind of joy I felt each time I woke and felt your embrace. I never believed I would get you back, Bruno." She was smiling, but her lips trembled and again there was a darkness in her eyes that did not come from their color. But before I could command my voice to answer, she turned merry again, marveling at how long a man could hold his water, and called Edna to help her lift me so I could relieve myself.

Usually I sank back to sleep after breaking my fast, but Melusine, having kissed me for eating well, made a moue of distaste and asked me if I intended to keep the beard I had grown.

"No," I responded, opening my eyes. "I long to be rid of it."

"I am very glad to hear it," she said, laughing. "I can get used to being stabbed by bones, even welcome it, but a mouthful of hair every time I kiss you—" She shuddered eloquently and told Edna to fetch the barber at once.

I was so delighted, I sat up by myself, wide awake. No one had bothered to shave me since Grolier's death and by now I had a bushy and untidy beard. But when the barber came, he pointed out that he could not shave me in the bed. I was so eager to be rid of that growth of hair, that I insisted I was strong enough to sit on a stool, but Melusine shook her head.

"Not for being shaved," she said. "For some other purpose, I could stand behind you and you could rest on me, but if I should move or you, the barber could slit your throat."

I knew it was true—not that the man would slit my throat but that he might cut me badly—and I knew too that it was perfectly foolish to care whether I was shaved now or a few days later, but still tears came to my eyes and I had to turn my head away. Melusine did not seem to notice. When she spoke, she was not looking at me but at the barber, and she asked him whether he could shave me if I sat in a chair. The man agreed to that, and Melusine went out. I felt a fool but also unreasonably happy, like a child who had received a toy he had despaired of getting.

For a moment I watched the barber run a fine pumice stone over the blades of his knives, which added to my feeling of well-being since a dull blade made a painful shave. Then I heard movement outside the door and the constable's wife asking angrily who had dared to take Lord Robert's chair. With the unstable reactions of the very weak, I flew from joy to rage, fearing that I would be cheated of a clean face—but I had underestimated Melusine.

"I do not care whose chair it is," my wife said. Her voice was soft, but I would not have blamed anyone who recoiled before it. "Just now my husband's lightest wish is of greater importance to me than your Lord Robert's, and your wishes, madam, I take delight in ignoring. How would you like your son back without his nose or his hands or feet?"

"My man will send an army to fetch him!" the woman cried.

Melusine laughed and asked, "Where? To the White Tower? To Jernaeve? To a cave hidden in the Cumbrian mountains? I said your son was Bruno's ransom—life for life—but I did not promise in what condition he would come back to you. Woman, if my Bruno is made unhappy by your stupidity, I will see that you mourn that stupidity every day of your son's life ever after. Now let me go."

The laugh and the voice in which Melusine spoke made my skin crawl, and it did worse no doubt to the constable's wife, who cried out that Melusine should take the chair. In another moment two stout womenservants entered carrying it and set it down near the bed. Until they went out, Melusine stood by the door looking out. That, I thought, was the face of the woman who had thrust a knife at my throat on the second night of our married life. I had almost forgotten that part of Melusine, but the memory pleased me. It made more loving, more precious, her gentleness to me, the tenderness with which she drew my bedrobe about me and with the barber's help moved me to the chair.

My legs trembled like the jelly that surrounds boiled fish, but I stiffened them as best I could and did manage the few steps to the chair. I held my head steady too, although Melusine stood behind me ready to support it. And when I was shaved, I leaned less heavily, not more, on Melusine and the barber as I went back to bed.

I felt wonderful and was just about to ask Melusine how it happened that at the moment I was hungry there was no sign of her pots and bowls when the king appeared in the doorway with the queen behind him. I suppose with the beard gone, I looked more deathlike than when the thinness and pallor of my face were hidden, for Stephen hesitated and cried, "No, do not move," when I pushed myself higher so I could at least bow from the waist. Then he came to the bed and took my hand.

"I have come to bid you fare well, my dear Bruno," he said. "You have served me more devotedly than I could have asked of any man. I am sorry to leave you here, but I must pick up the reins of my bolting kingdom and bring it to order, and it will be, I fear, many weeks before you are fit for service."

"Yes, my lord," I said. "I am to follow you when I am well?"

But the queen touched Stephen's arm and then came forward. Our eyes met. I tried to hide the despair in mine, but Maud had always been able to read me better than most people, and I knew she saw my horror of what was to come. For just an instant I thought I saw a similar horror mirrored in her eyes, but then, to my surprise she bent and kissed me and stroked my hair as if I were her child in need of comforting.

"You will be too busy serving the king in another way for a long time, dear Bruno, but your place will always be held for you. When you are ready you will be most welcome to us. Stephen, he does not understand what we mean. Give him the charter, for goodness sake."

The king looked mulish for a moment. I am sure he had been about to extract a promise to follow him before he offered my reward; however, he drew out a roll of thick parchment, heavy with a wax impression of the great seal, and handed it to me.

"It seems very little for what you have done," Maud said, "but Melusine insisted that Ulle and the other smaller manors were all you desired even though the lands and people have been misused. I know that is truly what Melusine wants, but if *you* would like some other, richer lands you can have those also."

"No," I breathed. "Ulle is what I desire. Thank you, sire. Thank you, madam. I have always been poor, so Ulle seems rich to me. I greatly fear power, and Ulle will bring me none. All I need or want is the peace of those great hills with their silver hair of flowing water."

"You must love the lands indeed to find words of such beauty to describe them," Maud said. "I hope some day I will be able to visit you and look on your hills." She touched my face gently and stepped back.

Stephen had recovered from his small pique, and he smiled at me and patted the charter that lay on my lap. "I do not expect to need to visit you," he said, grinning—meaning, of course, that he was sure I would be faithful and he would not need to attack Ulle again. "But you will have to come to me to do homage some day."

"I will come whenever you send for me, my lord," I promised. "I have already sworn my faith to you, and will do so again at any time."

He was very pleased with that, and leaned over and kissed me before he and Maud left the room. I stroked the parchment in my lap, hardly believing what I held and looking at Melusine, who held her deep curtsey by the door, I suppose until the king and queen were out of sight. Then she flew to me and embraced me and kissed me and began to weep, whispering, "Free! Bruno, we are free!"

"I hope so," I said, "but when the king and queen are gone, we will be fortunate if the constable or his wife do not murder us."

"I do not fear for that." Melusine sat upright. "I have their precious son safe, and if you and I together do not

appear before Sir Gerald at a particular time, which I will
not say lest there be someone listening at the door, Sir
Gerald will send one of the prisoner's ears. After that, he
will send other, more important, parts until we come."

"Melusine!" I exclaimed, "that is monstrous. What if I
am slow to gain strength?"

"I cannot help that," she said. "I did not expect to find
you half dead owing to their cruel neglect. But if you are
worried about what will happen to the young man, you
must strive to get well quickly." And then she winked at
me. "Besides," she went on, "the queen is not leaving
with the king. What was arranged was that Stephen would
be freed and the queen and Eustace would remain here as
hostages. When Stephen arrives safe in London, Robert of
Gloucester will be freed, leaving his son, Lord William, as
hostage for the queen's release. When Lord Robert arrives
here, the queen and Eustace will go, and when she and her
son are with the king, Lord William will be freed."

I shook my head. "Once Robert of Gloucester is here,
we will need no other assurance of gaining our freedom.
He is a very good man."

"Well, I had no way to know that," she said pertly,
"and it does no harm to be doubly sure."

In spite of her wink, which I took to mean she had never
told Sir Gerald to dismember his prisoner and was only
using that as a threat, I felt uneasy. I had found that
women could be terribly cruel and spiteful. She must have
seen that I was troubled, for that night when we were abed
and there was no danger of being overheard, she told me
that the young knight was safe and sound at Ulle in Sir
Gerald's care. She had seen the constable's wife listening
by the door while the king and queen were with us, which
annoyed her, so she decided to give the woman an earful.

As if one irritation had made her think of another, she
then told me that Sir Giles would be gone and Ulle restored by the time we arrived. A copy of our charter and a
letter from the queen as well as a full pardon for anything
Sir Gerald might have done had gone with him to Ulle,
together with permission for Sir Giles to give up his charge
of the estate to Sir Gerald.

"I have promised Sir Gerald that you would invest him

with Irthing for his life," she went on. "I hope you do not mind, Bruno. King David offered him a fine estate in Scotland—"

"King David!" I echoed. "Do not tell me you induced him to be part of your army. I will not believe that."

Melusine giggled. "I will not ask it of you. No, it was Sir Gerald who captured him after the rout at Winchester, and David offered the estate as a bribe to allow him to escape." She explained the circumstances of deciding not to hand King David to the queen and that Hugh had concealed David among his men and taken him safely to the Scottish border. "But Sir Gerald did not want to go to Scotland. He said he did not wish to begin anew among strangers. You are content for him to have Irthing, are you not?"

"Good God, of course I am. I would not have cared if you wished to give him the property outright—I will offer that. It would have been dreadful to lose him. I will need him badly, for example, to tell me the manner of giving justice in Cumbria and such things which I suppose your father did not teach you."

"There are many things he did not teach me." I thought I heard resentment in her voice, but it was too dark to see her expression. "He said beautiful women did not need to know . . . many things."

I kissed her. "You are certainly beautiful, but I think a woman needs to know everything she can so that she can protect herself. If I am to be away in service to the king, who will hold Ulle? You must be able to defend it—" My voice faltered when I realized what I had said, and I hurried on, "—and give justice and do all things as I would."

"I prefer to be ignorant and have you there," she said, but her voice was light again and she cuddled closer against me so that I began to think of the main purpose for lying two in a bed.

Unfortunately my body was not yet ready to follow my thoughts, but I did not mind. The night before, I had not even been able to think about coupling. By then I had forgotten all about the constable's son, but I would have had no need to worry even if Melusine's grisly threat had been true because I gained strength far faster than I had expected after my inability to recover when Grolier had cared for me. I suppose the difference in my spirits was the reason; I was very happy, happier each day as that strange terror that seemed to lie behind Melusine's smiles ebbed.

Later I learned that the lightness and laughter, the pretense that I was not sick—and the terrible fear that darkened Melusine's eyes—were all learned over the year it took her mother to die of a wasting sickness. It seems I looked as her mother did toward the end. At first Melusine was sure I would die and all she could do was to ease my way, so she behaved as if my weakness was a game I was playing to amuse her. But I was not dying; I was recovering, and I felt happy with her teasing that I was lazy rather than weak so that it made me much stronger.

Whatever the cause, in a week I was walking about in my room and two days earlier I had managed to put to its proper use the marital bed in which we lay. First when I began to caress her, Melusine seemed stunned, but a timid exploration soon assured her that Sir Jehan could stand by himself very well, even if Sir Bruno could not. To save my strength if not his, Melusine mounted me, but she rode me so well and so thoroughly that I needed a day's rest before I tried again. My enthusiasm grew with my ability, and I played much longer the second time, longer still the third, and I needed no rest day between that and our fourth coupling.

The middle of the second week, I went down on a fine day to walk in the garden. As I came through the bailey, to my joy I was greeted by Merwyn and Fechin. I was quite cross with Melusine for not telling me they were safe and had been with her all along although I grieved that Cormi was dead. Melusine apologized; she had forgotten that I did not know that they had escaped at Lincoln. She told me then how Fechin had put on Gloucester's colors, but she did not tell the whole story, so when we left the garden and found Fechin waiting with Barbe, whom I had long given up as lost, I wept.

That was not the last of my surprises. When Robert of Gloucester arrived a few days later—I had already been riding on Barbe and found riding hardly tired me at all, although I needed help to mount—he sent to me my armor and my sword. I did not weep over them, but I was very glad to have them back, not only because they were the best of their kind and would be costly to replace but because Sir Oliver had given them to me and they were dear to me on that account.

That gesture, however, seemed to me like a polite hint to be gone. I knew from the fact that Lord Robert had not summoned me to give me the armor himself that he must find my presence a painful reminder that his party had lost all the great advantage they had won in the battle of Lincoln—and, from what Melusine had told me, largely because of the pride and stupidity of his sister, which must have been a bitter cud to chew. By his chaplain, I sent Gloucester my humble and heartfelt thanks and the news that my wife and I would depart the next day.

Melusine was aghast when I told her, but she could not deny me when I pointed out that it was very late in the year and if we did not go within the next few days, at the latest, snow would close the passes near Ulle. I proved stronger than she feared, however. I did not faint with weariness after a day's riding; I just ate twice what I would have without the exercise. I did not take a chill from the cold air either, not even when we met snow before we reached Rydal.

Melusine made me laugh by the way she kept brushing the snow off me and the way she plied me with hot ale until I was nearly drunk. But I was surprised and much less pleased when, after the bailiff and his wife had withdrawn so Melusine and I were alone beside the fire, she said suddenly, "Let us stay here for the winter. The way to Ulle will be too hard for you in the snow, too cold."

"The snow is not deep," I replied, surprised. "As for too hard—it is poor Barbe who does all the work. And I do not mind the cold. I can pull a fur around me if it grows colder. We will go to Ulle."

Melusine did not answer, only searched my face for a moment and then turned her eyes to the fire—but I had seen again that darkness in her eyes and a dreadful thought came to me. I sat frozen, unable to bring out the words I knew I must say, but our life would truly be together now, no longer a few weeks of play between long partings. We had now what I had promised her I would get when I had taken from her the knife with which she tried to kill me. And in all our years of marriage, there had always been those moments in which she drew back from me. Did she still want me dead?

"Melusine," I said, "if you cannot bear to see me sit in your father's chair or drink from his cup, I will go back to the king and trouble you no more."

"Oh no, beloved, no," she whispered, slipping from the bench on which we sat and kneeling before me, her hands gripping my arms. "No! Not even if it was by your hand papa died. I know you did not kill him apurpose to get Ulle."

"I did not kill him at all!" I exclaimed. "Melusine, in God's name, have you carried that fear—that you were lying abed with your father's killer—all these years? My love, dearling, I *know* I did not harm your father or your brother. I was not even *at* Wark at the time of the battle. I was with the king, and we came too late. Why did you not ask me?"

A weak smile trembled on her lips. "I did not want to know."

"Is that why you never would say you loved me, dear heart?"

She put her head down on my knee then and whispered, "No. I am afraid to love. What I love, dies."

I pulled her up into my lap and held her tight, remembering all the cruel losses in her life, but it would do her no good to yield to her fears. "All men, and all women too, die," I said. "Will you withhold joy from me during my life because of that? You once asked me if I thought I was God to make and unmake the fate of kingdoms. Must I ask you the same question? You are only a woman. Whether you love or not, I will live or die as God wills."

"But we are so near home, so near safety. I cannot believe my happiness will not be snatched away from me."

"That is gross superstition," I said, laughing at her. "And you are not the only one who feels that way, so do not put on airs."

She laughed a little then, although I felt tears on my cheek where hers rested. "Oh, very well," she said. "We will ride on to Ulle."

So we pressed on early the next morning though the horses were fetlock deep in snow. A few times, when the trail seemed to disappear completely, I wished I had not insisted, but Vinaigre knew every foot of the way and led us without once faltering. We arrived safely as dusk was falling to find my dream turned real—a roaring fire of winter blazing on the hearth of a well-lit hall in which a tall polished chair stood empty at the head of a long table from whose filled benches a tumult of greeting rose as Melusine walked in.

This time I stood in the doorway apurpose, waiting for her to look at me. I could not bear that there be any shadow between us. Well, I no longer feared to lose her even if she did remember. I was sure now that I could soothe her hurt. But when she looked across the room, she smiled. For a moment I thought she did not remember and I would have to tell her in words, but she came to me, held out her hand, and led me to her father's chair. There she kissed me and said, "Be welcome, beloved invader. Be welcome in your own home."

EPILOGUE

Melusine

I HEARD this afternoon that Queen Maud was dead, and I thought back eleven years to the day I had last seen her when she said she would like to visit Ulle and see its beauty. Although she remained at Bristol keep for nearly two weeks more, I was busy with Bruno and did not go to her. And she never came to Ulle. I wept for her. Poor queen, those eleven years had been as bitter for her as they had been sweet for me. As Bruno had feared, the war continued all that time. Oh, there were truces now and again, but they never lasted long and treachery piled on treachery.

In Ulle, we lived in peace—at least after Bruno righted the wrong of Magnus's murder. Mary's dead husband's father and brother are dead now, their lands divided between us and Mary, whose sons have been restored to her. Bruno went to the king to swear fealty for Ulle and the new lands and to receive quittance for having done justice without proper warrant. I almost died of fear until he returned, but he begged continued leave because the lands needed his attention and Stephen did not hold him.

Even so, for the next year, I was terrified that the king would summon him. I was carrying my first son by then and could not have accompanied him even after the boy was born, for we had no one fit to rear a child in our manor. Bruno must have felt the same, although he never said so, and at last, in our fourth year in Ulle after our second son was born, he went to the king to offer his service if he were needed. I quarreled with him bitterly before he left, but he was right. Stephen seemed barely to remember him, thanked him warmly for the offer, accepted his fealty and his homage for Ulle—and released him from his promise, except for the military service any vassal might be called on to perform. But he was never called.

When Bruno heard the queen was dead, he too was sad. Later when the children were abed, he said it might mean trouble for us. He did not think that Stephen would long survive his wife, and Eustace was not fit to be king. Yet if Henry, Matilda's son, took the throne, which seemed most likely, we who had been steadfastly faithful to Stephen might suffer for that.

"No, we will not," I said, "for Henry Plantagenet is indebted to King David." And I brought out what I had kept quietly in my chest for all these years—two more charters, one from King David confirming those he had given to my father long ago, and one from Henry, David's son as overlord of Cumbria, for Ulle and the other manors.

Bruno shook his head. "Little rebel," he said, "how did you come by these?"

I reminded him then of Sir Gerald's capture of King David and how Hugh had hidden the king among his own men and taken him safely to Jernaeve. "I did not ask for these," I said, touching the sealed parchments. "They came with a letter from Audris, saying that it was King David's wish that I and mine not suffer, no matter what the outcome of the war."

Although Bruno shook his finger at me—it is the harshest punishment he has ever visited on me—for keeping the matter secret all these years, he was pleased. I am glad we are well protected because I have four children now, Malcolm is our eldest, Hugh our second, Audris our first daughter, and Bruno, the baby, is two years old. I think our Audris will be the next lady of Jernaeve, for she and Eric are already fond of each other and it is Hugh's and

Audris's dearest wish (despite the consanguinity) that our
families be bound in the next generation as in this. It will
be a little confusing to have two Audrises in Jernaeve, but
Bruno's sister is eager to take our daughter, who is already
a skilled weaver and—to my horror—a great climber.

That frightens Edna even more than me. She is still with
me and loves my children with the passionate devotion of
a woman who cannot bear her own. She nursed Fechin too
in his last illness—with surprising tenderness when one
considers how sharply she always spoke of him and to
him, but he died last year. Bruno and I were grieved, but
he went quickly and without pain. Merwyn is married to a
girl from the village and is now our master-at-arms. We
keep more men-at-arms now. The smaller manors are adding to our wealth as are the lands that were Magnus's
blood money, so we can afford a small private army, and
we might need it. Cumbria is at peace, but Bruno fears
that the war will grow fiercer now that Henry is grown
from a boy to a man. Well, I write the truth here. I look
forward gladly to the time when Henry Plantagenet will be
king—though I do not say it to Bruno.

I am healed of the trouble that fell on me when I was
thirteen too. Even when I lost a daughter, my little Melusine,
though I grieved bitterly indeed, I did not suffer again the
guilt and terror that had haunted me for so many years.
Well, I am *almost* healed; when Bruno asked me if I
would not name the child I am carrying now for our lost
daughter or one of my brothers, I would not hear of it. If it
is a boy, it will be Oliver; if a girl, I will name it Maud,
for the queen. I hope the babe will be a daughter, for it
was the queen who forced Bruno on me—and gave me this
new and very precious life.

AUTHOR'S NOTE

For those readers who are familiar with the use of titles in English society, I feel it necessary to explain that it is not ignorance that allows me to call Melusine, the daughter of a simple knight, Lady Melusine. In the early twelfth century, titles and their use had not yet been formalized. All women of the noble class were "lady," with no distinction being made between the daughter of a simple knight and that of an earl. A man who had been knighted was "sir" to his equals and superiors, but he was most often "lord" to his own servants and inferiors who did not know better.

I feel I should also mention that in the first half of the twelfth century, there were no such titles as Squire of the Body or Knight of the Body. However, the positions—both requiring close attendance and service to the king—did exist. I have used the titles as a matter of convenience, because they make clear the duties of the hero without explanations that might impede the action.

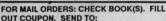